ALSO BY LEIGH EVANS

The Trouble with Fate
The Thing About Weres

The Problem
with Promises

LEIGH EVANS

St. Martin's Paperbacks

For Katie's kids: Bob, Susan, and Melanie

This is a work of fiction. All of the characters, organizations, and events portrayed in this novel are either products of the author's imagination or are used fictitiously.

THE PROBLEM WITH PROMISES

Copyright © 2014 by Leigh Evans.

For information address St. Martin's Press, 175 Fifth Avenue, New York, NY 10010.

ISBN: 978-1-250-00642-4

Printed in the United States of America

St. Martin's Paperbacks edition / March 2014

St. Martin's Paperbacks are published by St. Martin's Press, 175 Fifth Avenue, New York, NY 10010.

10 9 8 7 6 5 4 3 2 1

Dinner at the
Trowbridge Manse

Approximately two hours after I sent my brother to Merenwyn—

Robson Trowbridge pushed away his dinner plate and knuckled his red-rimmed eyes. There wasn't much left on the chicken carcass. The bones had been picked clean.

He ate a whole bird. On his own.

I poured another measure of maple syrup into my bowl. Not too much, just enough to coat the bottom of it. I was saving some space for the white chocolate macadamia nut cookies that sat on the counter.

"You need to sleep," I said quietly. My mate was all cheekbones and blue eyes now that he'd lopped off his dreads from hell. It made his skin look thin and taut, and only served to emphasize the blue smudges under the line of his thick black lashes.

Despite his exhaustion, he was still utterly beautiful.

Trowbridge nodded. "I will after I—"

"Uh-huh," I cut in. "After you've battened down the hatches. Set the picket lines. Shored up the defenses. Got all that. But anyone could see that you're about to do a face-plant into your plate. You might want to talk fast."

I'm hell with the love talk. But we were both exhausted, even though it was only eight P.M. It was taking everything I had not to crack my jaw into a yawn. I wouldn't mind going to bed even if it meant lying flat on a mattress and going "ah."

Gorgeous sat up straighter. "I don't need much sleep."

I licked at the spoon, tasting the sweetness of the maple syrup. Damned if Trowbridge's gaze hadn't shifted to the point of my tongue. A little flicker of a single blue comet did a quick circuit around his widening pupil.

I gave him a faint smile before my gaze drifted to the black felt bowler sitting on top of refrigerator. I'd done very well not looking at my twin's hat through the meal, but now its presence could not be ignored.

My palm went from warm and safe in Trowbridge's grip to a trifle damp and sweating.

I slipped it free.

Goddess, spare me. I'm going to Merenwyn to rescue Lexi. Where, according to the few facts I'd chiseled out of Trowbridge, there were no four-lane highways that had service stops every hour or so, where you could pee, and buy some coffee, and order a sandwich. Nope. Apparently, the Fae rode horses. And they shot arrows at people they didn't like. Silver-tipped. Who does that? An arrowhead piercing your spine had to hurt worse than a bullet. Hell, just shoot me and get it over with. Having something stick out of you and bob with every one of your breaths? I've done that. It sucks. I don't ever want to do that again.

If the Fae don't get me, the wolves will.

I'd demanded to be there when the Old Mage destroyed the Book of Spells. And I'd made a pledge to myself—yeah, we all know how well Hedi sticks to pledges—that I would destroy the old wizard's soul, and in so doing, free my twin's.

Sounds noble. Until you deconstruct the act. Take it down to a step-by-step event. First, I had to summon the Gates to Merenwyn and travel to the Fae realm. Usually, calling the portal to this world posed a real problem for me (as in hah-hah-impossible), but now, finally, Hedi Stronghold Peacock Trowbridge had the means to call the gates. All because last night—*Goddess, was it only last night?*—a man named Knox tried to kill me. He'd been sent by the NAW (the Council of North American Weres) to call me on the carpet for a blatant case of treaty-breaking plus two counts of murder.

For the record, I only killed one person and she totally deserved it. Though on reflection—and I try so hard not to waste time doing that—I don't think my guilt or innocence really mattered. There had been a whiff of kangaroo to the trial that had followed.

The outcome of that inquiry hadn't ended well for my accuser, Knox.

He'd died. I lived.

C'est la vie.

But before he was dispatched with a one-way ticket to the happy hunting ground, the fool had actually captured the Fae portal's materialization—from the first notes of the summons all the way to the end of the big event—on his cell phone. With his last breath, he'd hit send, and a copy of the video had been delivered to his girlfriend's e-mail address.

I'd seen the tape. Trowbridge had played it for us once during dinner. In the last frame the Gates of Merenwyn hovered over the fairy pond like something out of a Disney movie. All myst and lights and magic.

What had seemed like a sour lemon last night—just who the hell was Brenda Pritty and what damage could she do to us?—had turned into big glass of sweet lemonade. Now, thanks to the video, all we had to do was hit Replay. The song would be sung, compliments of the recording, and the portal would appear. Trowbridge and I would step through the gates *(whoosh)*, then take a st through Merenwyn's countryside *(Who me? Sure I bel*

there) to find my twin *(no sweat)*, and somehow maneu-
ver to be in the right place *(beside Lexi)*, in time to watch
the Book of Spells being destroyed *(tadah!)*.

Following that, I planned to effortlessly transport my
soul to Threall where I would tear the Old Mage's soul
free from what remained of my brother's and earn freedom for all.

All of which would be doable if I wasn't Hedi, the
mouse-hearted.

"Stop thinking," murmured Trowbridge. His hand lay
lax on the kitchen table. There was an odd callus on top
of the first knuckle of his thumb. *I should ask him about
that,* I thought, studying the way his veins forked like
warm tributaries.

Truth? I could stare at his tendons, scars, large knuckles, and oddly callused skin all night. To me, his paw was
beautiful, even if the world deemed it ugly because it only
had a thumb, a pointer, and an f-u digit left.

It was the hand that stroked my hair *and* killed Knox.

It was a very good paw.

The tap ran as Harry filled his glass. His white hair
gleamed in the light as he tilted his head back for a long
drink. Once finished, he used the back of his gnarled hand
to wipe his mouth dry.

Biggs scratched his shoulder as he stifled a yawn.

"Close your mouth, Chihuahua." Cordelia brushed past
him, pen and notebook in hand. She's big on lists, and sub-
lists. She sat, adjusted her red wig, then put nib to paper.
"What do we really need on this trip, Bridge? Can we
take weapons across the portal?"

They shoot at people in Merenwyn. They trap wolves.
And they've probably never met a six-foot ex–drag queen.
All right. That. Was. It. I fixed her straight. "You're not
coming with us. It's just going to be Bridge and me."

"If this is about me being—"

"This is about the fact that I'm not losing any more people that I care about."

Especially not another mother. I stared her down. Gritty-eyed and stone-faced. I'd accepted that I couldn't change the course already set for me and Trowbridge— our lives would always be irrevocably entwined. It's the downside, the hidden clause to the wonder of the mate bond: if a Were dies, his chosen mate soon follows.

But their lives—Cordelia, Anu, Harry, and Biggs— would not be added to the butcher's list. I wasn't giving up another family member to satisfy retribution's appetite.

I've lost too much, and I'm a very sore loser.

It took three "Mississippis" before my mother-who-wasn't lowered her eyes.

Feeling a sweep of queasiness, and a general unwillingness to catch my lover's penetrating gaze, I took refuge in the deep contemplation of the dregs of syrup coating the bottom of my bowl.

All hail, Hedi.

Queen Bitch of the Trowbridge kitchen.

This sudden need to assert myself—where'd that come from? Last week I'd been the slacker. Now, I was kept trembling on the edge of hear-me-roar-Hedi. Had some until now untapped portion of me finally realized the urgent and somewhat tardy need to haul ass?

Silence hummed in the room—appliances' motors filling in the place where words should be spoken. Feigning calm, I picked up my spoon.

Don't say anything, Trowbridge.

Let it be my decision.

I knew it must be mine, just like I recognized that I needed to catch up to everyone else in the worst way. Yes, Hedi had been a slacker; not doing much more than dozing over the last ten years. Okay, we're talking figuratively now—I didn't spend a decade lying on some posy-strewn bier, pale hands folded over my maidenly chest, eyes closed, lips sealed, whiling my way through a fairy princess's enchanted snooze.

But nonetheless, I'd not been here either—participating in life like other people my own age, getting my requisite bruises, learning how to self-heal. I'd been both awake and asleep. You can do that—move through life in a dazed semicoma. Seriously. People do it all the time. They go to their job. They come home, watch television, or read a book. They eat, and drink, and shower, and do the laundry, and play who-gets-paid-now with the bills, and sometimes, they watch people from a window, wondering what it would feel like to embrace life again . . .

I traced a circle in the bowl with the edge of my spoon.

Yes. You can do all those things without being really here. Three-quarters asleep. Just doing the stuff you needed to do, while some part of you dozed and waited to be brought to life.

That sounds sad, and I'm not a sad person.

Biggs suddenly asked, "Do you think Whitlock doesn't know that Knox is dead?"

"Oh dear God," I heard Cordelia mutter. "The longer I'm around you, the less I'm convinced that you have anything between your ears other than the cheat notes for Skyrim. Do you really think the head of North American Weres doesn't know that two of his men are dead? Of course he knows. Reeve Whitlock probably knows what we had for dinner."

"I have thoughts," said Briggs, clearly aggrieved. "Deep thoughts."

I listened to someone pick up the liter of pop and give it a cautious shake.

"Anyone want the last bit of Coke?" asked Biggs.

I felt for the point of my ear, traced the sharp peak and felt absolutely no cessation of anxiety.

"There's one more thing I have to do," my mate said.

"What's that, boss?" asked Harry.

"I have to call the Sisters."

The silence that filled the room after that pronouncement was simply deafening.

Chapter One

Trowbridge's belly button was kind of amazing—the tip of my baby finger fit perfectly in its shallow divot. Underneath it, the muscle was a hard slab. I stroked it again, marveling how two opposites could be such a good fit.

For instance, if you're talking navels, I have to admit mine is deep. Only my Goddess knows exactly *how* deep. I've never stuck my finger in it to check, possibly because you don't do that sort thing when you have an inner-bitch taking a snooze by your spine. She might bite it. Or worse—my Fae might grab it because she's the type of ride-along persona given to doing "gotcha" crap like that.

Shortly after Biggs had drained the bottle of Coke, Trowbridge and I had come upstairs to our personal sanctuary to catch a couple of hours of sleep before "the Sisters"—what the pack calls a certain coven of witches who practice dark arts—arrived at eleven.

To be honest, I'd anticipated lust—after all, he'd given me a slightly worn wink as we'd stumbled up the stairs, and let's face it, Weres are randy as hell—but by the time I'd come back out of the washroom from my presleep tinkle, he'd crashed into a sleep that bordered on coma.

I knew he was exhausted but how does a person do that? Close their eyes and fall instantly asleep? I wish I could do that. But sleep was an avenue for dream-walking, and that activity was a potential doorway to Threall. Unfortunately—given that most of us mystwalkers found the realm of souls kind of fascinating—every trip to the land of myst was akin to playing roulette with a loaded weapon. Why? Because every time a mystwalker traveled to that realm, she reduced her chances of remembering how to return to her own.

Goddess, this feeling I keep smothering—a touch of self-hatred melded to worry and fear—better not be the new normal.

"Trowbridge?" I whispered to my mate. "Will it get better?"

No answer. The bed hog lay flat on his back, one arm folded over his head, the other loosely wrapped around me. He's pretty, my Trowbridge. Though, in my opinion, he was too thin, even if he was sporting some new and disturbingly magnificent muscles.

I wrote "Move over, Stud-muffin" on his chest. With my nail. Very lightly. Because there's such a thing as poking a stick at a sleeping bear. And because he had a thatch of hair between his nipples. Not terribly dense. Just enough to say "Here be a manly man," and I enjoyed the feeling of the curve of my nail sliding through it.

I glanced at the clock, wishing someone had reset it. How much longer before the witches flew in on their brooms? Neither Trowbridge nor I had any love for women who practice dark arts but we required their services. Tomorrow at sunset, we planned to summon the Gates of Merenwyn. Ideally, we wanted to do that without the pack noticing because the return of the portal would prompt awkward questions, like "Hey, are they breaking the treaty again?" Or "By golly, have they brought back her brother? I thought he was dead?"

Either topic is a line of inquiry we'd like to avoid.

However, keeping our trip to Merenwyn on the down

low was going to be difficult without some help. The portal has a distinctive floral scent that even a Were with a head cold could detect. And then there are the pink-white lights and the chime of bells.

No. We needed another illusion ward, set precisely where Mannus had ordered one cast six months ago—right over the entire fairy pond. That way we could go to and fro without anyone being the wiser.

Though for the record, there was an additional and far less optimistic reason that we required a sheet of magic pulled over the pond like a piece of plastic wrap—failure. What if our seminoble quest ended in disaster? What if we couldn't rescue my brother and destroy the Book of Spells? Bad things could drip into this world through the Fae portal. Trowbridge worried that the lives of his wolves would be threatened. I couldn't quite muster the same level of concern.

It would require more saintly qualities than I possessed to forgive people who'd tied me to the old oak tree. The scent of their blood lust had filled my nose.

Enough. I need to move. If only to get up and trot around to the other side to restart the whole roll-over game.

Merry was hanging from the lampshade, right where I'd placed her before turning the light out. I hadn't wanted to put her on the bedside table because the wooden surface hadn't been wiped down with Pine-Sol (the cleaning-product choice among Weres), and there was still a touch of the fugly Mannus scent to it. An oversight on the part of the cleaning team who'd karate-chopped the throw pillows?

I think not.

Score another point for the League of Extraordinary Bitches.

Ralph, the amulet beside Merry, hung unmoving beside her on the parchment shade, either asleep or pretending to be.

Trowbridge said something like "Mrrrph" as I squirmed over him to reach for her.

My amulet gave me a little wink of light as I pulled her chain over my head. In another life, Merry would have done well as a mime. She can't talk, as she's imprisoned inside a hunk of amber that's been set into a pendant fashioned from a nest of Fae gold, but she manages to express herself very well through movement and color shows.

She hadn't interacted much with Ralph since she'd returned from the Fae realm. Which was interesting as her amber stone used to pinken at the sight of him. Understandable, to an extent. The Royal Amulet was astonishingly pretty, what with his brilliantly cut jewel and his manly Celtic setting. Though, in my opinion, even the artistry of his setting couldn't make up for the fact that personalitywise, he was a pain in the butt.

Evidently, she no longer considered him the rock star among her people.

I wish I knew why. One day, maybe she would tell me in her own way. I hope so, because I count her as my friend. Matter of fact, I don't like going anywhere without her. Even if all I needed to do was pace the threadbare carpet that still carried the faint scent tones of the master bedroom's former occupant.

Put that on the list: replace all soft furnishings and strip the wallpaper.

The second I rolled off Trowbridge and swung a leg over the side of the bed, he woke up—fast. None of this bleary-eyed stuff for my guy. He went straight from limp to warrior. Lunging for me as if someone had snatched me right out of his arms, at the same time blindly reaching for something beside him. Which wasn't there. With a

downright feral snarl he turned to check for the weapon
that he'd obviously grown used to sleeping with. The one
he'd evidently left in Merenwyn. What was it? A blade?
An axe? A wooden staff?

His gaze did a lightning sweep of the room, taking in
all the doors—the bedroom, the closet, the bathroom—
then the window, and finally, me and Merry.

"Go back to sleep," I told him. "The witches aren't
here yet."

But that was as pointless as expecting a Jack in the
Box to fold up and close his own lid. He was awake. Tired
blue eyes studied me.

I tugged my arm free with a wince. I had a bite wound
that I'd received in Threall and it was throbbing again.
"I'm going downstairs."

"Stay," he said.

"That's got to be your favorite word."

"Don't go."

"Second favorite word," I said, walking to the window.

"That's two words." He swung his feet over the side of
the bed and scrubbed his hands over the stiff bristles of
his hair. "I'm awake."

*But you shouldn't be—not with those purple smudges
under your eyes.*

"Come back to bed," he said, his tone all butter and
temptation.

I eyed his body in all its near-perfection. The few scars
he'd kept looked good on him. "If I get in that bed, you're
going to make love to me."

Even in the half dark of the room, I could see his decidedly naughty grin. "And that would be a bad thing?"

Normally, all I had to do was inhale the clean scent of
him, and I was a goner. And if he'd been awake when I'd
sashayed out of the ladies', we'd have enjoyed each other.
But I'd had time to brood. Guilt asked, in a withering

voice, "Hedi, do you have any right to enjoy being held and loved, after you sent your twin to hell?"

My face must have reflected my answer to that puzzler. "Oh," he said.

"Oh," I echoed, a tad sadly.

Trowbridge's wistful gaze dipped toward the girls and I turned back to the window before all parts of him woke up. "Do you know what time it is?"

The mattress protested as Trowbridge got up. He came up behind me to wrap an arm—muscled, hard, warm—around my ribs. He eased me against his hard body as his hand slipped upward to cup my boob. He lifted it, so that it plumped in his palm, as he considered the night sky. "Around eleven."

"Does the sky look the same there?" I asked him.

"In Merenwyn?" His chest rose and fell. "No, the stars are different. There's no Big Dipper or North Star."

"What does it have instead?"

"The moon is lower and bigger." He studied the sky silently, perhaps lost in his memories. "There's a cluster of smaller stars called Caitlin's Daughters. People make wishes on them."

"Do their dreams come true?"

"Not that I can see." His palm slid along my skin until it encountered the chain I wore low around my hips. That sent the soft leather pouch hanging from the end of the bride belt, swinging. Inside the little bag were seven stones, clear as diamonds but far more valuable. "Why can't you sleep?"

I gave him a mute shrug.

"The first obstacle has been passed, Tink," he said softly. "The Old Mage must have succeeded in merging his soul with your brother's." His thumb absently brushed my nipple. It hardened.

Hedi, the mouse-hearted.

Hedi, the betrayer.

"What makes you so sure of that?" I asked.

"We're not dead," he said with his usual bluntness.

"Good point."

Trowbridge rubbed his chin against my shoulder. "You're worrying about him."

I nodded.

"Did you get any sleep?"

I shook my head. "I can't stop thinking."

His exhale spoke volumes. "We're going to have to work on that." Then he leaned back a bit, so that he could gather my hair and draw it over my right shoulder. He set to gently untangling the knots in my rat's nest. Immediately, my nipples beaded—the backs of his knuckles were warm on the slope of my breast.

I let out a sigh, part pleasure, part sadness.

"Tell me what's bothering you most," he said, working on a difficult snare.

I swallowed. "I spent ten minutes as the Old Mage's nalera . . . and it almost drove me insane. You're naked. Every secret, every weakness, everything you like to hide from others, it's there. Accessible for your mage's interest and use." I waited for him to say, "Don't feel bad," or maybe, "Clearly, love of my life, you had no choice."

Instead Gorgeous finished with the knot, then said gruffly, "Go on."

The stars blurred.

"Lexi's the Old Mage's bitch now," I said in an anguished rush. "Every single thought he has is being examined—"

"Hedi," Trowbridge cut in. "You have to remember that your brother lived a long time in the Fae's Royal court. He's had lots of practice shielding his thoughts."

I slumped against him, thinking how we'd waited until

Lexi was so weak that he couldn't stand, couldn't talk, couldn't walk.

"Sweetheart," he said, moving his leg so that I could be cradled closer. "One day you will be required to become a leader, and there are going to be things you'll need to do that will leave you awake at night. It will harden you. And eventually you'll wonder if you have any humanity left inside you. But you'll have to push past that. You'll have to force yourself to grab sleep when you can. To eat when you must. To keep going, no matter what."

"What are you talking about, Trowbridge?" I turned, lifting a shoulder. "I have as much interest in leading people as I do in sitting for a group sing. I'm not a leader. I'll never be one."

He said something under his breath that sounded a whole lot like "Not yet, anyhow."

I pushed away and leaned against the window frame. The glass was cold. I covered Merry with my palm and she sent me a throb of heat.

"Sweetheart, look at me."

I considered that, and didn't resist when he turned me gently to face him. Gravely, he cupped my face. For the longest moment, he studied me, with an intensity that made me feel like he was memorizing my features.

"What is it?"

"If I could keep you like this," he said fiercely, "untouched and safe from everything harmful, I swear to God I would. You are perfect, just like this." Mouth set in a flat line, he stroked my jaw. "But I can't keep you out of trouble, no matter how much I want to, Hedi Peacock."

He was freaking me out.

I gave him a weak smile. "If we live through all this, I'm going to turn into the most boring person in the world. I'm going to take up knitting. And baking." Then I tipped my head toward the window. "Also, I'm going to fix your front yard. It needs flowers, Trowbridge." One corner of his mouth lifted, so I added, "After that? Maybe Tai Chi."

"Good luck with that." My lover tucked a strand of my hair behind my pointed ear. "Tink. You're attracted to danger."

"I am not. Whenever I see it, I run like hell."

"No you don't. You run right into trouble."

"Do not."

Real amusement softened his tone. "Let's see what you've done in the last twelve hours. You bargained with a mage and stared Cordelia down. Of the two I don't know which is the bigger deal." His gaze went to my mouth, clung there. "Sweetheart, you defy me every chance you get. You wrote 'Stud-muffin' on my chest."

"I thought you were asleep."

"I was concentrating with my eyes closed." A ghost of a grin flitted across his face. "You came close to losing me with the double *f*'s." He gazed at me, face somber. "We're heading for a shit-storm, Tink."

"I know," I whispered.

Blue eyes turned predator cold. "Remember this. Whatever happens—whatever it takes—we can't allow the Black Mage to walk through worlds. That bastard has no place in ours."

Unsettled, I dragged my gaze from him. Searched for something calming, and found it in the blue flower sprigs peppered across the wallpaper. Very small, very sweet. *Oh Goddess, let me be wrong.* "You're going to Merenwyn to kill him, aren't you?"

"There will be no peace for the Raha'ells until I do."

I closed my eyes briefly. *Them again.* "The Black Mage has magic. And guards. While you'll be armed with nothing more than hatred and the notion that his death will right a wrong that's based on prejudice and fear. I know you miss your Merenwyn pack and feel responsible for them. But risking your life—"

"That's what an Alpha does for his pack."

I'll never think that way. "Would killing the Black Mage change the Fae court's opinion that wolves are a lower order? Would it stop the trapping, or the—"

"It will buy them some time." His fingers soothed my tense jaw.

"Until what?"

"Until I find the safe passage."

I'd sent a rogue across the gates six months ago. In some ways, he'd been easier to deal with than the "Son of Lukynae." Never in a million years would rogue wolf Robson Trowbridge have lifted a clenched fist in the air and cried, "Freedom for all!"

"Trowbridge." I paused to pick my words carefully. "If there really was a portal keyed to recognize and accept Were blood, wouldn't someone have used it by now?"

"Are you saying there is no Safe Passage for the wolves of Merenwyn?"

"I'm saying that . . ." *The Raha'ells are no longer yours to lead.* "My wish list is a lot shorter than yours. I'm not trying to save the world. I just want the seven of us safe," I said. "That's all I want, Trowbridge. You and me, Lexi and Anu, Cordelia and Harry . . . even Biggs. Everything I do is for that, and because of that." I bit my lip. "You're confident you can take on everything that comes your way. While I . . . What if I haven't got what it takes?"

Knuckles brushed my cheek. Callused. Heated with blood. Smelled like forests and the wild. "Stop worrying," he said softly. "We can do this. And you have everything you need inside you to finish this."

"How can you be so sure?" I whispered.

"I just am."

I forced my lids open and lifted my chin to gaze at Gorgeous. *I love you*—that's what I tried to telegraph.

He frowned. "You look really tired."

"Go ahead, Trowbridge," I said sourly. "Keep drowning me in compliments."

His thumb lightly grazed the circle under my eye. Then naked as a jaybird he gave me a smoldering look. "I've got an idea."

Trowbridge steered me into the bathroom, his hand warm on the small of my back. "I could spend the next year in a shower. Hot water. Lots of towels. Soap . . . damn, I missed good soap."

The League of Extraordinary Bitches had gone over the en suite with their sponges and Pine-Sol. The tub gleamed, the sink had been swiped down.

"I'm not sure if I want one right now." An absolute truth. Though a lot of our conversations seemed to take place in one bathroom or another, we'd only really ducked under the spray once together. And that had been in a motel that had smelled of strangers, puke, and booze. Not one of my warm and fuzzy memories. Robbie Trowbridge had turned the water to cold, then held me under it.

"It will relax you," he murmured, pulling aside the curtains.

Sure it will. I leaned against the bathroom vanity.

His body was marble. All tendons and definition. Thanks to his zero body fat, even his veins were on display—blue ribbons beneath golden skin. One led a trail down his massive bicep, curved into his elbow, then forked—three times—on his forearm.

Sexy beast.

My One True Thing turned on the taps, then stood, holding his hand under the spray. On one level, he was just a man waiting for his shower to warm. Palm turned upward to accept the dancing spray. Weight balanced on one foot, hip cocked. But this was My One True Thing. I didn't even know how to describe the way his hip and groin met. He looked like a Ken doll, except for the fact he is an awesomely functioning male, and Ken has the anatomy of . . . well . . . a Ken doll.

Poor Barbie. She could have done so much better.

Trowbridge plucked the desiccated soap from the soap dish. His bicep flexed—*pumped*—as he lifted the cake of Irish Spring for a sniff test. Goddess. With Trowbridge, watching my man wait for the shower to heat was a mouth-drying, pussy-tightening *event*.

"This stinks of Mannus," he said in disgust, before pitching the bar into the empty wastepaper container with enough force to overturn it.

I did not bend to right the wicker basket.

But I did spot an item that had escaped the league's attention. Head tilted, I stepped back to get a better look. Half hidden under the skirt of the vanity was one of Trowbridge's dreadlocks. I leaned to pick it up. Fuzzy. Surprisingly soft. Smelling of him and Merenwyn. Should I get one of the crafty bitches to make a bracelet out of it?

"What's that?" he inquired.

"Nothing." I slid it off my wrist and tucked it in the drawer.

When I lifted my eyes, I caught him watching me in the mirror. Oh, goody. He'd offered me a full frontal. Ever the happy homing pigeon, my gaze traveled to the thin line of hair beneath his amazing navel, following the trail all the way to the promised land. I can't help it. If he's naked, I'm going to do a status check. Why? Because there's really such a thing as male beauty and it can be found in a pair of heavy balls and a cock that was growing thicker under my approval.

"Sweetheart," said the guy in the mirror. "When you look at me like that I want to—"

"Eat me up?"

The man doesn't blink when he wants sex.

"That's my T-shirt," he said.

"You want it back?"

"Uh-huh. Take it off."

"You're a bossy man, Robson Trowbridge."

His eyes gleamed wickedly. "Sweetheart, lose the shirt."

Boring but true: when you're tired and alone, disrobing is all about minimal effort. With far less grace than efficiency, you tip your head to one side, grab the neckline of your T-shirt and haul upward. It's not a particularly exciting thing. Your va-jay-jay doesn't flood with heat. Your nipples may or may not bead. (In my case, that depends on room temperature, my general level of exhaustion, and whatever I've been reading). You're stripping for yourself. Who cares?

But when you've got a man watching you with heavy-lidded interest, the shedding of clothing requires some contemplation.

Like how it might be best to arch your back first. And suck in your gut until your belly button kisses your spine. And perhaps you'll opt for crossing your arms when you reach for the hem of your T-shirt—knowing that when you finally peel the jersey up over your head, your arms will be twined above you.

I'm a dove. Yours to love.

That might be when you'll pause to allow *him* a moment of art appreciation. And his breath might hitch as his gaze travels from your crossed wrists, down to the column of your throat, and from there to slip lower to the curve of your breasts.

You may hold the pose, because the night before last, you'd discovered something of breathtaking importance—

your lover had an unexpected appreciation for all things visual.

Bottom line, don't talk, just give the man a diagram.

I held myself poised like a well-padded water nymph, all arched back and lifted chest. For him. And for me. Because when Trowbridge looks at me like that, I'm not fat, I'm not short, I'm not average.

I'm Hedi, Pocket Venus and Destroyer of Men.

I held the position until my lungs screamed for air, then slowly lowered my arms. The shirt wafted to the tiles. My hands tensed, then relaxed.

I gave him my best come-hither.

Ravish me, Big Boy.

I could have said it out loud. Just like I could have turned to face him instead of watching him in the mirror. But silence, I realized with growing wonder, was so much sexier. And seeing him prowl toward me? All predatory intent? That was *beyond* erotic. Particularly as he was doing the same thing as I was—watching the two of us in the mirror. Except my gaze kept sweeping from him to me, while his was fixed on the short girl in the mirror. A hungry wolf, he was, eyeing his game.

"You're creamy," he said.

Startled, I raised both brows.

"All over," he said, his voice rough. "I used to think it was because you had some Fae in you. But I've seen them and none of them can match your skin. You're so . . ." He shook his head, his voice trailing away.

"Creamy."

"Just perfect. Pink and clean. So . . . soft. Female. *Clean,*" he repeated, "and—"

"Creamy," I said, a smile flirting.

He walked toward me, still shaking his head. As I pivoted to meet him, he murmured, "No. Stay like that. I want to look."

Well, if you twist my arm.

Pheromones did a dance of joy when he eased himself behind me. I'm not sure whose they were. His. Mine. In the end, it didn't matter. All that was important was the fact that the air stirred moodily around us—sex, salt, woods, and wild—as he invaded my personal space.

"You're perfect," he repeated.

"I am." Disbelief, covered with a layer of jest.

"Yes, you are." Certainty, unvarnished by civility. "You're made just for me," he elaborated.

You feel that too?

Eyes glittering, he reached for my hips. Slowly, he drew me backward, bending his head, to observe how my body fit against his. He was fully aroused, his penis an insistent and hot presence pressed hard against my buttocks.

My inner core slicked.

"Look at us," he said.

Easy enough to look at you, My One True Thing. You are beauty personified. Once pretty, now honed into something raw and beautiful. While me . . . my attention shifted to the short girl being held by a broodingly handsome man. I considered her, trying to evaluate her as a stranger would. She wasn't as plain as I thought. In fact, she was . . .

Well, hell. Standing comfortably inside the circle of her man's embrace, she was pretty damn close to being hot. That is, if you liked flaring hips and a nipped-in waist. *I think I do.* And her face? While definitely not classically beautiful—and, if one wanted to be tedious about details, not even pretty—it was . . . arresting. Yes. That was it. *Arresting.* Both baby-faced and inexplicably bold. What was it? Because of her full upper lip? It was literally puffed with desire. Her brown hair? Nothing extraordinary there, except if one's gaze lingered on how its tangled lengths parted to reveal softly rounded shoulders.

Touch me, that's what those white slopes said.

An impudent Lolita. With extraordinary eyes. Almond shaped, faintly tipped upward. Pale, pale green. Sea foam cresting on a long, deep blue ocean roller.

But now, little bright flares spat from inside them.

Insistent. Impatient.

Son of a gun. I look so much better naked.

"Hey, I—"

"Shhh," he murmured, his cheeks flushed as red as mine. "Stop talking."

"But I—"

"Let me play," he insisted.

"Okay," I said faintly, my nails curling on the vanity.

He nodded, then, his gaze intent, his knowing hands started to roam. Such intrepid travelers, they were. They slid up either side of me, exerting a steady pressure that both branded and inflamed.

In his arms, I'm almost beautiful.

Up, up, they moved, lovingly following the outline of my hourglass shape. *My waist is so small. Under his caress, its exaggerated dip is darn right provocative.* His hands lingered there—a rest stop before they roamed to my breasts. Strangely solemn, he cupped their weight, his thumbs teasing my areolae.

He was so much warmer now. A veritable furnace warming my back.

My head fell back on his shoulder.

Slit eyed, I let him play.

Intensified by the shower's steam, the scent of sex wove around us. Licking my skin, with its sensuous tongue.

His gaze slipped from the girl in the mirror to the live one in his arms. Plumped in his palms, my pale breasts were visibly swollen, their tips tightly beaded and berry red. He swallowed hard. And then my man went berry picking.

Oh Goddess, yes, Trowbridge. Pinch them again. The right pressure—a tiny bite of mild pain—the right upward tug. I started to pivot, seeking the wet, sucking, irresistible pleasure of those chiseled lips.

"No," he said firmly, turning me to face the mirror again. Another squeeze, another pain-pleasure pinch to berries already ripe and red.

Goddess, look at us.

"Let me make love to you." Blue comets spun in his eyes, as his palm slid over the soft swell of my belly.

My breath caught as supple fingers slid to my mound and dipped low. *Yes.* With a hum of pleasure, I arched against him, lifting my chin to nuzzle his cheek. A love-starved wolf demanding the long stroke.

"I want to see you come," he told me, his voice rough and low. "I want to watch you break apart in my arms."

No. Problem. I turned my leg outward and tilted my pelvis in silent demand.

"Don't you want to make it last?" His clever fingers moved from the aching part of me to the soft silk of my inner thigh.

My thigh trembled.

"Next time," I said a tad breathily.

Mouth quirked, he continued to torture me, tracing teasing circles on my leg. "But I'd like to hear you moan in my ear."

"Trowbridge," I warned, slowly turning in his arms. Between us, the flushed engorged head of his penis. At the slit, a pearl exuded the scent of sex and salt and . . . him.

Mine.

I stretched on my toes to press a reproving kiss on the corner of his hard mouth. "You're a terrible tease."

"I know," he murmured.

And then he sank to his knees.

We lay on the floor of our bathroom, utterly spent, listening to the water ping off the shower stall. The last orgasm had been a heart-pounding, sweaty shared one— "You're perfect," he'd kept repeating, over and over. A two-word love song. Or three, depending on how you counted the contraction.

"How big is the water tank?" I lifted my leg off his sweat-drenched one.

"Not that big."

"We should get up before all the hot water goes."

He folded his arm under his head. "There's no showers in Merenwyn," he said reflectively. "No baths either."

"None?"

"They've got lakes," he said heavily. "Fed by the mountain streams."

"That sounds cold."

"Like ice," he said, adjusting his balls.

I rolled, pillowing my head, to face my mate. My mate had a long nose, made even more interesting by his flaring nostrils. A rock-hard body too. *Perfect for me.* I reached over to stroke those fascinating abs, then smothered a smile. Trowbridge wasn't above the vanity of sucking in his gut.

I should tell him he has no body fat. It would be a kindness.

I traced the ridges of his abdomen muscles.

Nah.

"Tink," he said.

"Mm-hmm."

Trowbridge rolled his head. Blue eyes, the color of the Mediterranean. Faint purple shadows below. A vein cut across the top of his right cheekbone. "Harry's coming up the stairs."

"Damn." I glanced wistfully at the tub.

Trowbridge covered his eyes with his forearm while we listened to Harry's footsteps. Our second stopped in front of our door. There was a long pause. Then coins jingled. *Harry's thinking.* The scent of our lovemaking must perfume the entire upper floor.

"What is it, Harry?" called Trowbridge, his mouth barely moving.

"They've found Newland, boss. They're bringing him in."

Chapter Two

The jeans that Trowbridge had rued as a size too small were yanked back on. By the time I'd tossed on my T-shirt and slipped on my panties, Ralph had been retrieved from his lonely splendor on the lampshade, and thrown over his head.

My would-be murderer, Knox, had come to Creemore with two thugs. While the thinner of the NAW's henchmen had been dispatched by the pack that very same night, the other—a burly guy I'd dubbed "Fatso" though his license had revealed that his true name was Kenneth Newland—had melted into the caves near Collingwood and had managed to escape capture for almost twelve hours.

Until now. Trowbridge had told Harry to call in their best tracker three hours ago when it was clear that the pack's search team of accountants and insurance adjusters wasn't putting their all into it.

At the door, my lover tilted his head to study me with narrowed eyes. "You might not be ready for this. This could get ugly."

Uh-huh. Me staying behind doing needlepoint. And pigs may fly.

I followed him. The moment we passed the first bedroom, my niece, Anu, came to the door. "Blah, blah, blah," the Alpha of Creemore said to her in Merenwynian. She halted, her green eyes wide, but when she saw me trailing behind him, her mouth firmed like a teenager denied Internet privileges. She fell into rank and filed behind me.

By the time we'd hit the landing, Cordelia's door opened. Somehow, after dinner, she'd managed to nip over to the trailer and change. She wore a dove-gray twin set and a pair of lovely trousers, tailored to fit her thin, six-foot frame. My former roommate had accessorized it with a couple of necklaces—just the right amount of flash against the cool and somber tones of her woolens. Cordelia was always tasteful, proving that not all ex–drag queens mince about draped in pink boas.

Trowbridge paused by the arch to the living room. "Hey, Biggs." When the dark-headed Were didn't lift his head, he raised his voice. "Hey!"

Biggs jumped and almost dropped the cell phone he had clenched in his hand.

"Is that Knox's phone?" Trowbridge asked.

Biggs nodded.

Trowbridge opened the door. "Bring it."

Biggs trailed me as I zipped up my sweatshirt and stepped outside to join Trowbridge and Cordelia on the front porch.

Harry had picked up a weapon and strolled out, well before my Fae ears had managed to track the sound of an approaching car. The hairs on the nape of my neck bristled. I'd never seen this side of my old cowboy before. He stood apart from us—his rifle balanced over the crook of his arm, his profile turned toward the road—a silent figure down at the far end of the veranda, hidden where the porch lights couldn't penetrate the gloom.

Everyone else's attention was centered on the Mazda that had driven at a funereal speed all the way to the mid-point of the long drive, and now waited, engine idling, for permission to advance. The passengers were two dark and indistinct shadows.

Trowbridge, arms folded, gave a nod, and the car resumed its approach.

The vehicle stopped in front of the house, rather than going to the back where the family parked. The engine was turned off, and the overhead lights went on as the driver, a big guy who I recognized as a pack member whose name was either Derek or David, got out. A moment later, the passenger door opened, and Rachel Scawens slid out.

Trowbridge's sister gave me her habitual thinly veiled look of hatred. When her son had become embroiled with the former Alpha of Creemore, Rachel had contacted her brother for help. He'd answered her call even though doing so had placed his life at risk.

But Stuart hadn't wanted rescuing and Stuart had ended up dead.

Rachel blamed me for that.

"Your sister took her vow to her Alpha, then?" I asked quietly. Swearing fealty to the new Alpha was a required act, performed by each member of the pack.

Trowbridge's nod was abrupt.

It was cold. I wished I'd lifted a jacket from one of the pegs by the door before I'd ventured outside.

The driver, Derek/David, went around to the back fender. (Henceforth to be known as Derek because he was tall as a crane, and about as pretty as an oil rig). He sent Bridge a sideways glance, read permission, then hit the button on his key fob to pop the trunk. Immediately, a stream of foul ripeness wafted out of the enclosed space. Fatso had been on the run for his life and he'd sweated a whole bunch.

"They didn't kill him," observed Biggs, from the doorway.

A statement that the occupant of the trunk couldn't have translated as a hopeful sign. Suddenly, a foot—no, not one, but two feet bound so closely together at the ankles that Fatso's legs looked like the bottom of a Pez dispenser—slashed out.

An understandable but completely futile effort. Derek was more than up to the challenge of evading flying Pez feet. Thus, the consequence of Fatso's escape attempt was a couple of nasty rabbit punches for the wolf in the trunk, before Derek and Rachel hauled their captive out.

Without much ceremony, they threw him at their Alpha's feet.

The last time I'd seen Knox's sidekick, he'd been a naked sprinter, hoping to break thousand-yard dash records as he fled the gathering field. Since then, he'd raided someone's clothesline, and he'd been well trussed—arms behind his back, double-tied with rope. His borrowed shirt had rucked up, and his gut gleamed above his jeans like the curve of whale's white underbelly.

"Is this the wolf?" Trowbridge looked down his long nose at the prey. "The one that led you to that tree?"

I thought back to the hysteria of the burn-the-bitch mentality that had begun with a trial and ended up with me chained to the old oak. There had been so many hands, so many scents. Had his been among them?

"Yes," I said, deciding it didn't matter. Fatso had hit me. He'd pushed me through the crowds, and he'd smiled when Knox had pulled out his knife.

Trowbridge jerked his head to the right toward the maple tree his mother had planted so long ago in their front garden. "Give me the chains and turn on the yard lights," he said softly to Harry, as Derek and Rachel began to drag their catch across the lawn.

Harry grunted, then bent to gather up the chains that Fatso and Know had used to secure us to our execution posts. I didn't know what was worse—the grim rattle of those fetters as Harry stepped off the porch, or the unyielding hangman's stare he leveled at the quaking wolf as he passed the bonds to his Alpha.

Trowbridge weighed a length in his hands for a long thoughtful moment. "Untie his hands," he told Derek and Petra, "then stand back from him."

Fatso must have realized it was now-or-never once they'd cut the ropes around his elbows and wrists. Handicapped by his Pez-feet, he lurched forward, possibly hoping to hop his way to freedom.

There was no setup, no slow burn. Trowbridge let loose his flare. Blue electric light burst from my man's eyes with the sudden blinding intensity of a lighthouse's searching beam. Fatso froze, hunched for the next sack-race hop, his sweating face twisting in panic as its heat bathed his features.

If an Alpha's flare is leveled at you with the sole intent of flattening you? Say hello to the dirt. Few can withstand that awful wish to submit, to grovel, to plead . . .

Fatso's belligerence held for three shuddering breaths before his mouth contorted into the downward droop of a man quavering on the edge of a chest-heaving bawl. On the fourth inhale, his resistance visibly snapped, and with a defeated, high-pitched whine, he shrank back against the maple's spine.

"Biggs," Trowbridge said, "use Knox's phone to film this."

The heavy chains swung from the Alpha of Creemore's fist as he walked across the grass. "Stand up straight," he murmured as he approached the flinching wolf.

The NAW's man lifted a meaty arm to block the light trained on him. "I didn't mean it," he cried before burying his face into the crook of his elbow. Even that self-defense move proved an inadequate shield against Trowbridge's unforgiving flare—Fatso's subsequent moan morphed into a broken hum.

I covered my mouth, remembering what it felt like to be under that surge of dominance. I didn't need to see this. I didn't want to see my own misery replayed in front of me. Nor did I want it videoed. There had been enough *recordings*. Knox had made one, showing my lover and brother leaping through the gates' round hobbit-sized window. "Trowbridge, you don't—"

"Hush, mate," he replied.

Did he just hush me?

Trowbridge considered the cowering Were for a moment. "Hey," he said. When Fatso declined the opportunity to trade gazes, the Alpha of Creemore tapped his arm. "Look at me."

It took Fatso a good two seconds to summon up the guts to obey.

Trowbridge nodded, then said evenly, "Hold this."

The NAW's goon whimpered, but he did as he was told—he accepted the end of the chain and held it obediently while Trowbridge did a slow, tight circle around the tree.

It's hideous to watch a person being bound like that. The chink of the chain, the frantic expression on the face of the person as it dawns on them that there could be and would be, no escape. Oh, sweet heavens, how could the pack have stood watching it happen to me? Hadn't the sight sickened a few? Wrenched a teaspoon of pity from at least one of them?

Fatso's flesh bulged over the links.

"The creature deserves it," I heard my Fae say.

So . . . she'd finally found her voice again. Following her bid for autonomy in Threall—now known as an epic fail—she'd fallen into a quiet, sullen funk. But I'd felt her, brooding and silent, watching me and mine interact. And sometimes, I'd sensed her sampling my feelings—admittedly fleetingly—while Trowbridge cuddled me post-sexual bliss.

Comparing things, I'd thought.

Was she right?

Perhaps Fatso did deserve all of this, but I found no joy in hearing his wolf pants of distress—those pathetic heh-heh-hehs—nor satisfaction watching him blink against the dribble of sweat that trickled into his eyes.

No, this wasn't what I needed or I wanted.

I need peace. I want a fairy godmother to wave a hand over all our problems and make them go away. But that wasn't going to happen, was it? I swallowed and walked across the crabgrass that was doing a damn good job of choking the last few clumps of civilized Kentucky blue.

Trowbridge was studying his captive, his head canted to the side. "You looked different," he told me, when I was close enough to hit him or kiss him. "The picture isn't quite right."

"Because, by the time you got there, I had a blade stuck in my chest." I lowered my voice to a whisper. "Let's not do this. Enough blood's been shed."

"You had something on your head," he said, as if he hadn't heard me.

"A blindfold." Actually a red bandana that carried Fatso's scent.

"That's it." Trowbridge peeled off his own shirt. He pulled it taut, then twisted it a few times so that the jersey was a coiled rope. Fatso—why can't I remember the wolf's name?—visibly cringed as my lover reached to blind him with the fabric.

Mouth flattened into a hard line, the Alpha of Creemore rocked back on his heels to embrace the overall picture. His flare died. He examined the shaking wolf for a long beat then said, "So you're Ken Newland. Somehow I pictured you differently."

"Biggs," I said quietly. "Stop recording this."

"You take your finger off that button and you'll lose it," said Trowbridge in a tone I hardly recognized.

Bile rose from my stomach. "I don't want a record of this—we don't need to see—"

"Not now, Hedi."

Unbelievable. He did it again. He shushed me.

"Want to tell me why the NAW sent you and Knox to Creemore?" Trowbridge asked the blindfolded Were.

Ken wet his lips. "We came to charge Helen Stronghold—"

"Hedi Peacock," Trowbridge corrected.

"Hedi Peacock," the other Were parroted, then with an overeager nod, "For crimes she committed in the absence of the true and rightful Alpha of Creemore."

That sounded wordy and well rehearsed. I had a mental picture of Knox and his two goons singing that chorus all the way up the 400 Highway to Creemore—three happy summer campers heading up toward the Muskokas for a spot of weekend fun.

"Did one of my pack lodge a complaint?" inquired Trowbridge.

"What?"

"That's the only legitimate reason the NAW could use to enter my territory. Unless we were behind on our tithes?" He lifted his shoulders in mock confusion and called, "Hey, Harry, come on over here."

The older Were was leaning against the porch column, filling in time by pruning his nails with a wicked-looking knife. "Coming." He closed it with a click and sauntered down the steps.

Trowbridge waited until his second was nicely framed

for the camera before asking, "Was the pack behind in the accounting?"

Harry's mouth pruned then he shook his head. "No, boss."

"So all the usual shit had been taken care of? The monthly meeting reports, the paperwork—all that useless bureaucratic crap that the council insists we send them like clockwork—had it all been done? Sent in on time?"

Not by me.

"Yes," replied Cordelia. I turned. She stood where I'd left her, underneath the soft golden glow of an old porch light. Harsh grooves bracketed her mouth.

"Then I'm confused," drawled Trowbridge. "Why would the NAW feel that my pack was in need of their assistance?"

"But . . . the pack didn't have an Alpha. They only had her . . ."

Rachel blew a huff of air through her nostrils. It was her only comment, but it carried weight, because Weres are all about the body cues.

"A mate can act on behalf of her consort in times of great need," he said coldly. "There's been incidences in the past where an Alpha's consort has done so for the pack's overall best interests. So, I don't see a problem."

"Yeah, for a week, maybe, but—"

"Irrelevant," my mate replied. "The precedent's been set. So, Kenny, you tell me who complained and we'll bring him or her here and give them a chance to explain."

I bet Fatso would have given away his entire collection of Guns N' Roses albums to have been able to produce a name at that precise moment. Any name would do.

Before he could fabricate, Trowbridge said, "Don't even go there, asshole."

Inspiration came to Newland. "There were formal charges! Signed by Whitlock himself! Knox read them in front of your pack before . . ." His voice trailed off as he realized the danger of completing that thought.

Before they tied Hedi to the old oak tree.

"What charges were read that night?" asked Trowbridge, his tone soft, deadly.

A pause as Fatso frantically tried to recall them.

I couldn't stand it; the scent of the trapped wolf's base fear melded to his urine; the way his chest rose and fell like he'd been run to the ground. I answered for Fatso. "I was charged with killing Robson Trowbridge."

"Yet here I stand," he said, his voice clipped.

"And with breaking the Treaty of Brelland."

My Trowbridge turned at his waist and looked over his shoulder toward Biggs and the cell phone that was recording every word, every lie.

And part of me wondered as I watched my man . . . did he know? That those cheekbones, those glittering eyes, that aquiline nose—even that shorn hair, which made him look tough and battered and three times the predator than the world-weary rogue he'd been before—all of it would play so well to the camera's eye.

The hero returns.

"The Treaty of Brelland," he said. "Jesus, I hate the word 'treaty.' It sounds like an agreement, but it's not. The Alphas that signed that treaty never had the option of choosing death over exile." He shook his head. "Making those men sign that piece of paper in their own blood . . . each one of those Alphas knowing that their own DNA would be used to key the portals to recognize Were blood so that no wolf could ever travel through the passages between the two realms again.

"My mate sent me through the gates. Not only did I survive the trip, but I'm back. Do I look weak to you?" His smile was grim and quick, just a flash of teeth. "The only person that seems to care about the treaty is you,

Whitlock. The Fae didn't retaliate. The Great Council has had six months to act and they haven't said squat. You know why? Half of those old farts remember the good old days when the portals were open, and trade between our races was profitable to both parties. They're watching and waiting to see what will happen. I can tell them what will happen—not a damn thing. It won't change anything."

A muscle tensed in his jaw, then he turned back to Ken Newland—the Were whose stink of welling terror was forming a knot at the base of my throat. "Why'd you really come here?"

"We were serving justice," the blindfolded Were said weakly.

That camp song is getting old.

Trowbridge's tone dropped to a threat-promising whisper. "I told you not to lie, you fucking asshole." He leaned in close until I knew that his breath must have warmed Newland's lower jaw as Knox's had heated mine.

"This is how I see it: the NAW waited until the last night of the moon, and then they sent in their team, waving papers and talking about trials 'by peer.' They gathered up the pack an hour before the moon's call—breaking I don't know how many council rules of protocol—knowing that few wolves can think beyond the hunt when they're that close to their change. They tried to strip the civilization from my Weres, which is no easy thing to do because most of my pack has been living the fat life for so long they hardly recognize their own balls." His voice was low, almost reflective. "My mate was supposed to die at the hands of her own, and when that didn't happen, Knox tried to finish the job with a knife." He dug into his pocket.

Ken Newland miserably wagged his head. "I didn't—"

"Why did you come?" Trowbridge suddenly shouted.

"Knox said we had to kill the fat little Fae bitch! It was

business—she was going to screw up everything!" Fatso rocked his head in distress. "I was just doing what I was supposed to. I was just—"

"Harry," said Trowbridge. "Give me your knife."

"Don't," I said, so quietly.

My lover stepped to the side, so that the camera could see both him and Newland; the Alpha and the condemned. "I am not this guy's peer, any more than you are mine, Whitlock. And I'm not a 'civil' man anymore. Nobody threatens my mate. Nobody sends a guy jacked up on sun potion into my territory. And *nobody* tries to take what is mine. I am the Alpha of Creemore. If you want my ass, you better come for me. Not fuck around threatening my mate."

Harry's bowie knife opened with a click. "This isn't silver," Trowbridge said, placing the tip of the knife to Kenneth Newland's belly. "And it's not as big as the one Knox used on my mate when she was helpless, but it will do."

Then he told me, "Close your eyes."

But I didn't. Even when he leaned in and sank the first inch of the knife's blade deep into the screaming man's belly. Though . . . I couldn't help myself. Even though I'd clenched my teeth until my molars hurt, the sound was building inside my throat. I covered my mouth with my hands but still couldn't quite smother my own high cracked whimper.

It is likely the thing that saved Fatso's life; that one thin note of absolute horror that I couldn't quite disguise.

In our absence, Anu had recovered the plastic barbecued chicken container from the garbage and was using my spoon to retrieve whatever fat dregs had been left in the bottom of the molded drip trenches.

"Can't we get her more meat?" I snapped.

A caring comment that prompted Anu and her ferret to perform a totally unnecessary avoid-Hedi circuit around the table to place the container on her kitchen chair. Disdain etched on her face, my brother's daughter's message was clear: that was *her* seat and *her* reclaimed pickings. As was her ownership of the window by the old pantry— even if she had to slide between Biggs and the wall to get to her favorite post.

Later, I'd find a way of connecting with her. Later, when I was steadier.

He knifed him . . .

Cordelia moved toward the cabinet that held the strong spirits. She uncapped a bottle and took a good, long swallow. It did the trick, judging from her discreet shudder. My ex-roomie wiped her mouth and muttered, "Does anyone else want anything to drink?"

"I don't drink anymore," said Trowbridge, hands braced on the sink. His jeans were slung low, his spine a long, deep groove in his well-muscled back. His rib cage swelled as he inhaled for a silent sigh, then he turned to toss the paper towel he'd used to dry his hand in the trash.

"You don't drink anymore?" I said.

He shook his head but he really wasn't seeing me—his gaze was distant, like he was Einstein on the cusp of adding "squared" to $e = mc^2$.

I should have congratulated him. But I didn't. I'd run the gamut of responses over the last twenty minutes. Being witness to a replay of what had happened to me in the backfield? It had left me off balance. It had been too real, too violent. I knew that wolves weren't boy scouts. I'd witnessed a few blood-speckled Weres trudging back from their monthly hunt on more than one occasion.

But this? It had been different. Trowbridge had done it wearing his mortal skin. A man set on a cold and deliberate kill. I couldn't imagine one of the Creemore wolves doing that. They were shopkeepers and café owners. Accountants and suits. They'd spent too many years blending in with the human populace and sitting in front of the boob tube. In their case, the cliché "you are what eat" could be modified to "you are what you watch."

I just watched Trowbridge deliberately knife a guy.

He was protective: this was very good. Though . . . the way he'd leaned into the blade, the smell of the wolf's terror and blood, the total lack of expression on my man's face . . . it had spoken to all parts of me. My Fae had been speculative. Mortal-me—good old Hedi, the mouse-hearted—had been appalled. But my wolf had flooded me with hunger.

You are what you watch.

"I need chocolate," I said. But I didn't move to check the cabinets. Truth was, I couldn't go another foot, so I remained where I was, just inside the back door. Four linear feet into the kitchen; two semimortal feet ready to haul ass out of it.

You know that old "last straw" metaphor?

That was two straws ago.

Trowbridge had left Fatso alive, but he'd also left the knife half in and half out of his prey's belly; the need for revenge inside him being so acute, my guy couldn't go so far as to personally remove the weapon from the wounded wolf. After, he'd pitched the chain's padlock keys to Harry and said, "I don't care if you have to put him on a plane in a suitcase or a boat in a tackle box, just get him off my land."

That was the good part: he'd pulled back at the last minute; giving me the illusion that he was—despite all claims to the contrary—still civilized. But then, in my opinion, he'd overcorrected. He'd moved from blade to telecommunications.

Standing shirtless and barefoot on the crabgrass, he'd used his scarred thumb to work the menu on Knox's phone.

"I don't think that's a good idea," I'd said, intuiting his intentions.

My mate hadn't deigned to answer. Brows pulled together, he'd scrolled to Whitlock's e-mail address. "Trowbridge, it's a really bad, bad idea," I'd murmured as he'd attached the video to an e-mail. He'd given me a sideways glance. A flicker of blue fire in his eyes. Daring me.

I'd said, "Don't do it."

To which he'd replied, "Have to."

Then the Alpha of Creemore had hit Send and with one squeeze of his scarred thumb, it was done. *No, no, no.* He already wore a "kill-me" sticker on his forehead, compliments of the Fae. One wasn't enough? Now I asked, with remarkable control, "Did you have to send the video to Whitlock? He's already got a reason to want to come down and hurt us."

The Alpha of Creemore had returned to his favorite seat. Blue eyes lifted and pinned me with a pretty good impression of Clint Eastwood—but back in the day when Clint wore a sombrero and smoked thin cigars. "Whitlock will gauge my strength by my reaction to the shit he put you through. I just gave him a visual." He turned to Harry. "Do a tour in an hour, check to make sure all the sentries' points are well manned."

Hello, Son of Lukynae.

By Goddess, here came the cue ball again. I could feel it there squeezed between the muscles of my throat—had felt it, on and off, ever since my brother and Trowbridge had come back. *Fear.* But I kept swallowing it down even as it kept rising up. Too large to expel, too uncomfortable to ignore. The strain of having it lodged there hurt my jaw and made the soft tender skin behind my pointed ears feel pulled and taut.

"It seemed to be overkill to me," I said.

"A strong Alpha doesn't hide, he doesn't wait, and he

doesn't apologize. He takes the offensive." My mate sat sprawled in his chair, his long legs stretched out, his arm resting indolently on the table's edge. He cocked his head to study me through those thick, black lashes.

My inner-bitch did a moan.

"Go big or go home," said Biggs, trying his best to mimic Trowbridge's sprawl.

"Quiet, Chihuahua," snapped Cordelia.

I sat down. Wanting to do something with my hands, I reached for the resealable plastic bag filled with Knox's last effects and held it up to the light. He'd traveled light: a heavy ring bristling with keys, a thin faux-alligator wallet, a leather cord from which hung a coin, and one small glass bottle.

One of these things does not belong with the others.

The vial was approximately three inches long, topped by a cork stopper. It was empty now, though once it had been filled with sun potion. A single dose taken before the moon would stop the Were's body from changing into his wolf. Which is a good thing if you don't want to turn into fangs and fur. But like every other thing in the world, there was a price to it. The longer you took it, the more you craved it. My twin, Lexi, had been an addict and healing him of his increasing need to consume the stuff was the reason I'd agreed to become the Old Mage's nalera.

Its presence had bothered me last night, but so many things were happening, rapid-fire, that I hadn't processed it then. But now I studied the bottle and asked myself some questions I might have asked earlier, if my world hadn't been tipped sideways. "I thought sun potion only belonged in Merenwyn. I didn't know that our Weres ever had access to it."

"They didn't," said Trowbridge. "That's contraband,

probably came across twelve, fifteen years ago. Whitlock must really want this territory because he could have sold that bottle for a fortune."

"Couldn't it have been Knox's?"

"He wouldn't have had that type of money." At the mention of Knox's name, two blue comets began circling Trowbridge's dark pupils. "No, this came from Whitlock. He knew that he needed to dose his man before he sent him into my territory."

"Why?" I said.

"Whitlock timed your trial for a full moon. He wanted Knox to appear as strong as an Alpha. So he had to make sure he would be the last to change into his wolf."

Trowbridge reached for the bag, then tilted back in his seat and kept going, until the chair was balanced on its back legs. He fingered the bottle through the plastic. "Knox didn't have Alpha in him—if he had, he would have gone after me, not my mate. Besides, he reeked of this shit."

I hadn't noticed, being somewhat preoccupied by my imminent execution.

My mate broke the bag's seal. He closed his eyes and took a long, deep sniff. "A female handled either Knox's wallet or the bottle." His pupils moved under his lids. "A halfling."

Upon that pronouncement, the atmosphere in the room, already tense, tightened into a thick soup of emotions. There were battle-ready aromas streaming from Trowbridge and Harry and a spike in Biggs's anxiety. But there . . . what was that? Deep disapproval. Coming from Cordelia.

Why? Was she dismayed that they'd used the word "halfling" in front of me? I've heard worse. To my mind it was an improvement over "mutt" or "half-breed." There was poetic fluidity to it. I tested it in my mind, breaking it into two distinct consonants: half-ling.

"I've never met another halfling," I said. "Are there a lot of us?" That question was greeted with as much enthusiasm as the trophy wife sashaying into the Old Wives' Club.

The lines bracketing Cordelia's mouth turned into grooves. "You're not one of them."

"I'm not? Then what's a halfling?"

Cordelia turned to my mate. "You need to explain this to her, right now. It's obscene how she and her brother were kept ignorant."

I hate this. Being three steps behind everyone. "Trowbridge?" I asked.

My mate rubbed his jaw, his eyes shadowed. "A halfling is sired by a Were and born of a human."

"So there's a subrace of half Weres, half humans?"

"No," he replied.

"Why not?"

The fanwork of lines around his eyes deepened. "Because they die young."

"How young?"

"For some seventeen, for others eighteen."

Before my mouth could shape the obvious question, he explained, "They die at puberty."

"Their puberty is delayed like ours?"

He nodded. "They don't have enough magic in them to survive their first change. That's why it's drummed into you. Don't have sex with a human."

They died? That speculation took me to a whole other place. *Son of a bitch.* "You told me to change into my wolf." I pointed an accusing finger. "Before you came back through the gates—when we used to meet in our dreams. You said, 'You *must* change into your wolf.'"

"I knew you could do it," he replied.

"You told me I *had* to try."

"You did," he shot back. "You couldn't run a pack without showing your fur. And I knew you could do it because your brother could."

"I am *not* my brother."

"There has been some—though very limited—interbreeding between some of the Fae and the wolf packs in Merenwyn. Half-Fae, half-Were kids can turn into their wolf."

But I can't. That's the malodorous statement that hovered over us like a stink bomb.

Biggs's chair squeaked as he shot to his feet. He went to the sink, turning his back on us to stare blindly through the window. His scent leaked angst and tragedy.

"What's up with Biggs?" I mouthed to Cordelia.

She flattened a manicured hand over her heart. Brows raised, she mouthed back, "The Chihuahua loved a halfling." I shouldn't have been able to follow that—that's a lot of silent speak—but all those years of lip-synching to Donna Summer tracks had left their mark on Cordelia.

Oh.

I'd attributed Biggs's lack of dates to his fashion choices—tonight's shoelaces were red. It hadn't occurred to me that he was nursing a broken heart. My memory stirred. "That's for Becci!" he'd shouted before pulling the trigger on Stuart Scawens.

I'd forgotten he'd said it until now—it was a detail that had been hazed over by bigger tragedies. But now, I felt a flicker of shame. I should have asked him about Becci.

One day, I will.

The door opened, and Harry walked in. He took in the scene, face carefully neutral. "So, what are the two of them going on about now?"

"Life, liberty, and—" Cordelia paused for an eye roll that set her fake eyelashes fluttering. "Love with a capital *L*. Our two lovebirds seem to enjoy sparring with each other as much as they do making those bloody bedsprings squeak."

"It's not the bed," said Trowbridge. "It's the chair."

Someone shoot me.

"What did you do with Fatso?" I asked.

Anu's head turned as Harry said in his low rumble, "He's hanging from a hook in the back of a refrigerated trunk that's on its way to Montreal." The pack's second gave me a reproving head shake. "Now, Little Miss. I didn't kill him. He's mostly alive and trussed up like Big Bird. The driver said he'd put pedal to the metal until he's over the provincial border. I told him to leave our friend somewhere inconvenient."

"Good," said Trowbridge, his voice clipped.

"Super," I added, rubbing my eyes. They burned. With fatigue. Not at all because the little comet in Trowbridge's baby blues was calling to my flare. I picked up the bag, opened the seal and took a whiff. To me, the contents smelled of Knox, blood, leather, sun potion, and . . . fudge. If we wanted to be specific about it, maple flavored.

Trowbridge tossed Harry the bag. "Take a whiff of this and tell me if you can recognize the scent." Harry sampled it, and shook his head before passing it to Cordelia. She didn't have any better luck and passed it across the table. Biggs rubbed his nose before he took a delicate snort.

"Well?" asked Trowbridge.

Biggs put the bag down on the pine table and stared at it. Silently, he shook his head.

"I hate thinking of a kid being around Knox," I said.

Trowbridge nodded, his eyes focused on the bottle of

sun potion. Absently, he flattened his hand over the scar hidden beneath his T-shirt. His thumb moved, side to side it swept, following the rough ridges of the now-healed wound.

Chapter Three

Both of the witches had long, thick auburn hair. That's where the obvious similarities ended. The older of the two was about Cordelia's age and perhaps four inches shorter than Trowbridge. She had an air of command to her, possibly because she was on the hefty side and her girth spoke all on its own.

Smart too, I thought, watching her size me up.

The other witch was a little taller than me. Small-boned, thin. When she'd got out of the car, I'd noticed that she'd forgotten to do up at least three of the top buttons of her chic white blouse, and somehow the way she'd arranged her arms made the cleavage of her high firm breasts look like a line that needed to be traced with someone's tongue.

But with any luck, she'd age like her mother.

"We're not related," said the older witch, regarding me with some amusement. "Folks see the red hair and they generally think Elizabeth and me are kin. We're not." She flicked a hard glance at the younger witch. "We just haven't resolved who has the rights to Garnier's Deep Auburn. Tell me, who do you think looks better in it?"

I'm a liar. Part of being a successful one is knowing when to bring one out and when to shut the hell up. I did the latter.

"I'm Natasha Sedgewick," said the older witch.

"And who are you?" I asked the younger witch.

"Elizabeth," she replied, but she pronounced it in the French-Canadian way—*Aleezahbet*. And she directed her answer to Trowbridge with the side dish of a well-practiced courtesan's smile.

I didn't like her.

"There's only the two of you?" I folded my arms over my chest. That served two purposes. Hopefully it made me look like a badass while at the same time it applied pressure to the bite mark on my arm, which had started burning again.

"The rest of our circle is already formed," said Natasha. "Once I know exactly what your pack is interested in, I'll phone it in." Trowbridge lifted his brows and she explained. "Our power comes from a community of minds concentrating at the same time."

At my cough of disbelief, she waved a vague hand toward the ground. "We use the earth's leylines to channel our magic."

"Uh-huh," I said. What balderdash—that's what I was thinking. If there had been a spiderweb of sorcery underneath the ground, wouldn't Mum have told me about it? She was after all a *Fae*, and that trumps any mortal with aspirations of conjuring greatness.

Natasha blew some air through her nose. "So, what do you need?"

"A ward set on the property," said Trowbridge curtly.

She lifted her shoulders. "Then how about we do a walk around the premises? I need to get an idea of exactly how large an area we're talking about."

The Alpha of Creemore nodded, started to lead the way, and then stopped. "Harry, you and Biggs go now," he said.

My old second stepped out of the shadows. Rifle

balanced over his arm. "You sure, boss?" It was clear that he didn't want to leave us with the witches, but one of the sentries along the route had rung in to say that they had bikers at Cash Corners. Why that made them all nervous, I hadn't figured out, nor did I want to know. There was only so much I could take.

Trowbridge nodded.

Harry swallowed his unease down. "Biggs," he said, tossing a set of keys to the younger Were. "I'll head east, you head north."

I looked up at the second-floor windows. Backlit was the shadow of a girl.

How will I say good-bye? What will I tell Lexi? That I left his daughter in the hands of one of my best friends?

Anu yanked the curtain closed. Trowbridge had told her to stay low. I wondered how long that would last. Her father would have taken that caution as a personal challenge to his general dislike of rules and regulations.

I have to stop looking for the Lexi in her.

The fat witch stood on the little wedge of cliff, overlooking the fairy pond. "It's larger than I remembered," she said when Trowbridge shone his torch toward the end of it where the lily pads and bulrushes grew.

I'd stood here, not six hours ago. Sat underneath the tree to my left and held my dying brother in my arms. Unbelievable.

This will work. It will all work.

Across the way, past the still water, past this place, and this patch of earth, was the Stronghold ridge, where once a home of gray brick and faded blue siding had stood. The pack had removed most of the traces of it. Someone had carted away all the brick and taken away the burned timbers of the home that once housed me, my brother, my mom, and my dad. All that was left of that family home was a foundation and the tall dried bones of an old maple tree that once was alive and thick with leaves and now was dead and bare.

A trailer sat beneath that old tree. Its silver skin gleamed under the waning stars. I had the sudden cowardly wish to slink back to the sanctuary of that silver bug. To shut the door to the little room I used to find claustrophobic. Zip myself up into the sleeping bag and cover my head with my old pillow.

The one that didn't smell vaguely of dust mites and Mannus.

Cordelia must have read my face, because she whispered, "Buck up, buttercup."

And least that's what I thought she said.

"*Ça sera très cher*," murmured Elizabeth, her head swiveling as she took in the area we wished enclosed. Then for us Anglophones, she enlarged. "Magic over water?" She garnished that inconceivable problem with a very Gallic shrug. "It is very difficult. This will cost you much."

All said in a charming Francophone accent.

I really don't like her.

A thought that grew when Elizabeth's gaze flitted from the terrain to my mate's damaged hand. Her attention focused on it for a beat, telling me in no uncertain terms that in her books, a man with blue eyes, a fairy pendant, and a few scars was a hell of a turn-on.

And bing!—I shuffled the little French witch out of my "dislike" column into my "despise" column.

Oh. Joy. Apparently, besides walking around with a cue ball lodged in my vocal cords, within forty-eight hours of my mate's return to kith and home, I was suffused by jealousy. Just another one of those wolf bitches who eyed every other female as a challenge to her claim to her mate.

Swallow that down too. Maybe the instinct will drown in the stomach bile I've got going on.

Cordelia placed her gas lamp on a stump. "Shall we get on with it?"

"I want the ward to be drawn all the way around this pond." Trowbridge illustrated what he wanted, using his scarred finger to trace the surrounding ridges. "It's got to enclose it completely. Make it tall, too. Like a dome. And we'll need a trapdoor that will open with a password." Trowbridge thought for a moment. "We'll use the word 'strawberry'."

"Where?" Natasha asked.

I shouldered between Elizabeth and my guy in order to slap the tree under which Lexi had fallen asleep. "Here."

The younger witch flicked me a disinterested glance, then bestowed upon my mate a charming shrug. "It can be done, but as I said, it will be very expensive." She dragged out the *r* in "very" so that we could get just a feel for how pricey such a request would be.

"How much?" I asked bluntly, already tired of them.

Elizabeth's blouse gaped as she used both hands to push her hair off her temples. "This is not of the ordinary, you understand?"

"How much?" asked Trowbridge tersely.

"Well . . ." The younger witch glanced again toward her silent companion.

Natasha's bonhomie disappeared so swiftly, so completely, that I realized that whatever pleasantry she'd offered us before had been of the false variety. Round and podgy can look surprisingly hawklike when the mask of good humor is tossed aside. "You don't have enough money in the world to pay my coven to put a ward around this pond," she said as if she was speaking the opening line of the dialogue of incoming doom.

"Calmes-toi," Elizabeth said in a soothing voice. *"C'est une bonne idée de réfléchir avant de refuser."*

Trowbridge's expression darkened. "Speak in English."

"Allow me to translate," Cordelia drawled. "This pretty bird wants the other one to stop and think before refusing our offer."

In response to Cordelia's language skills, Elizabeth used a French word that caused my BFF's right eyebrow to lift in a way that usually had me running for the hills. The contest of wills between Elizabeth and her was over in an eyeblink. Cordelia was a full-blown Were, and she'd held the title of Toronto's Best Drag Queen for five years in a row back in the late eighties.

A moment later, the young witch dropped her gaze and hid her loss by readjusting her collar with a quick jerk.

Natasha's chest had risen during this skirmish—almost impossible when one stopped to consider how massive a feat of engineering that was. "You have some gall," she said.

She's going to blow, I thought, taking a cautious step backward. Merry slid out of my lace cup, and started hauling arm over arm for a peekaboo. She likes to witness a good explosion here and there. Always had, always will.

And I didn't even try to stop her—she had few enough perks in her life.

A few scratches as she made her summiting move, then the top curved portion of her pendant crested the vee of my blouse in time for her to witness the fat witch jab a stubby finger at Trowbridge.

"You want to think back, chum?" Blotches of red mottled Natasha's cheeks. "When was the last time the Creemore pack asked for some assistance from my coven?"

Her little digit trembled in rage. "Do you remember what happened ten years ago?"

As a question, that one was right up there with who killed Kennedy. Of course he knew, just as I did, what occurred that night. We'd both lost our families in one swift hour of violence and blood.

The real question was, what precisely had her coven to do with the events of that evening?

Evidently, Natasha thought we knew. Because she was clearly insensible to the way Trowbridge's eyes had narrowed until they were two blue slits above sharp, sharp cheekbones. And utterly dismissive of the way Cordelia removed both earrings.

Natasha was having her moment.

"When your uncle asked us to summon a ward for this pond, I thought the request was being made on behalf of your father, the Alpha of Creemore. So of course, we did as required—your pack had been our biggest source of income."

Oh crap. The *Sisters* had placed a ward over the pond that night? They'd been responsible? We'd always thought it had been my aunt Lou. And we'd asked them to come help us?

Someone shoot me. Or better yet, shoot them.

Cordelia pocketed her hoops.

"But that wasn't the case, was it?" Natasha said with magnificent outrage. "Your father—the Alpha of Creemore—died as a result of our spell and your uncle used the protection of *our* ward to pass through the Fae's gates unnoticed." Her tone slipped into the death-and-doom register. "Do you know how much trouble answering the call of Creemore wolves brought unto me and my coven?"

Spitting with rage, she was. Air bubbles of spit collected by the corner of her mouth.

Her fury was a sickening visual contrast to Trowbridge's sudden stillness. So, he hadn't known either. Did his hands itch to throttle her like mine did?

"Good must be balanced with bad," Natasha pronounced. "Your uncle connected us to deaths and destruction. For five years every member of my coven suffered. We had everything from cheating husbands to Revenue Canada coming after us for tax withholding. We lost our homes, our side businesses. Not only was our Karma screwed over but our livelihood went up in smoke. First your uncle Mannus threatened our lives, then he sent out word that we weren't to be trusted. After that, no pack would come near us. It didn't matter that for twenty-five years our magic had kept the wolves safe from humans' eyes. All the cloaking spells, all the hide spells, all the wards we conjured to protect your private hunting grounds—forgotten. Suddenly we were too close to the dark side. All our contacts with the Weres—every single council we'd ever done work for—dried up overnight and the wolves started using another coven."

She lifted her double chin. "And now, you come knocking on our door, again, after all these years. You've got the nerve to ask us to make another ward for this fairy pond. You have balls of steel, wolf!"

"Nastasha," said Elizabeth in an undertone.

But the fat witch was busy giving us the evil eye.

Which was absolutely no match for the Trowbridge preflare, spinning-blue-sparks glare. "Then why'd you come?" he said, his voice too low, his body too tightly coiled.

Natasha said, "Some messages must be delivered in person."

Trowbridge's head reared back. Time for an intervention—no matter how much we both wanted to ass-kick them to the curb, we needed them. We could strangle them later. I touched his rigid arm, felt the stone-hard muscles beneath his warm skin. "Let me," I said.

This type of woman, I well understood. My Fae aunt Lou had been prone to long, dark periods of deep sulking, followed by explosions of anger. When I'd been an easily spooked kid, those rages had scared the crap out of me.

Not anymore.

"Let's be real blunt," I said to her. For the first time in the last ten minutes, I felt on top of everything. I'd seen the view from this particular mountaintop before and knew how to navigate the way down. Easy peasy: ignore the bluster and carry on.

"You're going to give us the ward. Because no one in their right mind would come here—in the dead of night, to the wolf's den—and dare to piss off the Alpha of Creemore, unless in the end, she meant to do business." I folded my arms. "Both you and I know that this is your coven's last opportunity to get back in favor with the Weres. And in the end, it all comes down to money, right?"

See? I wasn't above stealing Trowbridge's words or logic.

"If you don't put a ward around that pond, there won't be 'further opportunities' with the Weres. This is your chance to win back wolf approval and go back to sending your kids to private school." And then, just to sweeten it, I said, blandly, "The money will really start to roll in after this."

Perhaps it was the bland that set me up. Or maybe it's because I followed up with the slightly smug, "Let's cut to chase. Tell us what you want."

Natasha's smile was cruel. "Cry for me, Fae. Give me a Tear and we'll call it even."

Whoosh. The air rushed out of my lungs.

"Think again," said Trowbridge.

Natasha shook her head, sure of herself. "No. That's

what I want—a Fae Tear. About the size and shape of a tear-shaped diamond, but many times more valuable." She smiled at me, the fat Persian cat thinking about moving itself for a spot of fun. "They say all you have to do is make a Fae cry and hold out your hand. Her tear will harden in your palm. Turn to a diamond before your very eyes."

"That is a myth," Trowbridge said, his tone as cold and harsh as driving sleet.

"No. It's not," she said. "And it's what we should have been given for the last ward we put over this pond. But we were tricked, weren't we? We didn't know that Mannus had a Fae in the background."

"I could kill you right now, right here, bitch," said Trowbridge.

"But you won't. The Alpha of Creemore doesn't call on old friends to visit near midnight unless he's desperate."

"*C'est vrai,*" said Elizabeth.

Natasha lifted her eyes to meet Trowbridge's fury with a cool that belied her earlier heat. "One Tear for one ward."

"That's not on the table," my lover said, his voice a low threat.

Revenge is sweet, isn't it?

The tempting probability of it had swollen Natasha's chest. She tipped back her head, and said, really slowly, "You better think about your options, Alpha. Because there is no other coven to turn to. The rest of them want to play it safe—keep it all goodness and light. And none of them are interested in dealing with your pack because they've seen what happened to us." She issued him a smile laced with equal parts satisfaction and surety. "Your mate's going to adjust the balance sheet. She's going to pay the bill that your kin should have paid. She's going to give me a piece of the Fae, crystallized into a diamond. It's the only thing I'm interested in and the only thing our coven will bargain for."

Then she turned to me and stared at my dry eyes.

Tell her you don't have them.

A lie. One that I couldn't carry off because I could see it in her eyes. *She knows.* How did she know I always carried them, safe in the small leather pouch, hanging from the end of the golden chain belt girthing my hips?

She knows.

About those perfect six stones birthed in acute pain. Five of them squeezed from my mother's eyes, one of them from my own—brought forth as I lay on Cordelia's bathroom floor, Trowbridge's hip warm against mine, knowing that I was falling in love.

They were precious beyond words. Personal. Private. Oh Goddess, to have one of those corrupt women touching them. Owning it. Using it to absorb evil.

No, no, no.

Trowbridge reached for me, and pulled me close. Arms wrapped around me, one shoulder protectively hunched against the witches' sight line so that I could rest my cheek against his chest in relative privacy.

He knows how I hate being watched. How does he know that?

We've spent so little time together.

His breath warmed my ear. "Forget it," he whispered. "They're just leveraging for more money."

I shook my head. I truly did know this type of woman, having lived with one. The Natashas of the world don't take a perceived grievance lightly. The cost to fix a wrong to a woman such as she would always outweigh the value of the original offense.

"We'll call the portal without a ward," he whispered into my ear.

My breath had nowhere to go. It came out of my lungs

in a slow exhale, hit his shoulder, and then returned to warm my face. On it, I smelled sweet syrup and Trowbridge kisses. "The pack will know that we've gone. And they'll be waiting for us when we come back. They'll see my brother—they'll know it's all been a lie. I've seen them turn—"

"I'm an Alpha."

"There's too many of them to nail with your flare all at once, Trowbridge." I swallowed against the knot swelling in my throat.

"I can find another coven."

"Not in time," I said miserably. I pushed away from the security of his hard chest. Slid my hand beneath my waistband, until my fingertips encountered the thin supple links of the chain.

The Fae inside me was angry. I could feel the whip of her annoyance, and worse, I could sense her dark interest in the magic these women promised.

Trowbridge smoothed my hair in a gesture filled with impotent hurting as I bent to examine the pouch. The leather was soft and worn, embellished with silver filigree. Gently I teased open the delicate strings. The stones seemed to wink at me from the bottom of the pouch. Six pale pink. One bright and clear.

Which Tear could I part with?

Trowbridge sucked his breath through his teeth as I pulled out the one I'd shed for him. It had hurt, knowing myself to be falling in love. A small agony as the tear had welled in my ducts.

"I'm sorry," he said, and I knew he meant it, even if I wasn't sure what he was saying sorry for.

I turned to Natasha and held out my closed fist.

She moved closer, until I could smell the sweat of her body and the rot of her soul. "You can't stay while we set the ward," she said. "Your magic will interfere with ours."

I dropped it into her palm and watched with dull eyes as she folded her fingers over the bits of him and me, and then, because I couldn't stay, not without birthing another frozen tear, I said, "I'm going inside."

Though of course, I didn't. Even though Trowbridge told me to lock the door until he was through with them, I was loath to go into the house, where Anu waited. So instead I sat down on the back porch's bottom stair, and stared at them from a distance while I slowly pried up a long sliver of crumbling pine from one of the rotting stoop's risers.

You'd think it wouldn't take long to cast a ward.

You'd be wrong.

An hour passed—the owl roosting in the beech tree hooted three times; a mouse darted along the line of overgrowth that edged the woods; something small and unidentified burrowed under a layer of leaves; and my ass started to send "damp" and "chilled" progress reports to my nervous system.

And *still,* the witches were working on setting the wards. Evidently calling up enough magic to envelop the pond and surround the cliffs in a ward was a complicated business. The first step was to establish the area that Trowbridge wanted protected by the ward. Thus, he, Cordelia, and the fat one had done a survey along the edges of the cliff running along the ridge of his family's property followed by a precarious duckwalk along the thin crumbling precipice that bordered the parameters of the cemetery— I'm thinking *that* was Trowbridge's punishment for the witch's general insolence—and then finally across my family's land and down our path all the way to the small pebble-strewn beach.

Natasha had made a big deal of using her walking stick to sketch a line in the earth.

Show-off.

The skinny one—"Aleezahbet"—had chosen not to walk beside them, opting instead to parallel their progress around the property. Strangely enough, of the two witches, she looked more engaged with the whole see-me-cast-a-spell process. Her mouth was moving, and her gaze seemed distant.

As the foursome had slowly inched past my porch, I asked innocently, "What's she doing?" Mostly because I wanted to poke Natasha with a bear stick. She would have been far happier if I'd truly gone inside the house.

The woman needed to learn to live with disappointment.

Natasha had said, "The leylines are a web beneath the soil. She's searching for the strongest ones."

Ah, yes. The infamous leylines.

A tad grittily, Natasha had elaborated. "As Elizabeth follows them, she becomes a satellite tower, beaming the coven's power up through this plane on the earth. I, in turn, feed from her power. We are all connected."

Hogwash.

Trowbridge had given her his own searing glance of disbelief. "I've got limited patience for this shit. This ward better be functioning—"

"It will be."

"I want a demonstration of that before you leave this place."

"You shall," the older witch had said, looking straight into his blue eyes.

My mate's nostrils had flared.

He could have scent-tested for a lie all he wanted. This woman was the mixologist of fibs. She knew exactly how to layer truth with falsehood, wicked ounce by ounce, so that all you saw was a seemingly innocuous cocktail. Smelled right. Tasted right. Felt bad in the belly.

I may have just given my first Tear to a bunch of no-good charlatans.

That insight in itself should have been enough to make me want to hit the maple syrup. But what really added to my misery was the fact that Fae-me was on high alert. Magic was being stirred, and she was acutely interested. Alive and speculating. Assessing things I could not understand with eyes far keener than mine. I could sense her working out a problem, as if it was string in her hand into which she kept tying and untying the same knot.

Was it me? Or did the air feel tighter? Thinner in oxygen?

I pulled out Merry, and cupped her in my cold hand to borrow a bit of her heat. My amulet let out a measure of energy that instantly made me feel warmer, but she didn't make me feel calmer, the way Trowbridge did. Even when things were bad, having him in the same room made me feel . . . safer.

I got up, dusted off the pine slivers from my jeans, and headed for the lookout point to check on the ward status. Down by the pond, forward progress seemed stalled. The four of them were by the water's edge, examining the little creek that fed into the pond. Cordelia's mouth was a thin grim line, her arms folded. Their voices carried well over the water.

Natasha said, "This creek wasn't here last time."

"It's always been here," said Trowbridge flatly.

She scowled at it, then shook her head. "I can't do it. I can't seal a ward over a stream. It doesn't matter if it's only two feet deep. Magic won't settle over moving water."

"So I'll get a couple of two-by-fours. Lay them flat over the stream," said Trowbridge.

"It can't be processed wood," she said, shaking her head side to side. "It will interfere with the—"

"Hocus-pocus," said Cordelia sourly.

Natasha's jowls shook as she pursed her lips. "Our talent."

Then she pointed over to the remains of a long dead maple. Its trunk lay split in two, half covered by vegetation on the slope of the hill. "That will do. Use them to make a bridge over the stream. But you'll have to seal any chinks between them with mud, or the ward won't set."

"Mud?" Trowbridge repeated. By the light of the lamp I could see his expression. Testy, he was. Very testy. "Why can't we just put a tarp over the logs?"

"It must be organic."

The gas lamp highlighted Trowbridge's sharp cheekbones. He stared at the duckweed-choked water with acute distaste.

"I'm out," said Cordelia.

"No you're not," he growled, turning for the hill. "Help me with these logs."

She straightened her cardigan. "This is a Simon Chang."

"I'll buy you two new tops. One in pink." Trowbridge used his boot to flatten the burdocks that grew thick on the slope. He bent them at the base, creating a passage for Cordelia. "One in a blue to match your eyes—"

"You'll buy me four." She huffed as she stepped gingerly into the path he was making for her. "In fine wool. With pearl buttons. From Holt Renfrew."

He half turned. "Can't I pick up a few sweaters from the Bay?"

"Four," she sniped. "From Holts."

The witches had requisitioned one of the gas lamps and had climbed halfway up the narrow trail that led to Trowbridge's house. A small landing of sorts had been created by a huge flat outcrop of rock.

Elizabeth put the lamp on it and shed her coat. "We

will need absolute silence as we concentrate. Nothing must interrupt us, or break our focus. We are calling to elemental magic."

Mortals playing with that stuff?

"It is powerful here," Natasha murmured. "Stronger than I've felt before. If we lose control of it, it will be very bad."

"How bad?" Cordelia turned.

"Bad," Nastasha said baldly.

"Wonderful," Cordelia drawled.

"Come on, Cordie." Trowbridge gave her a little shove. "The sooner we make their damn bridge, the sooner they can enclose the pond with the ward."

Chapter Four

Casperella was having a spook-out. There was no other word for it. The Fae ghost kept bouncing from end to end of her little home on the spit of cemetery land that overlooked the pond, for all the world resembling one of those shameful Canadian flags that had been left out all winter to become national eyesores. Taunting relics of a brighter day; tattered edges fluttering with each stiff breeze.

I rubbed my ear looking for ease.

The parameters of her final resting place were delineated by a low wall, built so long ago that whatever time and effort the original builder had invested in the careful placement of each fieldstone was now moot. The barricade had fallen sometime long ago, and now pine needles accumulated against the low imprint of the once-firm wall.

A sigh was building inside my chest.

I could go inside. Then I wouldn't have to watch her fluttering back and forth like a demented moth.

I had mixed feelings about the Fae ghost. Two days ago, she'd stolen some of my magic. Fortified by it, she'd transformed herself from a mute, ghostly apparition to a far more substantial specter. With form came voice, which she'd used to call the Fae portal.

Yes. A damn ghost knew the song and I didn't.

However, Casperella's summons had set Trowbridge's

and Lexi's homecoming into motion, as well as serving as a hell of a distraction when it looked like it was curtains for me.

Technically, I wasn't sure if I owed her or not. She did thieve from me, but stealing isn't really a big, black negative on my moral checklist. Perhaps that was the reason I couldn't escape the feeling that I should tell her the Merenwyn-bound train was pulling into the station. The gates were going to be called in an hour or two. It could be her last chance to go home.

Karmawise, it seemed like a good idea.

I know I said that I'd never be Karma's bitch again, but that doesn't mean I'm not aware she's there, waiting like the sister-in-law who really hates you and is just dying to see you do something that deserves a huge, public smackdown.

And—much harder to deny—I was my mother's daughter.

Part of me is Fae.

Unless someone warned Casperella that she needed to be inside the ward boundaries being drawn at that very minute around the fairy pond, she was going to be forever locked out of her homeland. Which could have been my homeland, if Mom had married a Fae nobleman instead of a Were brewery worker.

Maybe I could encourage her to move past her walls.

Head to the light, Casperella. All will be welcome.

I held the lungful of air for one more resistant second, then let out a long, heavy, why-me exhale. Making a detour to the porch, I picked up my flashlight, and headed across the lawn for the path that led through the swath of mixed woods that delineated the Alpha's private residence from the pack's gathering field.

The second I stepped on it, the kid's bite mark flared.

Pain, sharp as if the little guy's molars were crushing my skin again.

"Fae Stars!" I sucked in some breath sharply and bent over at the waist, protectively cradling my arm in the universal "damn that hurts" pain comma.

Crap. I could smell sweet peas.

Grimacing, I pulled aside the wrappings. The bite had reopened again. A bead of floral-sweet blood now decorated the deepest imprint left from the kid's eyetooth. But even worse? The surrounding skin beyond those two oval half rings had a slight—though definite—green fluorescent glow to it.

My arm's green. That can't be good.

Kind of unsettling. No one wants to look down at their arm and see illumination. But there it was. *I've been marked.* He'd left something on me, that kid—besides a troubled conscience and a bucketload of guilt. When his teeth had pierced my skin in Threall, either some of his magic or some of Threall's magic had seen an opportunity to find a new home.

But what was with that sudden, needle-sharp pain?

I walked to about the spot where the bite had suddenly redeveloped teeth, and then, arm out, I did a blind-man shuffle. Nothing. No crushing pressure. Not even a twinge. I took another step in the general direction of the path, and then another, and then . . . bingo, the bite throbbed. Acute and rather miserable pain.

I retreated and the nasty throb ratcheted down to a thrum.

Merry extended the tip of her vine to snag my jacket's collar, then did a rather inelegant scramble to my shoulder for a better viewing point. Her body twisted this way and that, as if she was expecting a mage to come strolling out of the woods.

"I think we just walked across a line of magic, Merry."

My amulet had a think about that, then patted me, kind of the way a mum might when she saw the line of D plusses on her kid's report card. But the heart of her stone was tinged with orange—her color for caution.

"Yes," said my Fae impatiently. "Magic."

Huh. So, leylines *are* a mesh beneath the crust of the earth?

Okay then.

And now, my arm pinged—or rather, imaginary teeth ruthlessly crushed my flesh—whenever I passed one of those leylines? That was both fascinating—hey Mum, look what I can do!—and frustrating because there was no other path through to the cemetery, unless I wanted to retrace the cliffside walk that Trowbridge had done with Natasha. And to do that? Well, I'd need to use my flashlight, which would definitely highlight the fact that I wasn't waiting patiently on the porch.

A roll of thunder. Sounding close, and yet the sky was still clear. There was no blanket of clouds drifting across the waning stars.

The path beckoned. How quickly could I nip down it? A minute if I walked fast?

I started off at a brisk trot, which quickly splintered into an anguished sprint. Twelve seconds later, I burst into the pack's gathering field like I was going for the blue ribbon, arm raised, bite mark flickering like a glow worm.

The meadow smelled of the pack, and of fear, and of recent death. The hair stood up on the nape of my neck as I walked past the tree to which I'd been chained before Knox had plunged the knife into my chest.

The long grass at the edge of the field still struggled to bounce back from the trampling of Elizabeth's boot heels. Some of it looked a little seared and dry, which was odd—almost as if someone had dragged a lit torch along it.

My gaze followed it all the way to—

That's when I had one of those moments. Edison with his lightbulb. Newton with his apple. Lady Gaga the first time she saw a pair of fake, bling-studded eyelashes. There are coincidences and *coincidences*. If Elizabeth was truly following the leylines, then they were extraordinarily conveniently placed. What are the odds that these magical underground ribbons of power would just happen to coincide with a path through the woods, and more extraordinarily, the only gap in the long line of the living fence created by old cedars?

That was no natural break in the shrubbery. I'd cut the hole myself, with a hedge trimmer I'd permanently borrowed from Home Depot. Aleezahbet wasn't following leylines.

So what was she laying a trail down of?

I turned off my flashlight as I entered the cemetery. I didn't need it anymore. Ghosts are inner-lit. Between my glow-stick arm and Casperella there was enough light.

The Fae ghost hovered near the edge of the cliff, where she could monitor the witches' progress. Judging how the tatters of her gown were weaving nastily around her, she wasn't happy about it. I crept to one of the pine trees, and using its trunk to hide my presence, took a quick peek. Trowbridge and Cordelia had just placed one fallen log over the two-foot span, and were heading back to forage on the incline for another.

I'd better hurry.

"Pssst," I whispered to the ghost.

She turned. Her face was a vague smear. Her hair, definitely unappealing, dark Medusa ropes that floated in a current I could not see.

I cut to the chase. "Before the sun rises, we're going to

summon the gates to Merenwyn. It will be open for a short time and then it will be closed." I put enough finality in my tone to infer that it will never be opened again. "If you want to return home, that will be your chance to go through." I pointed to the crumbling edge of her wall. "You'll need to cross this wall, though, before the ward the witches are setting is complete."

She silently regarded me.

Being mute has it drawbacks.

A quick glance toward the pond. Trowbridge, face set in a snarl, was entering the water. Expression grim, he bent over and scooped up some mud. He waded back toward the improvised bridge he was fashioning.

He's going to need a shower after this.

"Come on, Casperella. Here's your chance. Just go." I gave her a little quick off-you-go wave to spur her on her way, and then when she didn't do much more than hover in front of me, I added my tight, Starbucks-barista's smile. The one that was shorthand for "Here's your drug-of-choice. Now, please, go swill it elsewhere while I prepare the next addict's drink."

It's uncomfortable to find yourself being studied by a ghost. And a little disquieting when the apparition decides to come closer for a better look-see. I backed up until my hip brushed a pine tree. "Well, you can make up your own mind. I've done my good deed for the day."

I thought she might touch me, or worse, try to steal some of my magic again. If so, I was going to do something. Punch her. Or run. Whatever worked.

But all she did was float past me, leaking sadness and longing, until she came to the edge of her wall. There she hovered, rags flapping around her, her back turned toward the pond and potential freedom, with her gaze fixed on the cemetery.

What on earth was she so focused on? Escape was in the opposite direction.

I pivoted. The cemetery was exactly that—a *cemetery*. Past the paint-flaking staves of the rotting picket fence that served as an additional barrier to this forgotten end of the graveyard there wasn't much out of the ordinary. We had a few trees—the oldest being at least a couple hundred years old. And the older tombstones—the first wave in a sea of them—thin and narrow, pocked with green moss now graying in the fall's chill. Beyond those relics, we had the circular road that led in and out of the cemetery. Two Were ghosts, who usually kept to themselves. And then a whole bunch more markers—a wavering line that followed the swell of the land.

I chewed the corner of my lip.

Merry got it before me. She delicately shook one of her vines free from the nest of gold surrounding her amber heart, and tapped me on the face. Lightly at first, then with enough pressure to turn my head in the direction she wished.

Look down, she silently urged me.

I did. Just beyond Casperella's reach, nestled amid the ruins of the picket fence, were five pint-sized monuments. The inscription of the closest read, "Absolom (1746–1747 Lamb of God)." My gaze went to the other names. Prudence, Samuel, Anne, Earnest. Five little graves. One for each infant loved and lost.

Merry climbed closer up her chain, so that the warm roundness of her belly fit in the hollow of my collarbone. "These are hers," I whispered to my friend. Merry dipped in agreement, and the heart of her stone turned the color of bruised peaches.

I glanced at Casperella, and then once more at the stone wall that surrounded her final resting spot. "You're trapped

here, aren't you? You can't reach your babies even if you
wanted to."

The taunting cruelty of it. Is this how a pack treats a
Fae?

Goddess, I've had my fill of trapped souls.

"I'm coming closer, so you don't need to do one of your
spook flutters," I warned Casperella, shuffling closer. "I
want to check something." I held out my bandaged arm
over the remains of the wall.

The moment I held my dandy new magic-sensitive
limb over the wall, it went weak.

I mean, *weak.*

Ever tried to use your arm after it's gone to sleep? Know
how it just hangs there from your shoulder and says "nah"
to all your body's demands to move? Well, whatever kept
Casperella chained to the confines of her stone prison
caused my whole arm to go limp and lifeless.

I stepped away from the stones, and almost immediately felt pins and needles revive my damn near useless
appendage. What crime had Casperella committed to jus-
tify the pack walling in her mortal remains in this little
spit of land? And furthermore, what kept her from doing
a spook-float out of this tiny spit of land?

Intuition prickled.

Mouth dry, stomach hurting, I aimed my foot at the
wall and started kicking. Hard and fast as if each one had
a name inscribed on it. *Here be injustice. Here be intoler-
ance. Here be cruelty.* I attacked the wall until it lay
plundered, and then I scuffed the ground until the long
line of spent pine needles that had accumulated at the
heels of that terrible wall were gone too. When the ground
lay bare to me, I grimly found a sturdy branch, and used
it to begin to dig.

Within moments, I spotted the rusted, riddled misery
hidden beneath the soil.

Pure iron.

Poison to a pure-blooded Fae. Proximity to it will cause most to feel like they've been tipped naked into an arctic sea—they'll writhe in the teeth of terrible cold until they're lucky enough to fall insensible and drift away into the endless sleep. But I'm a half-breed, and for me, up to this moment, my reaction to the ore was milder. Close contact produced a sense of biting cold—the swift shaft of numbing hurt you'd experience if you were dumb enough to touch a steel flagpole in the dead of winter with the tip of your bare tongue—followed by a drugging wave of deep fatigue that fortunately never sank me into anything more than a dazed slumber. Past experience had taught me that touching iron didn't kill me, or take me into the dreaded never-never land.

So, unlike Casperella, I wasn't terrified of iron. But that didn't mean I wasn't wary around it.

Filthy stuff. I tried to pry the piece from the ground, but the rusting chunk was awkward to lift—what with my right arm being so inconveniently weak around it. With a smothered curse, I found another sturdy stick, and fashioned myself a pair of clumsy chopsticks. Teeth clenched, I set myself to the task of teasing that festering misery out of the ground. I'd got the pointed edge of one stick under the piece of ore, and was fumbling to lift it with my improvised chopsticks, when my bite wound started whimpering again.

I glanced down at it. Yup, right through the bandage, each tooth indent was radiating an eerie light, just an increment less brilliant than a green glow stick. Lovely.

"Move to the side, Casperella," I said. "I'm going to toss this thing."

I suited action to words, and watched with grim satisfaction as the iron piece flew a few feet closer to the cliff, showering flakes of rust. A curious skunk watched me

repeat the process twice more—plucking the cold poison
from the ground and chucking it to the side—until there
was a path two feet wide of clean earth, untainted by iron.

"There you go," I said to Casperella, sitting back on
my heels.

It was like someone had pulled the trigger on the start-
er's pistol.

The cemetery's ghost didn't gracefully glide to the
objects of her desire—she streaked toward them, a gray,
shimmering blur that almost outpaced the speed of light.
"Geez!" I hissed when I realized that I was in her direct
flight path. With a grimace, I huddled tight over my knees
and winced against the blast of chill that ran along my
curved spine as she flew right over me.

A ghost flyby. That's a new one.

I counted to two, then lifted my head.

Casperella weaved through her children's headstones,
helpless to embrace them. It hurt, seeing her do that. Her
tattered gown and her long ropes of hair—I'd seen them
flutter wildly around her, I'd seen them snap to an invisible wind, but I'd never seen emotion expressed like this.

This grieving flow of faded fabric and dark tresses.

"You're free now," I told her softly.

She turned toward me. Mouth, an indistinct gray slash.
Eyes, dark holes.

"You can stay with them—and I'll make sure no wolf
imprisons you again—or you can go. Do what you will."

She thought about that, then, to my amazement, she
floated deeper into the cemetery, moving toward the old
ancient oak that brooded, alone and somehow miserable,
in the oldest part of the graveyard. She touched it with her
hand. Like Mad-one did with her old beech tree in Threall. Probably like I had during my first soul-ball commune in the land of myst.

As if that gnarled and ancient tree contained a soul.

"She's a mystwalker, Merry," I whispered, feeling all sorts of awful.

Oh Goddess, she's like me. If I made it to old age, this is the prize at the end of the rainbow? I'd end up here? Stuck forever in the segregated part of the pack's final hunting ground?

Past me the grave markers rose and fell like buoys on the swell of an ocean bay.

That's when I heard a loud, long metallic groan that made the hair at the nape of my neck stand up.

Merry flashed two pulses of red light.

"It could have been a trick of the wind," I whispered. But there was no breeze. No movement of air. Nothing except the stillness before a storm. I canted my head to the side so I could listen, trying to isolate the sound. Another long screech. The sound of the cemetery gates being pushed wider open—distinctive and discordant.

Normally, those cast-iron gates were padlocked, firmly sealed until yet another brief internment service. Merry, frustrated by her inability to see, unwound a strand of ivy, nabbed the end of my blouse, and did a quick hip-hop toward my shoulder. She braced herself against the wind, straining to see through the gloom.

Was that a car engine idling?

"Try to make like a pendant," I told Merry tersely, as I picked my way over the ruins of the picket fence. Strangely obedient, she slid down her chain until she dangled from its end, then doused her light. We headed up the hill toward the dirt road. The old soft stone markers gleamed in the night. I tilted my head back and let the aromas come to me. Eyes sealed, I concentrated, shuffling scents like a woman going through her mail. New stuff. Old stuff. Wolf stuff—a lot of that from the nearby field. But then— hello—fresh scents. Pungent and real. Two males. One brought with him the stink of body spray, leather, and weed. The other was musty with old sweat.

Neither bore the slightest whiff of wolf.

Humans, then, not emissaries from the NAW.

My ears picked up the sound of a car being set into drive, then the soft whisper of grass hitting the underbelly of a vehicle. Thinking to warn Trowbridge that we had unwelcome company, I started to backtrack. The vehicle was moving faster than I'd calculated. Before I'd gotten to the end of the road, headlights swept around the bend.

I dove for cover, which in that section of the graveyard amounted to two narrow and tall markers. Both leaned to one side. I went for the straightest one and hunched behind it. Fae-me curling into a tight coil around my waist. Merry's gold, a stiff sea urchin against my throat.

My Asrai friend was upset. She felt I should not have investigated.

I was starting to agree with her.

Particularly once the driver took his foot off the gas and doused his headlights. The big truck passed us slowly, gravel crunching under its tires. A newer model, pricey even to my inexperienced eyes. Dark—either black or navy blue. Tinted side windows. A lot of chrome on the grill. Overall—oversized in every way.

The foolish part of me—the section of myself that could rationalize anything, and pray for the most unlikely—was hoping beyond hope that the vehicle would keep going and follow the curve of the road all the way back out of the cemetery.

The truck braked three feet past our hiding spot.

Crap. Who were they?

I could smell the spicy grease of the burritos they'd eaten earlier right through the glass, and there were no taco stands within a dozen kilometers of Creemore.

A low *brrr* as the passenger's electric window was pressed. "This is it?"

The speaker's chin sported a soul patch that was thinking about branching into a goatee. His eyebrows were mean and dark, and absolutely flat like someone had balanced a ruler on the bridge of his nose, and then used a permanent marker to make two thick bristling lines.

Biker or ex-con—it was written all over him.

"Yeah." I saw the dark shadow of the driver's silhouette give a nod, and watched him drape his arm over the steering wheel. The star's weak glow picked up the silver gleaming on every knuckle. Rings. Ugly and gothic.

Another rumble of thunder. The sound of the storm was bearing down on us, moving too swiftly to be natural. Now it no longer rumbled, it rolled: one continuous sound, its volume rising and falling, like an argument overheard from a great distance.

And yet, still, no wind, no rain. Just the peculiar feeling of a vacuum slowly being strengthened.

"I hate this shit," complained Mean-eyebrows. The passenger door opened, and a booted foot flattened some grass. The silver-toned buckles on the side of his boots were scratched and gouged.

Shit kickers.

"Why couldn't we have used the main road and come in directly?" He cleared his throat and spat a wad at a nearby grave. "This sneaking through the woods makes me feel like Daniel-fucking-Boone."

"Shut up, Itchy," said the other guy. "They've got good hearing."

"Not even Rin-Tin-Tin could hear us over this storm." A jagged white line of lightning flashed in the sky as Itchy made his way to the back of the truck. "Man, this place gives me the creeps."

The biker was right. My hearing was more enhanced

than theirs, but I could hear little over the sound of the storm bearing down on us. Not the witches' chants. Not Cordelia's sighs. Not even the slap of mud being thrown on the chink between two fallen logs.

Bad magic was being drawn from the elements.

My ears hurt with pressure, and my arm was blazing, casting a here-be-magic glow right through the bandages. Inside me, my Fae positively vibrated with the need to come out and explore.

Now I recognized the night of the witches for what it was. The knife edge—that moment between before and after.

Itchy double-tapped the truck's bed cover. "Unlock the tail, Gerry," he called to the driver.

Gerry did.

Itchy quickly lowered the back gate to access the truck's bed. The interior light flared as the driver shoved open his door. "Watch out, man. That rollback cover isn't even a week old. I'll kick your ass if I find a scratch on it tomorrow."

Gerry was what mortals called middle-aged but that felt optimistic. He had cadaver written on his basset hound's face, and each inhale was a wheeze.

"What are you going to do if she starts kicking the shit out of your cover from the inside?" Itchy asked as he pushed back the truck bed's cover.

Gerry said in a faintly bored voice, "I'll shoot her."

Chapter Five

Her? I hate that word. When it's said in that negative tone, it almost always ends up meaning "Hedi." Geez Louise. Exactly what *is* it about me that made a person think, "I'm going to smack her upside the head and kidnap her. No, I'll knife her. Hell, forget that, I'll just shoot her."

That was it—I needed help.

I cast a quick glance to my right. The nearest cover was about fifteen feet away. I'd have to run fast, stay low.

Get to Trowbridge. Warn him and the others.

"I can't see squat," said Itchy, feeling around in the truck bed.

I tensed for the sprint, then froze as light played over the nearby headstones, narrowly missing me. Gerry heaved a big sigh and slid out of his truck. "I should have brought someone else," he said, lumbering to the back of the vehicle, his flashlight in hand. "Because you, my friend, are a big pain in the ass."

Itchy grunted. "Don't blame me because the fucker moved. I told you we should have kept the weapons in the backseat." A smothered curse, then another as he stretched to reach deep inside.

The wind, which had been so still and absent despite the rumbling sky, returned. A fitful stir of the tops of the cedars. Then, as if an angry God leaned down to blow a

·mouthful of hot temper, the current of air suddenly grew
hard and vengeful, shaking the sumacs, until their bare
branches chattered in distress.

I didn't want to be here—playing hide and seek in the
tombstones—while the ward was being set. And I didn't
want the bikers sneaking up on those dear to me. Clapping
my hand over my glowing arm, I shot across the grass toward the first group of markers. And made it safely. Nobody pulled a trigger and came thudding after me.

And so it went. For the next four "Mississippis"—as
Itchy bitched and Gerry sighed—I made progress. Hop-
ping like a hare with serious commitment issues, zig-
zagging from one marker to another, but still making
definite progress toward the cliff, and my guy.

I was about three tombstone groupings away from a
clean escape when Itchy backed out with his prize. "Holy
shit. It's a heavy mother when it's loaded. I feel like Robin-
Fucking-Hood."

When someone says "loaded," a person can't help but
think "with what?" So, even though I was half crouched
behind a distressingly narrow marker, I couldn't squelch
the knee-jerk instinct to peek.

What the hell was Itchy crowing about?

Fae. Stars.

My stomach curdled. A crossbow? Worse—one that
was preloaded. The bolt was long, metal, and capped with
a silver-toned head. A bolt like that would tear through
you, piercing flesh, mangling important organs . . .

I mentally tapped Fae-me. "I need you," I told her. She
impudently brushed past my inner-Were, and surged
upward, a merry little stream of Fae magic coursing
through my veins. At the base of my throat she did a high
five, then split to run down my arms. My Fae talent fat-
tened the ends of my fingertips—paused there for less time

than I could summon up the tally-ho—then streamed out of the ends of my hands, a long, supple coil of bright green light. A serpent, whose scales shimmered with lovely bits of pretty iridescence.

"There is magic in the air," Fae-me breathed.

It is bad magic. You pay attention to the guy with the bow.

Fae-me heard the phrase "bad magic"—tested it, found that it made no sense, and decided to look for herself. Which is dumb, because she's blind, and her "sight" is limited to whatever I'm looking at. She took a brief comprehensive look, then did a periscope pivot toward the cliff and all the delights of the bad magic. *No!* I gave her a jerk. She whipped around, clearly annoyed, and in so doing, dislodged a small stone that had been propped on the edge of the tombstone behind which we hid.

It landed with a nice loud click on the grave marker's cement footing.

"What was that?" hissed Itchy.

Old instincts made me roll myself into a ball. *I am a small little mouse, invisible behind this tombstone.* Light played over the gravestones. The golden beam slowed on the monument stone to my far left—*maybe he didn't see it*—then outlined the stone next to it—*surely he can't see me curled up like a hedgehog behind this marker*—and then finally on mine.

"I can see you," I heard Gerry say.

Make yourself smaller.

"I can still see you." To prove it he played a circle of light on my knee.

"Don't fucking move!" Itchy shouted, precisely at the same time Gerry told me to put my hands over my head.

Screw that. I had magic. I raised my hand—

* * *

I never saw the horseshoe coming.

The biker threw the piece of iron at me like a prize-winning ring tosser. I saw the briefest glint of metal, then the U-shaped piece of misery landed with a thump and minicloud of dust around the stake of my size-six sneaker. Immediately, my big toe began to burn with cold, and I had that same sinking sensation I got the day I put my wet tongue on the frozen flagpole.

Iron. Pure and terrible.

My Fae recoiled like a cobra meeting a mongoose. "Poison!" she hissed. Then she took off in full retreat, skimming the tops of the tombstones, heading toward the safety of the pond—all very much, Good-bye, Hedi.

She got ten feet and no farther. Because, well, she was attached to me. I gave her another hearty jerk, and she returned.

"Attack them," I said through my teeth.

"Poison!" she sobbed, curling herself behind me.

I'm not the only coward. A wave of languor swept over me. Numbing, drugging cold right through the canvas of my shoe. I told my foot to move. My toe said, "Forget about it."

"That saved us some time." Gerry ambled up, carrying a light-colored blanket, and a length of rope. "What the hell was she doing in the cemetery?"

Trying to even up with Karma.

I counted to five, and when Itchy didn't fire, I raised my gaze. To find myself staring at the end of the cross-bow pointed at me. To be honest, it's not a good feeling. He'd embellished the end of the bolt with what looked like a handcrafted arrowhead. I stared at the dull sheen of the silver-toned flange, knowing someone had told him to come loaded for Fae.

"Son of a bitch," said Itchy. "Is that really her?"

"Think so."

"She walked right into our arms. Damn, how's that for luck?"

About par for the course, thank you very much.

"This is going to be a whole lot easier than we thought." Even so, Itchy approached me cautiously. "Don't you even breathe. I know all about you Fae bitches."

Yes, because there are so many of us. Myth-believing asshole.

"Watch her other hand," said Gerry.

"I got it." Itchy balanced the crossbow in the crook of his elbow as he reached behind himself. The bolt wavered as he struggled to unhook the other horseshoe from his waistband. "That should do it," he said, pitching it near—but thankfully not on—my other foot.

Gerry tossed the blanket on the ground. "Put this over your head. Be careful doing it."

"Why?"

"Because we want your hands immobilized."

Change in plan. Nail him with your mighty flare.

I lifted my heavy gaze, feeling the burn in my eyes. But no matter how willing I was to strike the spark that heralded a flare—thanks to the iron in the horseshoe—I never got past a really mean, very mortal, impotent glare. The ore was sucking the magic out of me as fast as my body heat was seeping through the wet canvas of my sneaker.

My foot was officially numb and licks of fatigue were already lapping their way toward my right knee. If I ran, I was going to be doing it one legged.

"You haven't got a prayer of getting out of the territory," I told Gerry.

The old biker gave me an agreeable nod, then reached for the gun he had tucked into the back of his pants. "Did you hear that, Itchy?" said Gerry.

"I'm shitting myself."

"Now, little girl, pick up your blankie or Itchy will do

it for you, and I'm guessing you don't want Itchy to do it for you."

Evidently, they did know *all* about Fae.

Mortals and their awful, awful touch. One accidental brush of their skin against mine could cause stinging burns. They healed, but they hurt. Like a steam burn. Or an oven burn. A hot, spiking pain that throbbed until the skin's blisters had broken and wept.

For one single inhale, I was frozen by indecision. Putting the blanket over my head was a bad idea. Going with the bikers was a worse one. If they didn't touch me now, they would later. A little privacy often leads to a lot more brutality. But doing so would lead them away from Trowbridge . . . and there were so many cross-points and sentries along the road. Surely one of the pack members would remember the truck?

Opportunity. It's always been my friend.

And for the life of me, I couldn't think past the immediate hurt—devastating, lasting, possibly final—of that arrow-tipped bolt aimed at my head. Nor could my Fae serpent. She drooped behind me; a serpent whose sparkly bits were dimming by the second.

Gerry's leather vest flapped in the wind.

Test a woman and her true nature will come out. Turns out, I'm a gambler. *There will be an opportunity to even the odds.* With my free hand, I slowly picked up the blanket and pulled it over my head, and immediately felt like one of those kids at Halloween whose parents opted for the dead-easy costume. Make two eyeholes, and I was a Casperella.

Itchy bent to pull the blanket evenly over me, then cinched the rope tight around my waist, trapping my arms to my sides. The horseshoe slid off my foot as he hauled me upward.

"Move," said Itchy.

It's hard to blindly walk up an uneven incline, dragging your reluctant Fae serpent behind you, while your amulet's anxiety is an uncomfortable ball of heat between your boobs and the right foot is still seven-tenths useless. But I did it. And by the time we got to the truck, I was feeling stronger.

I heard one of them shove the rollback cover wider.

Oh hell no.

I shouted, "Trowbridge!" and made a break for it. I even made it past a couple of headstones (though one caught my hip) before I was tackled.

Gerry said something about mothers and fuckers, then Itchy grabbed me around the waist—*change your cologne, buddy*—and threw me, none too gently, into the truck bed. A second later, he tossed in the bonus. The horseshoe did a cartwheel down the length of the truck bed.

Merry moved against my breast as Itchy closed the back gate. I bit down on the sting of a scratch from her ivy as she worked in close quarters to unfurl a vine. She planted two feet on my breastbone. My T-shirt tightened as she began to tear at the rough blanket's fabric.

Before I could ease myself onto my side, the rollback made a *tick-tick* noise as Itchy pulled it closed. I steeled myself against the claustrophobia that would surely come. "It won't close," he said.

Thank you, Goddess.

He threw it wide again, then pulled it back with enough force to shake the truck.

"Don't mess with it!" snapped Gerry. "Let me see." He tested it. "There's something blocking it from closing." I drew myself into a ball as his meaty hand patted the area. "What's stuck?"

My Fae, you asshole. My Fae is stuck.

"It's this place," said Itchy. "This place is all wrong, man."

Gerry figured it out quicker than Itchy. "Nah, she's do-ing something," he said, after another couple of experi-mental tests of the lock. "Shoot her with your crossbow."

And with that, my Fae must have finally appreciated the fact that our destinies are tied together. The hard tug on my aching fingers eased. I felt her brush against my legs, and follow the curve of my hip, all the way to my waist. She rested in the dip of my waist as the lock clicked. Faintly twitching. Kind of like a hungry cat sitting on her human, wanting to be fed.

Together again, huh?

Evidently, this week's chosen theme had something to do with pairs. Twice now, I'd been tied up and threatened. Coincidence? I think not. One-and-one-equals-two was evidently going to being worked and reworked until I picked up on whatever the hell I was supposed to learn from this life lesson. Of course, that's only if one believes Oprah and subscribes to the idea that all events in life are lessons.

Some lesson. All I'd figured out from the last few body blows was that bad things for me seem to come in twos. Two bad guys. Two mages. *Two* trees.

"You got it now?" Gerry said. "Stay here with the girl. I'm going to take care of the other problem."

What other problem? Merry stiffened, and so did I.

"Liam said no guns," Itchy reminded him. "We're sup-posed to use the crossbows."

"Like I give squat what Liam says," said Gerry. "I'm using my piece."

"I'm not shitting you." Itchy's voice was strained as he shouted over the moaning wind. "They need the Alpha alive, so they can prove that he's dirty. Gerry! Don't fuck up the bonus," Itchy shouted.

Then I heard him curse, and felt the vehicle dip on the passenger side as he reclaimed his seat. A second later, I

heard a loud thump, as if someone had brought their fist
down hard on the dashboard. Then there was no more
talking or movement. Just the wind's cry.

Gerry's going after Trowbridge.

No, no, no.

In my mind I pictured him heading down the slope toward the cliff overlooking the pond. Finding the perfect
place, amid the pine trees and utter darkness, to aim his
gun.

Scream. Even if he can't hear you.

I opened my mouth for a howl to rival a banshee—

And with one invisible tick of the world clock, the
witches' ward went from an improbable premise to an immediate promise.

The hags had called to the elements, and they had answered.

Suddenly, we could sense the leylines, my Fae and I.
Right there. So close. Even with my eyes closed and my
head wrapped in a blanket, I could see them. They lay
underneath the soil, thick rivers of mystery and magic,
as invisible to most mortals as underground springs. Untapped by the average man but ready to be exploited by
sorceresses with payback on their agenda.

One flowed nearby.

Hell, if I wasn't trapped, I could have walked out of the
cemetery, knelt down on the road, and touched the exact
place it crossed to the side. That's how strongly I felt the
connection between my magic and the earth.

Those leylines were calling every piece of magic in
me. Fae and wolf.

In my mind's eye, I could see a thick band cutting
through the northeast edge of the bone yard, moving
straight through the riot of growth of what remained of
my mum's herb garden. Knew with absolute sureness that

it went straight through the roots of the old maple on the edge of our point.

And then—oh, the sweet irony of it—proof that the witches knew squat about real magic. Can't make magic over water, huh? I knew without a doubt that the thickest line ran right under the pond. The last ice age had left my pirate rock sitting right on top of it.

Stupid witches. Elizabeth had been close as she searched for the leylines, but she'd been as useless as a mortal sniffing for smoke. So easily distracted. She'd only caught a faint, distracting whiff of it. Enough to know it was within reach, but unable to detect its originating source.

Imagine what the coven could have done if they'd actually tapped into that hidden reservoir of power square-on?

As it was, they'd unleashed something evil.

Chapter Six

The pressure in my ears and sinuses turned into a swift agony when Fae-me and mortal-me met the vile corruption unleashed by the coven's summoning.

I couldn't see it. But I could sense the evil. An intangible presence as frightening as if a hoof-footed, scaled creature had crawled up from hell. Now, it floated in our world, and it sucked in deep hungry breaths. Tasting the air for magic.

My Fae slid off my hip and found a place to huddle against my belly.

Those stupid, stupid, ignorant women. This unseen entity—this manifestation of bad—was so much older, so much stronger than any coven of witches. And he would demand such payment that a thousand Fae Tears could not absorb his evil.

I would not pay that bill.

Nor could I protect my Fae or myself from the pain of his desire. So we endured, the four of us. Merry, sparking at my throat. My Fae, a flinching coil of misery. And my wolf, who howled and bayed, as if she'd seen the opposite of the moon and now knew true terror.

My eyes ached in their sockets. Goddess, they could burst under this pressure.

Don't surrender to this evil. Don't give it anything.

You'll lose pieces of yourself forever if you do.

But it was a literal agony to suffer it. I rolled, looking for release from its call. And as I did, my Fae spasmed and thrashed with me. Hitting the sides of the shaking truck with dull thuds that released a scent of crushed flowers. Filling my head with her high cries of hurt and fright.

The vacuum grew stronger. Winds that once howled now shrieked.

I flinched as something clawed at the cover over our heads.

Stay away!

There was a bang, followed by a quick, sharp crack as the wind sucked away the back window. "Shit!" I heard Itchy shout—his curse almost simultaneous with the sound of the hailstorm of glass hitting the cover over my head.

Don't come in!

The air was too thin, and I cried out in fear as an object, solid and heavy, hit the back bed hard enough to fold the side panel inward and send the car skidding to one side. Itchy shouted—though I couldn't make out what he said—and the truck lifted on both wheels.

Please, no.

I felt sudden, bowel-loosening fear that the unseen evil would pick up the vehicle like it was a Matchbox car and toss it right over the edge of the cliff, and then we'd drown in our very own fairy pond, trapped in the back of some biker's vanity truck.

That's when absolute panic broke loose inside that truck bed. My Fae went bat-shit. And me? *Can't breathe! Can't get out!*

I guess I went a bit crazy too.

"Trowbridge!" I screamed over the howling wind. "Cordelia!"

"Harry! Biggs!" I frantically swung my legs, trying to break Gerry's precious rollback cover, but I couldn't get enough swing to do much damage. With every desperate kick, I screamed another name. Trowbridge. Cordelia. Harry. Biggs.

Then finally, even Casperella.

With every wild flail of legs and core, my Fae swung wildly from the end of my hand, thumping against the lid and the lift gate until she met the infamous rounded hump of the tire well with a loud hard smack that I felt from wrist all the way to the bottom of my spine.

She fell limp as a discarded sock puppet.

Fear is never good and panic is never a thing you want to endure. But doing it alone? It's fertilizer to your anxiety; water to your worry.

I'm alone, I'm alone.

Stay small, stay quiet.

It took going that low—to the gut-level despair of a terrorized mouse—to fan anger in my Were. She did not like the wind, or the noise, or my whimpering fear, or the fact that my Fae—who'd always been so dominant and proactive—was out for the count. If me and my Fae weren't on the job, who the hell was looking out for Trowbridge? She growled, deep in my belly. Her obsession with him was the thing that transcended every other reason in her entity.

Wolves protect their own.

Mine, she snarled, swelling inside me.

Sensations so strong, my sweet heavens. It wasn't a flood, it wasn't a tide, it was an immersion in animal heat. My heart was no longer a skittering, fluttering thing inside my chest. Now it felt like a giant muscle, squeezing and clenching. And with each contraction it poured another measure of rich, feral-spiced blood into my system.

My wolf was rising. *Let her come.*

A sense of superior physical strength—something I'd only felt vaguely once before—flooded inside me. All the things that I took for granted and never really thought of unless they were letting me down—my muscles, my balance, my sense of space and hearing—coalesced. *This* is how a natural athlete feels. Attuned to his body, confident that it could meet any challenge.

I'm invincible. Even blinded and tied, and locked in a truck bed. We're so strong.

We listened to the sound of the cover shuddering. The lock sounded weak; it clicked against each tug of the wind. *Weak things can be broken.* I brought my knees up underneath myself.

Do it.

I surged upward. My shoulders hit the cover with the brute impact of a linebacker going for the block. The cover lifted, I could hear the lock being tested, and then the plastic gave. Cold air swirled around me as the lid was torn away. *I'm free—Dorothy without the farmhouse!*

I struggled to stand. Anger and terror streaked through my belly as two very real hands bit into my shoulders. I squirmed, I kicked, I wriggled. His grip slid and bare human skin touched the vulnerable half-Fae flesh. On contact, blisters bubbled.

"Stop fighting me, bitch! I'm trying to save you," Itchy yelled hoarsely.

So that he could kill me later?

Sir Galahad caught me around my knees and threw me over his shoulder.

I am not a thing to be grabbed and hauled and hurt and told what to do.

I am Hedi.

And I am as angry as my inner-bitch.

Like a cornered wolf, I went with what I had—my teeth. My incisors bit down on his skanky ass while Merry went for his shoulder. His glutes flinched under our two-pronged attack and his spine went stiff as a poker—but I didn't let go of my mouthful of blanket, dirty denim, and stringy butt cheek.

Itchy took four more running steps, then tossed us. My own well-padded ass met the soil first, then my back hit something solid and flat, and finally my head met a surface far denser and harder than my skull.

FYI. Never, ever slam the back of your noggin against a tombstone. Vomit rose, got halfway to my throat, then slid back to rejoin the bile in my churning gut. "Stay there!" Itchy shouted in my ear. His thigh brushed my hip as he hunkered down beside me.

Mortal, do not touch us.

Teeth clenched, I stretched my head back so that the blanket's surface was tight, and Merry dove back to work on chewing a hole through the fabric. *Hurry. I need to see.* Red light flashed from her belly, as she struggled to enlarge the hole. The fabric gave, and I used my head to enlarge the aperture.

Wind. It blinded me. Whipping my hair around my eyes. The smell of sulfur burned my nostrils. Evil was here. Its breath heated my face.

I heard Itchy scream, "Jesus!"

I opened my eyes and knew with sudden acuity the exact nature of the entity I'd sensed but not seen. Not a devil as humans understood him. No curling horns, no red glowing eyes or cloven feet. This beast was an oily shadow, gray as the smoke from a tire fire, coiling over us. A huge hulking mass, denser over the pond, but reaching all the way beyond the lines that Elizabeth had drawn in the earth. It was angry—I knew that instinctively right down in my Were bones—just as I understood that the creature would consume me and Itchy before it slunk back to the fire below.

Because those witches—those women I'd dismissed as charlatans—had done it. They'd caught the vile and foul beast in the web of their intent.

I struggled to my feet, frantic to free my arms. Itchy was staring upward at the twisting darkness above him, his expression frozen into a mask of stark horror.

The beast's mouth opened.

I'd only succeeded in freeing one arm, and my back was against hard granite. Rapid-fire, my brain sorted the options. They were depressingly pitiful. Either sink into a ball and pray that the beast didn't have a taste for Faes, or feed him a canapé.

I'm a big fan of no one going hungry. I bent at the waist and charged into Itchy. My head hit his stomach with enough force for me to feel the jolt all the way down to the base of my spine. The biker staggered backward with a high scream, his arms flailing uselessly. I almost felt sorry for him—that biker who wished me harm—as tongues of darkness reached for him.

I'm a bad, bad girl.

Unrepentant, and probably damned, I fell to my knees and closed my eyes as the dark shadow swallowed him whole.

Here's what you do when you've used up your last match. You put your faith in a divine force. I hunched up my shoulders, and silently prayed.

Dear Goddess. Save me. And Trowbridge. Cordelia needs some help, and—oh yes, Lexi needs major rescuing too. Do this for me, and I'll make it worth your while. Whatever you want, I'll do it. I'll be good. I won't lie. I won't cheat. I won't flinch from what comes my way. Promise.

A heavy gust of wind clawed at my blanket burka and tore it away—another token offered to the beast. I could feel the claw of him on my clothing, the stink of him on my skin. My Goddess was being curiously quiet. *Screw it.* I would not meet evil on my knees. I staggered upright, bent over against the wind.

The wind, the wind. It sucked, it plucked.

I clenched my teeth and forced myself to stand relatively straight. Or as vertical as you can, when the air is raking at you with claws of hunger and death and corruption.

Make it fast, make it fast.

There was a terrible roar, louder than a subway train hurtling past the station. I clapped my hands over my ears with a scream, and rocked on my heels.

Do it. Don't toy with me.

Evil's terrible exhale didn't last long. That's the way of it—screams and exhales never do. With a quiet moan, the cacophony died as quickly as it had come. Within two heartbeats, the anguished howl had died away, and the thunder had petered out to low grumbles.

A shudder went through me.

I waited. For the birds to commence tweeting or the other shoe to drop. But nothing happened, except it became marginally easier to breathe now that my lungs weren't trying to suck air inside a vacuum and definitely harder to stand upright now that reaction was knocking at the door, requesting an audience.

I opened my eyes. Broken branches had gathered at the base of the nearest grave marker. With a strange detachment, I found myself thinking of Mad-one's barricade of twigs around the old elm up in Threall. And I wondered if she'd watched my soul-light blink in stuttering terror and if she worried in her own cool, detached manner that I wouldn't come and lead her back to Merenwyn.

Close one. Mad-one.

I heard a bang. Somewhat muffled. I tilted my head. It

wasn't quite a bang; it was more of a ping. What would make that noise? *Gunfire?* Which led to . . . *Trowbridge.* Two unformed thoughts once linked together that hit the panic button all over again.

Bang, bang.

I slapped my hand on the top of the nearest hunk of granite and vaulted over it like I was a hopeful for the Canadian Olympic track team. Fear can make feet so fleet. See Hedi sprint. Flat out I ran, boobs bouncing hard, my serpent a dazed streamer from my pumping arm. *Go faster.* Merry pulsed red at my breast as I tore around the markers and sailed past the old tree.

Trowbridge. Cordelia.

Hell. I didn't even bother to navigate around the last fence—I did a hurdler's leap over the rotting pickets, landed neatly without breaking stride, and tore to the end of the cemetery's cliff. There, I stood staring, stunned and disbelieving, at the scene in front of me. There was so much to absorb. And so much being absorbed.

Looking back, I'm sure that I only got half of it.

Lightning still flickered over the pond.

I paused and shielded my eyes and searched, then—oh Goddess—I saw my guy and Cordelia. There—down by the edge of the pond. They'd retreated to the large boulder I called my pirate rock, and were crouched low by it.

The water still roiled. A body, twisted, broken—Itchy's—was impaled on the broken spar of one of the sumacs.

I tore my gaze from that visual reminder of my misdeeds and looked upward, searching for the beast. I found the echo of it in the membrane-thin wall that was rising just beyond where Trowbridge had made a bridge out of two fallen logs and four pounds of muck. The ward's growth was blisteringly fast—it was already rolling its edges, turning upward and outward, sinuously following the serpentine curve of the ridges.

Such a thing is supposed to be invisible. That's the whole point with wards. You can't see it and you can't detect it. And up to now, I'd been the dupe that had believed it to be a benign device. Protective and harmless. But now, the proverbial scales having been wrenched from my eyes, I *could* see it. Evil had been siphoned, intent and magic had communed, and now the coven's creation was in its final throes of birth.

Stop the bad from happening. That was my instinct. Helpless and hazy.

But in truth, I was as powerless as the flock of finches that were trapped in the interior of that setting ward. They wheeled in confusion, their course changing direction with every terrified tip of the wing until the leader bravely went where no bird should go. They hit the ward, full on, then, stunned or dead, the finches plummeted, brown missiles, legs folded. Horrible.

But what was happening on the beach was far worse.

The demand for a bridge over the creek had just been a piece of fiction manufactured to keep Cordelia and Trowbridge toiling deep inside the parameter of the ward—a diversion to trap them inside while the ward was drawn— and an opportunity for the witches to quietly move to safety before the beast was called.

Trowbridge lifted his arm and looked up at the things carried in that cyclone over his head—the spinning air above him carried the accumulation of anything that could be torn free from this world. Broken branches and stinging dirt. Wet leaves and the whipping ropes of lily-pad roots.

All of that debris made it far easier to see the ward rising like a dark film behind him.

He turned. Saw, just as I did, that the edges of it were

flowing, stretching, searching for those lines drawn by
the witches. Already the growing barrier was racing toward the path that wound up the ridge toward the Trowbridge home.

It was the only avenue of escape.

Trowbridge caught Cordelia's arm and looped it around
his shoulders, and then he hauled ass for both of them.
Somewhere during the interim between bridge-building
and beast-raising her tasteful gray sweater had been color
dipped. Underneath her armpit, the fabric was red as my
mother's blood, but far less sweet.

Gerry's shoulder bunched, then he pulled the trigger
again.

I'm going to kill him for that. It was the simplest
thought, but one of the clearest I'd had all day. I had tunnel vision. Long and narrow. There was only one thing at
the end of my spy viewer: one gut-bellied biker with cadaver written all over him. My Were was engaged, and
my Fae was conscious and with me again. She'd been
longing to hurt something. To make something bruised
and small, as she'd felt since the Old Mage had duped her
and the beast had threatened her.

Her wish to maim and hurt sang to us. More cunning
than any portal song.

"Yes," she agreed, uncoiling herself from my wrist.

Three-strong I spread my legs to steady us, then with a
flick of my wrist, I cast my coil of magic toward the closest heavy thing.

Lift.

Raining earth, the tombstone rose jerkily in the air. A
split second to aim, then we sent that heavenly marker on
its mission.

Perhaps Gerry's sixth sense for danger—honed from
years of his good standing so close to the devil—warned
him. He turned, saw incoming, and ducked. Not fast

enough to escape damage completely though. The rounded edge caught his shoulder. He lost his footing, but did not go down.

Old bikers are used to being under fire. And I guess a tombstone of vengeance is no different than any other assailant. Coolly, he turned and shot at us.

Blindly. *At us.*

I saw the flash first, then a piece of granite flew right off the headstone to my right. My brain noted them, but distantly.

"He is mortal, and therefore weak," my Fae murmured. *Hide from this, Gerry.* I felt my face split into a dreadful smile. I don't know what the biker read, but I was able to relish the fear that made his eyes round, and his eyebrows lift, and his stupid headband suddenly look too tight for his sweating face.

He did a crouching run for safety, but he was fat, and old, and slow.

And the tombstone followed.

You can't outrun a grave marker with your name carved on it. And in my mind, oh yes. His name was etched on this one. The first blow caught him between the shoulders. It felled him. The old biker collapsed on his hands and knees, and—oh sweet joy—lost his gun.

Up in the air the tombstone went, down it came again. I hardly felt the strain on my wrist. There was no holding back. Howling "shits" and "fucks" like they were his own personal mantra, Gerry futilely tried to protect his head.

Say good night, Gerry.

Pleasure. I felt nothing but grim, rolling satisfaction. Up and down went the heavy stone, a clumsy hammer nailing shut a coffin.

Over and over again.

"Strawberry!" A loud voice cut through that mist of rage and anger, and jerked me back to the present. Where

I stood, flanked by small tombstones for long-dead babies, my arm extended, my magic glittering from my fingertips.

The joy—the savage, pure happiness of hurting someone—rolled away.

My hand felt hot, and heavy.

"Strawberry!" I heard someone shout. And then again, far louder, "Strawberry!"

I blinked dully, noting that there was a tombstone in my hand—no, not in my hand. Attached to my paw through that part of me that was not me, but was me . . . and it had done something. *Oh Goddess! Look at that.* I shook my head, appalled and sickened. Fae-me sighed, peeved that I'd turned semimortal again.

Enough, I said in a whisper.

She let go of what remained of the tombstone. It was far smaller now, having broken in two at some point. It fell, with a hollow thump.

I stared at the biker's remains. How long had it taken me to turn his head into something terrible? Five strikes? Four? A handful of seconds to turn a man into that.

"Strawberry!" I heard the man howl in fury.
Trowbridge.

In the space of time it took to pulverize Gerry's head, my man and friend had almost made it out—they'd covered the distance from edge of pond all the way to the top of the path and the old oak tree, where there should have been an exit point. A trapdoor in the magic. Keyed to recognize the secret password "strawberry."

Trowbridge unlooped Cordelia's arm from his neck. He walked right up to the near-invisible barrier, and repeated the password, one last time. But the barrier never fell.

They were trapped.

The witches were long gone. Betrayal complete, they'd probably made tracks when things turned ugly with flying tombstones and raging Weres. Back to their car, and their lives. To their coven that at some point I would hunt down, and, one by one, eliminate.

I imagine they will protest.

That some of them, prior to their death throe, might point out that they'd done pretty much everything else we'd asked. Trowbridge had requested an enormous dome-shaped ward that followed the ridges surrounding the fairy pond—his, the Strongholds', and the one I stood on. Well, they'd given it to him. The freakin' thing was monstrous. And it looked so innocuous—hardly more than a faint shimmering skin over an otherwise unchanged landscape. But it encapsulated everything. Water. Frogs. Crickets.

Mates and friends.

And there was no doorway. No exit keyed to the simple word "strawberry."

Feeling heartsick, I left what remained of Gerry-bloody-Gerry and walked like a girl caught in the teeth of a very bad dream all the way to the edge of Casperella's stone wall. I could have spared my demolition attempt. If the Fae ghost had stayed within her spit of land, she would have had easy access to the portal because the shimmering veil of the ward extended all the way to the crumbling ruins of her wall.

I stared at it, thinking dumbly, it's a wall. Between him and me. A final one, unless I could think how to break it. Slowly my gaze traveled from it to My One True Thing. "You okay?" I asked my mate.

"I've had better days," he said, glowering at the wall in front of him.

I saw the muscles on his back bunch.

"Don't touch it!" I cried. "It's foul!"

If he heard me, he didn't pause. The Alpha of Creemore punched at the shimmering wall with all his considerable frustration. His knuckles met something solid—I saw the recoil of his arm—and the witches' net spat out a shower of red sparks.

But unlike me, it didn't call to his magic. Trowbridge danced back, rubbing his knuckles. He said some words, and then a few more. Clearly, he was more furious that he'd been rendered impotent than appalled by the darkness sensed on contact.

"I will hunt down the witches," I told Trowbridge, striving to sound hopeful. "I'll leave now."

"I don't think you can," he replied, confirming my private thoughts.

"We'll find them, Trowbridge."

But it will take time.

My man stared sightlessly down at his feet for a moment, then he gave himself a brief nod and squared his shoulders. He pivoted to give me a strained smile. "Get Harry, Sweetheart. Tell him we're looking at Plan B."

"What's Plan B?"

He exhaled, as if he was very, very tired. "Go find Harry, Tink."

Chapter Seven

And you know what? For once I wasn't behaving like an impetuous teenager. For the first time in my life I wasn't that dimwit girl who went down into the basement because she heard a strange noise.

Instead, unbelievably, I was going to do all the right things.

I was going to follow his suggestion—for once—and find Harry. I was going to do what was sensible after that—for the first time—and listen to my old geezer's advice.

We would find a way to fix this.

Even if I couldn't see how.

That was my intent.

Trowbridge was just damn lucky that one little finch had the heart of an ultimate survivor and I have the attention span of a gnat.

Here's the thing about aftermaths. When you're three-quarters numb and only just beginning to appreciate all the ramifications of what's happened, part of you is pissed that the world is still spinning indifferently on its axis.

Doesn't the earth know that it should stop?

Right then? Right there?

As I picked my way past the ruin of Casperella's old

stone wall, I was fighting to process the fact that my guy was on one side of the ward and I was on the other. He couldn't stay there. Slowly starving once he and Cordelia had consumed every frog in the pond.

Common sense told me that sooner—rather than later—he'd have to hit play on Knox's phone. He'd have to summon the portal and travel to Merenwyn. Where he and Cordelia would stay, for the rest of their lives.

While I stayed here. In Creemore.

Without them.

And Lexi? Oh Goddess, what of him?

My distracted gaze kept flitting to the little bird who wheeled alone inside the dome. The last survivor of the flock was the unlikely Mensa candidate. The little brown finch must have tailed at the end of the stream of birds, taking notes on what worked and what didn't. And unlike the other birds of the same feather, this dull brown finch had learned a thing or two. For instance, the ward was clearly bad. And those birds that flew willy-nilly into that invisible shield died.

So she'd avoided doing both those things.

I wish I was that bird.

The little finch did a slow lonely circle over the pond. Some lives are not lived well alone. The final survivor of a once noisy flock did one final quick circuit, gaining speed, and then she made a sharp turn.

My heart tightened as I took in her flight path. The bird seemed to be moving at full speed directly for me. Her altitude was low. I stopped, stricken, the helpless flight deck crew watching a fighter jet coming in too fast for their landing.

Don't, I thought. At the very last moment, a hiccup away from death, the little bird made the smallest, slightest course adjustment midair. She turned on the edge of a brown wing and swooped low.

Really low. Like she was aiming for my knees.

I tensed, ready for the inevitable, knowing she was seconds away from turning into an explosion of feathers and broken beak.

She hit the wall of magic, but instead of bursting into cinders, her dash to freedom seemed to slow—I swear she hung in the air for a moment or two, caught in a ward that wasn't solid, but . . . solidifying.

I grabbed the stick, sucked in my breath, and made a careful slash. The membrane tore and the bird fell, released from its grip. I could smell the pond—swamp rot now perfumed with sulfur—through the hole I'd created.

The finch hopped to its tiny feet, tilted its head at me, gave an avian WTF, and then the smartest bird in Creemore beat her wings. She streaked right past my shoulder without so much as a bye-bye and she got the hell out of town. For all I know she made it all the way to the deep forests of northern Ontario without once stopping for a nosh of mosquitoes.

My mouth opened. Closed. My Fae rolled into a question mark by my shoulder.

I made a hole in the ward.

And bang! I went from grim to hopeful. Heart thudding, I bent down and started tearing and slashing with my handy stick. Further investigation told me that the rest of the ward was quite solid. Except for one crucial place. The small opening the bird had aimed for—the gap in Casperella's prison wall.

Some people think every Canadian has an igloo in their backyard. For the record? I've never seen one, never been in one, and never owned one. That's probably why it took two more seconds and a whole bunch more prodding with the sharp end of my poker to figure out two things.

Thing #1: Like an igloo, the ward had an escape tunnel going straight through the part of the wall I'd dismantled.

Thing #2: But the escape chute wasn't going to last. The magic kept trying to seal itself over the perplexing residue of Fae magic left in the ground within the stone enclosure.

Given time it would close. But that's not right now, and so—

"Trowbridge!" I hollered, dropping to my knees. "I found a hole."

"What?"

I did a quick crawl through the tunnel, cleared it, went a couple more feet, then very cautiously sat back on my heels. I gave him an impertinent hand wave. "Hey, Big Guy," I said, giving him a kick-ass proud smile. "Looks like we're all going to Merenwyn."

"No!" he shouted.

I paused, dumbstruck. Hair hanging over my eyes. "What?"

He made a gesture with his hands. "Go back!"

"I'm already here," I said. "You want to explain to me why that's a bad idea?"

"Because there's no getting out of here, Hedi," he shouted. "We'll never be able to return to Creemore. We'll be marooned in Merenwyn."

A realm without humans? Let me think about that. "Well, I'll learn the language," I said, starting to rise.

"No." And this time there was no doubt about what he meant. No, as in no means no.

"Don't be an ass," I said.

His expression was unforgiving. "Go back the way you came and keep that ward open. We're coming to you."

"Well, you better hurry up," I said, feeling all kinds of cold. "It's closing."

"Keep it open for us."

I kept swinging at the stick, trying keeping the hole open—one eye on their progress, the other on the aperture that despite my best efforts was getting smaller by the minute. *Hurry, hurry.* I came to a decision. I went back down on my knees and charged through. "Look alive, Trowbridge. I'm sending a piece of me your way."

He looked up.

Cordelia—the only wolf I've known to see magic—saw my rope of magic coil out into space. "Catch it," she muttered. Trowbridge grimaced, and swiped blindly for it.

My serpent fell short. I needed more—another few feet at least—but there was no *more*. We were at the end of every cliché known to man. At the bottom of the well. At the end of the tether.

Out of rope, out of hope.

Goddess, if only I had more magic, I'd . . . I looked up at the ward. Yes. I raised my arm and the long coil of light streaming from my fingers hooked upward. Delicate as a serpent's tongue, it licked at the inside of the dome.

My Fae sparked, shooting out infinitesimally small stars of brilliant green. The coven's magic slid into me, through my magic, through my hands, into my bloodstream. It fought its way up my arm and almost stopped my heart.

I rose up on my knees. Hope can make you stupid. I didn't slow down. Even as my Fae was bracing for impact, I ran headfirst and headstrong, right into the nearly invisible ward. Sparks flew, as fire bright as a hard rock struck upon a ready flint, and the web that the witches had spun revealed itself, a blazing net of glinting evil encompassing the pond, the ridges, even Casperella's sad burial ground.

In response, the bite on my arm flared, hot and tight. Painful, but not as unsettling as touching that dome of foul magic. On contact with that, my body registered all kinds of insults. The ward's shield felt both solid and tacky to me—like the bottom of a filthy sink covered by a slippery ooze. Its essence slimed my skin. My hand, my cheek, the side of my chin.

But worse? It connected to them. Suddenly, I could see the coven. Sitting in a darkened room. Wearing normal clothing, in a normal living room. Mouths silently chanting. I blinked, and blinked again, trying to exorcise the haunting image of them.

My vision darkened. I saw darkness, and something—someone—whose presence filled me with the type of terror that stops your breath.

And then it—or he—was gone.

Then I saw Natasha and Elizabeth in their car, driving on a two-lane highway. Natasha sat behind the wheel, her mouth pulled down in worry. The younger witch's elbow rested on the door. Her thumb beat a restless tattoo against the filter end of the glowing cigarette she held pinched between her fingers.

They have sold parts of their soul to something as liquid and awful as hot melted tar. And it is watching them. It will always watch them. It will wait until they pass into the eternal darkness, and it will be there, waiting to greet them.

Revulsion swept over me. Whining, I shrank from it, my good hand automatically going to shield Merry from its contamination.

"It's foul," I cried. "It's . . ."

Evil, but I could not say that word out loud, for fear the soul that was darker than tar would hear it. It was inside me. The shadow of the beast and the magic of these foul women was inside me. No white magic this. No good intent formed this witchcraft. This was dark. Like a fruit, once sweet, that had been crushed into a pulp and then held in a dark jar until its rancid juice fermented.

Goddess. Use it fast and get it gone.

I cast again, and this time, the magic stretched. Trowbridge flailed to catch. He pulled it to him—the power that was the magic portion of us stretching, stretching. Cordelia's face contorted in pain as it wound itself around both of them and tightened. Eyes narrowed, Trowbridge threaded his arm around it, as if it was a lifeline, not a cursed thing.

Lift, I told my magic.

Sudden, intense pain from wrist to shoulder.

Heave.

Hands flamed. They were too heavy. Too big a burden.

Try harder.

I closed my eyes and concentrated, willing myself back into communion with my Fae. *We are sisters. We are one.* Fae-me stiffened, flexed, stiffened, then she lifted them, a few feet, and carried them a few more. *Too heavy. Too much.* She faltered, slipped, and grazed the water.

Trowbridge and Cordelia went into the pond up to their waists. My Fae screamed inside me, feeling the faint traces of iron still left in that once-fouled pond.

Don't break. Don't splinter.

"Mine," growled my Were.

"Ours," I moaned to my sisters. Three strong we fought to lift them from that contaminated soup of slick lily pads and iron-tainted water. It shouldn't have been so difficult. We had them, as they had us. Surely it should be as easy as belaying them upward. But the mechanics were so very wrong. We were above them, on our knees, stretched to the limit. Weres don't weigh the same as humans; their bones are loaded with their own heavy version of magic, a requirement of their monthly need to break, and grow, and reconstruct each month while obeying the moon's call.

My half-breed status made me featherlight compared to their combined poundage. I needed more magic, or more weight, or more strength. Because the shield was sealing and the beast would take that which was mine.

Sweat rolled down into my eyes, making them sting. If I could get to the tree behind me, I'd be able to loop my magic around its trunk and that would take the brunt of their weight. But I'd need to back up eight feet if not more. It might as well be a hundred and eighty feet. As it was taking everything I had to hold them steady.

"Trowbridge, I can't lift you." My voice was strained and shrill. "Can you climb up it?"

A savage tug on my rope of magic. My arms were being pulled from their sockets. Horribly, slowly. Like being on a rack, except there was no rack, no one standing beside me, turning the wheel. The only thing that was rescuing them was me.

Me.

Gasp-inducing agony. Panting, I leaned back on my heels, trying to counterbalance. The bed of pine needles beneath me was soft with age. The knees of my jeans skidded on them. And I heard another series of splashes.

This time, my Fae didn't even scream when she grazed the water.

"Give up, give up," I could hear her plead. Another hard tug on my magic, and then the pressure eased.

"It's too slick," he called. "It's no good, Hedi."

Like hell it's no good.

My wolf swelled again inside me, reaching out for her sisters. She welded her strength to ours, and we joined. Three strong, my spine felt stronger—not in danger of

breaking in two. Now completely whole—in balance
with all three of the mes of me: wolf-me, Fae-me, mortal-
me—my arm was roped with muscle. My courage a bucket
without a bottom.

Impervious to pain.

Unwilling to heed reason.

Three strong.

Teeth clenched, we shuffled backward on our knees,
gaining two feet, then two more. "You hold on, damn you,
Trowbridge. I am pulling you out." The line of magic
jerked as Trowbridge readjusted his grip on her. Our Fae
sister was so thin. Vibrating with the strain. *You will not
splinter.* A shuffle, a squeeze of muscle, and pure pig-
headed pissiness.

"That's it, Tink!" yelled Trowbridge. "Keep going."

Yes. Back we went. Soon we lost sight of them though
we could hear them—water churned in their wake as we
dragged them through the pond.

A fieldstone bit into our kneecap as we reverse crawled
through the remains of Casperella's prison walls. *Go faster.
Hurry.* Ass first, right arm extended as if we were trying
to perform some impossible yoga position, we kept going.

I'm burning. I'm burning. My fingers are on fire.

Keep going.

My heels hit something soft. A quick glance over my
shoulder. A thing—a body. We navigated around what was
left of Gerry. Hardly breathing. Shoulder screaming. As
fast as we could.

Back, back. Before the ward seals.

We reached the tree. Did a lunge sideways. Our magic
looped around its sturdy trunk, and immediately, some of
the spine-shattering strain eased. Reverse progress became
marginally easier. Heart pumping like an athlete's, we kept
going, now in a diagonal line, our magic rasping against
the fissured bark with every foot we gained.

Don't think. Keep moving.

Past four tombstones for four dead babies and a hole torn in the soil where once there had been a marker for a fifth. Over the rails of a broken picket fence. Right up to the tree that Casperella was waiting by. We did a circle around her and the tree for good measure. Why? We weren't sure. Put it down to instinct. But as we passed her, Casperella touched the scaled serpent of our magic.

And this time, she did not steal. Hands sprouted from her torso, white-ghostly, strong. They wrapped around the battered coil of magic and pulled with us.

Ghost help. Yes.

Now it was child's play. We were the four-girl-strong version of Gumby.

We didn't stop our backward locomotion until our heels hit the first pack member's double-wide monument, then we experienced a sudden release of a near unbearable weight, as if someone had clipped the belaying line.

Let them be safe.

With that thought, my long rope of magic shattered. Silently and invisibly. Fairy lights glittered in the low light of a gray morning. The air around us smelled faintly acrid. I opened my mouth, and felt all those little bits of magic slide down my throat.

My wolf gave one single whine, and then padded over to comfort her sister-Fae.

Go ahead. You guys rest while I roll into a ball and commune with the pain radiating from my hand. Merry— ever the St. John's ambulance–trained rescue amulet— began her descent, ziplining along the links of her Fae gold chain, heading for the square of skin above my heart, but I caught her with my other hand. The paw that absolutely wasn't smoking and smelling like hamburger just set down on the grill. Feeling nauseous, I forced out one word. "No."

Nausea roiled, acidic and bitter, as I rolled over. Flat on my back, I stared up into the sky. The moon was gone. The stars had faded. The world was as gray as the owl watching me from the oak tree.

Do owls fall into the category of carrion birds?

"Fuck off," I told the bird, before I forced myself upright. The tombstones around me seemed to spin, and that detached, shit-I'm-going-to-faint feeling momentarily swamped me. To keep myself in the here and now, I bit the inside of my lip. Hard. I refused to faint, pass out, or swoon. There's got to be a limit on how many times a girl can do that before she's labeled as weak.

I am not weak. And I'm beginning to be very label conscious.

"Trowbridge?"

"I'm helping Cordelia. We'll be up in a moment."

So, I sat back on my butt and chewed on the inside of my cheek until I tasted blood, while I allowed the smooth, slick marble of William Culley's monument to support a spine that felt remarkably spineless. A time-out period. Where I wouldn't pass out. Where I could sit, hunched over, my good hand cradling my bad wrist as I waited for the payback pain to stop hammering.

"Natasha took my Tear, Merry. And they tried to trap Trowbridge." My amulet slowly crawled up the Matterhorn of my right boob and found a comfortable summit perch. A yellow light flashed out a question. Blip, blip, blip. Was healing required?

"I'm good," I rasped. "It's moving off."

That was a big-assed lie, but we let it stand between us.

Gerry's body lay in a long trail of blood. "Who the hell sent bikers for me?" I asked my amulet in a shaky voice. "Bikers. Why bikers?"

My hand was a throbbing source of misery. By all the glory of all the Faes in Merenwyn and Threall, it hurt.

Feeling curiously faint, I rested my head back on the cool marble. Air whistled through my teeth as I fought to bring my breath under control. I studied the inscription on the opposing monument ("Kerry Butcher, Beloved and Cherished") until two legs came into my field of vision. With a harsh exclamation, Trowbridge knelt beside me. My gaze roamed restlessly over him, cataloging every insult to his body. He was dripping wet, the beauty of his chiseled jaw somewhat marred by a thick streak of mud.

"You are a crazy, crazy, girl." For all his tenderness, a current of suppressed violence stung my nostrils.

Trowbridge is concerned. I rolled my eyes toward his. "I'm mad at you."

"You're always mad at me."

"Boss!" Harry yelled.

"In the old part of the cemetery," Trowbridge called. "Check out the bodies on your way over here. I want to know who did this."

"Bikers," I said, carefully breathing through my mouth. Fae Stars, I wanted to puke. "Someone sent bikers to kidnap me. Why humans? That's just low."

Casperella drifted over to us, the hem of her gown brushing against the grass. She'd absorbed some of the magic in the air and now I could see her hair—long, dark, beautiful. Also the details of her face, delicate features, with a softly curved chin.

"You're such a thief, Casperella," I mumbled. My mouth felt rusty. So dry that my tongue was thick and fat. Like some dried-up cow tongue inside my mouth. Leathery. Reluctant to crisply form the sound of an *s*.

Trowbridge's long fingers teased a strand of my hair off my wet face and tucked it gently behind my pointed ear. *I must be crying. Strange I don't feel sad. Just beginning to hurt real bad.* His thumb stroked my jaw. "You keep getting beat up, Tink."

"I know," I said peevishly.

His face hardened as he swiveled to stare at the pond. "The Sisters set us up. They must have called Whitlock right after they spoke to me."

A pair of cowboy boots strode into my line of vision. *Harry.* He cleared his throat. "You don't look so good, Little Miss," Harry said.

I don't feel so good. I'd kept my hand tucked into my chest, but now it burned so badly, promising that this payback session would be an utter bitch. If it looked as horrible as it felt . . . I took a quick peek and wished I hadn't.

"Jesus wept," said Harry.

Oh. Fae. Stars. My flesh was as red as a skinned rabbit ready for the pot. Fat blisters distorted my knuckle. The palm was worse—a bevy of blisters had met at my lifeline fork for a gang bang and the resulting single bubble was damn near obscene.

Trowbridge swore—one short word—then he said, "Someone's going to pay."

That would be me.

"Who were they?" the Alpha of Creemore demanded.

"Bikers," replied Harry.

"Told you." Well, I tried to say that, but my lips were rubbery and my words came out without the benefit of consonants.

"They were wearing Liam's patch," Harry said. "Whitlock uses him for personal stuff. Things he doesn't want traced back to him or his pack." He pivoted on his heel, wiped his nose as he studied the pond. "The air doesn't smell right."

Trowbridge looked up to Harry, suddenly all business. "Get on the phone. I want everyone out on the road looking for the Sisters. If they find them before us, they're to stop them, and hold them. As much as I want those bitches to die, they're not to kill them. We need them alive. They are going to punch a door through that ward."

"Little Miss is going to pass out," said Harry.

"No I'm not," I promised them.

But then again, I lie a lot.

Chapter Eight

Drowsily, I opened my eyes. I was facedown, my head pillowed on my good arm. My other was stretched out on the brilliant green moss. The air smelled . . . sweet. Lightly scented with flowers of a type not found in my world. A blue myst played lightly over the contours of my swollen knuckles. So gently, its touch felt like a cool breath on heated skin.

Threall.

I must have fainted in Creemore.

So, I'm here. In the realm between the mortal world and the Fae's.

My mum's genetic imprint had gifted me with more than the ability to toss a tombstone or two. I'm also a myst-walker, which is what the Fae call those born with the unique ability to tear their own psyche from their mortal shell. Capable of travel to here—this secret realm, this sacred place—where the souls of the drowsing Fae hang from ancient trees.

Lucky us.

The Fae call us deviants and horrors too, but that was from fear. In their place, I guess I would be wary of someone who could see into me, know all my secrets, hear all my longings, taste all my memories, just by placing a hand on the spine of a tree.

Souls. Goddess, so many souls in the sky above me.

Shaped like balls, or maybe moons. Encased in vellum-thin skins. Each cyreath a glowing sphere, inner lit by the Fae's essence. Each soul-light was unique, in some way. Be it the subtle pattern on their skin or, more obviously, the hue of their soul. And of that . . . oh Goddess, so many shades. Yellows and golds, peaches and pinks, reds and angry purples. If I lifted my head from this bed of moss, I know I'd see a handful of brilliant blue soul-balls, in the far distance.

They called to me.

The whole damn place did—this realm between the mortal world and the Fae's. It's the downside of my mother's gift—if a mystwalker travels too often to this world, they become too detached from their true world. They forget how to return home.

There were a few upsides though. My right hand should be a throbbing mess. I'd burned the crap out of it doing all that magic by the pond. By rights, it should look more than a tad scalded. But it didn't. Threall's blue myst was like a magic eraser, easing the pain, and with each gentle touch, it painlessly peeled away the old skin, leaving soft, pliable new skin underneath it. I watched, feeling a smile pluck at my lips.

"The thumb," I coaxed. "Fix the thumb."

Evidently, my word was its pleasure. It slid from knuckle to the Delta of Venus, twining itself around that ruined digit.

Goddess, that feels good.

Movement in my peripheral view. I saw a skirt—long, thick blue velvet. And feet. Small, very dainty, in sandals that a Greek goddess might have coveted.

"Nice feet, Mad-one." I rolled over onto my back. "But then again, I guess you don't use them all that much."

The Mystwalker of Threall prefers to fly.

I gazed at her.

She returned my regard, wearing her usual expression—mouth set in a stiff smile that was absolutely bankrupt of humor. Wide mouth, lips well defined and somewhat pink. A nose that would do well on someone who had a double-barreled last name and an Oxford accent. Blond hair that never seemed to misbehave, even when she was hurling fire bolts.

"Why don't I ever wake up near my own tree?" I asked her.

"Mystwalkers never materialize by their citadel. It is one of the few protections we have against those who wish us ill."

"You fixed your dress," I observed, before I sat up. Last I'd seen her, the hem and most of the skirt had been muddy. The nap on the fabric had been seared into a dark brown streak over her hip.

She'd conjured a makeover—her gown was lovely once more. Couldn't blame her. Who wouldn't avail themselves of the magic in this world? In truth, it never failed to distract me. I could feel it on my skin. Smell it with my part Were nose. It was like drinking sweet wine. Each mouthful prodded you into taking another. And somewhere between all those sips? You forgot. Things you shouldn't.

Goddess . . . the ward!

"Do you know how to break a ward?" I asked.

"I am not a sorcerer."

"One day we really must sit down and write out a list of the things you can and cannot do. Starting with being friendly. Do you remember friendly?"

She raised one brow and managed to keep her face grave, but I saw a flicker of something almost like amusement in her eyes. "You were summoned," she said. "Why did you not come?"

"No one sent me an invitation."

Silently, she pointed to the kid's imprint on my arm. In this world the wound glowed even brighter, as if it was absorbing energy from the air. "That's you?" I said, staring at my glow-bright arm. "I thought the bite mark was reacting to the magic down in my world." *Wonderful. Now I'm on Mad-one's speed dial.* "Is this permanent? Once we've concluded our business, will it fade?"

"I have been calling you for an age," she said.

"Uh-huh." I leaned to the side to look past her full skirt. Two black walnuts—immense and powerful—used to anchor the edge of Threall's world. Now, only one tree remained. It was enormous and solid. Thick trunk. Boughs so heavy they looked like a giant's muscled thigh. Its cyreath was lodged high in its branches, casting a brooding light. Purple and mottled reds.

The Black Mage's soul lived in that tree.

And FYI? He was a bad, bad man.

Murder, cheating, naughty wizardry—by my brother's account, the Black Mage had done all of that in Merenwyn. Ordinarily, that wouldn't bother me too much, as I lived in my world, and with any luck, the Royal Court's evil wizard would stay in his. But, unfortunately, the bastard had a deep desire to kill me or my brother. And as we are twins, the death of either one of us would amount to a tidy two-for-one deal for him.

If I'd never come to Threall . . . if I'd listened to my mum . . . I'd never have met him or the other wizard, and then my life would have been dull, and simple . . . and somewhat more abbreviated than I'd anticipated. But it would have been mine. And I wouldn't have known what hell was coming my way.

And Lexi? His life—for what that was now worth—would have been his too.

My gaze traveled to the torn-up ground a few feet to the right of the nasty wizard's hulking citadel.

Damn. I'd kind of hoped I'd dreamed it.

But that hole—that large depression in the soil that still sprouted the jagged edge of torn roots—was very much proof that once another huge and ancient tree had squatted at the end of Threall's world. Or rather, better said, had held on to life there. And now it was gone and my brother was the Old Mage's temporary nalera.

Well done, Hedi.

I stood and wiped my hands clean on my pant leg. "Why did you call me?"

Mad-one's mouth pursed, in exactly the way you don't want someone's lips to shape before they respond to a very important question. "Your brother—"

All my anxiety? It was like the pressure inside the soda bottle well shaken. It spewed out in a torrent of words. "He didn't make it, did he? He's stuck in the portal, right? He's never getting out—"

The Mystwalker lifted an imperious hand. "Stop. We have limited time."

But I was a horse without a bridle. "What about his mind? Is he all right? All there? Does he know that I had no choice? Does he understand my decision? Does he know that I'm coming for him? Does he know . . ."

That I'd willingly sent him into puppet hell?

"Which question do you wish me to answer?"

And there it was: her careful query was my answer. I rubbed my face with my hands. Stomach sick. My twin knew I'd conspired to send him into the arms of the Old Mage.

Lexi *knew.*

"Mystwalker," she said. "Your brother desires to speak to you. It is your mage's wish that you do so immediately."

"He's healed?" I said, mouth dry.

"I only know that I must bring you." And with that, she

gave up on standing. She rose in the air, with the grace of a thistle seed. "We have no time, Hedi of Creemore. Follow me."

Sickly, I turned for the hole in the hedges. *Lexi wants to talk.* I almost tripped into a tree stump thinking about that conversation. *Hey, Lexi—sorry for the whole bait and switch.*

The Mystwalker clapped her hands, hard. I glanced at her, too heartsick to even tell her to take her empress tricks and shove it up her—

"We will fly," she informed me.

"What?" I gaped at her. "How do I do that?"

"You are a mystwalker," she said. "All you need do is to wish it."

"I wish you'd fall on your ass."

She lifted a brow. "You cannot wish ill on me."

"A girl can try," I said, studying her.

Fly, huh?

Yes, I'd flown before, but with as much self-determination as a lead ball being belched out of the mouth of a cannon. I'd shot across space, holding a mage's soul in my arms, terrified that I was going to lose trajectory before I saw blessed ground beneath me.

Truthfully? I'd thought the old man had been doing the steering.

But it was me? I'd flown? *Well, call me Supergirl.*

Mad-one gave me an irritated glance. "Mystwalker, we must make haste."

She adjusted her altitude, elevating a few feet higher so that her gown wouldn't get caught on the hedgerow's wicked thorns, and took off. Heading for the wild side of the clearing, where there was a little glen and one medium-sized black walnut tree that had one solid taproot and two trunks.

"Wait!" I said.

But being "the" Mystwalker, of course, she didn't.

I tested the idea. *Fly.*

Butterflies fluttered in my stomach. As if my core was terribly empty and wings—tiny and easily broken—were brushing against my guts.

And then came the lightening.

But from within me. *I* was light, so very light.

And supple. And free.

I rose in the sky—*look at me, I'm levitating!*—and then made the newbie mistake of bending over to see if my feet were still on the ground, and almost a did a very graceful somersault into the tops of the hawthorn hedge.

Whoa.

A quick correction of spine and head adjustment, and then I was more or less vertical.

"Hey!" I shouted to Mad-one.

The Mystwalker did a graceful turn—the swan on a placid river. A curl of blue myst twined around her swaying skirt. She made a mocking "come" gesture with her hand.

"Up, up, and away," I said grimly.

And then . . . oh sweet heavens . . . I flew.

Mad-one had a lead on me, which I never managed to shorten. There were trees to avoid, and I had constant issues with keeping my elevation steady, but I did follow her progress to the little clearing.

From the edge of the glade one could mistakenly believe that there were two separate trees growing in that odd little open space. But in truth, the two young black walnuts shared a low thick trunk and one single long taproot.

Twins. One trunk, two trees.

I came to a wavering halt. It was still arresting—the joined trees, the quietness of the clearing, the sway of the waist-high grasses that ringed the space. And most stunning of all, the aurora borealis—flames of light that spoke of mystery and history—cast by the glow of our cyreaths.

Lexi and I were twins, but not identical. The hues spun from my cyreath were gold and green, with tiny flickers of intermittent blue. While Lexi's came from an altogether different spectrum . . .

How much time has passed in this world? It's only been a few hours in mine.

Previously, the lights weaving around his tree had been picked from a royal palette—plum purples and midnight blues. But now red—a dull, throbbing crimson—had tinged those shades. Purples had been darkened to the bruised heart of a pansy and blues had been reddened to the shade of damson plum.

I looked upward.

There were three soul-balls hanging from our citadel's branches—a single cyreath on my tree, two on Lexi's. In the boughs of his tree, one soul had been placed a little higher than the other so that all of its sagging weight was balanced on the firmer soul-ball.

That's not how it was supposed to look. How on earth will I separate them?

I'd envisioned a tidy seam where the two cyreaths would join. A straight and obvious line that could be cut with surgical precision. But the Old Mage's soul wasn't adhering itself to Lexi's neatly. Instead it was . . . melting on it. His vellum sheath was slack, while Lexi's was still firm. And now gravity—did Threall even have gravity? Whatever. His soul was enveloping my twin's.

A sick feeling swept over me, and it damn well drowned whatever lightness had been working the magic of flight. Faster than a balloon with a pinprick, I went from high-flyer to ground dweller.

"Speak to him," Mad-one said, her voice flat.

I wanted to just stay there. Standing on the edge of the glade, deferring the reckoning between my twin and me for infinity and beyond. Or better yet, to will myself back to the real world. The moss was soft under my feet as I slowly walked to our trees. Lexi's was taller than mine and less foliaged. His bark was more striated and textured.

The green-gold light of my own cyreath bathed my skin.

I lifted my trembling hand and touched my twin's tree, not knowing who I'd meet, my brother or his mage.

I couldn't find him at first. Nothing was ever easy with Lexi, and this was no different. I should have been able to access his soul with a simple touch—that's how I'd done it before. Flatten my palm on the trunk, and there I'd be. In the thought streams. Wandering the soul's memories and feelings.

But instead, all I encountered was a confusing cloud of blinding color. Swirls of the vivid blues found in a peacock feather. Tongues of vermilion. Swaths of purples, some so dark they were almost ink-black.

He's waiting, I thought.

Indeed he was. Suddenly, an invisible hand tightened around my throat. Panic rose. Though I was frantic to claw it away, I couldn't move—my palm seemed seared to the rough trunk.

I was sightless. And trapped.

"Lexi," I gasped, "it's me."

A moment of consideration before the pressure around my throat eased. I sucked in deep whoops of air and borrowed strength from the tree I'd sagged against. When my lungs no longer felt afire, I tried to move away, and discovered that I was still held firmly in place. Caught, but no longer being actively punished.

Is that how he's feeling? Like he's begging for air?

"I don't beg," said Lexi.

My twin's soul was on the other side of that spectrum of color. Hidden from me. And he'd never let me touch it. Or know him again.

My eyes burned.

And then I heard my brother's voice say, "Come."

The swirls of color around me melted into one another and grayed. Shape was born. First, rough outlines. A square of dim light. A block of something solid.

I blinked, and then my vision cleared.

Lexi had conjured up a meeting room of sorts—a modestly sized room, cluttered and filled with curiosities. I'd visited the Old Mage's wizard snuggery once before in a dream, standing a little to the right of where I was now, while I watched Mad-one's heart break.

My brother stood behind a lectern, studying the pages of the enormous leather-bound tome that lay open on the stand. Patently ignoring me, he flipped to another thick page in the Book of Spells.

I studied my twin. Here, in the world created by his mind, Lexi required no natty bowler; he suffered no tattoo inked above his ear, any more than he sported an unfortunate, asymmetrical coiffure. His straight hair was uniformly long. He wore it unbound—a sheaf of wheat, the ends of which brushed the top of his hip.

Like Mum's, I thought, and my gaze swept the room. I half expected to see the Old Mage standing in the corner, arms crossed, cheeks mottled like the last time I saw him, but we were alone, Lexi and I.

It's so dim in here.

Natural light struggled to pour through the thick panes of wavy glass. Shelves flanked the window, and they, like the rest of the room, were cluttered, filled with a hodgepodge of strange collections in earthenware pots and baskets. But the bottom shelf—the one closest to the oak table that had been pushed against the wall—was the single place in the entire room where there was precision and order.

The shelf was lined with clear glass bottles. Feeling ill, I stared at those vials, noting that each one had been filled to exactly the same level with a colorless liquid, with the precision you might have expected from a factory.

Sun potion.

Had they been there the last time I'd found myself pulled here by a dream? I cast my mind back. *No,* I thought. They hadn't been here. But evidently, they were still very much part of Lexi's dreaming mind.

I chewed the inside of my lip. "Are you free of your addiction now?"

Sparks spat as he ran his palm over a page. "The wards still hold," he murmured. "The Black Mage must be beside himself."

I watched him repeat the process. "Why here?" I asked. "Why bring me to the Old Mage's den?"

"These are the Black Mage's quarters, though I suppose once they belonged to the old man." He lifted his gaze. Cold eyes. Greener than mine but cast from the same mold. Slanted slightly and heavily lashed. "Why wouldn't I bring you here? I spent more time here than anywhere else in my life. For the first ten winters, I rarely left this room, unless my mage did, and then I followed him. Never less than five paces behind him, never closer than two. That's how I earned my name the Black Mage's Shadow."

This room—the cold room with its stone walls and single narrow window? My gaze traveled, taking in the stone floors, the single chair, the door set in one of the walls. One wall was dominated by a large fireplace; its hearth was a dark hole that needed feeding.

It's a prison.

"Where did you sleep?" I whispered.

He nodded to the corner to his left. The thin, worn blanket that lay on the stone floor had been folded with exquisite care. On top of it rested a mug, a bowl, and a single spoon.

"That's it? In the corner?" Another press of grief and sorrow. I'd had a pink comforter—a prize that was plucked from the Goodwill charity drop container. My finger found the peak of my ear.

He closed the book with a shrug. "I soon grew used to it."

I'm sorry—that's what I wanted to tell him. For so many things, I couldn't even begin to write a list. For the fact that the Fae had stolen him and not me. For his blighted youth under the Black Mage's control, and for those lonely years spent in a Royal Court that had left him bitter.

And finally, I was deeply remorseful for yesterday's lies and deceptions. Filled with guilt that I'd held my twin in my arms and listened to his heart slow and then skip a beat, and I'd known what was coming for him. Feeling so damn sorry, but understanding, in a clear, cold way, that there was no choice.

Lexi had been watching my face as I worked my way through my list of sins. That's the problem with twins—we become such superb readers of each other's facial cues.

"Guilt is a useless emotion," he remarked, closing the book.

"So I've heard." I inhaled slowly through my nose, in an effort to make the burning sting go away. I turned my head left, right. "Where is the Old Mage?"

"He's left us alone so that we can speak in private." He nodded toward the window. "He's waiting out there."

I squinted at the window. Was that him out there, that dark shadow, underneath the tree on the hill? *Stay there.*

I needed time to explain, to make my twin understand. "It broke my heart to send you back into that portal, knowing that he was waiting for you."

Lexi shrugged and moved to the nearby table. Its top was as disorganized as the rest of the room, but a space had been cleared in the middle of the muddle for a large copper container. In the shadow of that sat a mortar and pestle. My twin ran a pale finger around the stone lip of the heavy bowl, his eyes downcast. "So you say."

My stomach clenched. "I did what I had to do."

"And you did it so well." He sorted through a bunch of dried flowers and settled on a sprig of faded lavender. "You let me believe that I was facing my own trial. I keep wondering," he said, using his blunt nail to strip the stem, "if that scene was really necessary."

I swallowed. "The pack needed to believe that you were tried and executed."

"Why?" He swept the leaves into his palm, then tossed them in the mortar's bowl. "Who cares what the pack thought?" He picked up the pestle. "Are you still measuring yourself against the pack? You'll never please them. You're not one of them." He flicked me a hot glance. "Nothing will ever change that. I keep telling you, but you're so—"

"The deception was necessary," I cut in, my tone getting hard.

"Careful, Hell, you'll start sounding like me. You wouldn't believe the shit I've done because someone told me it was 'necessary.'" He started to grind the flower petals. "What you really needed was a limp body. You could have had that easily. After a few hours sitting in that holding room, sweating through my withdrawal, I would have swallowed a bottle down without any coercion from you. It would have ended up the same way. I would have been unconscious and the wolves could have witnessed my departure." He gave the crushed lavender one more go with the pestle, and then added a drizzle of fine oil. His movements were easy, fluid almost. He'd performed the same task many times before. "So, my question is, why am I here, and you are not?"

"I went to Threall to solve a problem and I messed up," I said baldly. "The Old Mage's cyreath was supposed to be merged with mine, but once he discovered we were twins, and that you were addicted to sun potion . . ." I gazed at him helplessly. "If there had been any other choice, Lexi. You must believe I'm—"

Sorry, I was going to say, but he cut me off. "You were the mage's nalera for the length of time it takes a cock to crow in the morning. I don't think you can compare your . . . association . . . with him to what I've been going through." My twin dipped his finger in the oil and lifted it to his nose. His nostrils flared. "Strange, I can't smell a thing."

"I never do while I'm dreaming either."

With a fastidious grimace, he wiped his finger on a rag. "So tell me. Did you walk in my dreams when we were kids?"

"Only a couple of times."

"And here I thought we shared everything." He pulled the stool over with his foot and rested his hip on the edge of its seat. "You know what I can't forgive you for? When you sat down beside me on the hill and said, "Go to sleep, Lexi, I'll wait with you."

"You remember," I whispered.

"Of course I do. It's the type of thing you don't forget. For the first time in a long time I thought I was in control of my own destiny." He crossed his arms. "It was finally over . . . I was going to go to sleep and never wake up. Imagine how surprised I was to find myself trapped in one of the portal's passages."

Lexi.

"The tunnel was barely tall enough to stand up in," he said. "No door. No exit. No way out. Then I started hearing this voice inside my head. And no matter what I did, I couldn't get him to shut up. I was hot, and shaking . . . on my hands and knees puking and still he kept talking."

"He said he'd cure you. You needed to be—"

"You sent me to a fucking mage," he said, bitterness an acid edge to each word. "I've been raped by one of those mothers before . . . but this has been . . ." His lips curled and he gave me an awful laugh. "So much more intense."

Raped.

"I'm sorry beyond words for what you suffered," I said, meaning it from the bottom of my leaking heart. "If I could change your past I would. If I could beat the Black Mage senseless for the pain he's caused you, I'd do that too. But I can't, Lexi. Any more than I can go back to the night when Mum and Dad died and you were stolen. I wish I could—you have no idea how much I wish I could—but I can't.

"Right now, we are here because of *your* addiction. Not mine. Not Trowbridge's. Yours. You were a couple of bottles away from overdosing. I saved your life. The mage said that he could pull the threads of your addiction from your body and mind."

"Threads," he repeated incredulously. "When a man has taken the juice for as long as I have—when you've depended on it for decades upon decades—it's not something that can be pulled from you. It is *part* of you. The Old Mage took a piece of me and he threw it away. I'm not whole anymore. There's no peace anymore," he said brokenly. "The juice used to give me that—for a few hours everything was numb and . . ." He closed his eyes. "I used to feel like shit when I came down. But even that low was better than this." The tip of his tongue wet his lip. "There's no high, no low, there's only this sense of grinding weight on my chest."

"The weight will be gone when I remove his cyreath from yours."

His face went blank, absolutely still.

"Lexi?"

My twin blinked—slowly, like a sleepy tortoise—and gave me a strangely cold smile. "I do not wish you to do so," he told me. "In fact, I forbid you to."

My mouth, already dry, went arid. "I have to—and soon, or the union will be permanent. It must be done before the waning of Merenwyn's next full moon."

He gave me the faintest reproving headshake. "You presume too much. What right have you to make decisions on my behalf? I will live and die by my own choosing."

"Even if you take me and Trowbridge with you?"

"That is no longer of immediate concern." Lexi went to smooth his cuffs, but he did it strangely, prefacing the motion with an odd flick of his wrist as if he was wearing a shirt with very long and heavy sleeves, not a piece of clothing that skimmed his body and buttoned at his wrists.

I stared at him, intuition stirring.

"My mage has returned my health to me," he said, "and my circumstances have changed. I have found myself presented the most glorious opportunity."

Dread was a worm inside me. My twin's posture was wrong, his speech pattern kept flexing between the familiar and the formal. Sweet heavens, no . . .

"Who am I talking to?" I asked. "My brother or the mage?"

"I am your brother," he said stiffly.

No you're not. You're a terrible mixture of both.

I started across the room, wanting to shake him, to slap

him, to do something—anything—to bring my twin back
to me. But before I'd taken two paces, hot pain tore
through my right temple. Horrible, acute, piercing. I
moaned, pressing a palm hard over the place where an
invisible spike was slowly being driven through my skull.

"Stop," I heard Lexi shout. "You said you'd wait."

Two more pulses of agony, the point of the blade digging deeper, before the torture ebbed.

It took everything I had not to cry out in relief. *Do not
give the mage the satisfaction of seeing you humbled.*
Shakily, I straightened. Lifted my chin. Clenched down
on my molars so that my lips wouldn't tremble.

Raw anguish briefly twisted Lexi's expression before
he turned away. He studied the scene outside the window.
"Don't come any closer, Hell. I don't think I can take it."

My touch? Or watching the mage punish me?

"Try not to let him in, Lexi," I whispered. "Don't listen
to him. Keep yourself safe until I can free you."

"Don't *listen* to him?" The slim control he had on his
anger broke. He swung around. Weak light haloed his hair.
Bright color flagged his cheeks. "I can't stop hearing him!
You tell me how to drown him out, and I will. What you
just felt? That dagger through your thoughts? That's only
a fraction of what I've gone through."

The tear that had been clinging to my lower lid spilled,
scouring a hot warm trail down my cheek. "I'll bring you
home. I promise you, I will."

He shook his head. "I told you before, Hell. I have no
place in your world. I want to live as a Fae, not as a wolf."

"You can be both."

"In what realm? Not here. Not even in your world.
When you go back to your realm, do me a favor and take
a good look around you. Just how well are you accepted
into the pack? Do you and the other bitches braid each
other's hair? Meet for coffee and cake? Can you walk into

Pederman's bar and know yourself welcome? Stars, do you wear blinders? There's a wall between them and us, and it will never come down."

"It can come down." It had to because otherwise . . . ? What life would I have, providing I had one to look forward to at all?

"Really?" The corner of his lip curled. "When you go back, ask your lover about the council's kill list."

"What are you talking about?"

"I overheard Mum and Dad one night. Mum was crying," he said. "Some woman from the pack told her about the halfling kill list. Dad was reassuring her, telling her that we weren't on it. Children born of Faes were exempt."

"I don't believe you."

"Ask your mate about that. Then you tell me what you have in Creemore that's better than the old man's offer."

I have a mate who loves me in Creemore. A mother-that-wasn't. An old geezer Were who calls me "Little Miss." I have everything.

And then I remembered what else I "had."

"I have your daughter entrusted in my care," I said quietly. "Why would you bring her to our world if there was a kill list for half-breeds? Why did you bring her to me?"

His mouth tightened. "She is exempt—she has Fae blood. Besides, she was facing an execution. Saving her was a whim."

No, it wasn't a whim. It was an instinct. Even a man as broken as my twin could be surprised by the unexpected pang of paternal interest.

"What has the Old Mage promised you?"

"The moon and the stars," he drawled.

That probably wasn't too far off the mark. What could I offer my twin that would come close to the unearthly powers that the old wizard possessed? Did all roads lead to my brother being a mage's shadow?

Only if you let it. Hedi, the mouse-hearted.

Only if you lack the courage to save him.

"I can't give you those," I said, staring into his green eyes. "But I can offer you my word."

"Your word," he repeated incredulously.

"I've lied to you a hundred and more times, twin. But I'm not lying now. And I won't lie to you in the future. That's another promise." I steeled myself as his gaze turned from cool to mocking. "When we were kids, I could tell when you were fibbing just by the expression on your face. Has it been so long that you can't read mine?"

He cocked his head.

"Look at me, Lexi," I demanded. "Am I lying?"

My twin's brows arched in consideration.

"I can't promise you that we'll succeed. But I do promise that I won't give up. Do you understand? Whatever happens over the next few days, I won't give up. Come hell or high water I will meet you at Daniel's Rock and we will destroy that book. Then I'll bring you home—"

"I have no home in your world," he spat.

"Then we'll find you a new one in my world," I said, without missing a beat. "It might not be a castle but . . ." I caught myself before I began embroidering his future with butterflies and posies. "No, it will definitely not be a castle. And you may never be rich—not in the way you measure wealth." My gaze traveled from him to his surroundings, taking in the pestle and mortar, the flagons of sun potion and the thick doors. "You'll never be 'the' mage either."

"No money, no talent, no prospects," he scoffed. "How could any man pass up such an opportunity?"

A thin ray of light penetrated the window's grime. It lit on a strand of his long golden hair, gilding it.

"You will be what you are meant to be—Lexi Stronghold, son of Benjamin and Rose," I said, my tone hard and unflinching. "Which means you'll be no man's puppet. No man's lackey. You will never be a mage's shadow again. You'll be free."

He inhaled sharply.

"Lexi," I whispered. "Don't give up. Not on yourself. Not on me."

"Already done, sister of mine."

"Then why did you come back through the portal to find me?"

He walked to where the Book of Spells sat on the wooden lectern. Mouth set, he touched the leather binding. "Come hell or high water?"

"Pinky swear."

He lifted his chin, then stared long and hard at me. "Hell, if I could—"

Suddenly, all his features tightened into a spasm of pain. The struggle was horribly brief. The wizard shouldered past my brother's defenses that fast—one moment I was measuring the modicum of hope blossoming in my brother's body language, and the next, I was staring at an arrogant man who wore my brother's face.

Revulsion roiled inside me, squeezing my gut, catching my breath in its sweaty grip.

"'Tis the Mage," breathed my Fae.

Shut up.

"I will give him power," he said, coldly. "That, and the opportunity to live to see the Black Mage humiliated and executed." He folded his hands at his waist as if he still was an old man with a potbelly. "Once our souls fully merge, we shall be the most powerful mage in our realm. We shall know glory beyond glory."

"The last time you sought glory, you reached too high."

"This time I will be cautious, I will be prudent."

Not with Lexi, you won't. The squeezing heartbreak of loss had been there, ever since I'd opened my eyes and found myself in front of my brother. But now? Anger melded itself to hatred.

"We will live a long life," he said, arrogance rolling off each word. "And a far more valuable one, respected by people of great influence. Let your brother live a life of honor and prestige. Release me from my vow."

I hate you, mage. With all my heart, I hate you.

"He's still a wolf. The moon will still call him."

"I will deal with that."

My gaze moved to the bottles of sun potion lining the shelf. "What are you going to do? Take him back to the portal for periodic rehabilitation?"

"I will cleanse him as needed."

You'll hang him out to dry, like a paper towel used over and over again. And over time, all that was Lexi— the brightness and the dark—would dwindle into gray. My twin would die a slow soul death and eventually the only entity left inside the husk of his body would be that of an old wizard.

"I won't do it," I told him. "I will not release you from your vow. You will keep your pledge to me, mage. You will wait for us at Daniel's Rock, and together we will travel to the castle and destroy your Book of Spells."

"You risk all our lives, nalera," he said. "Do you not understand how dangerous it will be for you to travel in the company of your mate? He is wanted by the Black Mage."

"He's evaded him before."

"But now, his own kind hunt for him, high and low. They consider the Son of Lukynae a traitor to his pack and now believe him to be a false prophet. They know his scent. They will run him to the ground."

"We'll take our chances."

"We will wait for you at Daniel's Rock. But if you do not hold to your part of the bargain, then mine is null."

The ward. Goddess, the ward. It has to be broken.

"Lexi, if you can hear me, remember: Strongholds hold."

The world started to dim, the colors to swirl, and the figure of my brother started to fade. "You will regret your choice, nalera," I heard my brother's voice say, as the darkness swept over me.

Chapter Nine

I woke. As fast as that. Return to this realm came hard, with none of the usual slow and drowsy crawl to reality. An unaccustomed weight pressed me hard to the hard-packed earth. Heavier than gravity. Solid. Sealing my mouth. Smothering me.

They're burying me! In the spit of land at the end of the wolf cemetery, behind a high stone wall. Just another trapped Fae spending eternity with the pack.

I lashed out. Feet, teeth—then, oh so stupidly—with my hands.

A pained grunt. Mine? His?

Don't bury me.

"Calm down!"

My flailing knee hit something solid and warm. "Shit!" swore Trowbridge. Throbbing arm pinned to my chest, I staggered to my feet. Wildly, I swung around. I was Hedi among the headstones. The worry and fear I'd felt for my brother—and had kept so carefully cloaked from the mage—now ran rampant inside me.

Trowbridge rose from his half crouch. "Hedi?"

I danced out of his reach. "No, no, no." Frustration bit at me, making me inarticulate with haste. "We have to break the ward. Right now." I started to stumble toward it. Perhaps I could tear it again. Make a hole in it large enough for all of us.

"Hedi, come back!"

But I was already running, slaloming between the tombstones. Sprinting toward Casperella's tumbled-down wall, praying that the ward's skin was still thin there, even as my Fae said quietly, "Haste will not help. The ward is sealed. It is done."

No. It is not *done.*

With blind hope I knelt before it, stick in hand. I gave the veil a prod.

Evil. Everywhere.

Trowbridge sank to one knee beside me. "Hedi?" Warmth, home, mate—those were the things I had, and my brother so lacked. I leaned into the heat of Trowbridge's chest. Accepted the strong, impenetrable shield of his protection. Inhaled the scent of him—wild, woods, with a subtone of something pure.

"You stopped breathing again," he said tersely.

"I saw Lexi in Threall," I said brokenly. "He's not really Lexi anymore. He's shadowed, Trowbridge. The mage is there with him, behind his eyes, censoring his words . . . he tried to trick me . . . tried to act like he was Lexi. Using my brother's mouth . . ."

Trowbridge eased me away. "Sweetheart, we have to make tracks. We need to bring the Sisters back."

A new worry hit me. "How long was I out?"

"Only a couple of minutes," said Cordelia. "But you stopped breathing again. You have to cease going to that place, do you understand? No. More."

Lexi, remember who you are.

The windshield was dirty and the wipers weren't any good. The air in the truck was redolent with tense Were, ferret (Anu sat behind me), blood (Gerry's and Cordelia's), and fragrant pine. The latter was due to the fact I was sitting in the front passenger seat, holding an ornamental pine shrub in my lap.

Another clod of soil fell to the floorboards when I shifted my leg. If we'd had more time before piling into Harry's truck, we might have thought of wrapping the roots in a green plastic bag. But it had been a scramble—Biggs had shown up in his own vehicle, just as we rounded the corner of the house. His radio had been blaring; his phone lay forgotten in the console between the seats. He'd said that he'd been doing the rounds and hadn't heard or seen anything. It was the way he'd spread his hands, and said, "What?"—trailing the *a* into three notes—that had done it.

Trowbridge's fist had swung. It was a lights-out punch, square to the jaw. Biggs went flying into the forsythia, down for the count. Trowbridge had told Harry, "We're heading south on the 400. Swing by and pick up Rachel. If we lose the Sisters' trail, we'll need her help."

Then he'd flown into the house and had come out approximately two seconds later, tucking Knox's personal effects into a knapsack. He'd hurled that into the backseat of the car, almost nailing Anu, and turned for me.

"Merry needs to be fed," I'd told him, expecting him to grab a can of syrup. But Trowbridge had simply spun around and uprooted the bush with one hand. Then he'd one-armed lifted me into the truck's passenger seat, and deposited Merry's snack in my lap with a terse, "Tell her to chow down on that."

Merry hates pines.

Disquieted, I searched for her among the pine boughs, and found her buried deep. Merry's usual bright light had dimmed; the honey tones of her amber stone had dulled to a sickly brown. She'd taken the worst of my hurt into her, healing me while I traveled in Threall. I stroked her with a finger that should have been disfigured, but now was only plump and lobster red. In return she issued a halfhearted blip of yellow.

It had been a tough night for the Faes.

I will hold but I wish things were different. That I was just an ordinary wolf, mated to an average Were, looking forward to arguing over wallpaper and whose turn it was to take out the trash. That I didn't have a brother stuck in some portal passage that no mortal—or Were for that matter—knew existed. That wizards belonged only to Hogwarts, that evil was vanquished with a swipe of sword, that fairy tales always ended neatly.

Lexi.

I gave Merry another stroke, trying to rid my brain of that new and ugly thought—what if it all came down to the same result? In the end—no matter how hard we fought—we lost. One us died, which meant the other two toppled over like dominos? Perhaps our fates were already set in stone, our destinies chiseled out by some stone-mason working for a displeased Goddess.

"You okay?" Trowbridge asked gruffly.

The Alpha of Creemore drove with a fierce competence that belied the fact that he'd spent nine years in another realm where horsepower meant *horse*power. The speed-ometer's needle had climbed steadily since we'd left the side roads and merged onto the highway. Had I ever been in a car moving this fast? One hundred fifty-five kilome-ters—thirty-five over the speed limit. *That would be a negative.* Thankfully, since it was half past midnight, the cops were conspicuously absent on the 400 Highway.

A small favor.

Luck hadn't smiled on Natasha and Elizabeth. Accord-ing to a mortal who'd owed the pack a favor, their escape from our territory had been slowed down by the need to buy fuel at his gas station.

Life is full of learning examples, and this was yet another. Something to remember: all good getaways require a full tank. I would bet my last Cherry Blossom that Elizabeth was ragging on Natasha for that oversight.

I knew it in my bones that we'd catch up to them soon. And then what? We'd drag them back by their fake auburn hair and force them to make things right.

Which reminded me of an important detail. "The bikers didn't want to kill me. Not there anyhow," I told Trowbridge. I stared ahead, thinking it through. "They wanted to take me somewhere. To meet someone."

"Had to be Whitlock," said Cordelia.

"And Itchy told Gerry not to shoot you," I added. " 'Don't lose the bonus,' he said. 'We have to make him look dirty.' "

"I'm done with this asshole," said Trowbridge. "When we get back from the Fae realm, I'm going to take him on. Whitlock wants war? He's got it."

Two hours ago, I'd been appalled at the thought of a deliberate kill. But somewhere back in the cemetery, I'd crossed some invisible line. I knew without a doubt that there had been no "oops" to what I'd done to Itchy or Gerry. I'd wanted them dead and I'd followed that impulse to the grisly end. The three of us—my inner-wolf, Fae-me, and plain old Hedi—had not been appalled and horrified when we'd battered Gerry's noggin with the tombstone.

The truth is ugly . . . in fact, we'd smiled.

Even now, the yen to spill some of Natasha's blood was as fierce a craving as I'd ever experienced. What had changed inside me? Was it because I'd turned my wolf loose? *Am I turning feral?* Did letting out my inner animal make me think like one?

Was that even bad?

Not if I'm going to run with wolves.

"Are you going to keep going to Threall every time

you close your eyes?" Trowbridge asked suddenly. "Is that why you didn't sleep back at the house?"

"Maybe," I said. My mate steered the car smoothly through a bend in the road. A long semi was hauling a silver trailer, its fumes redolent of swine.

"Poppet." Cordelia heaved a deep sigh from the back-seat. "It scares the crap out of him when you stop breathing." She sat stiffly, her hand pressed hard to a dark blue towel held against her flank. A gun lay by her hip. Before we'd all piled into our cars, she'd stalked into the Trow-bridge house and came out with ugly-dark-and-deadly. The weapon smelled of gun oil with a hint of Cordelia. But the *other* Cordelia—the stripped-down one, before the heavy foundation and powder.

The towel appeared wet. "Are you still bleeding?"

"I am fine," she said, lifting her brows as if to dare me to contradict her. "Don't worry about me."

I lifted mine and turned back to face the road. Trow-bridge cast me a swift glance, his face carefully neutral. "Do you have any control over going there?"

"I'm not sure."

Up ahead, the pig hauler lumbered in the slow lane, leav-ing a trail of dust and swine stink. I dipped my chin into the midst of the pine, letting the soft candles of its branches brush my nose, as we overtook the long semi. The side of the trailer was a dull façade of grillwork and peepholes. The swine were pale pink shapes. The driver wore a cap, and a disbelieving expression, as we blew past him.

All the little piggies going to market.

"Is there a kill list for halflings?" I asked abruptly.

Trowbridge shot me a quick look. "What?"

"Lexi said there was a kill list." I watched a ruddy flush creep over his cheeks. "You told me that they died early because they couldn't survive their change. But that's not the truth, is it? Are they given a little help to their ends?"

"Do you really want to go into this right now?" He pressed the pedal completely to the floor, and the pig hauler disappeared in our dust.

My voice grew tight. "I need to know."

We traveled another half kilometer at rocketing speed before he sighed and lifted his foot slightly off the gas. "Listen to the whole story before you make up your mind." He scowled at the road. "We have rules, made to protect our race."

"From contamination?" I asked stiffly.

"Will you listen?"

I tossed my head. "Go on."

"From the word go, a male wolf is told to avoid human girls because they are way more fertile than ours. But a very few wolves . . . they don't listen and in some cases, they get a human girl pregnant." He shot me a quelling glance. "We don't take that lightly, okay? In my opinion any wolf that knocks up a human should be taken out and shot."

"What happens?"

"The guy responsible is expected to inform his Alpha, who in turn must pass the information on to the council. The woman's name is put on the watch list."

"They kill her?" I asked, shocked.

"No," he said. "Hedi, I don't agree with this, okay? Any guy who gets a human girl pregnant deserves to be shot. I don't agree—"

"Just tell me," I said tightly.

He exhaled through his teeth. "If she safely delivers the kid, the child's name is added to the list. Then it's the wolf's duty to stay out of the kid's life but to keep watch. You always know where your kid is, and when he or she's just about to enter into their puberty—"

"How would the wolf know the kid's ready for puberty?"

"Their scent changes just before their instinct kicks in.

They can feel their wolf inside them and the need to run.
The kid will feel compelled to head north, for the woods.
Doesn't matter if they've never been out of the city. They'll
hitchhike if they have to."

I tried to imagine some suburban teen thumbing her
way up north. Not knowing why, just being driven by a
need she didn't understand. "Those poor kids."

"The father must follow his kid into the forest. Two go
in, one comes out."

"That's barbaric," I whispered.

Trowbridge's mouth was a flat line. "It's a severe punishment. For a man to kill his child—"

"Yeah, I'm crying for him." Disgust roiled inside me.
"What about the kid? Doesn't he or she have a right to
life? What about the human mother? How does she feel
about losing her child?"

Goddess, those poor women.

"It's wrong all the way around. I know that." His tone
hardened. "But the kid's going to die. There's no stopping
it. A halfling's body doesn't have the magic to heal. They
literally split apart. Gaping wounds, torn bellies. They don't
have the magic to re-form into their wolf." Trowbridge, now
committed to telling all, kept talking, his voice a low, flat
monotone. "The halflings die screaming. Slowly torn apart,
their muscles—"

"How are they sure that every halfling will die?"

Regret in his eyes. "They just are."

"Fae Stars," I said, my voice a thin thread. "Why didn't
you just kill us at birth? Drown us like kittens?"

"You're not a halfling. You can change into your wolf.
I've seen enough Fae-Were crosses in Merenwyn to know
that."

It was a long way off, but the question had to be asked.
I stared at him, taking in the dark eyelashes, the high cheekbones. The shadows that lived under his eyes, and in his

eyes. *Tell me the truth.* "What if we have children?" I asked softly.

"We will love them." He smiled as if he saw them in his mind's eye. "Their mother will teach them to swim, and their father will teach them to hunt. They won't grow up like you did—that I can promise you. If I have to re-educate every wolf in my pack, they will be accepted."

That's when we saw the taillights of the witches' broom.

The 400 is a provincial highway, well used as it links the city of Toronto to cottage country. It has three lanes going north, three lanes going south. Between them, a steel barrier and a thin strip of asphalt reserved for breakdowns. It's a fairly straight road, and after leaving the pig hauler in our dust, we'd hit another long straight section of highway, which afforded us great visibility, as it was well lit. The witches' broom— an old Impala—had funky taillights. Shaped like a cat's eye, or maybe half of a mocking smile.

Trowbridge's smile fell away. "Got them," he said, pressing the gas pedal to the floor. The truck rocketed forward. Ahead on the road, the Impala suddenly surged forward.

"They've seen us," I said.

Natasha tore down the highway like a parole violator outrunning the law, but in the game of who's got the bigger engine, Harry's truck was the clear winner. The distance separating us steadily narrowed. If we didn't draw abreast of them by the time we got to the overpass, we'd get them half a kilometer later.

Cordelia opened her window. "You better cover your ears," she said, "in case I actually need to pull the trigger."

I flattened a pine bough to see better. Were those rear lights in the shadows beneath the underpass? "Trowbridge, there's a car there—no, it's a van. Is it one of ours?"

Trowbridge swore, and his hands grew tight around the
wheel, and several things happened all at once. The van's
interior lights suddenly blazed. Natasha stood on her brakes.

He shouted, "Cordie!"

A flash of rapid gunfire up ahead, coming from the
side of the van—*they're strafing the Impala*—and then
the road ahead of us turned into an obstacle field. Natasha
swerved and lost control. Her vehicle did a long screech-
ing slide—I almost thought she was going to recover, but
then the back end swung out and hit the road divider.

That's when Natasha's pride and joy, so solid, so heavy,
became as weightless as a Matchbox car. It rolled over—
once, twice, three times—shedding sections of metal as it
did. On the last bounce it hit the steel guardrail once more.
The nose slammed a kiss on the pavement; the back end
tipped like the *Titanic* going for its last dive.

In that fleeting split second, I saw a dark shape fall out
of a gaping door.

What is that? A sweater? No, larger than that. Metal
torn from the car? Suddenly, it hit me. *Oh crap. Not a piece
of debris—that's a person being thrown from the car!*

Natasha fell in an untidy heap on the asphalt.

Meanwhile, the car that had spat her out kept going,
end over end, heaving bits of metal with every strike. On
the third roll it slid onto its side and still kept going, skidding down the road on what remained of its passenger
door, presenting us with a long lingering view of its
undercarriage as it went.

In a piece of the surreal that would never leave me, I
saw the witch heave herself upright onto one elbow, to
watch it go.

Then it was our turn to pass the van hidden in the
shadows of the overpass. Trowbridge stomped on the gas.
Anu yelped as Cordelia roughly shoved her onto the
floorboards. "Get down!" she screamed before she fired.

In that enclosed space, the gun's report was agony—
eardrum-shattering pain to my sensitive ears. I screamed,
Anu cried out—I think even Trowbridge yelled. It was
too hard to separate, all was noise, all was a cacophony of
anguish and violence.

Cordelia's actions won us a short reprieve from return
gunfire. Our truck was already three-quarters past the van
before the shooter's bullets rat-tat-tatted into the rear of
our truck.

Trowbridge said, "Fuck!" just as someone—Anu or
Cordelia?—let out a low, guttural grunt. A piece of
debris—heaven knows what—smashed into the windshield with a sharp crack, leaving a starburst hole in the
middle of it.

We slid out of control on a direct path toward Natasha.
We're going to flatten her like a bug. She pivoted on her
hip. I caught a quick glimpse of her face, eyes wide open,
small mouth shaped like a big empty O as Trowbridge
jerked the wheel savagely to the right.

I steeled myself for a bump or a jolt.

But there was nothing—not even a scream that I could
separate and identify—because someone cried out—
maybe me—and then the back end of our vehicle was
skidding, swaying wildly. A second later, our front tires
left the pavement, and our truck hit the soft shoulder of
the road.

"Bugger!" I heard Cordelia cry.

Movement felt slow, time fractured, as my gaze slewed
over to Trowbridge. I'll never forget the picture of him.
Head lowered, mouth set in a snarl as he fought to control
the skid. We were going too fast. And ahead there was
soft erosion—a place where spring runoff had bit into the
emergency lane. Our front tire sank into it, and then we
were lost.

The right tire went down, the left tire went up. Me,

Merry, and the ornamental pine were thrown violently against the door. Earth rained. Glass shivered.

And I had time to think quite clearly.

We're rolling.

It's odd to see things out of context. The spiked buds of furled daylilies as a visual surprise in a field that was suddenly turning itself up on its end, sky where it should be ground, the dark gray blur of earth . . . and I thought, *If we just keep rolling along on the grass, we'll be fine.*

Something slapped me on the face, really hard, before I was blinded by the billow of gray-white balloon. We did one more roll. Then finally, we stopped.

I'm alive.

And everything is upside down.

The top of the truck's cabin was below me and dented, and so much closer than it should be. Unsettling. I shifted my gaze to the incongruous picture of Harry's portable coffee mug sitting needle-deep in a broken bough of pine.

Then the dust rolled in.

Chapter Ten

I'm almost positive I didn't pass out. Because I know that I didn't go to Threall.

Though I think I took an itty-bitty, involuntary, mental time-out. I was beyond exhausted, and my senses had been assailed by too many noises and horrible sights. For a couple of minutes, I shut down. Didn't hear anything. Didn't see anything. Detachment—thorough and complete—was mine.

I roused to the sound of a stifled groan.

Trowbridge?

I tried to lift my right hand and discovered that it was trapped, pinned between me and the broken plastic of the door rest. The jagged edge bit into the bandage on my wrist.

Who moaned?

Me?

Dust had indeed flown, and earth too. It was in my mouth, on my tongue. Sprinkled across my eyes. I blinked against the grit in them until my vision cleared.

I'm still upside down. Something dug into my stomach. Something pressed my head. *Trapped.* My heart started slamming in my chest. I hung from my seat belt. Head tilted at a ninety-degree angle, neck awkwardly twisted toward the blown-out passenger window, knees jackknifed to my waist. My intestines felt deeply bruised, probably because somewhere during one of the Ford's revolutions, my seat belt had moved from low on my belly to high across my waist.

"Trowbridge?" I croaked.

Someone moaned. Low in their throat.

"Trowbridge?" I repeated, louder this time.

I smelled sweet peas. *Blood. Mine.* Anxiety squeezed me, telling me that there wasn't enough air; there wasn't enough space to breathe; I was probably hemorrhaging and they'd need the Jaws of Life to get me out of this coffin of metal.

I've got to get out.

I moved my leg then hissed when my right knee hit something solid and jagged. Dashboard? Engine part? I wanted to turn my head to see, but something hard and unyielding was pressed to my left temple. Boxing me in.

So much metal.

All around me. *Don't throw up.*

Why couldn't I move?

Neck stiff, I slanted my gaze toward the driver's seat. *Sweet heavens, it was the roof.*

It had pancaked inward when the vehicle finally ceased rolling and had come to a rest upside down. What had once been a spacious cab now was a crushed sardine can—one that had been crumpled by the fist of a furious giant.

"Cordelia?" I called, my voice rising. "Anu?"

Listen for their heartbeats; there should be three besides my own. I strained to catch them—caught one beating very rapidly, and then another slower and farther away, but I couldn't count them all because someone was hyperventilating in what remained of the backseat—their panicked breath coming out in short gasps. *"Huh-huh-huh."*

Anu. Alive and well enough to pant.

But I can't hear Trowbridge's heart. I can't even sense his heart.

No. Not today. Not yet. There was too much to do. Rescue Lexi. Save the world. Make babies.

"Trowbridge!" I screamed.

My wolf grew large inside me, her hackles raised in an attitude of protection. Metal tore at my calf as I struggled to pull my right leg up to my chest. *I will kick the windshield out if need be. I will tear this sardine can apart with my magic and my will.*

There is too much to do. Too much to live for.

I will not die like this.

"Hedi! Talk to me!"

Relief surged over me. So strong I almost peed my pants.

"Trowbridge?" Hearing his voice wiped out any care about halflings or kill lists or wolves that should be taken out and shot.

"You okay?" he said, sounding hoarse.

"I'm alive." Though I couldn't see him, my ears told me he was on the other side of that flattened roof. "Are you hurt?"

He grunted, then there was the sound of tearing metal. "I'm good."

"Is Cordelia okay?" I asked. "And Anu?"

"I'm here," said Cordelia, sounding bored. On the heels of that, a stream of Merenwynian erupted from what used to be the backseat. So. The four of us were accounted for.

Thank you, Goddess.

A movement out of the corner of my eye.

A second later, the ferret poked its head through a hole. Its whiskers tickled my cheekbone. "Go away," I said. I could have sworn it smiled at me before Anu yanked it back to her side of the wreck.

Five alive then.

Yup. Happiness. It surged over me, and for about two seconds, I was the girl with the winning lotto ticket, the miner with a pan of gold.

I wasn't even that worried about being trapped anymore. Yeah, I was squeezed in the mangled framework of the car, but I was among Weres. Strong, healthy, *unhurt* wolves. Give them a pry bar and enough motivation and they'd get me out. We'd shovel up the witch. Get the ward broken. Collect Lexi. Everything was doable. I was poised on the edge of euphoria, making half-solemn promises— *henceforth, I will never tell another lie*—and then all bonhomie was shattered by a sound that can be summed up in one single four-letter word.

Bang.

Not like a car's backfire or a smack of meaty fist on metal. Nope. "Bang" as in "bang-bang, you're dead."

"Who's shooting?" I whispered.

"Be quiet, Hedi," hushed Cordelia from somewhere to my left.

There was a short pause, followed by two more bangs; the interval between the gunshots frighteningly deliberate. Like someone was taking their sweet time to aim before firing.

The one upside/downside to the way my head was tilted toward the blown-out passenger window was that I had a partial view of the road above us. I watched it, heart going thud-thud, thud-thud in my chest, and sure enough. Someone walked to the lip of the road above our wreck. *A human rescue person?* The wind caught his aroma and brought it to me.

Crap. He smelled like a Harley.

A biker? That had to be bad. Had they found out about Itchy and Gerry already?

Crap, crap, crap.

The overpass's lights provided me with some helpful details. For instance—I could see that he wore motorcycle boots. Square toes with a faint upward curl. Oh man, was the whole gang after us? Was another biker creeping on us from behind?

I'm trapped. Cordelia's trapped.

"Trowbridge." I whispered.

"Shhh." From the backseat—*not* Trowbridge.

I strained to listen. What was the biker doing up there? Taking stock of the situation? I heard a hollow metallic click—a sound effect that needed very little interpreting if you've ever watched *Reservoir Dogs*. My stomach clenched. The shooter was reloading.

No, no, no.

That's when it occurred to me that if I could see the shooter, he could see me. *Hell, no.* I fumbled with my belt, scrabbling for the release button. Found it. Jammed two fingers inside it. And then, just as I saw his knee flex— *he's assuming the firing position*—I caught a glimpse of Trowbridge slinking up the incline, ready to tackle him. *He's got a gun, Trowbridge!*

I tensed for the weapon's report.

There was a long, spine-chilling scream of air brakes. Rubber being burned on the pavement, and then, horribly, the squeals of terrified pigs.

It happened so fast.

The man in motorcycle boots spun around, then the biker was gone—becoming a grill ornament to the semi that whizzed past us, its long silver pig hauler balanced on one set of wheels.

Enough. I closed my eyes again.

I had no wish to see pigs fly.

Open your eyes. If you can't stand what you see, you can go to Threall.

"Hedi?" I heard my mate softly say.

I peeked. Trowbridge, crouched outside my window. From my point of view, upside down. Shirtless. Grimy. Stubble on his jaw. Eyes fierce. "Hey," he said, touching my face with two very gentle fingers.

"Hey." That came out rusty sounding—my mouth was so dry—so I worked my tongue against my teeth, then asked, "Who shot at us?"

"Bad guy." His hand was checking me over; sliding along my arm, moving to my ribs.

"Biker bad guy," I corrected. "How many bikers are in a gang? Are we done yet?"

"Does anything hurt?"

"My gut hurts, my neck aches, my wrist is . . ." Quick alarm flared in his eyes so I threw him a bone. "My mouth doesn't hurt."

"Why does that not surprise me?" he said, tenderly touching my lip. But his face wore a big, relieved smile, and I knew that he'd been as afraid for me as I'd been for him. Matter of fact, despite his calm voice his eyes were fierce. And his scent? My, oh my, it was bristling with male pheromones. *My mate's feeling protective.* My inner-bitch stretched her spine to luxuriate in the heady pleasure of me-mine-us.

"Is everyone all right down there?" some random human called. "Do you want me to call an ambulance?"

Go away.

Trowbridge hollered, "We're good."

"Is that the truth?" I searched his face. "We're all good?"

"Yeah. I got Cordie and Anu while you were passed out." He tested the door handle, then shrugged, evidently having low expectations of success.

"I didn't pass out."

He canted his head to the side. "You were out, Babe."

I was? "What about the shooters in the van?"

"Dead."

"Who shot them?"

"Cordelia doesn't miss when she aims a gun."

"Even when she's aiming from the backseat of a skidding car?"

"Nailed one, left the other needing life support. I finished him off."

That's a relief. I thought of something that made me frown. "Did you just call me Babe? I'm not a Babe, a baby, or a—"

"Hey, Tink," he said with a wink. "Just testing. You hit your head."

"My head's fine." I thought it was anyhow. Though my cheek was sticky. Automatically, I patted my chest for Merry, and felt another blip of awful when all I encountered was boob. Where was she? She'd been feeding when we rolled; her chain spooled in a golden puddle on a pine bough before we were hit.

"I can't find Merry!"

"Calm yourself." Cordelia's feet walked into view. "She was thrown clear. I've got her. We have declared a partial truce."

"Now, close your eyes," Trowbridge said, "We're going to pry open the door."

"Hey, Trowbridge," I said before I did.

"What?"

I felt my lips curl into a beatific smile. "I didn't go to Threall—if I really did pass out, I stayed here. In this realm."

"One problem down, ninety-nine to go." Trowbridge gave me a wink. "Give us a second, and we'll get you out of there," he promised, gripping the car door as if he was prepared to tear it open himself—a display of supernatural strength that would have gone viral on video.

He can't be thinking right.

"We've a minor setback," he said, once I was out. "Not the end of the world—we'll just have to—"

"I want to see." Glory be. What a sight waited for me when Trowbridge had helped me hobble up the ditch's incline. Carnage, death, and hogs gone wild.

A cloven-hoofed porker trotted past me, snout lifted, little piggy eyes fixed on a tempting clump of vegetation. Mr. Pig was not alone. There were at least a dozen examples of liberated porcine, many of whom had already spread out on the highway, in search of grub.

The hauler was some fifty feet down the road, on its side, still attached to the jackknifed cab. The biker's broken body was caught beneath it. Through the crazed glass of the semi's enormous windshield, I could see the driver standing upright in the overturned cab, trying to push open his door like it was the emergency hatch on a space capsule.

Slowly my gaze traveled back to where Natasha's body lay prone, a small dark whale draped across the dotted line painted on the road. A lank hank of auburn hair floated on a pool of crimson. She was dead.

My mouth was dry. "Did we hit her?"

"No, she was shot."

I remembered the biker standing at the lip of the road. "Why did they kill the witches?"

Trowbridge didn't know. "Could have been a deliberate hit. Could have been a case of wrong time, wrong place." He shrugged. "Bikers don't like witnesses to their drive-by shootings."

Elizabeth. I turned. Oh Goddess. More devastation. A human crouched by the Impala's twisted wreck. As I watched, he rose, shaking his head. The sick look on his face telling me all I needed to know.

Two dead witches.

How would we break the ward now? We'd have to track down the rest of the coven, and shake them like a bunch of castanets until they spilled their magical beans. But that would take time. Lexi had three days and no more before the temporary bond became permanent.

"How do we find their coven?" I asked him.

One side of his mouth pulled down. "I'll have to make a few phone calls."

"How long will that take?" I asked. *If we can't break the ward, I can't cross the portal. What will Lexi do when I'm not there at Daniel's Rock? He'll think I gave up on him, he'll think this Stronghold broke.*

"Not too long. We'll get there, Tink." Trowbridge's arms tightened, and I felt the weight of his chin on the top of my head. His heart, which had been thumping hard, picked up for ten beats then slowly leveled out.

"Come hell or high water," I said. "We will."

Underneath the underpass, the van's running lights glowed, the engine idled. Spectators were clustered there— the three or four people in the cars that had been behind us on the road, who'd watched us going through that underpass as if we were the thread going through the eye of the needle.

Trowbridge murmured, "I want another look at their van. I want to know why Whitlock's going to all this trouble."

"I'll come with you." But I didn't immediately lift my ear from his chest, and he didn't release me. "Trowbridge?"

"Yeah, Tink."

"I want my Tear back."

"Stay here with the others." Trowbridge kissed my

forehead—warm lips that belong on mine. "I'll get it for you." Then he left. The crowd gathered near the van parted at his approach. Altogether, not terribly surprising when you considered that the Alpha of Creemore wore an expression that would have scared the snot out of Billy the Kid.

Anu sat on the grass, my ex-roomie sat on a rock. Cordelia lifted her head at my approach and gave me a fierce nod. But Anu was hunched over, crying quietly into her hands. Her ferret was curled in her lap, its normally inquisitive expression set into one that damn near looked like reproach. I looked away, and then stared at the top of my niece's head, wondering what to say, what to do. Noted that her part wasn't straight, and that she had the same cowlick at her crown that my twin had.

Has to be a family trait.

I sank down to the back of my heels. She didn't flinch as my knee brushed hers, but she didn't turn for a hug either.

I've done a great job of looking after her these last twenty-four hours, haven't I, Lexi? I touched the shoulder of the kid who'd known dangers that I had never been asked to face, and was probably going to be left alone in this foreign world in a few years, without family or without anyone who cared. I said, "It's going to be okay."

Anu wiped her nose with her hand. She had streaks of oil on her face—it must have been on her hands and now it was on her nose, on her chin, by the corner of her trembling mouth.

She's just a kid. My brother's kid.

My niece pulled in another shuddering breath as a pig trotted past us, its jaw working. I gave her a weak, encouraging smile. Then I garnished the moment with a rough pat on her shoulder.

"It's going be okay," I repeated.

She gave me a searching look. The air was filled with scents I never wanted to put together again: burned tires, spilled fuel, heated engine oil, witch blood, wolf death, Were anger, and human curiosity.

We were all a bunch of liars.

Nothing was going to be okay.

Trowbridge said, "We need to get off the road before the cops come. Since the cars are totalled, we'll have to hoof it. We'll cut across the fields until we find a secondary road, then find a phone."

I nodded, knowing that he was right. The highway patrol would come soon, if they weren't already on their way. Southbound traffic was gridlocked behind us. Gawkers had slowed the northbound lanes to a crawl, to gape at the accident and the solitary pig that had managed to squeeze through the break in the torn road divider.

Anu stood, but Cordelia remained seated, arms still wrapped around her gut.

"Your shoes are going to take a beating," I told my mother hen. The field was deeply furrowed, the farmer having tilled the ground following the harvest.

Cordelia nodded but didn't get up. "That's why I'm staying here. You'd better hurry."

It was the way she said it. The tone so quiet and dry. Her face so still.

"Cordie?" said Trowbridge, turning.

She looked up at us, her face white. "There's something wrong with me."

I crouched by her, scanning her for a new injury. "Where are you hurt?"

"The bullet I took back at the pond came out in pieces." She worked her throat, then swallowed. Managed to muster a dry smile. "Silver pieces. I can't run. I can barely stand. I'll stay here."

"You're coming with us, even if I have to carry you," I said flatly.

Trowbridge spun on his heels. A white vehicle was tearing down the breakdown lane, heading for us, caution lights flashing.

I stepped in front of him. "Let me talk to the cops. I do helpless really well."

"Like hell you do," said Trowbridge.

"Trust me. I can do Bambi really well. It's all in the eyes."

"You won't have to," my mate said. "That's Rachel's truck."

Chapter Eleven

"Get that teacloth out of my face, you useless Chihuahua," snapped Cordelia, except she spoke in a low forced baritone, all her usual deliberately soft modulation stripped away. "If I require something to bite down on, it won't be some mildewed rag."

Biggs flinched and backed away.

Cordelia had revived long enough to get tetchy. Can't blame her. Her blood was on the linoleum floor, a line of wavering crimson drops, pitter-patters of awful, leading from the door all the way to the sixties dinette table on which she'd been placed.

The indignity of it all. She—a woman of feathers and silk—laid out on a slab of pink and black Formica like a trout ready to be filleted. They'd locked the table's leaves into the up position, hoping to make it long enough to support her body, but it was still inadequately short; her long feet hung over the table's chrome edges. Cordelia had bunions.

I never knew that.

In terms of avoiding any deep conversations with the provincial police, we'd made good. Rachel had gunned the vehicle as soon as she'd navigated around the wrecks and steered past the most intrepid pig (tail up, heading down the road toward Toronto at a steady clip-clop), and we'd rocketed back *up* the 400 until Harry had banged on the rear window's glass and pointed to the exit ahead. Rachel's truck was large, but it could seat only so many people. Thus Harry and Biggs had endured the Great Escape sitting hunched in the truck's open bed.

In the short interval it took to get Cordelia into the backseat her color had leached from pale and interesting to gray and terrifying. Five minutes down the road, her head had unexpectedly drooped. I'd caught her before she melted into a puddle on the floor of Rachel's Ford. She'd roused enough to essay an attempt to straighten, but when I wrapped my arms around her, she'd leaned into me. Her breath had turned shallow shortly after that.

The silver had to be removed. Immediately.

Harry had known "someone" in Thornton who lived above the general store and had a small building behind it that a real estate agent might have optimistically dubbed a mother-in-law suite. Trowbridge's brow had wrinkled at the lingering scent left by that long-gone tenant. "He is 'Other'?" he'd said, mildly enough, but his intonation had put finger quotes and caps around the word.

Harry had nodded.

I could have asked, "Other what?" but I didn't because my own nose told me that the guy Harry had roused from sleep wasn't human or Were. To be honest, the guy wearing a sweatshirt pulled over plaid pajamas smelled a little like one of the dressed rolls of roast beef that Cordelia used to pick up for her Sunday dinner. That was a trifle worrisome—raising misgivings of germs and bacteria. But Ferris was one of the two medics trusted by the Weres, and of the two, he had a complete lack of response to silver, so here we were. Doing makeshift surgery in a room that smelled like a cross between a deli and an abattoir.

Trowbridge's sister Rachel had barely spoken, except with her eyes, and they had lots to say whenever they focused on me. Condemnation and disapproval mostly, as if I'd somehow brought all of this on the pack, and on her brother, though I wasn't sure which bothered her more. She hadn't uncrossed her arms since she'd wedged a soup can under the window sash to hold it raised, and opened the back door.

Her nostrils looked permanently pinched. Being a first-rate tracker must have certain drawbacks.

Biggs turned to me—opened his mouth to say something—then quickly swung away to puke into the sink.

Lovely.

I wanted to go away from it all—to escape if only for a few minutes. Or at least curl up into a ball and fall asleep, right there, right then. Threall or no Threall. It was the scents. And the sights. You put those two together and memories were stirred.

Of death and loss.

I wound my fingers around Cordelia's clenched fist. Though she didn't open her eyes, she gave my hand a fierce squeeze. A silent Cordelia? Lying there with bra and belly exposed, and not saying one damn word? Anxiety wormed its way into my heart, found a ventricle and started drilling. I'm not sure if I could stand losing two moms. And for better or worse, that's what Cordelia had turned into. This tall redhead with her patented scowls and arched eyebrows had become my mom-that-wasn't.

"Why does she keep bleeding?" My voice sounded rusty, even to my ears.

My mate's jaw tensed, then he worked it loose. "It's the silver. Our bodies work to get rid of it but can't. Her stomach muscles are constantly spasming and that shreds you up inside."

It does?

My gaze slid to the scar above Trowbridge's taut

navel—a rough jagged line that was the only visible remainder of the night he'd been tortured by Mannus. I'd watched them cut him and lay fine filigree chains of silver inside the wounds. Most of them had been removed. All except the one that had lain below that scar. Had he felt agony?

"How did you get rid of the chain they left inside you?"

My mate lifted his shoulders. "I didn't. It's still inside me."

I firmed my mouth, but Trowbridge must have read the horror on my face. "I felt pretty bad until I got to the Pool of Life, but the water neutralized the pain, and did some other shit."

"What 'other shit'?"

"Don't know exactly, but the silver's still inside me and I don't feel sick at all."

Ferris, the medic, said, "I need to get a look at her back. You're going to have to roll her onto her side."

Trowbridge and Harry moved into position. I placed my hands on either side of her clenched jaw and stared into her arctic-blue eyes, their lashes weighed down by heavy and repeated coatings of Max Factor mascara—no false lashes today, for my Cordelia.

"I've got you," I said. Underneath the pads of my fingers, I could feel her muscles tense.

"We're going to do it slowly," said Trowbridge.

"How wonderful," she said, on the crest of a ragged breath. Then my friend, my hectorer, my mother-who-wasn't set her teeth. "Do it."

"Smoothly now. On three," said Trowbridge.

Don't be sick, Cordelia. I need you.

Her chest rose as she drew in a big breath. Trowbridge and Harry tightened their grip on her shoulder and her knees. She hissed through her clenched teeth as they rolled her, and her back flexed into a painful arch as Ferris probed the terrible exit wound. My forehead was drenched in sweat before they'd rolled her back flat on the table. Her gaze sought mine. She gave me a sickly smile. Then finally, very quietly, my six-foot mother hen fell insensible.

And I was glad. Because the really bad stuff had only just begun.

It's a good thing I'd used up my daily faint allotment. Otherwise, I would have hit the deck when Ferris said, "The wound has to be kept open while I work. She has the smallest hands."

Oh. Joy.

I'd never really wanted to inspect the inside of Cordelia— so pink, so wet. Plus, her body was reacting just as Trowbridge had warned me. It worked double time to extrude the bad thing buried deep in her body; her tendons flexed; her muscles twitched against the tools I held.

Do not throw up.

Trowbridge's sister remained silent, but I could feel her eyes boring holes into my back. *Stop looking at me.* How long had we been doing this? How much time had this taken? It seemed like forever.

"I think it is done," Ferris finally said, tossing the mushroom-shaped plug of silver into the trash.

Not a moment too soon, my head swam. "Can I take these things out of Cordelia now?"

He did one more poke with his improvised tool before he nodded. That's when Anu volunteered a sharp comment.

"Wait!" said Trowbridge sharply.

I didn't understand a word of her reply because she spoke in Merenwynian. "What did she say?" I said through my teeth.

Trowbridge shook his head, then raised his gaze to mine. "She thinks there's still silver inside Cordie."

Crap.

"How could she know that?" Rachel asked, suspiciously. "She can't see from where she's standing."

"Can you see anything?" I asked the medic.

He bent his head to reexamine the obscenity of a hole that marred Cordelia's flesh. "No. I think it's clean."

Anu had her game face on, but I'd worn a few thousand of those over my life, so I recognized it for what it was—a borrowed mask of feigned indifference—and knew as surely as if my hand was slapped on her tree up in Threall that she doubted anyone believed her.

I stared at my brother's kid, my thoughts swirling. *Could Aunt Lou's gift have found a new home in my niece?* My aunt Lou had been a Collector, which meant she'd been able to call to any of the seven precious metals with her voice and hands, and it would liquefy and stream toward her like a sinuous snake to puddle by her feet. Hers for the taking.

But that was a talent acquired after puberty—when the full measure of your Fae magic woke inside you. And Anu was only thirteen. Way too young to be able to *call* to the seven, but perhaps she was already aware of it.

"Trowbridge, ask her if she can sense the seven," I said. "Use as close a translation as you can."

Anu's response was simple: an inhale and a nod.

"Look again," I told the medic. "Our Cordelia's not clean yet."

Four sweating minutes later, Ferris exclaimed, "I see it." The air fouled as he mouth-breathed in concentration. A flex of his wrist, then he placed a silver fragment smaller than a newborn's fingernail on the plate we'd been using to collect the pieces.

I said to Anu, "Good call, niece."

Pleasure fired in her eyes, almost immediately banked, and then she cast a superior look toward Rachel. Truly, a huge, massive "Up that, bitch" that required no effort to interpret.

Ferris had been paid and had left us to our own devices. Cordelia was recovering on the couch while Rachel partook of the fresh night air outside. Predictably, Biggs was brooding. He'd retrieved the backpack from our car wreck. Though, in terms of go-bags, it wasn't particularly useful. Two sweaters, a knife, and the bag containing Knox's personal effects. Biggs had removed Knox's necklace and was studying the coin with a level of bleakness that a tarot card reader might summon for the hangman.

Harry said, "I need her number. Call me back as soon as you get it." He glanced to Trowbridge, who gave him a hard nod. Then he added, "There's a thousand bucks in it for you if you can get it for me within the next twenty minutes."

We needed to find a link to the witches. Right away.

Or I was going to splinter apart in an anguish of failure and grief. But, quietly. Inside, so that no one could see.

Lexi.

Trowbridge hovered, as discreetly as he could. He leaned against the counter, as if he just happened to find that its metal edge made a comfortable backrest. His scent broadcast his emotions more strongly than his actions. It spoke to me. Of comfort, and worry.

I hate blood. I detest the color of it, the sticky texture. I loathe the scent of it—particularly when it belongs to someone I love. It seemed to me that I was covered with it. Streaks, dots, dribbles, smears. Some of it mine, some Cordelia's, some Gerry's, and perhaps, a fleck of Natasha's too.

I wanted to strip off my clothing, but I settled on

unwinding my soiled wrist bandage and plunging my hands into a half-filled sink of warm water. That ball of woe rose in my throat again as I flexed my fingers and the water tinted rust. Silently, Trowbridge pulled the plug, then ran the taps and handed me some soap.

I lathered, finding a measure of solace in the act.

Rinse me of it. All of it.

The skin where the kid had gone pit bull was now smooth and almost unblemished. No blood, no spooky green light, no scabs. Four faint silver dots formed a half-moon pattern just above my wristbone.

"Almost good as new," I told my mate, offering my arm for inspection.

"Mmm-hmm." He tore a towel from the dispenser and handed it to me. A faint whiff of mortal clung to the T-shirt that he'd rescued from the back of the closet. BUD'S PAINTING (FRESH'N UP YOUR WALLS!) was emblazoned in rainbow ink on a V-neck that was made for a much smaller man. The jersey was soft; his body was tight. It was a nice contrast.

"I like that T-shirt," I observed. "Brings out the blue in your eyes."

"You've got some stuff on your face," he said, tearing another sheet from the roll. *More blood,* I thought as he dampened it. Tenderly, he wiped the dried streak at my temple. Once wet, the sweet pea scent of my blood re-bloomed. It was the gruff kindness that did me in. My eyes filled.

"Lift up your chin," he said gently.

Obediently, I tipped back my head. He daubed and patted. Tender strokes. Loving touches. *You have this, Hedi, the mouse-hearted. Enjoy it. Take it. Hold it. It won't last forever. Life will not go on for infinity and beyond.*

My mate's brows knitted together. "What's that?"

"What's what?"

"You have a red mark on your throat." His expression, though not thunderous, was definitely presquall as he eased my shirt aside to take a better look at my neck. "Another here. Son of a bitch . . . they look like fingerprints."

"That's where Itchy touched me."

"They're bruises?" he asked, perplexed.

"No." I tugged my collar back in place, faintly embarrassed. Full Weres heal faster than I do. "They're what's left of the burns. They've healed, but my skin is so pale the marks will stay red for another few hours. They'll disappear soon."

"He burned you?"

"When a mortal man touches me . . . I burn."

"Son of a bitch," he roared.

It was an explosion of raw anger. One second Biggs was sitting, slumped and moody, on a dinette chair, and the next he was being dragged to his feet and pinned against the wall. Cheeks flushed, Trowbridge tightened his grip around the spluttering wolf's throat. "You were responsible for the old cemetery road," he said through his teeth.

The back of Biggs's heels drummed a frantic tattoo against the wallboard.

"Where were you?" Trowbridge demanded in a low growl. "What happened?"

Incapable of speech, Biggs caught Trowbridge's rock-hard wrists and tried to do a chin-up.

"You didn't warn us," said my guy. "You let bikers drive right into my territory and threaten my mate."

"Trowbridge, you need to put Biggs down." The hairs on the nape of my neck bristled, reacting to the simmer of violence. "He can't answer you if he's got a crushed larynx."

"He'll heal," he snapped. Then perhaps to prove the point, the Alpha of Creemore tightened his grip until the

tendons stood out white on his hands and Biggs's throat
darkened to puce.

"It's enough, Trowbridge," I whispered. "I've had
enough."

He put his face right up to Biggs's sweating one. "She
is my mate. My. Mate." Jaw rigid, he held on for one last
choking second before he released the younger Were.
Biggs slid down the wall, boneless and gasping, his shirt
pleating up behind him. Trowbridge stood over him with
clenched fists. "If you'd been one of my Raha'ells, I'd have
killed you for that."

*I'm tired of hearing about death. I've had my fill of
threats, and fear, and violence. No more. I can't take any
more. I refuse to absorb one more thing.*

"Cordelia needs to be taken home," I said to Trowbridge
wearily. And that's when Ferris tried to turn the reno-
vated garage into a set from the St. Valentine's Day
massacre.

The first bullet tore through the wall near Biggs. Anu
darted, a yearling panicked by sounds that had no frame
of reference in her world, but in her crazed panic she was
going in the wrong direction, heading toward danger instead of out of it.

In that moment, she was Lexi.

Instinct kicked me. I hurled myself for a tackle and
felled her. We slammed into the floorboards as bullets spat
from an unseen automatic weapon, chewing up wallboard,
sending pieces of wood and insulation flying.

Things fractured around me. Time, bones, thoughts.

My body dimly registered the crack of my knee hitting
the floor, my elbow's sharp protests, the clawing girl writh-
ing beneath the cage of my body. Then a solid, heavy,
muscular weight landed on *me*. Strong arms bracketed
me, male thighs twined over mine, a hard jaw pressed my

head downward until my cheek felt the imprint of the linoleum's pattern.

"Stay," he breathed in my ear.

Ferris did another sweep. I cringed under the abuse
of the noise, a poor defense against the horror of Anu's
shrieks, the *chug-chug* of automatic fire, the thuds of
things falling, the pings and zings. I saw a line of leaden
slugs pierce holes in the table's steel legs.

Trowbridge's body—so warm, so hard with protective
tension—gave a sudden series of violent jerks. He stilled
on top of me. My hair stirred with his low moan, and then
he breathed no more.

He was a dead weight, pinning me to Anu.

Tears flooded my eyes, stung my nose.

It can't end here. Not like this! Not in this room! His
heart was silent . . . *please, Goddess* . . . not doing its job
of circulating oxygen, and magic, and life . . . *I'll do anything* . . . And yet . . . his heart did not beat. Not for the
count of two, not for the space of three.

He's still warm . . . I pressed my trembling palm against
his chest. Was that a flutter?

"Mine," my wolf howled.

I will not give him up. I will not let him die. He was so
heavy on top of me. I couldn't lift him. I couldn't squirm
from beneath him.

Pinned.

"Please," I whimpered to my Goddess.

"Please what?" said Ferris, setting his blue-plaid slip-
per on my mate's shoulder.

My gaze swung up. "Let me help him," I begged.

Ferris shrugged, then heaved with his foot. Limply,
Trowbridge's body rolled off me. I scuttled after him,
Merry shining red. My mate lay on his back, one arm awkwardly tucked under his hip. His chest had a line of small
round dots, like a rusting seam of rivets.

Don't be dead. Please don't be dead.

"Don't move," said Ferris.

"Shut up!" I screamed. "I need to listen!"

Trowbridge's eyes were slits, but so, so very vacant. *He's not breathing.* I forced his chin up with hard fingers. Clawed open his slack lips. Sucked in a deep breath, then bent to deliver to him the kiss.

Live . . .

I lifted my mouth. Felt my air trickle through his nose. Mewling in frustration, I pinched his nostrils, then blew again. *You come back,* I silently told him. His chest lifted—shallowly—with my borrowed breath. *Don't you dare leave me here,* I warned him.

I did it again—a long harsh *heuh* that filled his lungs— willing his heart to restart.

Hoping—praying—bargaining.

Nothing.

"No!" I shouted, raising my head. "You don't get to die first," I said, threading my fingers together. "You don't get to leave me here." I lifted my fisted hands high, poised over the strike zone. "I die first!"

And with that, I hit him with everything I had.

Once, twice, three times I pounded.

Panting, and sobbing.

Please. I flattened my palm on his chest. *Please.*

His heart issued one isolated thud, as tentative as a timid puppy's tail against the floorboards. "That's it," I coaxed, in a thick voice. "You come back." Another flutter from his heart. Faint and weak as his body was testing the concept of life over death.

His breath warmed my lips. Very light, very shallow.

"Very touching," said Ferris, sounding bored. "You do realize that they're just ordinary bullets, not silver, right?"

The "other" stood over us. Smelling of meat.

His scent called to my wolf. To tear. To shred.

"I shall kill you," I heard myself say flatly.

"He's a Were," he said, daring to smile. "They always come back. Guaranteed. Unless you take off their heads."

Or gut their bellies. Or poison them with silver.

Ferris moved to the front door. A cautious man, he kept his body protected by the frame.

I slumped over my love, breathing hard. One hand a plea on his chest, the other fisted by my thigh. "Why did you do this?" I bit out when I could speak. "Why heal and then kill?"

"Because I always back the winner," Ferris said, without turning. "You people are hot tonight. So hot you could burn my house down and everything I've got with it. It was a bad move messing with Liam's club. And a worse one to stray from your pack when you've got all kinds of wolves looking for you. Whitlock's people are all over this territory, and I don't plan to become collateral damage."

"Whitlock's behind all this?" I flicked a glance to my right—Anu was on her knees beside us. She seemed shaken but otherwise intact. To my left, I could see Cordelia's foot. Alive, too, I thought, noting its tension. "What does Whitlock want from us?"

"You."

"He'll have to take a number."

"Here they are," Ferris muttered, opening the door.

He stepped aside and two guys wearing boots and leather vests thundered into the room, carrying with them an explosive wave of bad energy, bike exhaust, and weed. One of them was a Were. He shouted to me, quite unnecessarily, "Don't fucking move!"

And then he pointed his bang stick.

At me. At Trowbridge.

And at Anu, who was on her knees beside us. Rage born of fear twisted her expression and she rolled upward,

screaming something unintelligible in Merenwynian.
Low on problem-solving skills, the biker-wolf raised his
boot.

Don't you touch her!

I blocked the swing of his foot with my knee. A clumsy
interception at best that just made him angrier. I'm not
sure what portion of my face he was aiming for—mouth
or jaw. What he got was my ear. My teeth clicked together
under the violence of his blow and sheared most of the fur
right off the side of my tongue. All was briefly blurred,
both sound and sight.

Cover Trowbridge. Keep him safe.

Ear ringing, I slumped over him, covering him with
my body. Merry scuttled to my neck, confused as to who
to heal, who to defend. She rapidly cinched up her chain,
turning into a choker at the base of my throat. I heard
Cordelia shouting. Some part of me dimly registered that
the flow of curses and threats came from a voice as deep
and virulent as a gunnery sergeant's. I turned toward that
welcome sound.

I had words too—*Trowbridge is hurt*—but they lay on
my bleeding tongue and expired. Right there on my spit.
Because now, with my gaze slanted to the left, I could
behold that which I hadn't before.

Harry had lost his head. His body lay with one arm
strangely akimbo, one leg bent at the knee. But his head . . .
oh, his head. Where there should have been a mane of long-
ish white wavy hair, where there should have been a griz-
zled jaw . . . there was ugly pulp and hideous vermilion.

He's lost his head.

Sudden grief—its touch so cold and swift that it left
my heart barren—caught up with my brain.

He's dead.

My gaze jerked away from his body and rolled toward
Cordelia. She was shouting, spewing swearwords and im-

possible suggestions as to who'd she'd fuck, and what she was fucking going to do, and how she'd fucking do it. The muzzle of yet another gun was pressed hard to her temple.

This can't be happening. Not now.

Did I say that out loud? I'm not sure. But soon after that thought, despite the gun to her head, Cordelia changed the direction of her shouting. She yelled at me. Or to me. But whatever she said, I lost because language was slipping away from me.

No more of this. I can't take any more of this.

Harry had lost his head. Trowbridge was down, with a line of rivets across his midriff. My mate's blue eyes were half open and half closed. No flare of light. No spin of comets. Alive, but barely.

Get up. Get up.

Chapter Twelve

Into that nightmare entered a man bringing with him an arctic chill. Like the others, he wore a leather vest with a patch, but his jeans cost big money, and his slicked-back dark hair was fastidiously styled. He carried a crossbow and had a quiver slung over his shoulder.

No Robin Hood, this one.

There will be no mercy, because it is a quality he doesn't possess.

His forehead was utterly smooth, his skin wrinkle-free. I got the sense that his body was a well-maintained vehicle for the brain that was working at top speed—accessing, cataloging, dismissing. He immediately focused on the back door. It was ajar, through which you could see the laneway with its rutted asphalt, and the sagging frost fence beyond it. The alley was empty—the open door the only evidence that once Rachel stood near it.

The new guy flicked his hand toward his grunt and said over Cordelia's shouts, "Peanut, check that out." Then he touched his ears, and told the wolf with the gun to Cordelia's head to "Ryan, shut her up."

Ryan hit her hard with his weapon. Cordelia crumpled without a sound. Anu cried out in fear and scrambled behind the couch.

My flare came in a rush, a torchlight suddenly flicked

to life. So fast, with such a powerful surge of heat, that my head snapped back. Green light, electric and eerie, spun from me, bathing his features, highlighting his prominent cheekbones.

I heard a click.

"Don't shoot her," he murmured to his boys.

His voice is too steady.

The world narrowed to him and me. His pupils contracted. His smile—that lopsided peculiar lift of lip and cheek muscle—turned into something almost feral. I tensed my neck muscles, then slowly, with a deliberation to match his, I lowered my chin, and nailed him, dead on, with all the power of my flare.

Bend to me.

I put everything I had into it. If he'd been a Were like Ryan, he'd have fallen. If he'd been spooked by the supernatural, he might have shot me in fright. But he was none of those things. He didn't even blink—even against the strand of hair teasing his lashes.

The man with the crossbow has got iron on him, I realized. A lot of it. Buried beneath that vest, underneath that denim jacket. Its drugging poison was a wave of numbing icebox air curling toward me. The real stuff too. Cold iron, or as close to pure as one could hope to find in this modern world.

My Fae sensed it and the soulless quality to his steady gaze.

"I'd have fun with you," he mused.

"No," I said, my flare licking his face. "You wouldn't."

He raised his arched brow another eighth of an inch. "Don't be too sure," he said, unzipping his jacket.

Neither Merry nor I was ready for it—though I should have been because the entire world had received the memo about Hedi Peacock. Small and round, doesn't like blood, has issues with a certain type of ore. The guy with the crossbow wore a big iron cross around his neck. Antique looking. Ornate and heavy. He walked toward me, holding the cross like a shield against my light, as if I was the bad vampire, and he was the good guy with the stake.

"I'm not a bloodsucker. I'm a Fae," I said.

"It's a multipurpose tool," he answered, sinking into a crouch in front of me.

He was too close. Polar air streamed from the crucifix. Merry shivered at my neck. My face stung, my belly contracted. Anu let out a whine, birthed from the back of her throat. She scrambled away from both of us.

"What would happen if I touched you with it?" he mused.

A tear slid down my cheek. "Get away from me."

He leaned forward. I could smell his breath—he liked mints and parsley. That was the last linear thought I had before he rested the cross against my skin.

That was when I should have gone ballistic. To the bottom of my empty heart, I wish I could say that I punched him, kicked him, or even flattened him with my flare.

Maybe before you act with courage, you need to think of yourself as a contender. You need to believe that you're a superhero that Marvel hasn't yet inked. You need to be confident in your ability to win.

I was none of those things. In the face of the iron radiating from his grasp, my flare winked out, and my Fae went shrieking downward into my belly, her cry as awful as the rasp of claws on chalkboard.

He smiled. He had a wide mouth and a good jaw, but the devil roamed this world when that killer smiled.

For a shattered moment, defeat stung and I allowed the iron to tinge every thought with despair. I lowered my head and curled myself over Trowbridge, hardly able to breathe because the loss—*oh Goddess, the loss! It's accumulating. Rising like dirty floodwater inside me.*

Trowbridge's hand didn't come up to cradle the back of my head. His lips didn't turn up. His eyes remained vacant. He lay beneath me, unresponsive.

Wake up.

The guy with the cross and bow said, "You're a little thing for so much trouble."

There was no answer to that. *The iron . . . it's making thinking so difficult. It's robbing me of me. Stealing essentials from me. My confidence, my hope, my grit.*

"Are you going to give Liam a problem?" he inquired. He used the edge of the cross to comb my tangled hair.

A trail of ice scored my scalp. "That depends on who Liam is," I said, bile rising. Trowbridge's mouth was slightly open. His breath was gentle on my chin.

"I'm Liam," he said pleasantly.

Of all the bad guys I've met tonight, he's the worst. Evil should have a smell, but I couldn't pick it off him. His body was permeated with hair product and the faint sweetness of dope. He looked human but he was missing a few ingredients that the best of the mortals carried.

I knew him to be hollow. A mind without empathy.

"Don't hurt the others," I said quietly, my dull gaze fixed on Merry. She'd slid onto Trowbridge. "Don't," I whispered. *Don't call attention to yourself. Not now. Wait.*

"What?"

"Leave them alone." I swallowed. "Please."

"Okay," Liam said easily.

I felt his gaze on me but I didn't lift my eyes to confront him. I didn't want him to have a reason to pull me away from my mate. Until Liam dragged me from Trowbridge, he was mine to hold, mine to protect.

That was the least I could do.

Liam rose. His heel ground into the linoleum as he pivoted for a slow three-sixty to take in the bullet holes and the body. "I told you to keep them here, not shoot them," he said to Ferris. "You could have killed her."

I glanced up. They definitely wanted me alive. Why?

"They were getting ready to leave," Ferris replied stiffly. "I had to slow them down."

Liam did something so mundane, I couldn't believe how it stoked my fear. It was the simplest mannerism—he dropped his chin to study the medic from under his dark, satanic brows. That's all he did; he simply considered Ferris, like he was a shark and the medic was the tourist who'd strayed from the boat. "You don't have the proper appreciation for life."

Ferris licked his lip.

Liam gestured to Harry's body. "I hope that's not Biggs."

Biggs?

My disbelieving gaze swung to the kitchen to where Biggs crouched behind the pathetic protection of an overturned chair. He'd wrapped his arms around his lowered head and had kept them frozen there. Waiting for the aftershock.

I eased myself into a sitting position. "What do you want with Biggs?"

Liam followed the direction of my eyes. "That's him?" He crossed the room, his crossbow dangling from his grip. "Hey." He prodded the cowering wolf with his weapon. "Where's the stuff you promised Brenda?"

Biggs slowly dropped his arms. Indecision and muted defiance flickered across his features. He tried to buy time. "What?"

Liam cocked his head. "Brenda's expecting Knox's stuff. I'm here to accept delivery. Where is it?"

"Biggs," I whispered, appalled. "What did you do?"

Biggs's gaze bounced from Liam to me, then he said numbly, "I don't know anything about Knox's stuff."

Liam shrugged and lifted the crossbow. "I'm very good

with this. I can start with the transvestite's knees, then move on to the kid's."

I opened my mouth but Biggs beat me to it. "It's in the backpack," he said. "In the front pocket."

"See how easy that was?" Liam murmured, moving to the bag. He carried it to the table. Tunelessly whistling, he placed the crossbow down to work the zipper. "Watch them," he told Ryan.

"You knew where Brenda Pritty was all this time?" I stared at Biggs in utter disbelief. "Last night when your Alpha said 'We need to find Brenda Pritty,' you just sat there and pretended—"

"I didn't recognize the name!" Biggs shouted, his guilt exploding. "We hung out for an entire summer two years ago and she would never give me her real fucking name—"

"Oh, spare me from that stinking pile of twaddle." Cordelia's voice as a low growl. "Harry's dead, you stupid, stupid—"

"Stop it!" I sucked in an unsteady breath, then swallowed. "You've known all this time where to find her. You told her where to find us. Did you call her and tell her that we were here? Knowing that she'd tell them and—"

"He texted her," Liam answered. Having extracted the clear plastic bag filled with Knox's things, he dropped the backpack to the floor. He rolled the bag into a cylinder and tucked it into his waistband. "Three times. Using Knox's phone."

There were no words for what I felt at that moment. I watched Biggs's eyes fill, and felt nothing but detachment.

"She was mixed up with Knox. You saw what Trowbridge did to Fatso," he said brokenly. He wiped his eyes with the back of his hand. "I needed time to think things through. I never thought anyone was going to get hurt."

"Tell that to Harry," I heard myself say. Biggs recoiled

like I'd whipped him. I wished with all my heart I truly had.

"You don't understand," Biggs said.

"No. I don't. Make me."

"No time for that. We have to make tracks," Liam said, casually lifting his bow. "Ferris?"

The medic turned.

Liam's bolt flew. Ferris didn't even gasp, he simply folded; a victim to a William Tell experience gone wrong.

Anu gasped.

"Shhh," I said automatically. But I didn't turn to console her. I stared blankly at Ferris's body, my hand resting on Trowbridge's hip. He was warmer than he'd been minutes earlier.

Hurry back.

"Only way to kill them," I heard Liam say. Then he clicked his teeth, the way you do when you want a mare to break into a trot. "Up you get. It's time to go."

I lifted my gaze. Liam smiled again—slow and confident.

He nodded to Ryan. "Put the wolf in my trunk."

Peanut, the mortal biker who'd checked out the backyard, returned. "All clear." He had a gun—*we're freaking Canadians, what is it with all the guns?*—which he waved at Cordelia and Biggs. "What about them?"

"Kill them, then set fire to the place," Liam said.

No. No more loss.

"What about this girl?" The biker reached for Anu.

In a smooth, almost amused tone, the devil said, "Bring her. She might prove entertaining."

That's when fear turned to bitter rage.

Chapter Thirteen

Merry worked tirelessly to guard me against the shivers, using her inner heat to warm the base of my throat. But still, I was cold beyond cold. The type of chill that goes to the bone. Being this close to a man carrying iron robbed me of energy and sapped the warmth right out of me. And yet the heater was on, the dial turned to the right, the digital readout set for 17 degrees Celsius. Colder for comfort for most drivers, but the man behind the wheel was wearing leather. Ryan drove with one wrist draped over the top of the steering wheel.

Harry's dead. Cordelia. Biggs.

The devil walker lolled in the front passenger seat, his body half turned toward me. He was polishing his crossbow with a strip of yellow cloth. He didn't lift his gaze from the task when he said in a casual tone, "How are the hands?"

Ryan had zip-tied my paws. Then, as final precaution, he stripped a pillow of its case and used that to sheathe my fists, securing it around my wrists with another zip tie.

My wrists hurt.

I turned my head and looked out the window again, my gaze following the gray steel road divider. In my mind's eye, I played the same segment of awful. The sight of the shack as we pulled out of the driveway. Flames, yellow tongues of fire, licking the side of the house. He'd set fire to the house. With Biggs and Cordelia still inside it.

"I know you're Hedi," I heard Liam say. "But I don't know who the other girl is. What's her name?"

"Katrina," I said, thinking of devastation. "She's called Katrina." I flicked a covert glance toward Anu. She turned her head sharply toward me, perhaps waiting for just such an exchange.

What could I say? With just my eyes? *Wait for an opportunity.* That's the message I hoped my gaze conveyed. Though I'm not sure if it did, because her gaze fell, and she went back to contemplating the tape around her wrists.

I had to get her out, if nothing else. I would see her safe.

And then I could be done. I could shut my weary eyes and go to sleep. Right after I killed them: the one called Liam; Ryan behind the wheel; and two other patch-wearing bastards who'd stayed to clean up the crime scene.

Merry had subtly changed her aspect during the drive, sharpening each tip of her leaves until it was piercingly uncomfortable. All her movements were covert, amounting to little more than shifts of her slight weight, but it was enough; her prickling needle nips had kept me from falling into a iron-induced doze.

As long as Liam was here, sitting this close to me, exhaustion was near smothering me. I wanted to sleep, and I wanted to kill. Too bad you can't kill in your sleep.

My Fae was quiet, too quiet. Did she think she could bury herself so deep inside me that the cold poison hidden on Liam could not touch her?

That's not how it works.

"Tell me," said Liam, tapping a bolt against his bent knee. "Were you the one who killed Itchy and Gerry?"

It took effort to turn my head. "Do you really care who did it?"

He thought about that, and lifted one shoulder. "Not really. Just curious."

Yes. I will kill them all. Because those I loved were not dead when Liam set fire to the little shack behind the general store. My inner-bitch said nothing, but inside me, I could feel her bristling fur. The predator, wary of danger, but determined to attack.

Given time, we would kill them all.

And then we'd go find my twin.

The driver put on his indicator. Up ahead, a familiar landmark loomed—a giant thirty-foot peach, topped by a jaunty green leaf, sitting on the roadside edge of a commercial property that sat a jowl to an acre of unplowed field. The Peach Pit: part roadside oddity, part bakery and restaurant. A huge billboard announced its name and exit number, while another sign, quite a bit smaller, informed the world that they'd baked over three million pies. Though, judging from the information collected by my olfactory senses, I'd say the greater balance sold were apple, not peach.

So said my wolf, anyhow. She'd moved into the empty hollow left by my Fae.

I was sitting straighter, feeling stronger, which could have been the result of my wolf's presence, or the fact Liam was in the front passenger seat and I was lolling in the back behind the driver. A fortuitous arrangement, because it put a modicum of distance between me and the iron cross. I didn't want to puke, though I wasn't up to handsprings either. Let's face it, an SUV is a closed environment. Liam still wore his iron cross, and it still streamed polar air. Bit by bit the temperature inside the Toyota had fallen—perhaps the vehicle's sensor hadn't recorded it yet, but I could sense it, even if the front passengers couldn't. I was about as comfortable as a model doing a swimsuit spread on an ice floe with a bunch of penguins. Chilled. In my case, inside and out. Skin goosefleshed, emotions suspended in a block of frozen water.

Though every time Anu shivered, I wanted to kill things.

A lot of things.

If Trowbridge had felt any measure of this implacable need to destroy something when faced by Ken Newland, then I owed him an apology. He'd pulled back from finishing off Fatso. If I got the opportunity to kill Liam, or Whitlock . . . I'm not sure I could.

Ryan got out of the SUV to open the gate. Simon yawned.

I bit the inside of my mouth again. It kept me awake.

I needed to be alert, not dopey.

Gate dealt with, Ryan slid back behind the RAV4's wheel. The private drive was long, flanked on either side by a line of scrubby swamp cedars. Signs bristled along the rutted road. Beyond the restaurant, thirty-foot peach, and bakery, the place had a near-empty petting zoo (MEET DUSTY OUR NEW ALPACA!), a mini-golf, and a miniature train (FUN FOR THE KIDS!).

Liam tapped on his passenger window toward a parking slot behind the restaurant. "Over there."

"Holy shit," Ryan murmured.

In an area that boasted no natural scenic attractions other than a stagnant pond, the owner had spread concrete. Any place where a path could be poured, had been. What made it weird was the proliferation of statues. I couldn't help but think of Narnia. The place was full of frozen animals—beavers, squirrels, and bears. Wherever he could reasonably plunk one statue, he'd squeezed in two. All of them oversized and none of them to scale.

Also—in a piece of irony that did not escape me—a grouping of wolves had been staged inside the miniature train track's path. I counted six. Five with snouts lifted for group howl. One set in a playful pose, head slightly cocked. Its gaze forever fixed unseeingly on the frost-fence that enclosed his pack.

Nice touch.

"That's weird," said Ryan, his gaze fixed on the wolves.

I scanned the area, hoping for a tombstone repeat. Forget the statues, the wolves were the size of one of the bikers' Harleys. Everything else that could have served as a useful projectile—picnic tables, litter cans—had been bolted down.

Not very trusting people, these Peach Pitters.

My gaze roamed. I could toss bunnies at them. The place was alive with free-roaming rabbits. They nibbled grass, both lazy and indifferent, until the wind shifted. Little pink noses lifted, a twitch of whiskers, and then stupid with fear, they darted for undergrowth and disappeared. I could hear their little hearts, under the sound of the vehicle's engine. Tiny little hip-hops of terror, pinpointing their exact location.

Their own hearts betrayed them.

An uncomfortable topic, betrayal. Biggs had done so—I knew that in theory, though I couldn't explain how his texts to his girlfriend, Brenda Pritty, had led to Trowbridge being sealed in the trunk and me being brought to the Peach Pit.

Why?

What was so important about Knox's things? It couldn't be the phone. From what Liam had said, Brenda had shared the contents of her texts with Whitlock. If he was privy to those, he'd likely received a copy of the video Knox had taken and sent to Brenda.

If the NAW had wanted evidence to bring to the Great Council, he already had it. He didn't need Knox's phone.

It would help if I knew what Whitlock wanted. He'd sent Itchy and Gerry to kidnap me. That suggested he didn't want to outright kill me, but it didn't preclude the possibility that my body would have eventually been found somewhere other than Creemore after he'd extracted whatever he wanted from me.

But now I'm here. Alive at the Peach Pit. I glanced at the clock. At four in the morning. With a wolf behind the wheel, my niece trembling beside me, and Trowbridge . . . *Goddess, please come back.*

"What does he want?" I asked out loud.

Liam leaned on his hip to twist around. I returned his gaze, hoping that he was seeing something that few save a dead Were called Dawn had ever seen. Hatred, of the coldest type.

That amused him. "What's it like? To have that magic inside you?"

"Busy."

"Even now? It's not . . ." He paused to choose a word. "Sick?"

"It's getting angry," I replied.

"And what will it do when it gets really angry?"

"It likes to kill things."

Liam gave me a smile, before swiveling back in his seat.

Another pair of lights turned into the parking lot. "There's Whitlock," said Ryan.

The leader of the NAW didn't fulfill my private expectations at all. Yes, Whitlock drove the obligatory Navigator. Check: it was black and had tinted windows. But he came alone, not with a bevy of fawning wolves. And I'd envisioned someone old like Mannus, but the head of the NAW was a spare, lightly muscled, blond man of indeterminate age. He had a flat mouth, bracketed by deep grooves that went all the way down to his stubborn chin.

I had to give the wolf one thing: he had presence. It was there in his body language and his scent. Thick as newly churned earth, his personal signature grazed my throat and touched my hair. "I will be King," it said. "I shall be obeyed." Anu must have felt the impact of his dominance too—she flinched and sucked in a sharp breath.

Smiling hopefully, Ryan got out to greet Whitlock. His Alpha gave him a terse nod as he approached, but his focus was on me and Anu.

"Why are there two girls?" he demanded.

Unruffled, Liam took time for a stretch and a yawn before he replied diffidently, "I may keep the younger one."

No you won't.

"That's not part of our agreement," snapped Whitlock. "I said total containment. No witnesses left, everything tidied up. Every single detail's got to be tied down before I meet with the Great Council tomorrow." He tested the air. "Where's Robson Trowbridge?"

"In the trunk."

"Dead?" said Whitlock sharply.

"No," Liam replied. "But he took a few hits from Ferris's semiautomatic. I didn't want him bleeding all over the upholstery."

Whitlock's mouth tightened. "Have you got it?"

Liam leaned on one hip to extract the bag he'd tucked inside his waistband. He passed it to Whitlock. "All of Knox's crap. Phone, wallet, watch, and the bottle you wanted."

The blond man bent to study the contents under the glare of the headlights. "This has been a nightmare," he said, breaking the seal. Gingerly, he removed everything except the bottle, placing each thing on the hood. He opened the wallet, riffled through it, then tucked it into his back pocket. The keys didn't interest him—he pitched those into the garbage.

Knox's cell worked a growl loose from him. Mouth turned down, he keyed it to life, then quickly worked his way through the menu. "This night has been a total clusterfuck," he said. "We've lost Brenda."

"I thought your people had picked her up."

His thumb stilled. "They had. She managed to escape."

"You want us to find her?"

He shook his head in irritation, never lifting his attention from the glowing screen. "You trying to hint that your bikers can find her faster than my wolves, Liam?"

Liam chose not to reply.

"She'll show up," said Whitlock. "She's got nothing. No money, no credit cards. She'll head for the meeting place and wait there." His lips moved as he read the messages on Knox's cell. "Nothing new here, except messages from me and the texts between Brenda and Biggs." Whitlock's mouth curled. "What is this shit? It's all abbreviations and cutesy emoticons . . . *C u last place we partied. Bring coin.*"

He shrugged. "Well, she's broke and shit out of luck. Biggs won't be coming. She'll wait for a while, then bolt again. We'll find her once she does. She'll need money, and we know her friends."

"What now?" asked Liam.

Whitlock pocketed the phone, then opened my door. He studied me for a beat, his lids lowered in calculation. "Get out," he told me.

When I didn't leap out, he said, "I'm on my last nerve, Fae, so don't piss me off."

"You've been trying to kill me all night." I drooped, shoulders rolling forward, head sinking so that my hair fell in a curtain around my face. The iron had sapped me. The night had drained me. "If you want me standing, tell him to ditch the cross."

"I haven't been trying to kill you," he muttered, reaching for my upper arm. "But I could change my mind." One haul, and I was out, standing on unsteady feet.

"I'm going to puke," I warned him.

"She's no good to me like this," Whitlock told the biker. "Take that thing off. Put it in the glove compartment."

"Not a good idea," replied Liam.

"Do it," snapped Whitlock. Before I got my sea legs, he half dragged, half carried me to the rear of the Toyota. "You've caused me a lot of problems. You're going to make things right."

He banged his fist on the rear hatch. "Pop it."

Ryan jumped to obey.

Be okay, Trowbridge.

Whitlock lifted the lid. Impotent fury roiled in me as I realized Liam had lined the inside of his trunk with a blue plastic tarp prior to tipping my mate into the hold. Trowbridge was folded up inside it, partially covered. His long legs were drawn up close to his chest and one arm covered his face.

Don't puke.

"At least he's subdued," Whitlock said.

Liam let out a low whistle. "You guys heal fast. His body's already getting rid of the slugs." He reached for a flattened bullet by Trowbridge's hip. "If I had more Weres in my club, we'd wipe out the competition." His eyebrow rose as he silently counted the pieces of metal. "He's pushed out three, looks like he's got another three to expel."

Wake up. Please. Wake up.

"Bring him out," said Whitlock with a jerk of his head. They extracted Trowbridge with the tarp and deposited him by our feet. I watched his chest and felt bittersweet happiness when it rose, slow and shallow.

Ralph lay dead center on my mate's chest, positioned at the lowest edge of his chain, right over Trowbridge's heart. His gold was dull, and the clear light in his stone had grayed. I knew then, just at the sight of him, that the Royal Amulet had been quietly transferring some of his Fae magic into the one man who held all the magic in my world.

Bless you, Ralph.

Whitlock sank down to his heels beside Trowbridge. Holding the base of the bottle through the plastic, he rolled down the sides of the bag until the vial was mostly exposed. "I need your help," he told Liam. "Come here and get his hand. Wrap his fingers around the bottle."

Liam cocked his head in inquiry.

"I need his scent on it. I can't do that without putting my own on it." Whitlock watched tensely as Liam squeezed Trowbridge's fingers around the glass. Once done, he dragged the curled rim of the neck of the bottle across my mate's lips. "That will do it," Whitlock said with some satisfaction. "Try sliding out of that, Trowbridge."

He rose and leaned on one hip to jam the bag down his front pocket. Then, letting out a huge sigh, he walked around the vehicle, kneading his back.

"Am I done here?" asked Liam. "You know I'm working on the clock now. Every minute I stay costs you that much more money."

Whitlock exhaled, put a foot on the railroad tie that edged the asphalt, and said to no one in particular, "Who's got a knife?"

Liam said, "Never carry one."

Ryan piped up. "I got one."

"Give it here." The knife had a bone handle and a release button for the blade. "Nice balance," Whitlock said, approvingly.

"Got it on eBay," Ryan said.

"Uh-huh," Whitlock said. "Everything's done online now, isn't it?" I held my ground as he approached. "Proof that I'm a reasonable man," he said. "Hold out your arms. I'm going to free your hands."

"She's got magic," warned Liam.

"And I'm an Alpha." Lip curled, the leader of the NAW inspected the pillowcase secured by multiple bracelets of zip ties. Ryan had taken no chances. My wrists were circled with more plastic than a geek's electronic cables. "For someone so young, you're really on the road to developing a badass reputation," he said, sliding the blade between cotton and plastic.

Not yet, but soon. Once my head cleared a little more.

A twist of the knife and the blade jerked upward. The zip tie broke. "The Weres talk about you. The Fae who can open the portals. Who'll stop at nothing to keep her man alive. Sending him to Merenwyn took balls," he said, stripping the pillowcase from my hands. "They say heads rolled when you came back to Creemore."

"Just one," I said, thinking of the former Alpha of Creemore. My fingers looked fat, not from magic but lack of circulation. I clenched my teeth as he inserted the knife's tip deep into the tight crevice between my inner wrists. One hasty snick and I'd be spouting arterial flow.

"Mannus was a pimple on my butt cheek, and I, for one, am not sorry you dispatched him," he said, making quick work of the last tie. "He needed to go."

"Why?" I attempted to force my claws into a fist.

Epic failure.

"He was nosy and greedy." With a glance toward Liam, he spread his paw on the small of my back and pushed me forward. "Let's go visit Larry the llama."

And leave Anu with Liam? I looked over my shoulder. Her face taut with fear, Anu stared at me through the back window. I worked up another smile, just for my brother's daughter, one ripe with false hope, as Whitlock propelled me down the hill toward the Peach Pit's attractions.

The owners had spent some coin on chain-link fencing, too. Both the miniature train course (a short snaking loop) and the fantastical world of the mini-putt were bounded by mesh and posts. Whitlock steered me down the short hill that led to them. Once we reached the cement path that bordered them, Whitlock turned right, following the trail as it led us down to the area shared by the petting zoo and the pond that smelled of oil and standing water.

We stopped before we reached the water.

Larry the llama slept on his side in the shadows of his shed. He was too long for the little house, his shaggy head stuck out of the doorway. One ear turned slightly toward us as we approached but he didn't wake.

Whitlock smiled faintly. "Ever eaten llama?"

"No."

"Neither have I." He rested his arms on the railing. "One day after this is all done and said, I may come back here. See how fast a llama runs." He batted away a fly. "When you first showed up, I thought you were a gift from heaven."

"You have an odd way of appreciating gifts." I rubbed my left wrist, trying to work the circulation back into it.

"A Fae showing up in Creemore who was capable of opening a portal—it was genius." He smiled, thin-lipped and smug. "You were my Canada Savings Bond. I let you sit there, accruing interest."

"And here we thought you didn't come hotfooting to Creemore because we wrote such a nice letter."

"That was a piece of work," he said. "Calling yourself Alpha-by-proxy. I could have—"

"Killed us," I finished for him. "Why didn't you?"

"Let's say having the Great Council occupied with

something other than my books was more important than my need to slap you down for your insolence. You were a great distraction. They haven't been that shook up since St. Silas took his seat on the council." The llama's front hoof twitched when he pitched his voice to falsetto. "What should we do about her? Where do we stand on the Treaty of Brelland?"

"Things weren't all tidy with the NAW's balance sheet?"

A half smile. "There were certain financial irregularities in mine that required topping up." He crouched, his body lithe and supple, to pick up a handful of pebbles. "Frickin' St. Silas looks like a rocker, but he's nothing more than a gray suit hiding in leathers. He's worked his way to the NAW's accounts."

If a Were becomes incensed just by someone swiping fruit off his apple tree, I didn't even want to think how they'd react to embezzlement. "You stole money from the Great Council?"

Tension thinned his mouth. "I *borrowed* from the contingency fund." Whitlock shook his head. "Accountants. When the world ends, there will be nothing left but cockroaches and accountants." He slanted me a smile that was almost winning. "And me."

And bad things will drip into this world. "I'm tired, Whitlock. I've been knifed, choked, kidnapped, car-wrecked, and shot at—and that only in the last forty-eight hours. Just cut to the chase. How do Trowbridge and I fit into this? What was all that about with the bottle?"

He poured a pebble into his hand. "It ties the Alpha of Creemore to sun potion."

"*This* is about sun potion?"

"No," he corrected, rolling the stone between his fingers. "*This* is about the cash you make hand over fist selling the shit to the right customers."

"You're selling it?"

"For a couple of years." He pitched a stone at the roughened plywood shed. Startled out of sleep, Larry the llama blearily lifted his woolly head.

He sells sun potion. Here. In this world. I thought of Lexi, before Trowbridge and Cordelia carried him to the portal and pushed him through. Lying under the tree. His eyes glazed, his heart slowing. I remembered holding him in my arms, knowing that he was going. "Why would they want it?" I asked in a dead voice. "So they can last a little longer against the call of the moon? It's not worth it. It's addictive."

"Well, praise Jesus for that," he said. "You wouldn't believe the money you can make if you have access to a constant replenishing stock of the stuff."

Constant replenishing? "You're not selling your stockpile," I said, slowly.

"No," he said, "that's long gone."

How could he continually resupply his stash? He didn't have access to magic. Sun potion belonged to the Fae, and the mages, and the cursed wolves of my mother's realm. Oh . . . it was so simple, so obvious. "You're getting it from Merenwyn," I whispered. "You're trading with the Fae."

"Just one."

Another Fae, who might be here in this realm, right now. Walking among us. I might have passed him or her on the street and never known. My hand crept to Merry as the full import hit me. *There has to be an open portal. One that wasn't closed ten years ago. A gate just waiting for a girl with an amulet and a powerful need to get to Merenwyn.*

Lexi.

This close to saving him. And this close to losing it all.

Whitlock brooded, oblivious to the chain of possibilities being crocheted in my mind. "I knew it couldn't last.

Guaranteed some halfling would screw the pooch. We tell them—everybody thinks you're dead. Stay away from the big cities, stay away from cameras—we give them a long list of things they can and can't do. But some brat didn't pay attention. The little shit was spotted at a café in Paris, having a beer, months after he'd supposedly been taken on the long walk." A certain peevish quality slipped into Whitlock's voice. "The halfling was supposed to be a corpse. Dead to everyone. His body buried in Algonquin Park."

He sells it to the halflings. Not full Weres . . . halflings.

Larry and his red shed, even the frost fence, disappeared, and I was back, revisiting the night Lexi sat opposite me in the trailer's dinette. He'd been weary, his eyes red-rimmed. "I don't want to turn into my wolf," he'd told me, lifting the flask of juice to his mouth.

My twin had a choice. Though it hurt his sense of identity, transforming into the four-legged did not present a life or death challenge for him. If he needed to, he could embrace his Were.

But at the age of sixteen or seventeen, halflings were faced with a completely different set of prospects. Prodded by an instinct they did not understand, they left everything they knew behind them and headed for the north. Goddess . . . they were babes in the woods, being followed by a wolf tasked with their murder.

What if they were told of the danger? Then offered false hope in the form of a draught that would block their bodies' response to the moon? They'd do anything, pay anything . . .

"If they're on sun potion during the moon's call . . ." I felt sick.

Whitlock nodded. "They stay human."

They don't die.

Death would come later.

"Paris," he repeated incredulously. "If I'd known the kid had access to that type of money, I would have squeezed his father for more." He clicked his tongue at the llama. "Hey, boy," he said, holding out his pebbles. "What have I got? Food? What's this?"

Larry the llama may have looked like a sheep with a giraffe's neck and legs, but he wasn't dumb as a mutton chop. He bolted out of his red shed, ears pointed forward, and careened toward the safety of the back of his pen.

Whitlock let the stones dribble slowly from his grip. "It was a thousand to one that a Were would pass him on the sidewalk," he said, watching them fall. "Maybe a million to one that he'd have recognized the halfling. A billion to one that St. Silas would recognize the halfling. Game frickin' over."

"How many?" I demanded.

"Hmm?" he murmured, moving along the fence in pursuit of Larry.

I followed him. "How many people do you have on the hook?"

"Enough that I was out of the red in seven months. You wouldn't believe the money. A man facing the long walk will cough up anything you ask."

"I find that hard to believe. I've seen no love for halflings."

"It all changes when the man knows his kid doesn't have to die." For the first time I saw a flicker of real emotion. Sadness, of the weariest sort. "Some of us can't produce kids. Not with our mates. Not even after years of trying." He lifted his shoulders. "But after that kid was spotted in France, I knew it was only a matter of time before I got an invitation to appear in front of the Great Council. Not only was the halfling sired by a wolf under my jurisdiction, but I had an Alpha-by-proxy leading a pack—a Fae who could open a portal. Time to cash in my savings bond."

"Me."

"You, the perfect scapegoat. The consort who sent her mate to Merenwyn." A semi whizzed by on the highway. Casually, he turned to watch its red lights wink out. "Your death would have tied everything up in a bow. A day after stepping into the role of Creemore's Alpha, Knox would have discovered your stock of sun potion. I'd have launched a take-no-prisoners investigation. Within a few hours, I'd have dredged up two more sires and halflings and served them dead to the council. Case closed."

"The money would never have been found."

"Oh, maybe a few thousand bucks, but that's it."

Yes, very tidy. I wondered just how far Whitlock's "containment" efforts would have extended. I glanced back to the parking lot Liam leaned against the RAV4's front door. His arms were folded, and he was watching Anu with detached interest. Suddenly, the biker lifted his head and looked at me from under those arched brows again.

A chill ran down my spine. "How did you come to find out about the open portal and the Fae? It's not like you can Google it."

"Knox had an uncle who was childless. As the years go by, dear Uncle Pat starts treating Knox like his own son. When he died, he left Knox a hat, a letter and map telling him about the portal and the Fae. Knox, being a smart guy, immediately saw the potential for profits. One of his responsibilities was to keep an eye on the halflings."

"And he came to you? Funny, I would have thought he'd have taken the map and run with it."

"I have no doubts he thought of it. But then he realized that sun potion without clients is about as useful as a wine bottle without an opener. He didn't know where to find the halflings and their sires."

The kill list. "So you gave him their names and addresses."

"Nothing as crude as that. I just gave him access to the NAW's database. Officially, he's listed as one of the list's two admin users."

"Who's the other one?

"Me, though I haven't been near that database since I gave him access to it."

"Keeping your hands stain-free," I said.

He made a show of dusting them off. "Seemed the smart thing to do."

I thought about it for a bit. "How did you know that sun potion would work on the halflings?"

"We did a test run. Knox picked through the list, looking for someone close to their change. Brenda's name came up. She'd split from her family, but her sire had tracked her down to Toronto. It didn't take Knox more than a week to find her." His voice turned reflective. "Even in the city, there are places that mimic a natural forest. Knox found Brenda testing her new hiking boots on the Don Valley trails. He said her scent led him straight to her—she was ripe and ready for the change."

Plucked like a piece of sun-ripe fruit from the vine. "He took her up north for the moon call and let her start her change. A few minutes into it, he gave her a dose of sun potion. He said it stopped her change just like that," he said, snapping his fingers. "She's been on it ever since."

What would it be like to have to take the sun potion, every month? Knowing that you were a puppet dancing on the strings held by a wolf who saw you as nothing more than a business prospect? How many years would it take before mild cravings turned into full addiction?

"How long has she been on it?" I whispered.

"Twenty-six months."

My stomach clenched as I imagined myself in her place. "I'm glad Trowbridge killed Knox," I said.

"Really," he replied, his voice hard.

"Yes," I said, staring him down.

"Well, I guess I won't ask you to sign the condolence card," he said, briefly amused. He scratched his neck. "Let's get to business. Tonight, Knox was supposed to be here, ready to accept the final shipment from the Fae. What I want from you—"

"Here?" I interrupted. "The portal is *here*?" Lou had dragged me everywhere during those first weeks following the night the Fae closed down all the portals. We'd trudged from Barrie to Hamilton to Peterborough—a four-hour trip that grew and grew as we paused for a look-see at various spots—but we'd never stopped here.

Maybe the giant thirty-foot peach had put her off.

"Where is it?" I asked, doing a three-sixty.

His expression soured, and he bent his head to examine the tip of his boot. Recognition of his problem made me smile—one of my cruel smiles, the ones I never wanted my parents to see. "You don't know where it is," I purred.

"I know it's somewhere here." His gaze lifted. "Probably over there." He gestured toward the pond. "These things are always near water, right?"

Lou had taken me to pools, a couple of rivers, even a secluded bay on the shores of Lake Ontario. How many places did we go? Eight? Ten? I couldn't remember them all. I'd been so beat up. Mum and Dad dead. Lexi gone. But yes, every place we'd visited had been near a body of water.

But this pond was empty of life. No lazy fish, no paddling ducks, no croaking frogs. Nothing except the tall blond stalks of wild sage and the broken, short spars of rotting water grass. I couldn't see a single sacred pine mixed in among the scrubby growth ringing the banks.

Whitlock studied the man-made pond with equal disgust. "If I'd known Knox would die without showing me how to call the portal, I would have planted some hidden cameras."

Welcome to my life. "You're an Alpha. Why didn't you make him show you?"

"The frickin' fairy placed a spell on Knox," he said. "I asked him a question, I told him to show me, but he just choked. Couldn't answer squat. He sat there, his mouth opening and shutting—no words coming out. Basically, all I got from him was what she wanted me to know."

"She?"

"That bitch of a Fae."

"You've met her," I said, interest stirring.

"You think I'm going to put out my neck without meeting her? Of course I did. I insisted on it. For all the good it did me." A bunny scampered across the grass. Whitlock went silent, his eyes narrowed until it disappeared under a shrub. He blinked and then gestured to the restaurant. "The three of us had a late lunch right over there. She ordered three pieces of pie. Smug bitch smiled when Knox choked. Then she told me that she'd only trade with him, and that I could ask all I wanted but his tongue was tied." He wiped his palms on his thighs and essayed an indifferent shrug. "At least he wasn't going to flap his mouth to anyone else. As long as I made money, I could let it go."

Whitlock could pretend diffidence but anger streamed from him. He jerked his head and left the fence. I followed him up the short incline, then along the path that led to the mini-golf and train course. Disgust rippled his face as he took in the montage of wolves. "Do you think they were trying to be funny? Stupid, frickin' humans."

My wrist ached where the kid had bit me. *Don't call me, Mad-one. Not now, when I've got the wolf at my door.*

I flicked a quick glance at my skin. It was pale and un-blemished by the slightest hint of ghoulish light.

I rubbed it, thinking about calling portals, and running to different realms. If it was just me . . . but it wasn't just me. By Ryan's SUV, supine on a sheet of plastic, lay Trowbridge. In the vehicle sat Anu. Two guards; one wolf, one whatever, watched them.

No running for me.

"Fae women used to be beautiful," he mused, watching me. "Your mother was a good-looking woman. The Gatekeeper looks like a troll with sharp teeth."

Gatekeeper? I slanted a quick searching glance in his direction but he'd gone back to brooding at the statuary.

"Here's what's going to happen," he said. "You're going to step in for Knox. You're going to call the portal and you're going to get me that final shipment."

"Final shipment?" I repeated.

"I'm done with this business," he said. "The money's no longer worth the risk."

"But what about those halflings? They depend on . . ." My voice trailed away. His expression was impassive. "You're going to let them die."

"No, I'm going to kill them and hide their bodies."

"Those are people you are talking about. With the right to life and—"

"They're incriminating evidence for a now-defunct business venture." He turned to study me. "If you feel a responsibility for them, then twitch your nose and do whatever you need to do. Open the gates and those half-lings will get enough sun potion to survive this next moon call."

Bile burned at the bottom of my throat. "I can't open the gates. Whatever you've heard, whatever you think you know about me—"

"I think you're the Fae I have over a barrel." He bent

his head to piece the ends of his jacket zipper together. "You know what I've learned about my product? A bottle keeps a halfling alive for a month. A mouthful makes a Were stronger. But you give the same wolf half a bottle of it, and that man's no damn good." Whitlock pulled the tab up to mid-chest. "You're going to fix my problem or I'm going to bring Trowbridge to St. Silas tomorrow at ten A.M. He won't have a scratch on him, but he'll be stoned out of his gourd on sun potion."

"The bottle's empty."

"I have one stored away for personal emergencies." He checked his wrists and adjusted his shirtsleeves so that a wedge of striped blue edged the leather trim of his jacket. "The Great Council is going to see what they expect to see—Robbie Trowbridge is still a drunk. Still a good-for-nothing responsible for the death of his family—"

"That's not true!"

"They'll see what they expect to see," Whitlock said taking my arm.

Ryan ground out his cigarette as we approached. Liam leaned against the bumper. That particular biker was turning into my personal Lex Luthor. I knew, just by the way my head began to pound, that he still had iron on him. Probably buried beneath his jacket.

I need to put some distance between him and me.

My mate had shifted positions in his slow crawl back to life. Tears blurred my eyes. For a moment, there were two Trowbridges, both so badly wounded.

Keep crawling back to me.

Whitlock studied my mate. "Bridge's going to meet them trussed up like a convict, with a Fae amulet around his neck, reeking of sun potion. I'll produce Knox's bottle—with your mate's scent all over it. I'll tell them that it was the three of you. Knox, Bridge, and his Fae." A faint breeze lifted the tarp. Whitlock flattened it with his heel. "You have another option," he told me. "Cross the portal. Bring back the Gatekeeper."

I shook my head. "Portals don't need gatekeepers. She's not going to be sitting there with a badge and clipboard. Whoever she is—she's not going to be hanging around the portal waiting for me."

"This one does," he replied. "Knox told me she always answered right away. You open the portal. You bring her and my shipment to me, and we call it a day."

As if it's that easy. "Listen to me. Walking through a gate isn't like walking through a door. The passages are complicated. You have to know the way. And even if I managed to get to the other side . . ." I knew from Whitlock's expression that he thought I was lying. "I'm telling you the truth." I forced steel into my voice. "I can't talk the language. I don't know where to go. There are a hundred different ways, I could—"

"I don't give a shit," he said.

Fail. "Even if I found her, and brought your shipment back. Once you had that, you wouldn't need us anymore."

"I'm a fair man," he replied, straight-faced.

"Tell that to the witches."

"They were collateral damage and all part of containment," said Whitlock with an indifferent shrug. "You come through with the shipment and I'll let you and Trowbridge return to Merenwyn. I'll tell the council that I tracked you all the way to here, but you escaped across the gates before I could close in." His smile didn't reassure me in the least. "I get my shipment, you get your happily ever after. And maybe we'll do business one day again. Except this time, you'll be *my* gatekeeper."

Bullshit. "You'll still need the scapegoat."

"Knox will do," he said negligently. "Tell me where his body is, and I'll present it to them. They'll smell the sun potion on his corpse. And I can show the computer logs to prove that he was accessing the halfling list since Brenda—something I haven't done in three or four years, so I'm square. I'll even wrap it up by producing Brenda Pritty's body."

"You don't know where she is."

"I'll find her."

"We're pawns to you, aren't we?" I muttered. "Pick us up, move us around, knock us over—"

Whitlock glanced at the sky and said, "You're wasting my time. Let's get on with it." He bent to twitch the tarp. It settled over the top half of Trowbridge again, like a shroud.

He keeps getting beat up.

Time after time, he keeps getting beat up because of me.

"I'll do it, but Liam has to keep away," I said quietly, staring at the ragged outline of swamp cedars and overgrown spruces near the pond. "He has iron hidden on him. It's interfering with my ability to call to magic."

And think.

Whitlock made an impatient noise between his teeth then spun around. "Do you have more iron on you?"

Liam lifted a silky brow. "Of course."

"Get rid of it."

Merry spat a bright, intense white light from the middle of her stone. A sharp brilliant explosion, like a mini-firework. Liam considered us for a moment, then slowly slid off his jacket. He looked around, walked to the fence, and hung it neatly. Cold stretched for me when the mercenary peeled open his vest. *Stand tall.* I bit down on my back teeth as he worked his buttons. He gave me that peculiar smile again—too intimate and taunting—then he held the shirt open, like an elegant, insolent flasher, so that we could get a good eyeful of the light, elegant chainmail vest he wore beneath his clothing.

No clumsy steel reproduction, this vest of chains. Real iron, each double link precise and thin, so that the overall piece was not a weighty burden. It began at his neck—did a high scoop just at the base of it—then skimmed his body all the way to where it disappeared under the waistband of his well-fitting jeans.

No wonder he'd made me ill. I locked my knees against their desire to tremble.

"You should be wearing one," he said to Whitlock. "It's the only way to keep the upper hand with the Fae."

"I don't need it," growled Whitlock.

"She is Fae. You shouldn't forget that." Liam reached for his jacket and sweater. "Since I'm not taking this off, I'll wait by the SUV with my crossbow."

"No!" I said sharply.

Liam pivoted, eyebrows raised.

"I won't be able to concentrate if he's left alone with her," I said to Whitlock, gesturing to Anu in the Toyota.

Whitlock looked annoyed. "Ryan! Come down here with the girl."

Ryan jumped to it, yanking open the RAV4's door to extract Anu. My niece was obviously shaken. She stumbled once, only to be brought up shortly by Ryan's punishing grip on her arm.

Whitlock waited until she and her escort had passed Larry the llama before he said roughly, "Go on, Liam."

The nausea at the base of my throat slipped an inch. I watched Liam insolently stroll up the hill, knowing that I would kill him, too.

"I need Knox's phone." My shoe sank into the fetid mud. "The portal is called by a song. Knox recorded it and sent Brenda a video."

"I've seen it," said Whitlock. A bunny scampered along the far bank of the pond, then disappeared down a hollow, its white tail a flash to all who would be interested.

"Open the file and hit play."

"Why should I do that?"

My cheeks heated. "I don't know the words to the song."

To the victor goes the huff. Whitlock's was an explosion of pure mirth. "That's rich," he said, extracting the cell.

Anu and I were alone with wolves.

Hurry. Find something to pitch at them. A spar of cedar lay broken near the base of its trunk on the pond's left bank. Too heavy. There was a largish boulder at the back end of the property, but Goddess knows how deeply it was buried or if my magic could stretch that far. What to use? All I had was grass, earth, and a pile of gravel waiting to be spread over the clearing. *Hello.* I almost smiled.

"Rise," I told my Fae.

"Nay," she replied, her voice distant and cold.

"Rise."

"What is she doing?" Ryan muttered.

"Nay. There be cold poison," my Fae murmured, tightening into a ball of refusal.

She will obey me. I shut my eyes, concentrating on her. Then with a cold hardness that was all Hedi Peacock's, I surrounded her. Held her in my mental grip, both to test her weight and to allow her to gauge my strength. *You will bend to me.* I squeezed, with the same implacable, steady pressure of Liam's finger tightening on the trigger.

I will be obeyed.

In response, her magic surged upward, as always, but now I wasn't the dry-mouthed witness, nor was I steeling myself against the sting of her heat. When my talent hit my heart, and did the roll through valve and ventricle, I inhaled deeply.

And felt stronger, not weaker.

I heard her cry. Felt the wild flutter of her distress. Now she knew how I felt in Threall. *You will obey.* My magic was mine, part of the flow of my rich, thick mixed blood. And for the first time in my life, I knew my Fae in a way that I had never before. Still a separate entity, but one who'd just been apprised of a very pertinent fact.

We may fight together, but from this day forward, Hedi rules.

Chapter Fourteen

When Whitlock hit play and Casperella's voice broke the dead silence, Larry the llama gave a bleat and disappeared once more into his little red hut.

Wolves can't swim. Magic simmered at the ends of both my hands. Jewels gleamed at my breast. I stepped into the water and Merry tightened into a nervous ball. Asrais and pond water—it's never a good combination. For reasons unknown to me, they fear it. Period. And Merry had good reason to be skittish. The last time she'd been doused with pond water, it had contained iron and contact with it had burned her badly. "It will be okay," I murmured. "I'll keep you safe."

I wasn't planning to take a swim. I just needed to get out of Whitlock's reach.

"What are you doing?" he asked sharply as I slogged through the first crop of battered weeds.

I could have told him, "Using the fact that showers are the only time Weres are willing to enter water to my best advantage." Instead I gestured vaguely to the middle of the pond, which I was praying wasn't very deep. "The portal opens over there. The amulet needs to be closer to call it." Total balderdash, a quick lie to pacify the Alpha. I kept moving deeper into the water, feet sinking into the sucking muck. When my jeans were soaked to mid-thigh, I said, "This looks about right."

Perfect in terms of getting out of Liam's sightline too. Standing up by the Toyota, he couldn't see me through the scrub of trees. What he can't see, he can't shoot. *This will work.* I turned to face them. *You can do this because you must. Break it down. Free Anu first because Ryan has the gun. Take Whitlock out next. Destroy Liam. Liberate Trowbridge. Open a portal. Find your brother. Kill the mage . . .*

Stop making lists before you freak out. Take it step by step.

Whitlock stood at the edge of the pond; Ryan was some five feet beyond him, guarding Anu. One thing I'd noticed about that biker—he was prone to aiming his weapon at things that frightened him.

He could be a lousy shot but that only happens in *Die Hard* movies.

Take him down first.

I lifted my hands breast high, palms outward, fingers splayed. I paused like that—the wicked witch ready to shoot a fireball. Sure enough, the Were's gun switched from being pressed to Anu's ribs toward pointing at me.

Go, I silently told the magic waiting at the tips of my right hand.

Anu's eyes rounded as the thin cable of pure magic streamed from me. I gave her a slight smile, before casting a significant glance toward the cover of the tree line. Would she have the sense to run? Her gaze narrowed thoughtfully.

Casperella's song had moved past the chorus, and now was starting the second verse. "Does it always take this long?" demanded Whitlock.

"Longer, as a rule," I said with complete honesty. Though

I was getting a bad feeling. If the portal was truly here, wouldn't the air be moving in a clockwise fashion above the pond? Yes, there was wind—the tops of the rangy cedars swayed in distress—but that could have been nothing more potent than a breeze. There should be lights by now. The scent of freesias. The tinkle of bells.

Seriously? If the Peach Pit's portal could respond to a lousy wolf, why on earth wasn't it showing some sign of recognition? A little flicker of fairy lights would be nice. Could it really tell the difference between a taped voice and a real one?

If that was the case we—me, Trowbridge, Lexi, and possibly every single living thing on this planet—were out of luck.

Suddenly, Whitlock's patience shattered. He shouted, "Then stop stalling and make something happen!"

No problem. The gravel was there, the mound of earth was ready. *Pick up the stones,* I told my Fae. A slight pause—probably to register her discontent—before she complied. Thinning herself, she streamed toward the end of her tether, to form an abbreviated question mark over the pile of gravel. I could feel her confusion—did I want her to shovel it up? Pick it up stone by stone?

I needed her to break apart. To become pure energy. The essence of my desire. Pure magic. *Become the cyclone of my desire.* I poured what I had into her—all my cold hatred, all my black anger. *Break apart. Become my will. Become a manifestation of me.*

"Ah," she breathed.

Heat inside me, then she ruptured into a haze of glittering pieces. She hovered for an instant, then fell upon the gravel like a starved Dirt Devil spying a debris-strewn carpet. *Take those rocks.* With one whoosh, hundreds of rock fragments rose in the air.

Ryan spun toward the chatter of the stones, his gun raised.

"Run," I mouthed to my niece. She took off like one of the Peach Pit's rabbits as I flicked my wrist to send the cloud of gravel churning through the air toward Ryan.

The Were had a gun and the natural inclination for target practice. Mouth gaping, he fired at the angry hive of gravel swooping toward him. A stupid reaction—he should have run—because the hurricane of gravel was impervious to bullets and fear. Screaming, he fell under the assault, balling himself into a defensive crouch. How many shots he got off after the tornado of dust, dirt, and gravel swallowed him, I'm not sure. But I caught the glimpse of flailing arms, the turn of a shoulder—and sadly the last doomed attempt he made for freedom. He tried to crawl away from it. But there would be no escape for him; his demise was cast, because the cloud of malcontent consuming him was partly Fae, and partly me, and mostly set on killing him.

He got five feet and collapsed. The cloud flattened, and settled over him like a low, heavy hailstorm. There was something ugly about the way it continued to torture the unconscious Were. Pitter, pat, pitter, pat. The rocks bounced off him. Grotesque and savage satisfaction swelled inside me. I was the wolf with the skin of the hare hanging from its sharp teeth.

Die.

I caught movement to my left. I swung around in time to see Whitlock wrench a sign—PLEASE DON'T FEED LARRY!—right off its post. Holding it like a centurion's shield, he came for me, racing down the low slope at top speed, his jacket winging out behind him.

"To him!" I yelled to my magic. She turned with me—my eyes, her vision—and perceived his threat. In a fluid motion, she re-formed our low cloud of gravel into the pointed V-shape of a dark and angry colony of wasps.

But this guy wasn't mortal, and he wasn't superstitious. He was a Were, of full age. Moreover, he was a *true* Alpha, and they are of different stock: judged by their willingness to act, weighted by their ability to quickly calculate the odds. Drowning and going down with a fight, versus being humbled by a cloud of gravel? I guess he figured the dog paddle would come to him.

Holding Larry's sign over his head, he plowed right into the scummy pond, each thundering step sending water spraying up.

Fool. My hailstorm could find him in the water.

"To him," I cried.

I should have said it silently. Because that's when the bastard played dirty—chopping at the water with the side of his Alpha paw, effectively blinding me with a spray of cold, stinking pond water. Merry received a wave of water and shuddered hard.

"Don't freak out," I hissed to her. "There's no iron in it."

But my usually fearless friend scuttled upward, taking herself up, up, up away from the evil water. Her chain shortened until it was uncomfortably tight around my throat.

Whitlock kept coming at us, smacking the water hard, sending sheets of scum into my face. Blinded, I twisted away from him and we retreated, heading deeper into the pond. It was a desperate, sloshing retreat, made complicated by the fact that my disembodied magic was looking for a target, and not finding it. Bottom line, if I was blind, so was she. And since my magic couldn't find the intended target—she swooped back home to me, dropping pieces of gravel in her agitation as she did. Overloaded, she whirled around me in cloud of chattering stones. Directionless. Volatile. Freaking out, Fae-style.

"Bitch, surrender to me!" shouted Whitlock as he fired his gun. Something very hot, and very angry, streaked past my bicep, stopping just long enough to take a searing nip before it zinged through the screen of my cyclone of gravel.

"Do you need me?" called Liam.

"I can handle one little bitch," shouted Whitlock. "I speak to your wolf, Hedi Peacock. Come to your Alpha. Lay down your arms."

I would have told him to go fuck himself but I was too busy choking. Mindless with terror, Merry had tightened to a strangling noose around my throat. Back I went, nails tearing at my skin, trying to loosen her stranglehold. Deeper I staggered, until my feet could barely touch the bottom. There wasn't much I could do, but stay *en pointe*, keep my balance with a one-arm dog paddle, and hunker over my amulet, offering my back to my enemy.

If Whitlock had known how close I came to blacking out, he would never have ceased his splash efforts. But he couldn't see that, could he? A tornado of stone still spun around me.

I don't know how long it took me to figure out that the deluge had stopped—possibly two seconds longer than it took Merry. She'd loosened enough for me to inhale.

I really thought I had a chance. You know? I really did.

But first, I needed to get Merry out of the water and beyond Whitlock's reach.

"I'm going to throw you to safety," I told her as I pulled her over my head. I dried my eyes as best I could with a forearm, and won my Fae and me partial sight.

"Make a hole!" I screamed to my Fae. My magic—still feeding off my emotions—puzzled over that command. "I need to see!"

Aha.

She reshaped her cloud to create a small opening. Through the gap, I focused on the massive willow growing at the edge of the pond. I made a short prayer that for once my aim would be true, did a quick high-speed flutter kick that raised me in the water, and threw.

Make it, make it . . . Oh Goddess, I threw too short, she'll never make it. She hit the crotch of one of the limbs that stretched out over the pond, with a hollow thunk, then free-fell for the count of two, bounced, slid for another terrifying half second, until a vine caught one of the slippery, trailing yellow branches.

She held, her Fae gold chain swaying.

Safe.

Now, to summon up a cyclone of dirty water that will drown Whitlock.

My back was turned. I didn't even see the bolt coming.

Pain. Hot, searing, stabbing. It tore through my right shoulder. So unexpected, so awful.

"Iron!" screamed my Fae. I heard her, as if she were me, wailing, loud and high inside the confines of my own head. Then with one broken sob, she gave up her outward shape—no longer a cyclone protecting me, no longer a tornado promising doom . . . no longer a tangible thing.

She was misery. She was fear.

Stones started to fall, pitter-patter, into the water, onto me. Pea gravel pinged, on my face, on my nose, cutting into my soft lower lip. *I should lift my arm to cover my face,* I thought groggily. I could taste the essence of sweet peas. I could taste me.

Semimortal, semi-Fae.

Stunned, I looked down. The rounded nub of an iron bolt protruded below my collarbone. The tip of it, having pierced through shirt and flesh, was red-glazed. My head turned, very slowly, because even the slightest tensing of neck muscle yielded horrifying misery. The part sticking out of my back was out of comfortable vision range. But between eyeblinks, I could just see it—a long stick of metal, coated with iron—quivering with each of my panicked breaths.

Not again.

I'm not a voodoo doll. People have to stop sticking things into me.

My knees gave out. One moment I was standing, safe inside the eye of a cyclone of gravel, thinking myself protected, and the next? I was part of the water, my legs floating, my arms nerveless. My face skyward, pointed ears covered by the awful water, tasting foulness as water surged into my mouth.

Oh Goddess, I'm going to drown.

Again.

The iron's poison had felt like fire on contact, but now its tentacles were hurting me with a different type of burn—numbing, biting cold. And the weariness.

Not a bad way to go, if one considered it.

My body weightless. The pain receding to a dull constant throb coming from my shoulder. Breathing took concentration. Thinking took more. The water lapped at the seam of my mouth, searching for entry.

My wolf let out a long mournful howl inside me.

Mate, she called for Trowbridge.

"Pull her out of there," Whitlock said.

Liam stood over me, wet to his waist. I floated, eyes slit. Waves of cold streamed from him. Iron vested, iron hearted, he studied me, without his habitual half smile, or even the spark of curiosity. His attitude was one of resignation. I was the bump that refused to stay flattened; the button that kept flying loose.

It would have been equally practical to seize my floating arm or snag my collar. They were right there, for
pity's sake. Even my hair would have made a better handhold. But his focus traveled to the bolt that stuck out of
me, and quivered with each one of my ragged breaths.

Don't do it. My gut twisted in fear.

Without expression, he wrapped his hand around that
slippery rod, and then he turned—without even a flicker
of glance downward to his limp prize—and began to walk.
Agony . . . *agony.* Dragging me toward shore with each
churning step. I screamed. Water rushed up my nostrils
and clogged my throat.

Choking. Thrashing. Crying. I spluttered and kicked,
trying to turn my head, unmindful of anything but keeping alive to the next second and the one after that. No
wily catfish was I; no great marlin capable of an inspiring
leap. I was the sunfish wiggling on the curved hook, tail
flapping. Truly caught. Weakly struggling, being pulled
willy-nilly to a place I knew I did not want to go.

It's tearing me apart. My shoulder will break in two.

"Let me go!" I screamed. "Stop!"

Liam dredged me through the slime of decomposing
weeds, dragged me choking through the stiff and broken
stalks of the lone clump of bulrushes. All of it was awful,
but nothing compared to the great rasping horror when he
reached the edge of the water and finally . . . let go of the
bolt.

"You want her any farther, you get her," he told Whitlock.

Maybe Whitlock planned to pluck me free a few chokes
before the last sayonara. Perhaps, once I'd choked enough,
he'd have reached for me and dragged me out of the water, and up the slope.

Whatever. He didn't spring to my rescue.

I sank, jaw first, into the soft shoreline muck. Eating

mud? It's worse than swallowing water. It's thicker; it's slimier. You can't expel it with a splutter. The mud creeps up your nasal passages, it slides past your teeth. And as it does, your panic level shoots upward faster than the red needle on a pressure cooker.

I can't cough. I can't lift myself!

Goddess, help me!

If ever there are moments in your life when you see the value of your existence in absolute clarity, this instant must count among them—that split second during which you are no longer a thinking person or a calculating entity; you are the animal on the brink of death. One who either wants to live or wants to die.

And by glory be—not to be redundant on this point—I wanted to live. I'd come all this way, never giving up, always ruled by two principles. Don't die. Find your family. Well, by Goddess, I'd found and lost a family again. At least I could stick to point one.

Let go of the pain.

Ignore it.

Choose to live.

Stubborn desire knocked the stupor right out of me. My neck may have felt weak, and my head heavier than a cast-iron pot filled with cement, but I lifted my chin free from that soft bed of stinking sludge. As soon as I did, brown water filled in the depression left by my face.

It was a powerful motivator.

What did one monkey say to the other? Roll over. Ordinarily that meant using my right arm, but that particular appendage was full of pins and needles. Everything's connected, right? The arm bone's connected to the shoulder bone. And the area south of my clavicle had a bolt rimmed with iron sticking out of it.

Before you drop your head, heave yourself over to your back.

My flopping arm was nearly useless in terms of bracing, so I threw it behind my back, and did what comes so naturally to others—I used my head. In this case, as a dead weight that helped my entire body roll over to its side.

Good enough. At least I could breathe. And feel throbbing, stabbing, heated agony radiating from my shoulder. My arm felt numb. Useless.

Breathing an exquisite self-torture.

Don't look at the bolt.

The hot knifing sensation in my shoulder had spread until my entire body pulsed with it. *If you're hurting, you're still in the game.* I tried to sit up. Couldn't because my spine had dissolved. I wished for Trowbridge. For Merry. For Cordelia. For Harry and . . .

Get up. No one's going to rescue you this time.

My world no longer included a six-foot mother hen who'd wade into the disgusting pool of stagnation, muttering under her breath about "Bridge's bloody girl." Cordelia would never complain again. Or fuss over my clothing, or tell me to eat some protein.

He killed her. He's going to do the same to you.

Try harder.

Too difficult to coordinate raising myself to my knees. *Then crawl like a commando if you must.* I bent my left arm—*Goddess, it weighs so much*—and lifted it with the clumsy, fixed concentration of a baby attempting her first feat of self-locomotion. I won progress—one short foot, before it sank deep in the sludge.

Don't think about it.

Shoulder screaming, pointed toes digging into the mud, belly catching on every sharp stalk there was, I used that arm like an anchor, and dragged myself to it.

So hard.

My shoulder screamed as I repeated the whole process

again. Heave. Pull. Whimper. Drag. I lost count of how many reps it took to pull myself out of that water. But I did it.

They were side by side, two sportsmen standing over their catch. Whitlock wore a pair of brown slip-on loafers—the type that vaguely resemble boat shoes. Liam wore the same motorcycle boots as his club—square-toed, black leather.

I'd lost my shoes.

My face was half buried in the crook of my left arm, and I was near blinded by the muddy rattails of my own hair, but I could see them out of the corner of my right eye. Two shadows hazed by the vapor of my breath.

Whitlock swore. A long string featuring cocks doing things that probably weren't physically possible, then he said, "Where's the other girl?"

Liam's voice sounded far away, and not at all distressed. "She took off through the fields."

"Well, don't stand there—go get her."

Anu, have some part of me in you. Run.

"She won't get far," said Liam. "I'll scoop her up when I'm ready to leave."

Whitlock's tone sharpened. "She's a wolf; she can run fast, and the highway's just over there. I don't want to take a chance of her getting away."

"She won't head toward civilization, and she won't get away. At least not from me," he said with absolute certainty. "I will find her."

"There are already too many loose ends. She'll go to the first human—"

"I said she won't," said Liam. "You know what a good hunter I am."

Whitlock let out a hiss, then said, "I keep getting fucked by the world." I saw his foot lift. *No!* Before I could brace myself, he used the toe of his slip-on to heave me onto my side again. My back bowed into an anguished arch as tender abused tissue and muscle—and for all I knew, tendons too—screamed against the friction of the bolt. The world went gray, and all the shapes around me became wavering shapes.

Vertical ghosts, floating ghosts.

"You stupid bitch," said Whitlock, prodding me again with his foot. "The next time I tell him to shoot, it won't be soft tissue. The next time, I'll tell him to hit bone."

"Something to look forward to," I said, my words slurring.

"Shut up," snapped Whitlock. "Liam, go get the amulet."

"I don't climb trees," replied Liam, intent on wiping his boot heel clean on the grass. "And the more distance you keep between yourself and a Fae amulet the safer you are."

"What are you? An authority on fairies?" Whitlock stalked over to what was left of the Were we'd pummeled with our hailstorm of gravel. He bent, picked up the weapon, then returned to his muddy catch. He stood over me. The gun hung from his grip. Black. Square looking. Lethal.

Why is it that whenever someone has a gun, they feel compelled to point it at me? Do I wear a sticker? Shoot me, I'm a deer.

"You are a pain in the ass," he said. "Frickin' fairies. I hate them." There was a perfectly round hole at the end of the perfectly round barrel. So dark. So lethal. You had to wonder if you'd see the bullet coming.

The hurting will stop then.

Whitlock's toe tapped in irritation. "You told me you needed the song, well, we played the song. Where is your magic?" he shouted. To emphasize my sad lacking in all things Fae, he toed me again. "Why can't you call the portal?"

So many questions. Where was my magic? Where was the portal? Before I had a chance to inhale, the gun did a slow menacing bob—the type of slow cocking motion a guy makes with his thumb and index finger. My stomach did an upward climb. The gesture looks dumb when some suit does it. It earns gravity when the scary guy actually has a weapon in his paw.

"This is not a game," he said in a low savage voice.

No shit.

When it's down to microseconds, you notice certain things in perfect clarity. The shape of a knuckle, and the three deep lines bridging it, and the blood flow or lack of it. His finger tightened on the trigger.

He's going to shoot me now.

"Where is the portal?" he said in a low forced voice.

Wherever the passage was, it wasn't over the pond. The song had been sung. The air would have stirred instead of whispered. My bite mark should have reacted to the magic, shouldn't it have? Before I could form a lie, Whitlock grabbed my shirt, and hauled me up—bolt bobbing and grinding through skin and tendon and bone.

I screamed, the high shrill sound of a creature being tortured.

"You're dead, do you understand?"

Sweet merciful Goddess, why? What have I done?

Whitlock gave me another shake then said in disgust, "She doesn't know where it is." He released me, and I slumped, my elbow raised to block another blow. "Dammit! Dammit all to hell!"

Don't sob. Don't throw up.

Liam walked to the edge of the pond, and stared up at Merry. His crossbow lay balanced over his arm. "Do you want me to kill her?"

"No. Not now. She's Bridge's mate and I need him alive for the Great Council. I need him to take the heat for sun potion. It will be over for her as soon as they serve their justice on him. You'll know when it happens. She'll start to fade and die within a few minutes." He tucked the gun in the back of his pants and jerked his coat to cover it. "Fairies. Freakin' fairies."

"What do you want me to do with her?"

Frustration laced Whitlock's voice. "Just take her somewhere and keep her stashed until . . ." He glanced at his watch and did some rapid calculations. "One o'clock."

"Then what?"

"Find a place to bury her."

Whitlock went away. He was there right beside me by the pond. And then his loafers moved and he was not there. I wanted to follow him. Because where he went, so did Trowbridge.

But Liam reached for the back of my shirt, and started dragging me up the hill, with his arm outstretched as if I was a garbage bag leaking sour stuff. The bolt grated at my shoulder. Within a few feet, the slow cold drain of his iron vest numbed the worst pain. I was Scott in the Antarctic, slowly freezing to death. My eyes kept closing, my heart slowing.

Fight to stay awake.

I blinked against sleep's seductive pull—but could only scrounge up a slow droop of my eyelids. Liam and his iron were too close.

Whitlock said, "I'll need your help. I want to move Trowbridge to my truck." I opened my eyes, tried to pin the voice to location, but everything was blurring. Liam didn't drop me and leap to Whitlock's call. Stubbornly, he dragged his burden—the inconvenient Fae—all the way to Ryan's SUV. He opened the door, then swung me face-first onto the backseat.

"Hurry up," called Whitlock.

Liam stiffened. This was one biker who didn't like dancing to the Alpha's tune. But then again, he wasn't a wolf. He was something other though. But what?

"Now!" snarled Whitlock.

Whenever Liam was within a foot of me, I had to fight against the desire to slide into a coma of sleep, the logical consequence of being so close to his vest of iron. But if he moved away, I started to revive. Not anywhere close to full capacity. I still had an iron-coated bolt sticking out of me and chaining thoughts together took heavy effort.

Go away, Liam. Do what Whitlock tells you to. Weak relief spread when he said something under his breath. He left me—my sprawled legs hanging out of the car, my toes hitched on a clump of stray grass—and went to help.

Thank you, Goddess.

I listened, identifying the sound of a rear cargo door being raised, then heard the slide of plastic and a thump that I hoped was Trowbridge's knee, not his head.

"I want this place cleaned up," snapped Whitlock. "Hide Ryan's body. Find the girl stat—I do not want her flagging down some trucker for help. When you get her, kill her. And I want that frickin' amulet."

"I don't climb—"

"Ten grand," Whitlock said flatly.

"Twelve and I'll do it."

Whitlock said some more stuff in the surreal haze that followed. I could vaguely hear the drone of his voice—like the hum of an angry bee—but here's what happened. I stopped listening and started thinking. Liam thought me weak. *I am not.* Liam thought me done. *I am not.* Liam thinks I can't move with this iron bolt inside me. *He might be a bit right on that.*

The bolt had to go. Could I grab that iron-tipped thing with my bare hand? Could I make a fist around it strong enough to pull the long shaft all the way through my body?

Without passing out? Before he came back? Maybe I could reach behind myself, and grasp it from the other side? Or what if I heaved myself against something hard, and drove it right through my body?

I'll pass out. Doing that, guaranteed, I'll pass out.

Shit.

While I was still pondering the possibilities, I heard the crunch of gravel under boot, a door shut—with a frustrated bang—and an engine turn over. My wolf surged inside me. Scrambled to be released.

Exploding into fur? I didn't know how to do it.

"Goddamn fairy," Whitlock muttered with disgust, putting his vehicle into drive.

I hung my head, as the black SUV carrying My One True Thing left the Peach Pit.

I would have folded into the mire of despair except someone chose that moment to drip molten lava on the underside of my upper arm. Each droplet, as hot as a sear of solder. I sucked in a shuddering breath against the sensation. What fresh hell was this? I opened my eyes, and discovered something interesting.

Iron was on the move.

Stunned, I considered the molten bead of the metal poised at the tip of the bolt that protruded from my shoulder. Was I hallucinating? *But no . . . look at that.* The end that Liam had so carefully coated with iron was turning liquid right in front of my disbelieving eyes. Melting right off the tip of the bolt. Each tiny drip of it—splat, pause, splat—sharp microbites of fire.

Another pearl formed. *Crap. Move your arm out of the drip path.* It was a simple, straightforward suggestion from my brain to my body, but damn, it took an enormous amount of effort to force myself to accomplish that simple feat.

Iron's on the move. It's been called.

The next bit always embarrasses me to remember. Truth? I'd seen too many ghosts and specters in one night. And simply put, I wasn't firing on all cylinders. My gaze traveled from the iron, to the seat's upholstery, past the door frame, beyond my splayed foot, searching for Lou. Yes, I knew she was dead, but hell, this was the night of spooks, and my brain was fumbling to supply an answer to the fact that melted iron was being summoned by a Collector.

There could be only one. Lou had returned to save me in my moment of dire need. Yup, that's what I was thinking. Because there had been only one Fae I knew who could make the seven metals do her bidding. So I was sure Lou had come back—the Jacob Marley of the Fae— filled with self-reproach and the desperate need to make things up to me.

What my bleary eyes found was Anu. Standing half hidden by Larry the llama's shed. Colt legs, big eyes, expression a meld of fear and determination.

I promised Lexi you'd be safe.

Chapter Fifteen

If she'd had any sense, Anu would have kept going, sprinting through the cover of the woods until she hit the highway where she could have flagged down help. Or hidden. Or done any of the things any sane thirteen-year-old kid would have done in the face of the bad guys. Instead she'd come back, and in so doing, she'd pushed herself into what should have come far later, when her body was ready for it, when the timing was right—all of it done in a place far, far safer than this one. My niece had gone straight to the claiming; that turning point for those with Fae blood where they received the full gift of their heritage.

For some that moment never comes.

But for those that it does, its arrival comes at you in a visceral rush. It courses through you—blood, heart, brain—filling you. Your Fae. Your magic. Your destiny. You cannot anticipate the full impact of it and nothing will adequately prepare you for that first introduction to your Fae. It changes your inner balance and even the way you stand.

I'd fallen to my knees when my gift had burst to life.

Lexi's daughter stood, more or less upright, her narrow back braced against the chewed-up board siding on Larry the llama's little shack. White-faced, she held her trembling hand aloft. Her mouth moved silently as she called to the iron.

Within seconds, she'd cleansed the shaft of the cross-bow's bolt of its iron taint. If I could have, I would have cheered as the molten ore pooled on the ground. Instead I watched, half numb, half dumb, as the round blob of melted misery elongated into a tear shape, and then funneled into a long spittoon of evil. Compelled by Anu's call, the slender rivulet moved in a slow but steadfast direction toward her.

Moving on out.

I slowed my respiration from dog pant to forced and steady breath. Getting out of the truck was going to be difficult. *You want your mate back?* I asked my wolf. She lifted her head from her paws and whined. *Stand up.* Butterflies in my stomach, then a squeeze, and I felt her expand. Her essence—that wild creature that reacted rather than planned—filled in the cracks left in my physical body. *This is good. But I need more.* I required every bitter bit of me. The good, the bad, and the awful.

"Return to me," I said. There was no doubt in my voice. No plea or petition.

She will obey.

"We will destroy them," I promised her. Whitlock. Liam. Every single being that stood between me and those that I loved. Every person who chose to stop me. Every wolf who made the mistake of thwarting me. I will get back what is mine. And then—

"Liam first," murmured my Fae, spilling down my throat.

Agreed.

The world did a drunken spin around us as I pushed myself upright. *Don't think about the hot pain. It will flare, but it will go.* Clenching my jaw against a whimper, I did an awkward turn in my seat. *Oh, sweet heavens.* I forced myself to butt-shuffle toward the open door. That minor flex of hip, spine, and torso was bad. In terms of body revolts it was very, *very* bad. Standing was going to be worse.

Do it anyhow. Don't think about the bolt. Think about Liam.

He of the bolt, and the desire to hunt Anu.

I stood, holding on to the door. Things tilted, then righted themselves.

Where was Liam?

Coming up from the pond, his back to me, his attention focused on navigating Ryan's corpse over the lip of a walkway without leaving a telltale trail of the red and the awful. He gripped the wolf's collar as he had done with me, but this time, he was straining. Ryan's dead weight demanded more muscle.

Cautious son of a bitch. He hadn't given up on the crossbow.

My Fae was with me—indistinguishable from me. In my blood, in my bone, in my thoughts. Magic streamed weakly from the fingertips. Goddess. We'd taken a heavy hit—my normally fat serpent of green was thin as a wafer; our fluorescence muted to tepid spits and sparkles of fire.

Not good.

I couldn't see strangling Liam with it. My gaze frantically swept the area. Next time I met a biker, I'd arm myself with an Uzi. Better yet, I'd order a flamethrower from Amazon.

Come on. Give me something, anything.

What can I turn into a weapon? There were signs. Wooden ones. Pounded into the ground with sharpened stakes. Giving directions, tossing out reminders, and warnings about perceived dangers. CHILDREN UNDER FIVE SHOULD NOT . . .

The closest one read BEWARE OF RABBITS.

My magic was an extension of me—of my hand, of my rage. It grafted itself onto the sign and tore it from the turf. Turned it upside down so that those worried about feral bunnies would be required to perform a handstand in order to read the caution. The stake had been honed to a nice point. A long sharp spear for stabbing, slightly encumbered by a tailfin of signage.

I lifted my hand.

Liam dropped Ryan's corpse. Fast as a zombie-killer, he raised his crossbow.

He aimed. My inner-bitch saw his eyes tighten.

We both fired at the same time. Two separate events, in two separate streamlines of intent, like a poorly scheduled synchronized swim event.

My sideways lunge would have made a stuntwoman proud. I registered air being squeezed by a fist of cold as his bolt brushed past us, but little else.

Unbelievably, he'd missed. Even more miraculous? I'd hit the bull's-eye. Or close enough. Okay, a fragile bond, at best—my bunny stake had torn right through into the meat of his thigh and kept going until the sign's rectangle would let it go no farther. But we were connected, Liam and I. This time I had him on *my* hook.

Before he could wriggle free from it, I willed my magic to slip off the dirt-smeared pointed end of the stake and wrap itself around his upper leg with the squeezing power of a famished python. *Gotcha, Hook, line, and sinker. You—thing that must be destroyed—are now mine.* My serpent was strong, tensile. Invisible, indomitable, damn near indestructible. She did another circle around his abductor muscles.

Any other man would have reacted to a DON'T FEED THE BUNNY placard nuzzling his package. Liam spared the briefest look for the stake skewering his thigh. Eyes slit, he reached behind to wrench another bolt from his quiver.

Doesn't he feel pain?

Fine. I'd give him a harsher lesson in remittance costs. I slashed my hand viciously to the left. My invisible cable of magic jerked his thigh right off the ground and held it raised, hip high.

Every joint from my knuckles to neck howled, "Son of a bitch, that bastard's leg is heavy!" My fingernails felt too tight and the bolt in my opposite shoulder took exception to sudden movement.

I swear I heard it grate across a bone.

Stake through thigh plus an invisible tourniquet tightening near his groin should have unmanned him. For crap's sake, his leg had been plucked, squeezed, and suspended in an awkward side lift.

The fucker smiled and swiftly rebalanced his weight to his other foot.

So standing like a crane was no big deal, huh? Resolve tightened my hand into a fist. *I will bring him to his knees.* I put everything I thought I had into my next move. Body, mind over matter, hatred, fear. I lunged to the left.

Liam offered no resistance to my savage tug— anticipating my reaction, he simply leaped in the same direction, using my magic's momentum to his full advantage. Baldly put, Liam went with it, going all the way to the edge of my serpent's physical limits, and from there, a scant inch beyond it. Without losing his grip on the damn crossbow.

He slowly lowered his leg, stretching the line between us until it trembled. Feet planted, sign fluttering from his groin, he calmly leaned back. That's the problem when your magic is a rope—strings have two ends. Fae Stars. I was the bantamweight in a tug-of-war game against a heavy hitter. My bare feet lost a layer of dead skin on the asphalt. I stumbled, did a few skittering steps in his direction, then found my balance.

Magic bound us.

Hate too.

Without lifting his hooded gaze from mine, he groped for the stake spearing his thigh. He yanked it out. Stood, frozen and silent as he absorbed whatever irritation that injury produced. Then he lowered his chin and threw the blood-smeared sign on the ground between us.

I knew what he was going to do. He was going to reel me in using the thin rope of magic connecting us. Once I was dragged past the gauntlet-sign . . . he was going to hurt me. Not with a bow, but his bare hands. His touch would sear my skin. Leave it bubbling with heat blisters.

My fingernails throbbed. My shoulder burned.

Screw him. If he was going to make me suffer more, he was going to have to work for it.

Feet, don't fail me now.

"Break!" I said harshly to my magic. I meant it to cut in two or to unravel from him. I wanted it to follow my retreat like a hive of bees. But worn to extinction, my wire-thin talent didn't splinter so much as dissolve. No good-bye burst of sparkles. No hovering mass of flickering bits of fluorescence sparkling in the air around me. It just . . . disappeared as if it had never been part of my soul.

It's gone.

Inside me I heard a terrible wail. "I'm dying," my Fae wept.

A horrible, knowing smile creased Liam's face, plumping his hollow cheeks and webbing the lines drawn from the corners of his eyes. It drew my attention to the fleck of glitter, glinting dully on his cheekbone. Another similar particle glimmered on the bridge of his nose.

My stomach squeezed. *Goddess, he's coated in bits of my magic.*

"I'm fading," Fae-me sobbed.

"No you're not." I shook my head, even as my frantic gaze traveled. More glitter on the ground. Bright specks on my sleeves. "I won't let you." A faint coating of magic dusted the feathers on the bolt protruding from me. A sheen of it clung to the wet, copper-scented patches of my shirt.

"Having a burnout?" inquired Liam.

A stone bit into my sole as I spun on my heel. Run. That's what I planned to do. Even if it was futile. Even if he caught me before I made it four feet. I wasn't going to stand like a sheep waiting for slaughter.

"You can't run from me," he called as I darted up the little hill toward the parking lot. He followed at an easy lope. "I can see for miles. I can track you—"

Headlights bit into the gray of the early dawn.

Karma, for all the pity in your mean little heart, throw me a freakin' bone.

Liam's head spun, his lips splitting into a delighted grin, as he took in the sight of a truck tearing down the Peach Pit's private drive. *What? More bikers?* The truck hit the speed bump at full power; its front wheels dipped and the undercarriage issued a stream of sparks. Undeterred, the driver stomped harder on the gas. The engine revved and the vehicle careened across the parking lot straight toward me.

Liam's smile faded.

A woman leaned out of the open passenger window. Her hair streamed behind her, a Valkyrie's mane. Her gun arm was solid and muscled, braced on the side of the car. Her wide mouth was set into a snarl. She fired. Once. Twice. Again. Very fast, very sure. But the vehicle hit a depression in the asphalt and the bullets went wide.

That's when Liam threw me under the bus. A few strides collapsed the distance between us. I didn't even see it coming—I was standing transfixed, not believing my eyes—and then I was being shoved right into the on-coming vehicle's path.

Brakes were trod, tires burned. The driver slewed the car violently to the left. Back end swinging into a skid, the truck's path altered at the last moment.

It almost missed me.

I'd have come out clean if I wasn't impersonating a felled tree. Liam's shove had caught me right between the shoulder blades, upsetting my center of balance. My head snapped forward, my hair flew. My mane—such as it is—slid over the mirror and got caught.

I cried out.

And things went briefly gray. Too much pain. Too many hurts.

It's a bad feeling falling backward, knowing you're bristling with a bolt. Mostly because under the right cir-cumstances (example: the potential for body injury) the same brain that can't make up its mind whether it wants to supersize the fry order proves itself perfectly capable of working faster than a computer. "You know that bolt?" it inquires. "It's going to be the first thing to kiss the pave-ment. And that, my dear friend, will feel comparable to being crossbowed all over again."

Shit.

"You may," it says dourly. "Particularly since the sharp end won't be the first thing to meet the ground. It will be the *other* end."

It's just too damn bad you figure out all of that before you have a chance to put your hands up to break your fall.

Not the feathered end. Please, not the—

On impact, an exquisitely awful blast of agony shud-dered through me, robbing me for 2.2 seconds of the abil-ity to breathe, to scream, to even think. Then I did an inhale and wished, with every strand of my outraged nerves, that I hadn't.

Sweet pea scent oozed from my shoulder.

I must be bleeding again.

Was it a call to arms? The speck of dull glitter on my knuckle sparked bright. And then another spitfire—tinier than a scintilla's wink—twinkled at me from the nap of my shirt. My magic was reviving?

Come to me. I need all parts of me.

A well-shod foot thrust open the vehicle's door. The shooter slid out, took three long strides, raised her gun and aimed. Bang. Bang. A short pause to adjust aim as Liam pitched forward, and . . . a final bang.

That's when the impossible happened.

His body exploded.

Literally. From the inside, as if he'd swallowed a pound of C-4. A blowout of skin, sinew, and bone. I shielded my eyes as gore pit-pattered on the hood of Ryan's car. The rainfall of Liam parts was mercifully brief. Something soft and light fell on the web of my fingers. I peeked.

A feather?

A long black crow feather?

My gaze slid to the epicenter of yuck. A huge bird—dark as a piece of wet jet—shook its wings, the way I'd shake an umbrella after a heavy deluge.

Liam's a bird? Am I seeing that? Or am I hallucinating that?

The crow erupted into flight. He—it—could have flown in any direction. The trees, the sky . . . but it swooped toward me. I rolled onto my hip with a stifled scream—*Goddess, stop the hurting*—burying my head under my elbow and doing my best to tighten into a snail. *Don't take me like a mouse from a field.* A sharp talon dragged itself along my exposed cheek, caught a strand of limp hair and tore it free. Then the bird wheeled away with a terrible scream. He—it—did a circle high above me, its cry loud and shrill.

Horrifying.

I watched it go. Thoughts suspended. The smell of cordite pinched my nostrils.

A tiny flicker of jade-green light glittered over me. *Isn't that nice. A piece of my magic's found its way home.* Another one joined it. Twins. Ah, now a cloud. Green. Shiny. Bright. My magic hovered over me, forming a low blanket of protection, if one was to subscribe to the idea of my Fae talent having any softer dimensions.

"Open your mouth," pleaded Fae-me. "Bring us home."

Okay.

I unhinged my jaw, and my magic funneled back down my throat. It warmed me, and heated my insides, as welcome as warm chocolate on a wet fall day. I held my lips wide until every particle of light was consumed, then swallowed.

"Better," murmured my Fae.

Uh-huh.

My gaze slowly—achingly, disbelievingly—slid to my left.

My rescuer stood under moonlight. Her clothing was in dreadful disarray. Her wig was askew. In the gloomy light, her hair color looked brown, maybe black, but to my eyes . . . I saw fire. The glorious vermilion, the wondrous golden, and the royal blue of the flames from which the phoenix rises.

"Darling," Cordelia said. "Were we late?"

Chapter Sixteen

The world blurred. There she was standing by the car, smelling of perfume, and blood, and home. "You're dead," I said flatly. Ghosts all around me. In the cemetery, and now—right here in front of my watering eyes.

Cordelia shook her head.

"I'm not dead," she said slowly. She started moving toward me, her gait mechanical, almost robotic. The way you walk when your arms are full, and your brain is preoccupied by a possibility that up to that moment had been imponderable.

"Liam said to burn the house—I *heard* a shot." I tried in vain to shape two fingers to imitate the barrel of a gun, but failed. Because I had a bolt buried inside me and moving my arm ignited nerve endings I didn't even know I had. And because my pointer and f-u fingers were too swollen to straighten, too painful to manipulate.

And finally, because I didn't believe it.

Any of it—men turning into birds, phoenix risings, magic reanimations. At any moment, the heavenly representative tasked with the job of informing me of my death would tap me on the shoulder and say, "Hey, babe, your mom and dad are waiting for you at cloud nine. Haul ass, okay? Your mother is motoring through our stock of maple syrup."

It had to be that. All this—everything since Knox had sunk his blade into my belly—was part of Hedi's personal hell. That or a hallucination that just kept going and going.

"Yes," she said tautly. "You heard a shot."

I lay there, unable to stand, my clawed hand hovering near my chest in a failed bang-bang pantomime, feeling the heat of stirring anger. I'd been the cursed yo-yo at the end of the Grim Reaper's string for over forty-eight hours, and I was tired of it. One flick of her wrist, and I was spinning toward certain annihilation. One tweak of her f-u finger, and there I went again, jerked back upward toward the mockery of false hope.

"There was a biker inside the shack with you," I said, my words missiles fired through clenched teeth. "He couldn't have missed."

"Hedi, I'm all right."

"You're a ghost," I said, with a negative roll of my head. "I'm hallucinating right now—"

"No you're not."

"Yes! I am!" I said, my voice rising. "I conjured you up because I want my mum and I know I can't have her. And you're my mom-who-isn't and the next best thing. So I've dreamed you up, because I need you . . ."

Ah shit. Was I crying?

My broken speech had stopped her in her tracks. Her mouth worked then she said in a low, rough voice, "Biggs was shot. Not me. Biggs."

"Is he dead?"

She shook her head. "No, he's not."

"He should be," I whispered. A tear rolled down my temple. "He betrayed us."

"He's in the backseat. It's your call, Hedi."

"No, I need to speak to him. He's our link to Brenda Pritty." I needed to blot my face but the idea of moving anything other than my head . . . *I'll lie here for a little longer.* I needed to do stuff. Pull out the bolt. Stand. Make a plan. Find Trowbridge. Gather all the parts of me, and do something.

Because I'd made a promise. To my twin, to myself. And because Strongholds hold. Even ones that gave up using their true name long ago.

I won't give up. Which means, I must rise to my feet.

And I would. In a second.

Cordelia's knees cracked as she knelt beside me. "Look at you," she muttered. "What have they done to you?"

"Used me for a dartboard." I flinched as her hand moved perilously close to the bolt. But all she did was to reach across my body for my good paw—the one that wasn't grossly swollen and bubbled with blisters. She held it, firm and warm in her relentlessly gentle grip, as if she reckoned I needed support and that was her job.

"I'm not that hurt, you know," I muttered to her. "I'm just resting."

"I know," she said.

Her heat penetrated. Her skin was soft, made so by the peach-scented lotion she purchased from a small apothecary outside of Collingwood.

So. Not a mirage.

Alive. Missing an earring that exposed one of her fleshy lobes to view. Kneeling here, beside me, after I'd written her name with blood ink in my grieving column. A band tightened around my chest. Is this what happens when you start loving again? When you open your heart and let people in? *Goddess, curse her.* I did not need another suspension bridge in my life. All sharp angles, and rusted arches, and thin wires that could snap.

"Harry?" I asked after a hard swallow.

"No, pet," she said after a long quiet moment. "He's dead."

Dammit. Is she tearing up?

"Did you leave him there?" I whispered. "Did you let them burn his body—"

"Whatever was Harry was already gone. The rest was just . . ."

"A shell," I said, remembering Dad and Mum. "Go find his bones afterward, okay, Cordelia? Bury them in Creemore. Near my grandfather's stone. Promise me?"

"You'll do it yourself," she growled, her gaze assessing the bolt, the shoulder, and my level of resistance.

"I'll be in Merenwyn, remember? Don't wait until his remains are picked up by some fire investigator. I don't want them sitting in a box in a coroner's office. No one but us should touch them." When she nodded, I demanded, "How did you get here? Why aren't you shot?"

"Rachel," she said shortly. "I despise the woman and now I owe her."

"Where is she?"

"Here," I heard. My gaze swung to the truck. Rachel stood beside the driver's door. She carried a weapon that looked very much like the sawn-off shotgun one of the bikers had carried. All the lines in her body spoke of edges. "We need to move," she said. "Shots were fired."

"We'll move when Hedi's ready," Cordelia parried.

I lifted my brows in inquiry. My mom-who-wasn't gave me a faint smile and continued. "When Biggs saw her through the window, he threw a chair at the man covering me. Rachel and I took care of the rest." She exhaled, then she asked, in a voice so careful I knew she dreaded the answer, "Where's Bridge?"

I slowly pulled my mitt from her grip. "Whitlock took him." *Wrapped in a plastic shroud.* "Help me up."

"Stay there." She gestured toward the bolt. "That needs to come out of you. It will be easier to do it if you're lying down."

I think not. I got a quick image of a smiling Rachel holding me down with her foot while a grim-faced Cordelia tore the bad thing out of me. "Even better reason to help me up," I muttered, lifting my head. How could one noggin weigh so much? It was impossibly heavy, and sadly, connected to my neck, which was connected to my shoulder . . . *There's a hole in the bucket, dear Liza, dear Liza.* While Cordelia's face pleated into a terrible frown, I breathed through my mouth, waiting for things to settle.

When I could muster words without gasping, I told her, "They're going to frame Trowbridge. And me too."

"How?" she asked.

"Whitlock and Knox have been trading with the Fae." I rolled onto my good side, biting down against the need to scream as I leveraged myself up onto my hip.

"You are ridiculously stubborn," she said, moving to support me.

She had a hard time finding a good handhold because the five-inch bolt that used to protrude from the front of me had lengthened into nine or ten inches of gore-covered arrow sticking out from my shirt.

"Don't touch it," I warned.

The logical portion of me had arrived at unpleasant mathematical certainty. The bolt was only so long. If that much was sticking out of the front of me . . . I risked a quick glance over my shoulder. Uh-huh. Impact with the ground had drilled the thing through me. Now the feathered fletch was buried inside me.

I cringed at the thought of the pain coming my way. Odds were, I'd pass out halfway through the extraction. Hell, I was that close to doing it already.

I can't do that. Not right now.

I'll faint later.

"There's a portal here," I informed her. "I thought it

would be over the pond, but . . ." I paused for a long steadying inhale through my teeth. "The gates didn't respond to the portal song. Maybe the magic knows the difference between an audio file and a real voice . . ."

In which case I'll never get to Merenwyn.

Tempting to swoon. I widened my eyes and focused on Cordelia's set chin—an uneven landscape of enlarged pores and hair follicles. "Whitlock wanted me to call the portal and find its gatekeeper."

"Why?"

"Sun potion." I reached to touch her cheek. Leather coated with the best foundation on the market. Her nostrils pinched as my finger traced the deep groove beside her mouth.

"You said Whitlock was going to frame my brother," prodded Rachel. "How?"

My gaze swung sharply (well, relatively so) to my right.

Somehow the wolf-bitch had snuck up on Cordelia and me. She stood uncomfortably close to us, gripping the sawed-off shotgun like she wanted to use it again. I ditched exploring Cordelia's face and hitched myself upright on one hip. Immediate remorse. *Shit, that hurt.* Life was better reclining sideways on the solid, if lumpy-boobed, comfort of my mother hen.

"Whitlock and Knox have been selling the potion to the halflings," I said. "A dose of it before the full moon will—"

Cordelia inhaled sharply. "Stop their transformation."

"Whitlock's going to bring Trowbridge in front of the Great Council, but first they're going to force-feed him sun potion. They're going to pour it down his throat until he's wasted."

"Robbie's reputation is lousy," said Rachel in disgust. "Once the rogue wolf, always the rogue wolf."

Some of the air went out of Cordelia.

"Trowbridge is not rogue," I snapped. "He's the Son of

Lukynae—and that means something in Merenwyn. And he's the Alpha of Creemore—and that should mean something here."

But Rachel hadn't finished smashing her bro's rep into tiny little hurtful fragments. "All my brother's known for here is his drinking, whoring, and violence."

Whoring? Violence? The guy who sauntered into my Starbucks hadn't been . . . okay, that was then. Now, he was . . . *He's mine. That's what he is. And Whitlock shouldn't have taken him.*

"He built a business in British Columbia," Cordelia murmured, her tone distracted.

A gate creaked. We all spun—weapons (well, in my case my blistered hand) ready to fire—but it was only Anu, emerging from Larry the llama's enclosure. My niece wore the vacant expression of someone who'd survived a perishing disaster. She surveyed us, then tossed her hair back in a gesture so achingly like Lexi's that I wanted to close my eyes.

Don't think about Threall or the Old Mage. You can't save your brother's soul if you and Trowbridge are dead.

She tilted her head to inspect me.

Words were necessary even if she didn't understand them. "Thank you," I said.

Her gaze sharpened on mine, wandered to the arrow, returned to my eyes, then looked down to the horror of my hand, and then back up to my face again.

"You'll be okay," I said. "I'll make sure you'll come out of this okay."

Anu's nostrils flared and she turned for the truck. The ferret was running along the dashboard. Back and forth, forth and back, desperate to find release.

"You brought the ferret," I said to Cordelia.

"It didn't leave us any choice." She gazed unseeingly over my shoulder, and then nodded to herself before raking me over with one of her all-seeing assessments. "You're a mess, my darling girl."

I glanced down. The light had faded from my arm, but there were traces—individual pinpoints of pink, in the heart of each tooth indent. As for my hand? Yes. It was grossly swollen.

"It's not bad. I hardly feel it what with—"

"You do and you will," she said grimly. "We need Merry on the job."

Merry. There had been a massacre on my chessboard— pawns had been forfeited, a rook overturned, the bishop had lost his head, the king was still in peril, and I'd allowed my friend Merry, the dark queen on my board, to be left swinging from a branch over a fetid pond.

My mouth was dry. "Help me stand. I left her by the pond."

"Don't be ridiculous. You can't walk. I'll get her."

"No," I said through my teeth. "I left her, I'll retrieve her." Waves of nauseating heat (*why does pain always feel hot?*) pulsed as I rose with Cordelia's help. Crap. The whole damn world turned into a shifting ocean. Trees swayed like hula girls, Cordelia blurred in and out, and the ground beneath me seemed to slope invitingly toward hell.

"Before I die, I'm going to kill Whitlock," I told her. "And any person who hurts my mate in the hours it takes for me to find him again."

Was that me? That cold, hard voice that sounded a bit like my Fae?

Yes. It's me.

All of me.

As I waited for my sea legs, Cordelia's gaze traveled over my features in a way that I will never, ever forget. Her mouth went from a grim slash to a smile that was slow, and full, and as wide and proud as any mother's when her child crossed the dais for the coveted diploma.

"That's my girl," she said softly. "You're back. The little upstart who stood by that pond and told them all to go to hell is back."

Damn right she is. And she's going to see Liam suffer too. Though there was the remote possibility that I might need birdshot for that. Unless that last bit really *was* a hallucination. "Did I see that right?" I asked, jerking my chin in the direction of the pond. "Did Liam blow apart and become a crow?"

"A raven," she corrected, her mouth pulled down.

"What the hell is Liam?" I asked, accepting her arm. "I didn't get any 'other' to his scent."

Anu scuttled around to my other side, to wrap an arm around my waist.

Her scent tugged at a memory. I wove on my feet, trying to place it. Woods after a storm. Earth newly turned. Cedar.

"You smell a bit like my dad," I told her. "In the morning. Before his shower." Had my brother recognized it? Scent it on her? *Oh, Lexi. Is that one of the reasons you brought her to me?*

I scanned my niece's face, searching for my mum.

Anu spoke. I watched her mouth move, thinking that the world was weaving around me. My niece shook her head, angered. She took a step, pulling me gently with her toward the pond. Still yammering away.

"Mum talked a lot," I said dreamily. "And she could sing. Can you sing?"

Evidently not. What came out her mouth was another string of Merenwynian. You don't really need to understand the language to appreciate the fact you're being chastised.

"The child is right," began Cordelia. "You are impossibly difficult."

"Uh-huh," I said faintly. Then, supported by a bitch and a bitch-in-training, I tested walking. To my vast relief, putting one foot in front of the other only nominally impacted my shoulder. "So, Liam," I said, swallowing down bile. "Returning to my original question—"

"Obviously, he's a shapeshifter of some sort," she replied testily.

The concrete pathway looked like it was floating. So did my feet.

"Why wouldn't you recognize his nature by his scent?"

A scowl twisted her face. "All I'm getting from his scent trail is human and wolf, a bit of—"

I shot her a sideways glance. "Could he be a halfling?"

"No." Her mascara-heavy lashes lowered, spiky shields against her thoughts.

Ah. The three of us crab-walked over the railway tie edging the downward slope to the pond. "So, basically, Liam smells like whoever he's been around." *Like me and Lexi.* "He has no scent then? He's a Fae? Or a half-breed like me or Anu?"

At the mention of her name, Anu's head turned.

"Possibly," said Cordelia evenly.

The payback pain was starting to make itself known. Throbbing to my heartbeat, swelling with the misery in my shoulder. "I could have saved Trowbridge," I whispered, lifting my eyes from the rough ground. "If I'd known how to open the gates, Whitlock would have done business with us and—"

"Only until it suited him," Cordelia whispered back. "*Only* as far as that. In the end, he would have destroyed you both. Men like him are—"

"Users," I finished for her.

My heart dropped when we reached the pond. Merry should have been clinging to a thick bough hanging over the water. Merry was not. No amulet bleated red flashes of belligerence. No glint of a Fae-gold chain. "She should be right there," I said, fear starting to crawl up from my gut again.

But she wouldn't have stayed there, would she have? Not with the water below her. She'd have climbed through that thicket of yellow branches, moving along that serpentine limb toward the heart of the tree.

"Merry?" I called. "Where are you?"

Cordelia chewed her lip as she scanned the tree with me. She didn't have to say anything; my imagination had already grimly leaped there. Without its summer skirt of hanging fronds, the willow was all thin whippets of drooping branches. Navigating toward the trunk, moving past the crisscrossed branches, finding a good grip—particularly when you didn't have opposable thumbs—it would be a definite challenge.

I should sense her. Fae gold calls to me. Was the bulk of the trunk interfering? Blocking the signal? I circled the tree. No such luck.

"Hedi," said Cordelia softly.

I turned to see her pointing to the mud slick my knees had left when Liam had dragged me up the hill. Three-quarters up the incline, just beside the gray-brown trail, stood Merry. A stick figure, with a belly flushed orange, bristling with prickly ivy, half hidden by a tuft of a small weed.

My eyes got wet because I was tired, okay?

I trudged—okay, wove—my way to her. "So, mounting a rescue attempt, huh?" As slowly as a dowager removing her gloves, she shook out the arm she'd fashioned from one length of ivy. The gold flowed, flattening the stiffly articulated ivy leaves, until her limb appeared surprisingly muscled. She left one leaf at the tip of her appendage. The end of it sharp as a needle.

I looked down at her, my fingers digging into Anu's waist. "Pissed with me, are you?"

A blast of orange light lit her up.

"Sorry for the pond," I said. And then because the ground was coming up to meet me, I let myself fall to one knee.

The bolt bobbed. And the ground swayed.

Kind of nauseating.

I gritted my teeth—*don't puke on Merry*—as my amulet pal climbed up my thigh. Said not a word as she hooked pincer-sharp leaves into my T-shirt to clamber up to my left shoulder. I did hiss through my teeth when she grabbed one wet hank of hair and did a running walk across my collarbone. (She could have smoothed the points on her leaves before her rescue charge to the bolt site.)

"It's not as bad as it looks," I said.

She tested that whopper by resting a tendril of ivy on the bolt.

"Okay," I said, when the urge to whimper like a little girl had passed and it was safe to unlock my jaw. "It's exactly as bad as it looks."

Merry picked up her chain and offered it to me. Quietly. The color inside her softening to gold. Wear me. We belong together. I dipped my chin. Hands—large, square—helped me draw Merry's chain over my head.

"Thanks," I muttered.

Cordelia cleared her throat. "So, do we have a plan?"

"First I'm going to rescue Trowbridge."

"Of course.

"And then I'm going to waste them all—"

"Well, obviously," she drawled, "Though I want to be the one to finish Liam."

"You can kill Liam," I said as my amulet pal reworked her vines from stick appendages to a nest of articulated gold, surrounding a belly of beautiful glowing amber. "But Whitlock's all mine."

"You're very generous."

"So I've been told."

Cordelia slid a finger underneath her wig for a thoughtful scratch. "How are we going to do all this?"

I knew where Trowbridge would be in a few hours. I knew what was waiting for him. I had to be there. With evidence to prove that Whitlock wore a black hat.

"Here's what we'll do." *Well, listen to me. All Hedi-knows-best.* I'd finally figured out how to make a plan. It begins with a simple statement. Not a hazy "I want" but a firm "I will." Funny that I should realize that here. Life lessons, compliments of the Peach Pit.

"Biggs is going to tell us where to find Brenda Pritty."

I looked up, searching the sky for a dark winging shape. "Liam will follow us." I knew that in my bones. "He's up there somewhere. We are his prey, and his anger is his hunger. He will hunt us. We've got to get out of here and find some secluded place where I can . . ." *Don't say "interrogate." At least not now when I can see Biggs through the rear window.* "Where Biggs and I can talk," I said, resting my hip against the back end of Rachel's truck. "I need two more things from you."

"Name them."

"Keep an eye on Merry's color." I glanced behind me, estimated the distance to the rear bumper, and allowed myself to slide ass-first toward it. "When it starts to muddy and turn brown, you take her off me, okay? Then you get Rachel to drive us as fast as possible to a stand of hardwoods. You find a tree and you put Merry on a branch. Stand guard, okay? I don't want some raven on an amulet hunt coming tearing down from the sky."

"Shall do, darling," she said.

I manufactured a smile for Anu and gave her a "go sit"

head wave. Once she was perched in the backseat, I turned my chin back to Cordelia.

"What's the last thing?"

I sucked in my breath. "Catch me?"

That's when I grabbed the bolt and jerked it free.

Chapter Seventeen

The gas needle had trembled in the red long enough. Cordelia had decreed that I needed something sweet so she'd instructed Rachel to take the exit for the next service station. In terms of quenching impulse buys, this place had it all—from sunglasses to diesel fuel, from chocolate bars to celebrity magazines, from rolls of chalky Tums to tacky T-shirts. As Rachel was the only one who'd thought to bring her credit card, she was elected to gather supplies while Cordelia pumped our gas.

I'd swum back to consciousness on the 400 Highway, somewhere after exit 85. The first thing I'd done was to cry out Trowbridge's name; the second to ask for Merry. Once she'd been placed in my puffy hands I'd quieted. Cordelia told me they'd fed her until she'd indicated she was full. Merry had been foolishly hasty on that one. Even after her feeding, her color was one shade off burned butter. I'd slid her clumsily into the confines of my left bra cup. Nuzzled against my warm boob, she had fallen into an immediate dreamless sleep.

(Okay, I don't know if my amulet pal dreams or not, but she didn't move. And since I was forcing myself not to think of her twitchless nap as a coma, I was going for dreamless.)

By the time the tank was full, Trowbridge's sister had

returned to the vehicle and I'd done a quick inspection of the area below my left clavicle. The puckered scab was larger than I'd anticipated, but, then again, I had nothing to measure it against. Just how large a hole should a feathered fletch leave?

I wasn't completely healed. Yellow fluid weeped from the site. *I'm going to scar.* That would make Trowbridge and me a matched pair of oddities among the Weres because wolves don't as a rule carry mementos of past injury unless we're talking complete amputation. A leg hanging by a thread? No problem. Just jam it back in place and ride out the healing.

Trowbridge really likes my skin. He's always stroking it as if it's fine silk. Now it's damaged. I'm no longer perfect.

Rachel handed me the shopping bag, and turned the key. "Where to?"

Goddess, I hadn't even got my arms and legs moving properly and Trowbridge's sister was asking me to think. *Welcome to life as a leader.*

"Somewhere private off the main road." I found the smallest T-shirt and passed the rest over the seat to Cordelia. "I want to speak to Biggs."

The accused was not innocent in my eyes. He was guilty as hell, which is why he didn't get a place of comfort to recuperate inside the vehicle. Rachel had offered him the cargo area at the back of the enclosed cab. It couldn't be comfortable, but I had a hard time drumming up any sympathy.

Trowbridge had been tossed into Whitlock's trunk wrapped inside a plastic tarp. Biggs should count himself lucky. I was not a betrayal novice. My aunt Lou had screwed me over, and the pack had done it to me twice. Sweet heavens, Karma had done it more times than I could count. But this—it was worse than Lou.

Biggs had been part of my new family—one of the misfits who I'd thought had been irreversibly tied together. He'd had his place at our roundtable. I'd been well on the way to developing fond and possibly deep feelings for him. I might have even grown to love him if he hadn't taken his sweet-ass time coming around to rescuing Trowbridge and me when Mannus and Stuart Scawens took turns hurting us.

Though my heart was never going to open wide enough for another brother, Biggs had been the equivalent of an irritating cousin. Alternately frustrating and amusing. Part and parcel of my daily life.

Here I'd been, thinking he'd had a seat on the same screaming roller coaster, and instead he'd been . . . what? When it all boiled down, what had he got out of betraying us? Two bullets. One of which came close to severing his spine, Cordelia had reported without expression.

I said that I'd kill every person who led to the hurt of my mate. Did he count as one of them?

Could I? Did I need to?

Why had he done it? Who was Brenda Pritty to him? How did he really know her? How deep was his connection to sun potion and Knox?

I glanced over my shoulder. Anu listed against the backseat door, the ferret wrapped around her neck like a fur stole. Cordelia, having tossed a water bottle and some bandages over the seat to Biggs, was methodically using a hand wipe to remove all traces of blood and smoke from her person.

"There's a good road." Rachel slowed the car. "Hardly any scent of human to it. Doesn't look like it's been used much."

"Take it," I told her, with a glance to the dashboard's clock. It said 4:57 A.M. How was time slipping through our fingers? How'd I lose another hour?

Here was another question—why was Rachel helping us?

I wasn't feeling the love.

Half turned in my seat, I assessed Trowbridge's sister. She had the same hair color but that was about it in terms of a sibling resemblance. His nose was long; hers retroussé. Her features were long like a fox, his were sculpted. But on the other hand? She won in the guess-my-age contest. Every hour of the thirty-seven years my man had lived was written on his face. While Rachel, despite the fact that she had to be in her early forties, could easily pass for her mid-twenties.

She'd reaped the rewards of the easy life. See? Changes in perception. I'd always thought Creemore Weres didn't show their age because they had Fae in them. Mom never looked a day over thirty, and she'd lived a full, long life before she ever laid eyes on my dad's twinkling eyes.

But now I was wondering how much of aging is part of the genes and how much is part of your life experiences. Trowbridge, my beautiful man, was still strikingly handsome, but he was no longer too-pretty-for-words. Nine years in Merenwyn—that's all it took to make him careworn.

I stroked the pointed tip of my ear, thinking about the life of a wolf in the Fae realm.

"Do you have to do that?" Rachel snapped. "You're always calling attention to your . . ."

Fae.

"We're never going to be besties, are we, Rach?" I asked, my tone idle.

Her glance was disgust-tinged. "The very sight of you makes me want to hurl."

"Well, dear sis, I'd pass you a hankie but I need it for the tears streaming from my eyes."

"You're never going to be my sister-in-law. You might

have sweet-talked him into mating with you, but he'll never stand in front of the others to marry you. You're not one of us."

"Old news, Bestie."

"Must we?" said Cordelia wearily.

"Let her get it out," I murmured. There were answers I needed from Rachel and this was the first time she'd exchanged more than two words with me.

"I hate the Fae. They've ruined my life. I lost my family, piece by piece, because my father allowed a Fae to live on pack land." Spigot open, words streamed from Rachel. "Every time I see you, I'm reminded that my son is dead. If you weren't my brother's consort, I'd have claimed my justice."

"I didn't go looking for Stuart," I said. "He came for me." Her darling son had broken down the door to the apartment I'd shared with my aunt. Then he'd beaten me up, and promised to do pretty much the same things she'd just threatened me with. In the end, I'd unleashed my magic on him. But I'd left him alive, though he'd been duct-taped to a water radiator, and had lost a few, much needed, brain cells.

If I'd only known how much trouble he'd turn out to be, I'd have . . . No. I wouldn't have killed him then. I hadn't crossed the line into murder then.

I sighed. "Rachel, I'm going to say this once. I did not kill your son."

"I don't believe you."

"How very predictable. If you hate me—and all things Fae—why are you helping us now?"

"If I don't, my brother will die."

"Sisterly love," I said slowly. "I can understand that. But I watched you yesterday. Where was all your family pride when Trowbridge asked the pack to pledge their loyalty? You should have been the first to step up—

Trowbridges united and all that—but you were the last to take your vows, weren't you?"

"I had to think carefully."

I snorted. "About what? Me diluting your family bloodlines? Are you really such a—"

"I'm doing this for Petra," she said.

"Your daughter?"

"She's developing a flare," she said, her tone pitched a half note below belligerent.

"Like your brother's?" I frowned.

"Like an Alpha's," she replied. "Like my brother's, and my father's, and his father's before him. Petra can already ignore the moon call longer than I can. At fifteen, she's stronger than most males her age." A cold smile. "Faster too. Every moon I have to force her to promise me that she won't be the first to pull down the prey. She doesn't understand. She thinks I'm trying to hold her back," she said wearily. "She can't help testing herself in other ways. She's already proved that she's a better tracker than me, and I'm one of the pack's best."

"Jealous of your own daughter, Bestie?"

"Never!" she snapped. "I am proud of her. She's the finest thing I've ever done."

And thus, Stuart's hero-worship roots for Mannus were exposed. With Rachel for a mother, his odds of being deemed the prodigal son were as remote as one of those child actors breezing past their teens without paparazzi pictures.

"Let me get this straight," I said. "You're proud of your daughter but you don't want her to become an Alpha. Doesn't that strike you as a tad retro in thinking?"

"Have you ever met a female Alpha?"

I'm guessing my tenure as Alpha-by-proxy didn't count in her recollection. When I didn't reply, she said tersely, "There hasn't been one in over seventy years."

"So they're rare." I shrugged. "It doesn't mean—"

"Edith ruled for less than half a year before she had an accident."

Edith the Alpha? Now there was a name to inspire fear. I raised my eyebrows. "Did she have a suspicious accident?"

"Very," she said grimly. "They killed her."

"Which they?" Her brain had more twists than a mountain road.

"They!" she snapped helpfully. "They—the men in charge. The NAW, or the Great Council. It doesn't matter which one of them ordered it. It could have even been someone from within her own pack." Her hands tightened on the wheel. "Our men are misogynist throwbacks. Each and every one of them."

I thought of Trowbridge's hands cupping my face. "Your brother isn't."

"How well do you know him?" Rachel shut up as a car driven by a mortal woman passed us, heading in the opposite direction, then added, "Humans have no issue with their women being equal."

There were a few million women who might disagree with that sweeping statement.

"Their women lead troops, rule countries, head companies, and make important decisions all the time. But our men don't want any part of it. They want us to keep to the pack. Stay home. Raise the kids. We're allowed to work outside of the home, but if any of us want a real career . . ."

Rachel was one froth away from spittle flying.

"Stay where we belong—that's what they all want. All we're good for is to bring children into the world," Rachel carried on, full rant. "And if we can't turn out a litter of boys then their eyes start to roam."

My gaze rolled toward Cordelia. She mouthed "TMI"

before rolling her lips back into one of her trademark gum-baring grimaces.

Trowbridge's sister's hands were claws on the wheel. "Our men forget that we're biologically engineered to protect. We can do the job because we know the value of what we're defending. And they know it . . . that's why there's no room on their council for a strong woman." Her gaze was fixed on some point ahead on the road. "Petra has everything required to be an Alpha. The bloodline and the natural ability."

I went back to stroking my ear. "And you're worried that if Bridge is gone, she'll want to step into the role."

Her nod was thoughtful. "She's not ready. She needs a few years to refine her abilities and to form the right relationships inside the pack. She'll need support when the opportunity is right."

"You coldhearted bitch," accused Cordelia.

We'd arrived at the same conclusion simultaneously. "You're using Bridge as a place warmer," I said incredulously. "You want everything lined up for Petra so that she can step into the role of the Alpha of Creemore. So much for Trowbridge collecting an old age pension." I didn't even have to glance back to Cordelia. Her scent broadcasted a swift shift from banked caution to flat-out aggression. "Are you nuts?" I asked Rachel. "Hello? I'm his mate. Do you think I can't read between the lines? When the time is Petra-ripe, you're going to wipe out your brother."

Her glance was swift and without any expression. "I won't have to do anything to Robbie. He makes enemies as easily as you do. Sooner or later one of you will cross the wrong person. I thought Mannus was going to bring the council down on us before I was ready, but my kid brother is twice as bad . . . Bridge got everyone's back up so quickly." The paved segment of the road ended and the car coasted onto a gravel road. "What I'm giving you is time."

"That's why you asked Bridge to come home," I said.

"Mannus was sick," she said reflectively. "As much as I loved my son, he never had it in him to be leader. No one in the pack could step into the job like my daughter. But she wasn't ready and if she stepped up too soon . . ." She shrugged. "I needed Bridge."

"Even though returning to Creemore was as risky for him as wearing antlers during hunting season." I stared hard at Trowbridge's sister. "Don't you have any real feelings for anyone other than your daughter?"

"I loved Robbie once," she said stiffly. "I half raised him. But he screwed up. He should have been there the night the Fae crossed the gates, instead of in a bar drinking."

"He returned home in time but he was knocked out."

"He was impaired and easy prey," she said, her tone inflexible. "You never saw the house after the massacre. You didn't fill up bucket after bucket with hot water and bleach. You didn't scrub the walls. Don't you make excuses for him. He was a party boy. Always looking for a way to escape his duties. My son turned out to be no better."

"Your brother is not the man he was. The things he's gone through have changed him. He's—"

"I am not interested in hearing you talk about my brother." She hissed through her teeth as the car hit a pothole. "I kept my ear to the ground. I listened. Robbie the rogue wolf behaved exactly like Robbie my spoiled kid brother. Irresponsible. Drifter. Drank too much."

The ferret chattered in distress.

"Robson Trowbridge may have been all those things you said he was," I said, holding on to my temper with both hands. "Maybe he was an alcoholic with serious commitment issues once, but he's not like that anymore."

"I don't see any change!" she shouted. "He chose you for his mate!"

"We belong together!" I shouted back. "And I'm damn well not going to apologize for being Fae or his mate anymore! Not to you. Not to the pack. Not to anyone."

Or to myself. That ends now.

The air in the vehicle was too close—a swirl of anger from Cordelia and Rachel and a hovering question mark of fear and misery from Biggs. I rolled down the window, and breathed through my mouth, silently counting to myself. *One Mississippi . . . don't hurt her . . . two Mississippi . . . I need all the muscle I can muster . . . three Mississippi . . . I have to deal with Biggs yet . . . four Mississippi . . . lunging at her throat would be a bad, bad thing . . .*

Goddess, I was exhausted. I leaned my aching head against the door frame just in time for the truck to hit a particularly deep pothole.

I straightened. Slowly, like my temple wasn't going "ow, ow, ow."

She'd aimed for the rut deliberately. A person with borderline Asperger's could figure that out with one glance at the satisfied curl of her lip. The pure childishness of her action should have enraged me—I'd been trembling on the edge of a good flameout— but all it did was make me look at Trowbridge's sister with detachment. *Emotional bitch, is she? Given to pinches and the like?*

"Let me hit her," Cordelia bit out. "Just one good slap."

"One of us needs to drive," Rachel said. "One of us needs to watch the traitor. And *she* can't drive because the steering wheel will burn her hand."

I couldn't help it—I laughed. "You're talking about

cold iron, right? Well there, you're partially right, Miss Misinformed. Pure Faes can't tolerate contact with cold iron. But I'll bet you my last Cherry Blossom against your entire stack of outdated encyclopedias that a Fae could sit in this truck and not feel much more than a tad faint-headed. You know why? Because the iron used isn't a pure cold element anymore. It's been melted—gone through a fire hotter than hell—and been mixed with stuff like carbon and sulfur and manganese. It's come out of the fire wearing a different name. Steel."

My tone hardened. "Your brother has walked through fire in Merenwyn. Whatever he saw and did there turned him into who he was always supposed to be—an Alpha of the most extraordinary kind. One with steel in his blood. So don't you *ever* speak negatively about him in my presence again." My heart started slamming into my chest. "You may be taller, you may be older, and God knows you've got more wolf in you. But I've got an inner-bitch who's fed up to her canines with hearing shit spewed about her mate, and a Fae who'd gleefully squeeze you until every single one of your ribs was broken."

Merry's chain bit into my neck as she pulled herself up out of my cleavage. My pal was still the color of burned butter, still cool to the touch, but she was mad enough to muster a rapid pulse of angry red light from the center of her amber belly. Blip, blip. Asrai for "Screw you, Wolf-bitch."

With a nod to the pendant looking about ready to self-ignite, I added, "Not only that, but I've got a personal bodyguard who has a personal prejudice against anyone named Scawens."

"And a surrogate mother," drawled Cordelia, "who has chewed through more chicken-breasted, bandy-legged divas than Elizabeth Taylor chewed through men."

Rachel stopped smiling.

We drove another thirty feet, a family road trip gone decidedly wrong.

She braked in front of a driveway that hadn't seen a set of tires for a good long time. "I will help you find Brenda and then I'm gone," she said. "The rest is up to you. If you fail, I need to be with Petra." All business, she took a snootful of the night air. "Kids come here. But only at night. No fully grown human has visited this place for a while."

"It will do," I said.

Beech trees had tried to embrace the boarded-up house. Their long boughs stretched over the tin roof, offering whatever protection gained by its leafless branches. Kids had partied here—teenagers who'd left the burned-out fire pit and several dust-filmed wine bottles stacked into a tower.

Biggs sat on the backdoor stoop. Sweat trailed down either side of his throat. His body had expelled one slug and was working on the other. "I didn't mean to betray the pack."

"You withheld the fact that you were acquainted with Knox's girlfriend," I said flatly. "You think that doesn't qualify? And you lied to your Alpha."

I didn't even know you could.

"She's *not* his girlfriend."

My hands fisted into two plump and swollen boxing gloves. "When Knox had zero seconds to send the most important video of his life, he sent it to Brenda Pritty, not his boss. Her scent is all over his wallet and that bottle of sun potion. She was his girlfriend." Bile in my gut, rising, rising. "Damn your hide. While we were running from the NAW, you were texting Knox's woman. You led them right to us."

"You think I was just going to hand her to Bridge on a plate?" he said, with traces of his usual beleaguered belligerence. "She was tied up with Knox, and the Alpha of Creemore is not the type of guy who forgives people. You saw what he did to Fatso."

"So you chose some girl you hardly knew over your own pack."

His expression hardened. "Isn't that what Bridge did?"

Cordelia sucked in her breath sharply.

"Believe what you want," he said after a beat. "When I met her two summers ago, she used a different name. I didn't connect the dots between Becci and Brenda until tonight."

A lie. Or a rationalization so deep that he couldn't see the light of truth from the bottom of the hole he'd dug for himself. He had to have known who she was. He was a wolf and their nose can recall every person they ever crossed paths with.

Rachel let out a snort of disgust. "What is it with you people? Don't any of you use your real name?"

"Only if absolutely forced to," retorted Cordelia. With a stage grimace, she turned from a bush she'd been inspecting. Near its base, a used condom hung from a spindly branch.

"Brenda Pritty's scent was on the bottle of sun potion, Biggs," I said. "And her personal perfume was all over Knox. That didn't twig your scent recall?"

"She's been drinking that sun potion shit. Her signature has changed," he replied, his eyes downcast. "Not a lot but . . ." He paused to lift shoulders that appeared to be heavily weighted with remorse. "Enough for me to doubt what I was smelling."

"This is bullshit." Rachel hissed, leaving the truck where Anu waited. "That one there"—she jerked her chin toward Cordelia—"can spritz himself all he wants but I can still smell the man under his French perfume. A scent is a scent."

A flush spread across Bigg's cheeks. "I couldn't believe my nose, okay?"

"Have you been sleeping with her?" I demanded. "Working with her and Knoxs?"

"No," he said sharply. "I told you. I haven't seen her in two years." A silent plea flitted across his face. "The girl I knew as Becci was supposed to be dead—don't you understand? The halfling I loved *died* two years ago. All this time, I thought she was gone. All this time I've been . . ." His expression turned to wood and his voice trailed off.

Mourning her, I thought, watching the shadows grow in his eyes.

"Who was Brenda Pritty to you, Biggs?"

"A really pretty blonde," he said, chin up, trying for flippant and failing.

So very badly failing.

His gaze sank and he bent his head to study the ground. Evidently, he didn't find any life answers carved in the dirt by the toe of his Keds, because he reached to pluck a small stone from the weedy base of a clump of crabgrass. "She was a halfling. And a runaway." He straightened, rolling the piece of granite between his fingers. "A girl who didn't know that she had wolf blood in her."

His mouth worked, making him look both bitter and broken, and then he shook his head. "I met her in Toronto. Two summers ago. I fell in love with her. We had a couple months together and she disappeared. Since then, I thought she was dead."

With a huff of self-disgust, he flung the pebble into the brush.

"I've been asking myself all day—why didn't she call me? She knew where I was. My cell number's never changed. She didn't even try to contact me to let me know that she was all right." He winced suddenly, victim to another muscle spasm. When he could talk, he said, "When I caught her scent . . . I couldn't believe what my nose was telling me. Becci was alive. And then I realized that if my Becci was alive, she'd been living with Knox under the name of Brenda Pritty. And that she'd been with him for a long time. Probably since the night she disappeared."

Truth, I thought.

"That's why it took me so long to accept what my nose was telling me." His voice was rinsed of all emotion. "That's why I didn't really want to believe it was her until I saw her first text on his phone."

"When was that?" Cordelia asked. "Last week? Last month?"

"Last night," he said. "Before Trowbridge interrogated Newland. You guys were upstairs. I was checking Knox's cell to see if it was fully charged when her message came in. I was going to call you but . . ."

Arms folded, Cordelia said dryly, "You stopped to read it first."

A rough nod from Biggs. "Brenda didn't know Knox was dead. Her message said, *Where r u????*" He examined his sweating palms with a fierce frown, then dried them methodically on the legs of his jeans.

"Biggs!" said Cordelia sharply.

"I was still telling myself, 'It can't be her,'" he said, staring blindly at the wet drag marks on his denim. "Then I saw it."

"Saw what?" I asked.

"She ended the message with . . ." He sighed with exasperation then grabbed the rickety railing and painfully hoisted himself to his feet.

"Careful," said Cordelia. "No sudden moves."

"I have to show you," Biggs muttered. He shambled

across the yard to drop to his knees in front of the fire pit. He gathered a handful of ash, which he carefully sprinkled on the ground. Then, using his finger, he traced "^-+-^" in the dust. "I saw that and then I knew. Brenda Pritty was the halfling I fell for two years ago in Toronto." He gently touched one of the symbols resembling a pointed roof. "She always signed off with this. Her wolf was calling and she just didn't know it. Those roof peaks are ears."

Rachel let out an impatient huff. "He betrayed the pack for some slut who didn't even give him her real name. Either kill him or make him tell us where she is."

"Shut up," I said, my gaze fixed on Biggs's perspiring face. We were moving both too slowly—what time was it now?—and too fast. Rushing toward a point where the winds of fate would collide in the perfect storm.

Cordelia cleared her throat. "God knows I hate to agree with Rachel but—"

"Don't make me tell you to shut up too," I said softly.

Biggs bowed through another muscle spasm. When it was over, he lifted his shirt to study his chest. The bullet's flattened point was visible just below the surface of his skin below his right nipple. It would break through soon. "I've got to take this off," he said in a distracted voice. Fingers trembling, he worked the buttons. When he'd pushed the final one through the last hole he sighed like an old man who'd slipped off his shoes.

He sank back on his heels, his shirt gaping. "We had sixty-three days together. A summer and a few days of fall as I watched her getting closer and closer to answering the call of the moon. I knew it was going to happen. Probably in the next cycle, her body would try to change into her wolf. And she was going to die. All torn up. I'd promised myself that I'd be there for her. That if anyone was going to take her to the woods, it would be me."

Almost impossible for me not to flick anxious glances at the flexing skin beneath Biggs's nipple. "I loved her," he said quietly. "I loved her more than any other girl I've met. I thought she was . . ."

His.

Biggs's shoulders slumped. "But a couple days before the full moon, she disappeared. I couldn't find her anywhere and I flipped out . . . When I couldn't find her trail I went to him for help. The little prick . . . he drank the beer I bought him, ate the wings, wiped his mouth with a napkin. Then he told me he'd found out about my 'skank' and that since I didn't have any balls, he'd done the right thing. He said, 'I put her down like the mutt she was.' "

"Who?" I broke in. "Mannus?"

Hate flashed over his face. "You think I'd go to him?" His gaze swiveled toward Rachel. "No, I went to her son. He was always going on about what a great family of trackers he came from." Loathing drenched his words. "Stuart said that he'd taken her up north and 'put her down.' The son of a bitch told me he left her body there for the animals."

"But Stuart was lying," I said.

He nodded. "I believed him. I should have made the prick suffer more before I killed him."

"It was you," Rachel said in a shaking voice. "You killed Stuart. Not my brother's bitch . . . you!"

"I should have gutted him," he goaded. "He was a worthless piece of shit!"

Words chosen to inflame. Rachel launched herself at him with a screech. He tumbled right over onto his back. She straddled him to choke the life out of him.

"Don't do that," I shouted, starting to reach to grab her.

My hands.

Rachel looked up, from under her lashes, a lupine shadow across her face. Her posture that of a wolf protecting her kill. With murderous intent, she tightened her stranglehold until all ten of her knuckles shone whitely. Biggs didn't fight back.

Oh no he doesn't. He doesn't get to choose death-by-bitch.

Faced with the fact that she was stronger than me and any attempt at hauling her off him was going to be an ow-fest, and about as effective as tearing a barnacle off the hull of a boat, I did what I had always wanted to do to Stuart Scawen's mother. I kicked her.

Hard as I could. Right in the ribs.

She pivoted to bare her teeth at me. *Go ahead, give me an easy target.* The next kick was aimed for her pearly whites. She intercepted my swinging foot, twisted it, and down I went. Another face-plant. *Has my Goddess got something against my face?* Then she was on my back faster than I could shout, "Who has reflexes that fast?"

Enough.

Green light streamed from my right hand. "Get her," I snarled. Spitting sparks, my magic swiftly formed itself into a cable of got-you-bitch, twisted over my shoulder, and—judging from Rachel's strangled gasp—hooked itself around her neck.

"What is that!" she got out before my magic turned itself into a twist tie. A second later, Rachel's claws slipped from my throat, and she became the Were-bitch payload in my catapult. Right over my head she went in a blur. Thump! She landed right in front of me. Kind of like a meal. On her back, still uselessly clawing at the green coil squeezing her neck.

"Kill her." That's what I heard from my inner-bitch.

"Yes," murmured my Fae.

Eyes burning, I stood. "Release."

My serpent gave the Were one more squeeze, then sulked off to coil presumably over my head. I'm not sure.

I was building up toward a well-deserved release. I let Rachel cough twice before I bent forward. "You want to know what that was? Tightening around your neck like a noose? That was me—my magic. You can't see it, can you? It's just above my head right now. Waiting for me to tell it what to do. Bam! You won't even see it coming." I leaned down until I could feel her breath warm my face. "And this, Bestie, is the *other* part of me. Say hello to my flare."

Chapter Eighteen

So much for being invited to Thanksgiving dinner. I released my inner light and not in a good way. That close, there was no way to avoid the glare of my fed-up flare. It didn't bathe her, it fried her. Before she'd even made a fist, the dominance duel was over.

Perhaps I held her pinned under the nasty for a moment longer than required. I'm not a saint. It felt good. It felt right. Fae-me preened, my inner-bitch swelled.

All of me was in accord. Turning her into charred bacon was the right thing to do.

A few sparks before total eyeball incarnation, Cordelia's hand touched my shoulder. "One would assume you've proved your point, dearest," she said in a carefully neutral voice. "The sun is starting to climb. We have so little time." A nail dug into my tense muscles. "Hedi, do you hear me?"

That would be a yes. But my inner-bitch was saying, "Turn that woman into a charcoal briquette."

On the other hand, my eyes are flaming.

"He killed my son," I heard Rachel rasp as my flare dowsed. "Over a halfling. I want justice."

Wearily, I slid off her. "You're not getting it now. Hear me? You will not touch him until I tell you that you can." I tested the concept of lifting my eyelids.

Crap. Cue the usual pain and misery. "One day, I will get mine back," she promised Biggs.

"Yeah, yeah." I squinted against the early morning light streaming through the base of the trees. *What time does that make it? Six-thirty? Seven?* Anxiety tensed a gut that already roiled.

Merry began to ratchet down her chain, heading toward my heart. "No," I said, capturing her. "You've pushed yourself as far as you can go. I'll get over this."

Biggs sat with his head buried into his folded arms. A shimmer of sweat coated the back of his neck.

"You stupid boy," Cordelia hissed. "You should have chosen from one of the bitches in the pack. A halfling! You knew there could be only one outcome to that story."

He raised his eyes to meet hers. "I couldn't stop myself. The first time I saw her . . ." Cordelia's expression was chilled, and his gaze wandered to the blank canvas of the clapboard siding. "She was sitting on the sidewalk outside the Eaton Centre and she couldn't panhandle for shit. I passed her Tim Horton's cup five, maybe six, times before she looked up and said, 'Why don't you take a picture?'"

Cordelia said sternly, "You should have kept walking."

"I couldn't have if I tried," he replied slowly. "I could smell the wolf on her and it . . ."

Don't say "spoke to me."

He fingered his mouth, trying to hide the bittersweet smile curving it. "I never believed in soul mates before. I'd always thought it was bullshit—putting a polite face on wanting to fuck someone. But when you meet the right person it's nothing like that . . ."

"My One True Thing," I whispered.

Cordelia's expression pained when Biggs turned to me with almost pathetic eagerness. "She listened to me, you know? When I talked she really listened." Then, weary disillusionment swept his features, and I got a teasing impression of what he'd look like twenty years from now if he was given the option of living them.

I said I'd kill anyone who stood in the way. Anyone who betrayed us.

"I gave her money," he said. "Found her an apartment and kept her refrigerator full until she got a job in a confectioner's shop off Queen Street. Never accepted a dime from me after that. I was proud of her independence but now I wonder if she was already . . . Anyways, it was the best and worst of my life." A small, bittersweet smile. "She always smelled like sugar to me after she started working."

Still does. There's sugar to her scent.

"You should have trusted us," I told him.

"After what Bridge did to the NAW guy? No way was I taking that chance with Brenda." Suddenly, he hunched over in acute pain, his palm flattened over the place where the bullet fought to break skin. A groan broke from him.

Don't touch him. Don't offer help.

"I hope it hurts like hell!" shouted Rachel.

"Be quiet!" I snapped in frustration.

"Keep it down if you can, Biggs," murmured Cordelia. "Anu is in the truck. She doesn't understand what's happening or why."

"I'm trying." Biggs moaned, rocking himself.

I paced a circle around him until he straightened. When he lifted his gaze, I asked in a hard voice, "Where is Brenda?"

He tilted his head to consider me. "So I tell you and you bring her in front of the council. And what will happen then, eh?"

"We'll explain the circumstances, and she'll give her evidence."

"And then they'll put the halfling down," he said harshly. *Yes.*

"I'll hurt you, Biggs. I don't want to but I will." Part of me—the one that was cold and distant—knew it would be like shooting fish in a barrel. Hell, all I'd have to do was squeeze the trigger a few times and then wait to interrogate him during the inevitable agonizing muscle spasms. Could I do that? Shoot the guy I'd shared more dinners with than I could count? Aim at his various body parts with the intention to hurt and maim? Hurt the guy who'd stood in line at Walmart to buy my historical romance novels?

A rivulet of bright Were blood snaked down Biggs's ribs.

The copper scent spoke to my inner-wolf (prey, weakness) but it said squat to my conflicted emotions.

He inhaled sharply through his nose. "All those times you tried to change into your wolf and you couldn't . . . I used to think, why her? How come Hedi can resist the moon? She's no more pure-blooded than Brenda." The trickle of blood—wolf and pain tinged—widened into a thin stream. "And then your brother shows up, and I find out that he can change into his wolf."

Biggs shook his head. "And then I knew you could face the moon. Transform into your Were. You just don't *want* to. Jesus, I hated you yesterday. When I knew that . . ." His tone turned venomous. "What makes you so special, Hedi? Why do you get the pass? You're a half blood, just like Brenda, and no one's put your name on any list." He shook his head in self-disgust. "All those months I stood by you because I thought you were like Brenda. But you're not like her at all."

"Where is she?

He lifted his gaze so I could read his condemnation and resolve. "I don't know."

"I will hurt you, Biggs. I will do whatever is necessary."

"You'd do it, wouldn't you? You and Bridge—you're no better than Mannus."

"Neither of us is anything like him."

"Yeah? You tell yourself that's why you're doing whatever it takes. Bring out the silver chains and the knife." He lifted his chin. "Go ahead. It won't help. I know jack."

Merry warmed, then unfurled a long strand of ivy. She lengthened it, flattening all the articulated leaves along the strand until there was only one at the razor-sharp tip. "Shall I?" she silently asked.

I could let her torture him. She hadn't minded turning Stuart's cheek into ground beef. Easy-peasy. I'd stepped back and let her wring information out for me before. *When I was dodging responsibility and self-knowledge like a cokehead avoiding rehab.*

Suddenly, Biggs flinched. The slug, having received one final push, tumbled to his lap. Without a word, he plucked the flattened bullet from the folds of his jeans, then flicked it into the open fire pit. Courage and stoicism—that's something I hadn't associated with him before.

I studied his set jaw. His expression telegraphed the desire to be noble, the determination to hold tough, the damn doggedness of the soon-to-be-martyred. He was going to push himself to the limits to protect the girl he loved. He was going to face the heartless inquisitor.

Which would be me. Hedi, the Torturer.

Goddess, he was right. I was Mannus, planning to use pain and disfigurement to get what I wanted. Mouth dry, I said to Rachel, "Get me the rifle."

"Let me do it," whispered Cordelia. "You don't know how to use it."

"I can point and shoot." I shook my head, grimly watching Trowbridge's sister lean into the truck to retrieve the weapon.

Just do it. When Rachel passes you the rifle, raise it to

your shoulder, aim for Bigg's thigh, and pull the trigger.
Then do it again, choosing body parts—foot, hand, bi-
cep, gut—until he breaks.
You must.
Otherwise Trowbridge will die, and then you will die.

Rachel handed me the gun. Over her shoulder, I saw
Anu peering at us through the back passenger window.
Her nose was flattened against the glass.

You had no problem killing Dawn when she went after
Trowbridge. This isn't much different. If you don't have
the information . . . And come on. He betrayed us. He
texted with Knox's girlfriend and didn't tell us he knew
her. He's been hiding things all night. He's still covering
up. I can see it in his eyes.

The gun weighed a ton. I fit my finger into the trigger
and lifted it.

"Butt braced in the shoulder," said Cordelia. "Otherwise you'll feel the kick." Her voice was too controlled,
too modulated. "Choose your target, then release the
safety."

Sweat rolled down my back as I picked a spot about
three inches above his knee. "Brenda's not worth it."

"She is to me," said Biggs.

Don't make me do this. "I order you as Alpha-by-
proxy—"

"You going to use your flare on me?"

I only wish I could. My Fae and I? We were depleted.

"I didn't think so," he said, lifting his hot eyes to snare
mine. "Stuff it, Hedi. Do what you think you have to."

Bile. Up it went, burning my esophagus. Why was this
so frickin' hard? It was simple: it came down to me and
mine or him. And—not to get too dramatic—the potential for the annihilation of mankind. Because if I didn't
save Trowbridge, then I'd die, and Lexi would soon wither

away—taking the Old Mage with him—and bad things could drip into this world.

Meh. I don't give a flying fig about the rest of the world. I did, however, dread hurting my slacker friend. Because he bought me books. Because he saved me once. When the odds had been against us at the pond, Biggs had come to our rescue carrying a shotgun loaded with pellets and a gut filled with repressed resentment. The former he'd used to blow a huge hole through Stuart Scawens, the latter had added rage to his cry, "This first one was for Becci!"

I should have asked him who she was but I never had.

"Do you know where the safety is?" asked Cordelia.

"Yes, I know where is," I said through my teeth.

This. Was. So. Unfair.

I used to be able to tick off those I called "mine" in this world on two fingers: Merry and Lou. The rest of the world's population could drop like flies and, providing they didn't turn into flesh-eating zombies, I wouldn't have given a rat's ass. But Trowbridge . . . damn him. He'd opened me up to feeling. Then he'd brought back my twin, the other part of my frozen heart. If only for a night, my Trowbridge had reunited us and, in so doing, had restrung the bonds between brother and sister. Making me almost whole again.

Now look at me. I had more "mines."

Bottom line, I loved them as much as Rachel loved her daughter. How's that for irony? She—the future Alpha's Helicopter Mom—knew deep affection for only one person. Not her brother, not her pack, and definitely not her errant husband. While I—the former Call-Me-an-Island—now loved five. Or six. No, five now.

Harry's dead and my hands are beginning to tremble.

I flicked Rachel a glance of loathing. She stared down

at the road, her arms crossed, chin lifted so that she could graze on the scents streaming by.

Wait a minute.

"Rachel?" I called, returning my gaze to the leg I was planning to shatter. "Is Biggs telling the truth? Does he really not know where to find Brenda?"

Two "Mississippis" before she reluctantly replied. "Yes."

"Told you." Biggs's voice sounded rusty.

The weapon sagged in my hands as I swung around to glare at Helicopter Mom. "And you were going to let me shoot him?"

Rachel lifted a shoulder. "There's evasion in his scent."

Cordelia sighed. "It's in his body language too, Hedi," she said reluctantly. "He's not telling you everything he knows."

Tell me something I didn't know.

I swung the business end of the weapon back toward my perspiring friend. "So in all those texts you exchanged with Brenda—did you offer to be her white knight?"

Bingo. Biggs blinked.

"I'm going to aim for high on your thigh. You might want to remember that this is the first time I've ever pulled the trigger." Biggs's hand shifted to cover his privates. "Where were you going to hook up?"

Defiantly, he clamped down his lips. Though his teeth were busy. I could see them gnawing away at the inside of his cheek.

"Tell her, boy," said Cordelia tersely.

I thumbed off the safety. "Think what Whitlock will do when he finds her. Then think what will happen when you don't show up and she makes a run for it—where's she going to go?"

"Make me a promise." The pulse beat frantically at his throat. "And I'll tell you everything."

Promises, promises. Everybody wanted to extract one

of those buggers from me. "Biggs, you know how good mine are."

"Yeah, I do," he answered. "Which is why I want you to give your word."

Talk about kneecapping your opponent. "What do you want?"

"If Brenda can give you the evidence you need, give me your word that you won't take her to the council."

I shook my head. "Sorry, I can't do that. I need to be loaded for bear when I face them. She's my star witness for our defense." And maybe soon after that, the condemned for the prosecution.

His gaze darted to Cordelia. "If we can find evidence at her home—"

"Biggs . . ." she said, shaking her head.

"Please," he said, turning to me again. "You know how good I am with computers." Now he was blinking. Rapidly. Almost as fast as words were tumbling out of his mouth. "There must be bank accounts or a client list."

Pity swelled to do a half lap with regret. "Documentation would be a bonus. But we'd have to find it and we—"

"It will be with her," he broke in. "She'll give it to us."

"Sorry, Biggs. They can say we doctored the evidence. Downloaded a file into his computer."

"They'll have truth sensors," he pleaded.

"But I don't have scent."

"Then I'll be your witness. I'll tell them everything I know. About her. About the texts. About what Knox did."

"Words, Biggs. Just—"

"I *do* have a scent and they'll know by that I'm not lying. I'll tell them the truth. Please, Hedi. I'll go to the council with you and tell them everything I know. The texts. Everything I've seen or heard."

"Chihuahua, they'll execute you for betraying the pack," said Cordelia.

"Biggs, it won't make any difference," I said, my wrist aching. "Without Knox she'll run out of sun potion. When the moon calls, she'll be alone in that forest again."

That's when the worst expression crossed his face. I'd hardened myself to anguish. I'd told my nose not to interpret the fox-sour scent streaming from him as fear. I'd held the gun steady on his perfectly formed thigh when my instincts were screaming, "This will ruin you." But this? I wasn't ready for this blank slate of a face. Or the fatalism behind his eyes.

This was the man he might not ever get the chance to grow to become. It all came down to me. Either I brought him in, or the pack dealt him justice . . . whatever I decided in the backyard of this forgotten house . . . it all fell on me.

The girl who might not grow up either.

"Not if you let me take care of her first," he said, his voice raw. "If you let me do it—not them—she won't be afraid. She won't feel pain. It will be fast."

Oh, sweet heavens. Now? Now he turns into Mr. Nobility?

"Don't be a weakling!" said Rachel, sidling up to my shoulder. "You have him where you want him." Her patience snapped and her voice rose to a near scream. "Shoot him! Make him tell you everything we need to know!"

"Back up and shut up."

"He's not important," she insisted. "He's just a—"

"Don't you freakin' say 'pawn.' No one's life amounts to being a 'pawn.'" And yet, that's what I was making of Brenda, wasn't I? If Trowbridge needed to gut Newland to show his strength to another Alpha, just what would the council feel required to do to showcase theirs?

Biggs said, "I swear, Hedi. I'll die before I let you take her to them."

"Shoot him!" Rachel screeched. "He'll break."

"I won't," he vowed.

"This is why Bridge should never have chosen you for his mate!" She was so angry I could feel her heat warming my right shoulder. "You don't have the guts or the mentality of an Alpha!"

"I don't need Alpha guts," I said, steadying the rifle. "Been there, done that, and burned the postcard. Trust me. If Bridge and I walk out of that council meeting, I will bow out of pack politics. You guys can knock yourselves out fighting over boundary lines."

"And you'll go back to hiding in your trailer," she said in disgust. As if that was worse than shooting someone you broke bread with.

"Haven't you heard? I'm living in the big house now. I sleep on your mother's side of the bed in the master bedroom. The mattress is little lumpy but I can get used to that. The thing I can't tolerate is the wallpaper in your old room. That's going. I want our kids to grow up with something a little more cheerful."

"You—"

Rachel's tirade was interrupted mid-foam by the sound of breaking glass. I turned just in time to see her do a tree fall into the fire pit. Cordelia shrugged unrepentantly and tossed the neck of the broken wine bottle to the turf. "She was boring me."

I licked my lip. "Tell you what, Biggs. If the evidence is sufficient to stand without her, and you come along to be the witness, we've got a deal." He nodded and I lowered the gun. "Where can we find Brenda?"

"She wanted to meet me in Bradford West Gwillimbury."

"When?"

"Noon."

And back we go—rats in a maze with no exit.

Glass tinkled on the rocks rimming the fire pit as

Rachel rolled to her knees. "Robbie will never see lunch hour." Her teeth flashed. "Neither will you."

"You never know," I said, baring my own pearly whites. "I might hang in till afternoon tea."

West Gwillimbury wasn't too far—just a few more kilometers farther south on the 400 Highway—but its population was at least ten times the size of Creemore's. Tracking someone by their scent alone would be daunting unless we had a better fix on their location. "Where in Bradford did Brenda want to meet you?"

"At the gas station on the corner of Holland and Ten."

Great. A public place, rife with petrol fumes.

Biggs read the dismay on my face. "But I think she might live in the town—right there in Bradford."

Cordelia murmured, "She and twenty thousand other people."

"Did she say she lived in Bradford?"

"No."

At his reply, Cordelia selected another grimy bottle from the cache of empties, which she began to tap menacingly against her thigh.

"She smelled like candy!" Biggs pitched desperately.

I threw up my hands. "So? Half the time I do, too!"

"Hedi—"

"Make it fast, Biggs." My goodwill had gone hunting.

His Adam's apple bobbed, then he said in a rush, "When we were in the kitchen, Bridge asked me to smell Knox's stuff—I wasn't lying—her scent *has* changed since she started taking sun potion. There's some weird sickly sweet shit to it now but under that I smelled candy . . ." His gaze pleaded. "My Becci *liked* working in that Toronto candy shop. She said it was the coolest thing."

It would be.

Perhaps my gaze marginally softened, because Biggs kept spewing, the car salesman seeing a chink in the armor. "She didn't have any other skills. She would have found a job—"

"Knox probably gave her money for rent."

"No! She wouldn't have let Knox support her. She never accepted a dime from me after she started getting her paychecks. Hedi, she *liked* being around sweet stuff. She liked making chocolates and truffles and . . ."

Come to think of it, I had caught the brief and welcome scents of sugar, butter, and maple syrup when Knox's phone was pulled out from the plastic bag.

"Who's got a cell?" I asked.

A pause, then Rachel said, "I do."

"Find out if there's a confectionary shop in Bradford."

She shot me one of her drearily familiar glares before pulling out her phone. A minute or so later, she said, "There's a Sandra's Sweet Fudge on Holland." She tapped her screen with a curved nail to enlarge the screen. "It's right downtown."

It was better than nothing. I started walking to the truck. "Heigh ho, heigh ho. To Bradford we go."

"Biggs?" inquired Cordelia carefully. "Trunk or back-seat?"

"Trunk."

There's nothing like the contemplation of a spot of B&B to make a girl unbearably conscious of the speed limit. I drove down Bradford's main street at a sedate forty kilometers. Cordelia sat beside me, worrying the lifted edge on her thumb's press-on nail. Rachel and Anu shared the backseat. They'd kept themselves occupied during the drive. Trowbridge's sister had trained a steady glare on my naked neck, while Anu, confused and sorely in need of a translator, had fidgeted.

Cordelia rolled down her window, and a rush of cold wind howled into the vehicle. She wasn't dressed for it—none of us were dressed for the weather. But I was the only one who shivered.

She rolled it back halfway up. "Sorry, darling, but Biggs is sweating worry."

I nodded and kept my eyes peeled.

"There," I said, jabbing a finger to the left.

Sandra's Sweet Fudge was the narrow shop tucked tightly between a small hardware store and Mazie's Consignment. It had a cheerful red awning and a window made for displaying bonbons.

Like the rest of the shops, it was dark.

There was a delivery alley behind the shop, a nice bay for Rachel's vehicle and absolutely no security. "I'll keep an eye out," said Cordelia, sliding into the driver's seat.

Sweet Fudge's sole defense against bonbon burglaries was a flimsy door with a lock that could be opened by a half blind dowager with a hatpin.

No time for finesse.

I kicked the door, aiming for just above the handle. Wood splintered, and the door swung wide on a room that functioned as a makeshift office and supply storage. We eased past a curtain and walked into the retail area.

"Careful!" I said to Rachel when she flicked the lights.

She shrugged. "We'll be in and out before they know it."

I let my gaze roam. Fudge, fudge, everywhere. Chocolate, vanilla, maple syrup. Saliva flooded the back of my mouth. $9.99 a pound? Geesh.

"I've got her," Rachel said.

"So soon?" I whispered, staring at the slab of the good stuff. *I will not steal. I will not steal.*

"Halfling scents are easy. Take a wolf and water it down." She blew some air through her nose.

Really? I inhaled discreetly, but all I could smell was the answer to my stomach pains. "Can you track her?"

"Of course I can," she said confidently.

Goodbye, fudge. I reached past her to flick off the lights. "Okay, let's go."

"Wait." She cast a furtive hard glance toward the truck. Cordelia's head was turned in our direction, her eyes narrowed. Rachel flexed her shoulders as if to rid them permanently of a cramp, then turned to block Cordelia from lip reading. "I can track the halfling, but I won't do it for nothing."

"Fine. I'll get Bridge to write you a check when he's free."

"I don't want his money."

Of course she didn't. She probably wanted our first-born child. "Cut to the chase, Bestie. What do you want?"

"Biggs said your word is good. Is it?"

"It never used to be."

"But it is now, isn't it?" Her smile exposed her white teeth. "This is what I want—for you to stay in Merenwyn. Once you go across the portal, you don't come back."

Life as a wolf among the Fae was not a good life. "No deal," I said through numb lips. "We'll find her without you. Cordelia can hunt her down."

"But as the Drag Queen likes to point out—you've got no time." Rachel lifted both brows in a taunt. "So? Do we have an agreement?"

I studied her, then said, "Yeah, we do."

"Good." She sauntered out the door. Hands on hips, she slowly spun to face west, head lifted, nostrils flared. Then she looked at me and mouthed, "That way."

There went one promise I wasn't keeping.

If I thought it was cold before, it was downright frigid driving along those country back roads, with Rachel hanging out of the open window. It took us fifteen minutes,

and a few backtracks, plus one stop for a tramp up to
a hill for a better sniff of the surrounding area, before
we found the right driveway.

Rachel pointed. "That's it."

I drove past the driveway and kept going for another
hundred feet or so, until we got to a place where trees
grew along the side of the road. I pulled over. Biggs's stink
was almost unbearable, and it was a relief to get out of
the car.

We all trooped to where we could get a good view.

Brenda Pritty's white clapboard bungalow sat on a long
rectangle of land, bordered by two farmers' fields. The
small house looked out of place, a Monopoly piece left
forgotten on an empty board. Someone had taken a chain
saw to the trees that used to grow along the driveway and
the grass around the home and separate garage had been
sheared down to a yellowing stubble.

I studied the place for a moment. "You sure this is it?"

Mouth grim, Trowbridge's sister said, "Yes. I can smell
her. She's in the house."

"Do you smell anyone else?"

Her nose crinkled. "Knox was here at one point, but I
don't smell anything else except her fabric softener." She
wiped her palms along her yoga pants, then said, "I'm
leaving now."

"What?"

"I said I'd find her and I have," she said with a wintry
smile. "The rest is up to you. You said you were worthy of
your position. Well . . . prove it. I'm going."

"If you do, you're going on foot," I said.

"I'm a wolf," she said, walking away. "I could jog all
the way home and not even get winded."

"There's a bald-faced lie," drawled Cordelia. "The coldhearted witch will hitch her way home."

Rachel's running shoes had candy-pink soles. "I'll be waiting to hear how it goes," she threw over her shoulder.

"You're not going to wish me good luck and God-speed?" I called after her.

"I don't believe in either." She took off at a brisk sprint, heading back down the road toward the town.

"Bitch," said Cordelia.

"Yup. In every sense." I gazed at the house, and the road, and those open fields.

My first combat mission, and I didn't have the foggiest idea what to do. Cordelia busied herself checking a weapon that was already in perfect shape. Biggs came up beside me, his hands dug deep into his pockets. Anu sat in the car with her ferret.

Evidently, Moody, Broody, and Duty were tactfully giving me time to think it out.

Though Cordelia couldn't resist putting something into that silence. "We'll have to watch the wind," Cordelia said, casually. "Otherwise we might as well just send a calling card out in advance. Biggs smells like hopeful hound."

"Shut up," Biggs said.

Cordelia slanted a look at him, her eyes narrowing.

"Don't fight now," I said.

From what I could see, there was only one door. It was on the side of the modest bungalow. Someone had cut down all the trees, so no one could sneak up on the place. And then—*who says watching TV rots your mind?*—I got a visual of one of those old war movies, where the British commander stood in front of a very large Allied map. The kind that always had big black arrows indicating a pronged attack.

"Biggs and you come in from the right flank," I said. "I'll drive up to her door in the truck. Hopefully, her attention will be focused on me, not you two." *I hope she doesn't have a gun.* "Anu will wait here until I give the all clear."

My mother hen gave me a good long look, and I read deep approval. "Right," she said briskly. "The brat and I'll come in from the right." Then she set off, moving quickly across the open ground, heading for the thin cover offered by the trees that edged the property line. "Hurry along, Chihuahua. Unless you want me to bring out the rhinestone leash."

Biggs exhaled, then pushed himself away from the car. He walked to the culvert ditch, stared at it as if he wished it was deep enough to drown himself in, then leaped across it. He loped along the tree line, half hunched over, his dark clothing melting into the shadows.

I got in the car. Made a careful U-turn, then headed up the driveway.

Hedi, the Promise Maker.

Hedi, the Almost Brave.

Chapter Nineteen

Talk about anticlimactic. No one twitched the blinds. No one even came to the door for that matter. It was painted white, with a diamond-shaped glass window, set like most of those sixties-era bungalows into the side of the house. I stood on the miniscule porch considering my options.

"Now what?" I whispered to Merry.

My amulet unfurled a strand of twisted ivy, extended it till the tip of the leaf touched the door, then mimed knock-knock.

"It's easy for you to say," I muttered, staring at the door. One kick, that's all it takes the brawny actor's stunt guy. But the wood looked fairly solid. I leaned to the right, cupped my hand and pressed my nose to the window. The television was on but the living room was empty. I laid my ear to the door, straining to hear anyone moving around inside the house. Nothing.

Then, with an inward shrug, I pressed the doorbell.

The ringer was circa 1970s or maybe even earlier. But before it had even got to the dong part of its familiar peal, I heard the sound of a window being pushed open. I lunged for the wooden railing and twisted over it, just in time to see a girl slide leg-first out of a window on the side of the house. She dropped almost soundlessly, then leaned back in to pull out a backpack.

"Hey," I said.

Her expression, on seeing me, could best be described as stricken, like the deer who'd lifted her head and spotted Elmer Fudd. That's all it took and then she darted for the garage faster than I could have said, "Be vewy vewy still."

Maybe it was the long streamer of fright she left in the air. And possibly if I hadn't been thinking about deer and hunters, it wouldn't have happened. But it did. Her dash for freedom sparked my very first "squirrel" moment.

My inner-bitch kicked in. Full force.

Prey—that's what I heard inside my head. *Hunt*—that's what instinct told me to do.

I vaulted over the railing, landing on one knee and one palm. I was in pursuit before my body had time to send a pain message. Hunt! What a glorious thought. No weighing of choices. No stopping to consider the why and whynots. Things were reduced to simple verbs. Run. Catch. Chew.

I tore after her, in a loping run, cutting her off before she'd reached the garage's back door. I slammed into the door with my body. She spun on her heel with a sharp cry and took off in the other direction.

Never do that.

Instantly, my vision telescoped. Everything in the peripheral view disappeared, and my sightline was reduced to one small focal point—her waist, where I knew the vital organs lay ready for my teeth.

Mine.

Brenda made the fatal error of shooting a panicked glance over her shoulder. That small miscalculation was all I needed to narrow the gap. I didn't just tackle her—I sprang—fingers curled like talons, teeth bared.

Touchdown. She let out a shrill scream as we collapsed in a heap.

My game was desperate with fear, and several inches taller than me. In theory she should have rolled on top of me and gone for my throat. Instead she tried to crab-crawl her way out from under me. It was an epic fail. She might have been leggier, but I was heavier. Plus I was in feral heat. Wolf driven, with a bloodlust urging me to rip things.

My arm curled around her neck, and my teeth went right to her throat.

And bam—the second my eyeteeth touched the raised hairs by her hairline she collapsed. With one cry she turned herself into a shivering, whimpering appetizer. Goddess, the sour-sweet taste of her sweat against my tongue filled me with the intense need to bite down. To break skin. To know victory in a way we'd never known before.

"No!" someone cried. "No, Hedi!"

She is my kill. I felt her pulse, right there, pounding against my lips. I could smell her fear, more tasty to me than even the best grade of maple syrup. Every squirm she made, every little ragged pant—it all inflamed me. I growled low in my throat then turned her head sideways so that the long column of her throat was bared.

"Get off her!" Biggs screamed. Hard hands tore at me. I twisted to slash at the interloper. He raised a fist to strike me.

Hit me *will you?*

Anger, so hot, so raw.

I lifted my jaws, felt the anticipation of another lunge, another takedown.

Hunt.

Cordelia came up in a blur of perfume, and swinging foot. Her kick caught him right in the kidneys. He fell to one knee. She grabbed the back of his collar and dragged him out of my reach. "Stay down!" she hissed to him.

I watched her, a hungry dog with juicy bone, feeling

possessive and uncaring that Becci was semimortal, a foot taller, and crying helplessly. Cordelia, no stranger to the hunt, gave me and my prize the space I needed. She picked a point in the air above me, and stared at it, as if it held the answer to some question she'd long wanted to pose.

Casually she said, "It's best if she's not dead."

I could smell the gum Becci had chewed in the morning. The glass of milk she'd drunk before that. My heart was still doing double time, but now I was starting to be aware of the fact that I was spread-eagled over someone who was very, very frightened of me.

Not the wolf in me . . . me.

"Do stop chewing on your toy," Cordelia said, very evenly. "Trowbridge needs her alive."

I reluctantly lifted my lips from the nape of my intended meal's skin.

"That's right," she said.

I breathed in and out from my mouth while my inner-bitch did three circles inside me, looking for a good place to rest. When the smell of Becci's fear struck me as defeat instead of meat, I rolled off her. She crawled away—head down, imaginary tail tucked between her toned thighs.

"Brenda." Biggs caught her near the frostbitten geraniums. "It's okay, it's me."

She stiffened in his arms. Then—and this killed me— her pretty face crumpled like a six-year-old's. "You brought the wolves here," she said in a Kewpie-doll voice. "You said you wouldn't." My wolf lifted her head in renewed interest as her voice got even squeakier. "They're going to hurt me."

Maybe. Maybe not.

"No." He soothed her. "You're safe. I'll make sure nothing happens to you."

Uh-huh.

And with that, she dissolved into another bout of chest-heaving tears. "I'm scared," she wailed.

Biggs curved himself over her. "It's going to be all right."

Everybody's lying through their teeth today.

She swiped at her tears with the back of a shaking hand. "Knox hasn't come back. He was supposed to come and get me and he didn't. I'm so scared."

Biggs's face turned to stone. "Knox is dead, Brenda."

I'd thought she'd *already* dissolved into a sobbing wreck. I was wrong.

The house was small, barely big enough to swing two fat cats. The front of it boasted an open kitchen and a living space anchored by a sagging couch and a brand-new La-Z-Boy. The back end had a bathroom and two bedrooms. The first had a king-sized mattress and smelled like Knox and Brenda. The last was locked.

"Don't go in there!" cried Brenda.

Cordelia's kick broke the lock and sent the door crashing into the wall. She stepped back to let me walk in. There was nothing personal in the room beyond a table strewn with paint tubes—no bed, no bureau, no chair filled with last night's clothing. But the room was a riot of colors and faces. Canvases were propped up against the wall, in some places two or three deep.

So many faces, so many eyes. All of them staring out at the viewer. Despite their elaborate costumes, their figures seemed naked. As if, regardless of some of their formal positions, they'd been caught unawares.

Oh Goddess. Their ears.

"They're all Fae," I whispered in horror.

Cordelia had followed me into the room. Now she abruptly turned to me. "There's no scent of Knox here," she said. "Let's check out the other bedroom."

I'm not a fool. I'd caught the way she'd tried to swing her body so that it blocked the sight of whatever had claimed so much of her attention before her brusque suggestion.

"Step out of the way," I told her.

She slid her hand under my elbow. "You don't need to see this."

I gave her an accommodating smile. "Okay."

She fell for it. The moment she relaxed, I ducked under her arm.

The portrait was exactly the same size as all the rest, roughly twenty-four by thirty-six inches. The subject in question stood in the center of bloody carnage. At his feet, the torn body of a wolf, a rope of intestine streaming from its belly wound. Behind him, a smoking pile of corpses, some of which appeared to be human in shape. Behind that a horrific funeral pyre, silhouettes of blazing trees, and a hellfire sky.

"It's a picture, nothing more," said Cordelia. "Don't let it shake you."

The subject wore a gray shirt, suspenders, a pair of tight pants, and boots. Jammed on his head was a bowler hat.

"Lexi," I said brokenly.

I spun to Brenda who hovered in the hallway. "Who painted these?" I cried.

Her eyes widened and she squeaked, "The fairy does."

"What fairy!"

She cringed. "The ugly one who guards the gates."

"The Gatekeeper comes here? To paint? Does she paint from memory? Do any of these people visit here?"

"Mmm-mmm." Brenda shook her head. "She comes here alone. We go to the pie place and we wait for her. And then she comes and we bring her here and she paints." She slipped into the room and tiptoed to an old-fashioned hourglass and she upended it. Sand dribbled through the narrow neck. "When it gets here"—she pointed to a line drawn on the neck of the glass with a black sharp pen—"we have to leave. The fairy has to go home before all the sand is gone."

"Or what happens?"

"I don't remember. I used to know. Knox told me." Mention of his name was enough to cause tears to well in her baby blues. "I don't remember things like I used to. And her English is weird."

"She speaks our language?"

"She's the Gatekeeper. She's supposed to be able to talk to the Weres. Knox said that's her job. To be there to . . ." Confusion etched three light lines on her forehead. "She's like one of those hostess ladies who show you where to sit at the pie place."

"A guide?"

"That's it!"

Again, I was struck by the same thought. Why would a portal need a gatekeeper? They were already keyed to recognize which blood could pass through their gates. As for having a guide? Wasn't that Merry's and Ralph's job?

"How does she know Lexi?" I murmured to myself.

"Who's Lexi?" asked Brenda.

I pointed to his canvas. "Him."

Brenda studied the picture for a moment. "He's trouble."

"He's in trouble," I corrected.

"Mhhhm-mhhhm," she murmured, with a mulish head wag. "The fairy paints the future."

"What?"

The halfling's eyes rounded and her voice dropped to an impressed whisper. "That's what she paints. She says it's the 'truth that hasn't been revealed.'"

"Total garbage," muttered Cordelia, with a sideways glance in my direction.

Lexi standing in the ruins of civilization?
Not going to happen. I won't let it.

I tore my gaze from Lexi's painting. "We don't have much time," I said to Cordelia. "Let's get what we need and get out."

The evidence was in the master bedroom. There we discovered a plain desk, a stack of bubble envelopes, and Knox's "book," which turned out to be an iPad, loaded with a whole lot of bang-bang movies and a spreadsheet app. The inventory was found inside the near-empty closet's top shelf—a cake box containing vials filled to the neck with sun potion.

Cordelia's mouth pursed as she did a quick count. "A baker's dozen of them." She rotated the bottle she'd picked up, watching the liquid lap against the glass. "Looks like water."

"You're touching it!" Brenda cried. "You're breaking the rules!"

On prodding, Knox's girl revealed that only she could touch the bottles. *After she'd washed her hands.* Because Knox said his scent shouldn't be on anything they send to someone else. That—merely the mention of her deceased beau's name—caused her to burst into loud hiccupping tears again.

And once again, Biggs had looked at me as if he wanted to do violence.

I could see why his protective instincts were stirred. She was about my age, but that's where any useful comparison ended because she was very, very beautiful. Big blue eyes, heart-shaped face surrounded by a nimbus of white-blond hair. But her gaze was vacant and an air of helplessness wove around her. She'd been alone for two days. She'd shown us her empty fridge with an air of bewilderment.

"Has she always been like this?" I asked Biggs.

"No," he said fiercely. "She used to be really smart but she's been taking the potion for more than two years. It's—"

"Turned her into a dimwit?" drawled Cordelia.

"Caused some deterioration," he retorted. "You saw Hedi's brother. The stuff's addictive. It messes you up but good."

Lexi. Be strong. Hold on.

We moved into the kitchen, bringing the iPad with us.

"See if you can find anything we can use to incriminate Whitlock on it." Over Biggs's head, I caught Cordelia's gaze and she nodded, moving into place by his right elbow. A precaution, in case he decided to delete something. I couldn't trust Biggs anymore.

"It's password protected." Biggs's hands hovered over the illuminated keyboard. He threw a tight glance toward Brenda. "Do you know it?"

"It's 'K loves B.' " Brenda sat cross-legged on the sagging couch. She made another knot in the pillow fringe. "He said I should choose something I'd never forget."

Frozen. That's what I'd call Biggs's expression. "Any spaces between the words?"

"Mmm-hmm."

Her murmurs were irritating.

Biggs flexed his knuckles before he tapped in the password. Two minutes later he said, "Here's something interesting. It's a spreadsheet listing the name and last location of every halfling born to a Were in North America." He scrolled sideways with a swipe of his finger. "It's got everything. Date of birth, sire, mother's name, addresses for both parents." He indicated the fifth column. "Even one for date of death."

"This spreadsheet is their kill list?" I said, surprised. I'd envisioned something more gothic and less mundane.

"So it appears." Cordelia shook her head with disgust.

"It's bloody obscene. All those randy bucks had to do was keep their pants zipped. Then none of these children would suffer."

How many times had Cordelia wished she could conceive? It was a new thought. One that caused me to reach under my hair to find the peak of my ear.

Biggs's expression hardened. "Hedi's on the list."

"I am?" I leaned in to see.

He rolled the page down to the particulars of birth for one Helen Stronghold. In my death date was the word "Pending."

Huh. I rolled my thumb along my ear's crease, wishing I had a Kit Kat. There's something undeniably off-putting about seeing your name on a kill list.

Cordelia lifted her penciled brows. "Darling, you're probably on a dozen kill lists." Then she smiled as *my* brows lifted. "Even I—as well humored as I am—have frequently wanted to strangle you. Despair not. I can report that the feeling always disappears after a glass of Beaujolais or two." She nudged Biggs aside and changed the entry from "Pending" to "Particularly Difficult to Kill."

I snorted. "You are truly irreverent."

"One hopes. The alternative is being 'well-meaning.'" She produced a convincing shudder. "God spare me from do-gooders."

The sudden flash of humor that had warmed me died as I stared at the entry above mine in the ledger. Lexi Stronghold was listed as "Deceased."

Hold, Lexi. I'll get there, I truly will.

Scowling, Biggs hit page end, and suddenly the spreadsheet sprouted colors. Rows were highlighted. Some blue, some gray, some green. He rolled his head, kneading his neck. "The green are the active clients." He pointed to the column filled with dates and numbers. "Those are charge card numbers and expiration dates."

"He has a good business." Cordelia tallied the numbers. "Twenty-eight clients in all."

"They were raking it in," I said. "Each bottle went for a thousand? That's $28,000, and . . ." *My kingdom for a calculator.*

"Three hundred sixty-six thousand dollars a year," Biggs supplied.

"Okay, then," I said. "We'll take everything. The bottles, the shipping labels, and the laptop."

Biggs stood. "And Brenda?"

I gave her a glance. She was doing woeful, woefully well. "Any luck resuscitating her phone?"

We'd found that abused device, in three parts, sitting on a bench in the garage beside a hammer. Brenda, having belatedly remembered Knox's suggestion to "ditch the thing if anyone comes sniffing," had used brute force.

She might have wanted to remember that nugget of advice before she'd started answering everyone's texts. Apparently, she'd spent the day holding her phone, trying to decide which man would best champion her—Whitlock or her old beau, Biggs.

Whitlock had wanted her location. Biggs had wanted to meet her. Dumb instinct had told her the second offer was a better one. Thus, when I'd rung the doorbell, she'd been getting ready to fly from her roost. Her side of the bed was littered with discarded clothing choices, and her gym bag was sitting inside the old Subaru parked in the double garage.

"No, darling," said Cordelia. "Her phone is Humpty Dumpty."

I rubbed my head. "But that thing can record stuff, right?" I asked, gesturing to the iPad.

Cordelia picked it up. "Yes."

"Okay, we'll do an interview and tape her confession

just like Trowbridge did with Newland. If she answers everything honestly, then . . ." My voice trailed away.

Biggs's swallow was audible. "You'll keep your end."

"Yup," I said, feeling bleak.

He dug his hands deep into his pockets, his shoulders hunched. "Let me be the one to interview her. Not you. Me."

I rested my shoulder against the wall, pretending to think about it. "I won't let you give her an easy ride, Biggs. She'll either tell you the truth or she'll—"

"I'm not asking for one."

Brenda/Becci made a pretense of ignoring us, but I could tell by the quiver of her eyelashes that her ears were tuned to the conversation. Just as I could guess by the way her body was slightly angled toward Biggs's that she'd answer his questions before she'd reply to any of mine. "All right," I said, feigning reluctance.

Taking the iPad from Cordelia, Biggs walked into the living area. Grimly, he placed the tablet on the small table beside Brenda, then angled it so that the video screen captured her face. She offered him a hesitant smile. Stone-faced, he dragged a chair closer to the couch.

He sat, then with a rough inhale, reached over to press record. "I want you to tell them your name. Your real one."

"It's Brenda."

"Pritty," he added, his gaze now fixed on the wood paneling. "And how do you know Knox?"

"He's my boyfriend."

His fist bunched on his knee. "Was your boyfriend," he corrected. "Knox is dead. Is this his house?"

"No," she said in small voice. "It's mine."

Biggs's gaze finally swung her way. Though she flushed prettily, she was quick enough to add, "He said I needed a place to work from." She sat up straighter. "I fill all the orders."

"And do you take sun potion too?"

"I have to," she whispered.

"Because you're a halfling, right?" he asked with a certain measure of cruelty.

"I don't want to talk anymore," she said in her Kewpie-doll voice.

"Well, you bloody well have to." Cordelia spoke up from the kitchen. "Harry's dead and someone is going to answer for it."

The girl squirmed deeper into her chair, her pillow raised like a shield. With all the guile of a ten-year-old, she issued me a look of entreaty. Big eyes, trembling lip. In response, I gave her my best Starbucks smile then followed up with a warning glance toward Biggs.

Biggs said in a softer voice, "Brenda, do you have a wolf inside you?"

She nodded miserably.

"And the potion keeps it away?"

Another dip of her golden head. "Knox gave me the medicine to stop the pain."

"Oh dear God," muttered Cordelia. She grabbed a sponge, wet it, and started going at a stain on the kitchen counter.

I had to give Biggs credit. Without flinching, he walked Brenda through the key events. She talked about the day she'd met Knox, and the night he'd brought her to a remote forest to meet her first moon call. "It hurt so bad," she said, her eyes dark.

They discussed her involvement with the business—the mailings, the location of the bank accounts. "He said that I was really good with the runaways," she told us proudly.

But the pay-dirt moment—in terms of incriminating bad guys—was when he delicately probed Whitlock's participation in the trade. Apparently, Knox had constantly grumbled about the uneven percentages. Whitlock had claimed seventy percent. "For doing nothing!" exclaimed Brenda, her eyes wide.

Biggs changed the subject. "Tell me where the money goes."

Money was a subject that Brenda felt comfortable talking about. And so, while I privately anguished over my brother's potentially black future (and mine), the inquisition carried on. The conversation was going swimmingly—details flowing about the location of bank accounts and the like—until Biggs asked her for the exact location of the Peach Pit's portal. That's when the blonde with lots of air between her ears turned totally uncooperative.

When Biggs sat back with a frustrated sigh, she lowered her eyes and returned to plucking at the pillow's fringe.

"She must know where it is," said Cordelia, tossing the sponge into the garbage. "She knows everything else."

"Why don't you get yourself a drink of water?" I told Biggs.

When he rose, I pushed a wheeled hassock closer to the couch with my foot. "You're exhausted," I observed, lowering my weight to the footstool.

Brenda sent me a sly glance from under her lashes, then added another knot to the length of twisted silk.

I ran my nail up and down the yellow stitching on the footstool's seam line. Heavens, she was worse than a kitten—her attention immediately moved from the fringe to my finger. *Follow me, my little airhead.* "Brenda, why wouldn't you tell Biggs about the portal? You know he's worried that you won't have enough medicine and will get sick."

"He's a wolf," she said. "And wolves might close it if they knew where it was."

"Brenda, I'm not following you. You're part wolf. Biggs is a wolf. Why would you—"

"There are good wolves and bad ones," she snapped.

"And you don't think Biggs is a good wolf?"

That confused her. So I moved in, to disarm her. Casually tucked my hair behind my ears. "I'm not a full wolf either. See my ears?" Then, I extended my wrist. "I'm part Fae, just like the fairy who paints the pictures. Here, take a sniff. I don't have a scent either."

A yearling approaching a salt lick would have had less reservations than Brenda did taking that first important snort of scentless-me. A quick snort, then she shrank back, her golden brows pulled together in confusion.

While she was still rattled, I said in my softest voice, "Brenda, you're going to need help opening the gates."

She thought about it, chewing on that poor lower lip of hers. With one last anxious glance toward my Fae ears, she revealed, "It's not too hard. Knox calls the fairy and the door opens."

"Over the pond?"

"That would be dumb," she said.

Yeah, I always thought so. I rubbed my nose and then pointed casually to the bedroom door. "So a door opens? Like one of those?"

"Nooooo." She dragged out the word, managing to infuse oodles of scorn. "It's a *magic* door." Her eyes were very wide, and very blue.

She's overdoing the damsel-in-distress act. "With smoke and bells too?"

She frowned, patently perplexed.

Evidently, without the usual bells and whistles. "Where does this door appear?"

"At the pie place," she said slowly. Then damned if she didn't give me that look—the one that implies that she was talking to someone a few marbles short of being a dimwit.

My stomach took that moment to growl. Cordelia was busy in the kitchen, examining the finger she'd run over the counter with a hideous grimace.

"Is there anything to eat in those cupboards?" I asked Cordelia. "I'm starved."

"I'll probably get flesh-eating disease," she muttered, using a tea towel to grasp the cupboard knob. "This one's empty."

"You're a wolf."

"Salmonella then," she said, moving to the next. "And don't tell me I can't get that. I spent a memorable afternoon poised over the porcelain after consuming a Caesar salad made by the now-deceased Lois Carmen Denominator." She slammed the last cupboard. "They're all empty. I'll get you some water."

Being hungry was low on the pyramid of doom facing us, I thought as the tap ran. Instead of thinking of fudge, I needed to group everything I'd learned about this portal into some sort of shape.

Important Fact #1: When Lou had dragged me from portal to portal, she'd always gone straight to the nearest water source. Ponds, streams, slow-moving rivers. But this portal didn't materialize over water. *Interesting.*

Important Fact #2: It didn't come with bells and smoke. *A no-frills discount version? Come to visit earth for half the price and twice the bang!*

Important Fact #3: This one didn't come when called by the portal song. *A gate with an attitude? Spare me.*

And finally, Important Fact #4—and perhaps the most fascinating deviation from things I knew about gates—this one came with a gatekeeper.

Hard not to think of *Ghostbusters*.
Concentrate.
Who was this Fae? Everything I'd been taught about portals had been consistent on one point: the portal's magic was keyed to recognize and reject those with wolf blood. Thus, tasking a Fae to guard the gate seemed a tad excessive.

And why would she answer a Were's summons?

When the truth hit, it felt like a sucker punch.

All but *one* portal rejected Weres.

I stared at Brenda, and saw not her little heart-shaped face, but a woman with a face like a troll, waving good-bye to the pack of Weres streaming past her. Knox's portal had to be the Safe Passage. What other gate would require a guide? More importantly, one who was receptive to wolves?

Darling Trowbridge, you were right. The Safe Passage is not a myth. And now we're going to use the pie place portal to tra-la-la to Merenwyn, and once the evil mage is vanquished, we're going to lead your Raha'ells to the land of freedom, fries, and—oh man, gird your loincloths—supposedly equal rights for women.

"Brenda," I said, trying not to sound wonderfully gleeful, "how did Knox call the Gatekeeper? Does he have to sing to call for her?"

"That's silly," she said, wrinkling her nose.

There really is a point when your pity for someone sours. Usually after they turn out to be no nicer as a dumbass than they did as a smart cookie. I could tell. Brenda of the Big Eyes was once a mean girl. "Okeydokey." I flashed some teeth. "If Knox didn't sing a song, then how did he call the lady?"

"He has . . ." Her china-blue gaze swung to Biggs. "Did you bring it? I need it! The lady won't come without the coin!"

Fragile, my ass.

Biggs hung his head.

"Hey!" I snapped my fingers to get her attention. "What coin?"

"The one on his necklace," she said, her tone indignant.

The coin threaded through the strip of leather Knox wore around his neck opened the Safe Passage? Not an amulet, but a *coin*. Of course they wouldn't let a wolf have an amulet.

Cordelia turned off the tap. "It was in the plastic bag with all of Knox's other stuff. What happened to it?"

"Simon gave it to Whitlock." I'd watched Whitlock remove everything from the bag except the bottle of sun potion. I'd seen him pitch the keys, pocket the wallet, and examine Knox's cell phone. . . . There had been no necklace. "Son of a bitch," I said slowly, "Knox's coin wasn't in the bag when Whitlock went through it."

Cordelia asked, "Liam?"

I focused hard, replaying what I'd seen. Liam had taken the plastic baggie out of the backpack at the shack, which he'd then rolled up and tucked into his waistband. We'd driven to the Peach Pit. When Whitlock had asked him for it, Liam had leaned back on one hip. . . .

Frowning, I shook my head. "No, Liam's hand never went to his waistband until Whitlock asked for the cell phone." I racked my brains. When was the last time I'd seen Knox's necklace? Did we leave it in the kitchen in Creemore? No—I distinctly remembered Trowbridge putting it into the backpack before the witches arrived . . .

Then, with a sickening slide, my memory transported me back to the shack. To those sweet moments before Ferris burst into the room. . . . Trowbridge's hands on my hips, his legs cradling me. Then past him, Biggs at the table, examining the plastic bag.

I turned to face my once-trusted friend. His eyes said everything I needed to know.

"You foolish boy," murmured Cordelia.

My mouth dried. "You keep betraying us."

"You didn't ask me if I took the coin. You didn't ask me anything about it!"

"The time to come clean was before. Not now. How many other things are you keeping from us?" I lifted my hand. "Don't bother. I don't believe you anymore. Answer one question: did you know why she needed the coin?"

"No," he started. Then he corrected himself. "I didn't know for sure, but it was the only thing of his she wanted. And . . ." He looked away.

"You're ahead of us on the track. You've had more time to put things together. So somewhere along the line— probably just before Ferris fired on Harry—you knew. And you didn't say anything." His misery was telegraphed through his scent. I wiped my nose with the back of my hand, and then swiped it twice on my thighs. He would not cling to me. Not in any way. "Where is it?"

Chapter Twenty

Biggs dug into his hip pocket and pulled out a handful of coins. The foreign one, with a hole in the middle of it, was slightly smaller than a loonie and much duller. He dropped it in my open palm.

"How does the coin work?" I asked Brenda.

She tensed—I hadn't used my happy voice—and her own scent changed very slightly. "You feed it the wolves."

I'll admit it: I blinked.

"What wolves?" Cordelia asked sharply.

"The ones that are there," she said, as if it was patently clear.

Enough. "I know you're a few bits short of all your wits, but do you understand the phrase 'I've had a day'?" She gulped and nodded, so I gave her a smile etched with acid. "Answer Cordelia's question. Right. Now."

"The stone wolves inside the train tracks."

The freakin' statues. I'd stood right beside them talking to Whitlock and neither of us had recognized them as anything other than a visual demonstration of Karma's twisted humor. "What happens after Knox feeds the statues his necklace?"

"The smoke comes and she walks through the door. We bring her to our place. He gives her some pieces of wood and she gives him the bottles. Then I watch the hourglass. When the sand—"

"You take her back."

She nodded. "Can I have the coin now?"

"No. You can't."

She turned to appeal to Biggs. "Tell her to give it to me. I need it!"

Biggs lifted a trembling hand to cup her jaw. "Don't worry, Becs. I'll fix it."

Merry climbed out of my cleavage. Her amber belly was dull, the usual warm glow of vivid light from her heart dimmed to a pinpoint of faded gold. "Hang in there," I said.

She slowly rappelled down the end of her chain, then did just that. She hung, not limply because she was too heavy and ornate to ever achieve that. But somehow, the way she'd tucked each articulated leaf tip underneath a coil of her vine—as if their points were fragile—made me think she was hugging herself in exhaustion.

"Where's Canada's national tree when you need it?" I tucked her into my palm, trying to infuse my heat into her cool stone, and threaded, hipwise, through the brush that grew near the fence.

The tree selection was not going well. I'd made my way across the back field because I'd noted a small clump of trees near the single strand of barbed wire. What I'd hoped for was a sugar maple sapling. All I netted was a single weak pine, a spindly spruce, and a white birch. The latter was a multiple trunk specimen. Never ideal as a food choice, what with its papery bark. More work to eat than a pomegranate.

"Best I can do, Merry." I went on my tiptoes, straining for one of the higher silvery branches. "You've got five minutes. Eat up."

Anu coughed. I rolled my eyes her way. Chewing on her lip—she'd started that right after the Peach Pit and hadn't really stopped since then—my niece held out her hand. She mimed placing Merry high in the boughs.

"That okay with you?"

Merry's tepid assent wrung my heart. I handed her to Anu who stretched to set her in a narrow fork, far beyond my reach. Immediately, Merry's gold flexed and changed shape, and by the time my niece was back onto the soles of her feet, my amulet had settled in for a hasty chowdown.

I leaned against the pine to watch her. Merry needs feeding—that's what I'd said when Cordelia had picked up her rifle and given me a significant nod. Then I'd almost growled, "Come with me, Anu."

I don't growl. Not usually. My wolf is finally stepping up.

Somewhat to my surprise, Anu had trailed me outside without ferret or any further prodding, obviously as anxious to leave the house as I'd been. Biggs's personal perfume had streamed anxiety and anguish.

Still was. I could smell it from where we stood.

A kinder or gentler person would have dealt with the situation back in the house immediately—put Biggs out of his misery—but I needed a couple of minutes to gird my loins. Or maybe it was better to say shore up my foundation, because I didn't have a loincloth to my name.

All I had was a crumbling infrastructure.

Anu stooped to pull a long shoot of dry grass. Into her mouth it went. The kid has an oral fixation, I thought, stroking my ear.

My brain was caught on a string of four words—much like a CD that had been left to cook on the dashboard. Warped by the sun, the disc's best track (and it was never one of the filler songs, it was always your personal fave) skipped. You got hung up on the tune's chorus.

Here's a killer one: Brenda had to die.

Or let's try that again: in about two minutes or less, Brenda *was* going to die.

I checked my wrist, now encircled by the watch Knox had thoughtfully left on his bedside table. Twenty minutes before eight. How long would it take to battle our way through rush-hour traffic to Toronto? Southbound traffic would be heavy. An hour and half? More?

Cutting it close. Time to witness the deed. *My blood's no purer than Brenda's.* Didn't matter. Either way, I was taking one of them to face Trowbridge's accusers.

"He's betrayed you," murmured my Fae.

"Biggs lied," I said. "To protect a girl he held above all others."

Like I had. Like I would.

I rubbed my gritty eyes, then winced. Had I said that out loud? Anu's gaze was fixed on me in a manner that might be best described as concerned bordering on cautious. I shrugged. "Ignore me. I'm just talking to my Fae."

Brows raised, she took a hokey-pokey to the left.

Well, why wouldn't she be careful? Without any language skills, how could she make any sense of the things that had happened to her over the last few days? Witnessing the events of the last twenty-four hours must have been worse than watching one of those Swedish flicks without any subtitles.

"I have a Fae inside me," I said with a faint wince. "She talks. Also a Were. But most of the time she's pretty quiet. Almost invisible."

Until she took Brenda down like a summer-fattened deer.

"You know, Anu?" I murmured, rearranging my hair to hide my ears. "This wolf thing that you and I fear? It might not be a bad deal after all. I had no idea how much hunting feels like stealing."

Her hum could have meant anything.

I nodded for her benefit and said for Merry's, "It's almost identical. I get the same quivery anticipation just before I boost something; the same adrenaline when I pocket it, and then precisely the same 'life is freakin' good' joy when I walk away knowing it's mine. No wonder Trowbridge likes being a wolf."

At the mention of his name, Anu's head canted sharply to the side.

The man collects females' hearts as easily as my white shirt attracts chocolate stains.

"It must be a rite of passage," I mused. "You're right on schedule. I started obsessing over him at twelve. Though, pay attention—he's My One True Thing, not yours."

My finger slid behind my ear and found the peaked curve again. "You want to hear a piece of wisdom from your old aunt? Once I believed I could melt everything down to one true thing. One person to love. One to protect." I shook my head. "I was lying to myself. But I'd lost so much . . . Mum and Dad . . . Lexi. In one night—they were just *gone*. I never wanted to feel that pain again." I looked above to where my amulet fed. "Truth is, Trowbridge's never going to be my *only* true thing. Merry was one of my first true things. And now I've got all these people . . ." I frowned, thinking it through. "Twined around me again."

Take them away and maybe I'd discover that I'm hollow.

My stomach squeezed. "I take lousy care of the people I love. Last night, my actions left Lexi in a special kind of hell. Tonight, I lost one of ours." My voice hardened. "And in two hours, I'm going to sacrifice Biggs after I watch him break the neck of the girl he loves."

I'm committed to seeing it to the end but—oh Goddess—am I right? There is so much collateral damage.

My gaze slid away to the ground.

"All this morality crap might come naturally to others, but you'll have to trust me on this—it's a relatively new preoccupation for me."

Pinecones rested near the foot of the evergreen. Small ones. Within them, the seeds of future evergreens, if they could only take root. It would take a lot for them to sprout. The right water. The right sun. The right nutrients in the ground. So many variables to consider, so many things to provide. I bent to retrieve one.

It smelled like Creemore and home.

"I'm going to leave you here now." Scales layered the cone. Hard. Woody. "You're going to stay and watch Merry. Because she needs to feed and because you're not going to witness another death." I tossed the cone, then looked up, giving her a stare that promised all kinds of hell if she disobeyed. "Not today. Not if I can help it. Goddess, you're only thirteen."

She let out a trill of Merenwynian.

"Sorry, Anu. I don't understand." Hard to smile but I gave it a weak try. "Do you think my stellar skills at language might be a problem when I get to Merenwyn? Maybe just a bit, huh?"

Frustration tightened her features and she unleashed another torrent of words.

With a sigh, I closed the gap between us. Reached out, took her hand. It was cold and larger than mine. "There are a lot of things I'd like to tell you. But if there was one thing I could make you understand—just one—it would be about Lexi."

Anu flinched.

Ah. She recognizes his name too.

"I know you hate and fear him. And maybe you should. I don't know how really corrupted he is, any more than I know the sum of the damage he's left in Merenwyn. But I do know that some portion of the brother I loved is still there, buried inside him. He cares about you. He brought you back here. Do you understand me?"

Perplexed, she shook her head.

"Your father brought you back to me." Perhaps it was my tone because she shrank away and I had to tighten my grip lest she peel off before I'd said everything I needed to. "He knew you stood a better chance here in this realm. Lexi brought you here and asked me to make sure the bitches and bullies wouldn't make you miserable."

And I'm pretty sure I can't.

Her eyes were wide. Green as the crest of a sunlit ocean roller. "He's not a terrible man," I whispered. "I wish you could know that." I gave her fingers a final squeeze and released them, then made a fork with mine. I pointed to my eyes and then to her, and finally to Merry. "You. Stay. Here. Guard her."

I said it one final time. "Stay."

An order that was drowned under a piercing screech.

The bird was neither hawk, nor sparrow, but a known enemy. He rode the air currents, tipping his dark wing ever so slightly—the fighter pilot with the lightest touch—to change his course.

Liam had found us. How? We'd hidden the truck inside the garage.

Crap. Change of plan.

"Run to the house, Anu!" I shouted, pushing her in its direction. I then ran to the birch. "Merry, we've got to go!"

In response, my amulet sparked orange-red fire from her heart.

"Liam's come. Drop to me!" She needed no further enlargement on the subject of danger, danger, danger! Vines whipping, Merry fell into my palm. I took off at high speed across the field, well behind Anu, whose longer legs had already carried her to the back porch. She held the door open and shouted a warning to the others.

In Merenwynian.

The kid had to learn English.

I was twenty feet from the house when the raven came hurtling down from the sky. Though I was panting, I could still hear the wind whistling through the feathery fingers of his wings. So I turned, quickly, to take a look, because that's what you do. You turn. You look. And whatever forward momentum you had slows. Because you're thinking of impact, so you cover your head, because the portion of your mind concerned with self-preservation is decidedly worried about those hooked claws and that long curved beak.

I zigged. He zagged.

Anu screamed. My heart thudded. Liam flapped his wings—*there's the stuff of a new nightmare*—and the porch never looked farther away.

Until Cordelia stepped out.

With her rifle.

Liam the bird evidently shared brains with Liam the bad guy. He wheeled off, with one quick tilt of one long wing. Five powerful flaps carried him swiftly skyward.

Cordelia pulled the trigger. The weapon flashed and a single feather fell. The raven flapped a tad harder and Cordelia swore. Virulently, with adjectives that sounded plummy but meant nothing to me. In her frustration, she'd reverted to the drag slagging for which she'd been famous.

Out of range, the bird of prey circled high above us.

And that's when—over the sound of my own harsh breathing, and Cordelia's curses, and Anu's panting, and Biggs's "shit"s, and Brenda of the Big Eyes's whimpers—I heard the rumble of motorcycles coming from the west. We all spun, heads cocked.

"How far away are they, Cordie?"

"Sound travels in the country," she replied. "A couple of kilometers at the most. There's time to run, though I don't how far we'd get. We'd have to head east over the dirt roads and where they'd take us—"

"It's a kilometer to the highway," said Biggs. "On these roads that will take a couple of minutes even with the pedal to the metal. Then two more kilometers to the next town."

"If we leave now," said Cordelia, "we might make it, but it's a long chance. Liam could have them coming for us from both directions . . ." Her mouth twisted then she shrugged. "We'd have to go now."

Brenda tugged Biggs's sleeve. "Are they wolves? Will they hurt me?"

His jaw hardened as he stared into her pleading face. "I can lead them away," he said, his gaze jerking to mine. "They'll be looking for Rachel's truck, not Brenda's car. We'll take the truck—the windows are tinted, they won't be able to tell that there's just the two of us. And with the dust kicked up from our tires . . . I can do this. Give us a chance."

All eyes were on me.

Let them both go and I won't have a witness to bring forward to support my claims to the council. Don't let them go and I have a good chance of losing it all here.

Screw it. I'd rather die beside Trowbridge.

"Cordie, grab the rifles and the keys to Brenda's car. Take Biggs and the others into the garage. Start pouring gasoline on anything and everything flammable while I get the iPad and evidence."

Never have I been so efficient. Merry scuttled to my shoulder as I hurriedly tucked Knox's tablet under my arm and grabbed the basket of bottles. No time for the mailing labels or the rest—not if I was heading to the portrait room.

Executive decision made, I was out of that bedroom faster than you could say "Haul ass, baby, the bad guys are coming."

I made a very swift detour into the kitchen, grabbed a knife, and bolted back down the hall to the spare room. One quick stab to pierce the tight canvas, four ruthless slashes, and my brother's face was cut out of that disturbing painting. All it took was five tearing seconds, then I was whipping out of there, intent on making it to the garage before (a) Liam decided to change from a bunch of feathers into a guy with a wicked smile and a grudge, or (b) the dudes in leather showed up with their weapons and total lack of moral fiber.

Either way, we were screwed. Unless I stepped up. Thought badass. Used wiles while there was still "a while." Goddess, I'd spent my formative years outthinking a Fae aunt and a dozen employers. I could outthink a bird.

Merry pinched me as I loped down the hallway toward the back door. Really, really hard. Grabbing that little soft swell of flesh that was neither breast tissue nor underarm—the flub that spilled over the side of my bra.

I skidded to a halt. "What!"

She jabbed an urgent pincer toward the kitchen.

"Fuck!" I said, spinning on my heel. Then because I didn't have the wit or the time to form a complaint, I repeated the same verb over and over again. All the way to the little box nailed to the wall beside the gas stove. "Fuck!" I said again, snatching up three wooden matches. And finally one last "Fuck!" when we breached the back door again, and I heard the sound of those twin-stroke bike engines.

Overhead, Liam wheeled.

Would he follow their car? Be faked out by the dark windows?

I darted across the lawn. Cordelia slammed the door behind us. The garage smelled of gas, exhaust, and worried Were. Brenda and Biggs were already in the truck, engine running. Brenda's old Subaru was idling. Cordelia hurried back to the double doors where she'd piled drenched rags and chair stuffing. Anu's ferret chattered at me as I slid past them.

I crouched by the pile.

My hands trembled. *I hate matches. I hate fire.*

I struck the head.

I couldn't control my trembling, though I wished I could because it made my whole frame shudder. *Heroes don't quake.* Smoke roiled, dark and oily, over the hood of Brenda's car. Blinding me. Making my lungs hurt, making me want to cough. And worse, the screen of flames was spreading. *Hurry, hurry.* I could hear them licking the side of the garage walls, imagined the orange-red river bubbling over the ceiling.

It took me back.

To when I was twelve, and little for my age. Small enough to crouch on my heels inside a cramped cupboard. Old enough to understand that the fire that consumed my family's home had a terrible hunger. And that it would soon eat me. Unless I got out.

But now—with this fire—I had to stay. I had to be strong and wait, straining my ears to track the sound of the motorcycles. They were getting closer: I could hear the rumble of their twin-stroke engines over the fire's pops and crackles

With all my heart, I hoped the bikers took the bait. A scant forty seconds ago, Biggs had gunned Rachel's truck and burst out of the garage. He'd driven like a wolf possessed, barrelling down the rutted lane, then taking a hard right at the end of the drive. The truck's back tires had caught in the soft verge and spun up a cloud of dust and gravel; evidence that Biggs had fulfilled one promise in a useless attempt to make up for so many broken ones.

I'd demanded a dirt trail, and he'd given us one.

Let the bikers see it. Let them follow it and Biggs down the back roads.

My hands tightened on the wheel as I listened to the bikers' engines slow down.

Don't stop. . . . Take the freakin bait. . . .

Suddenly, with a sudden collective roar, their engines throttled back into gear. Relief bathed me—the fleeing *ah* before the roller coaster's next dip. *Hold.* I waited, blinking against the smoke, trying to ignore my shaking knees, slowly and methodically counting to twenty. When I reached twenty-one, I hit the accelerator hard.

Brenda's ancient Subaru surged forward, and me and the sedan shot through the smoke and out of the garage. The first fifteen feet were driven in a state of mechanical horror. Had Liam's gang left a biker or two at the bottom of the drive? Perhaps a welcome party for Hedi and company? I couldn't tell—tears blurred my vision.

I swiped my eyes with the back of my arm.

Another *ah*, just as fleeting as the first. The road was clear, empty of Harleys and men who wore shit kickers.

Keep going. Put some distance between yourself and the garage.

I drove, not like a madman, but like a girl pursued by one. The Subaru made it three-quarters down the drive—all the way to the stand of tired poplars—before Liam swooped down from the sky.

Escape had been prepared with the knowledge that Liam the raven still cruised high over the house—he was, after all, the bikers' eyes in the sky. If all had gone to the original plan, he'd have followed Biggs's vehicle when it had torn down the road. But all the cursed bird did was wing his way to a higher elevation to get a longer-range view. Even with a brain the size of a wizened walnut, the raven thought like the mean-spirited evildoer that he really was.

Now the bird of prey plunged from the sky, beady eyes intent on his prize.

Shit. I hunched over the wheel.

A sudden, frightening blur of black wings, a glimpse of horned legs tipped with three curved talons. Thud. The car dipped as the bird of prey landed on its hood with a rending scrape of claw on steel.

Go away! I hit the gas harder and the car coughed, then lurched forward.

I'd hoped to hit him—to make him insensible or better yet, the carrion equivalent of bug guts. But a hooked talon slid into the vents, and another wrapped itself around the wipers. And for a horrifying second, a yellow eye—small, beady, angry, evil—stared at me through the glass.

Impossible to see past him.

"Get off," I shouted.

I hit the windshield wipers. One blade swept, and windscreen fluid jetted. Liam ignored his bath, continuing to flap and caw and jab his yellow beak at the shatterproof glass *(oh, please be shatterproof)*.

His wicked eyes gleamed. "Got you, bitch."

Feather-off, dickhead.

I jerked the wheel to the left, taking the car off the drive and onto the quarter acre of field. The ground was rutted and softer than the drive. The wheel bucked in my grip, the mirror vibrated, and the change in the cup holder chattered.

I was losing traction and speed.

No, no.

Ahead, the field dipped sharply. I could avoid it by hanging a right (*but I'd lose speed!*) or I could think rocket. I opted for propulsion. *Fly, Subaru. Fly.* Just before liftoff, I gunned the car and hit the windshield wipers one more time. Blue fluid jetted over bird and glass, and I went airborne in my seat. The Subaru's flight was brief. *Bam!* We hit earth with a spine-wincing jolt. The car's front end dipped, and—*thank you, Goddess*—the outraged raven slid off the slick hood in a flurry of wings.

Visibility won, I jammed the pedal back to the floor. Dirt spun up behind me. The tires bit, grudgingly found traction, and then me and Mr. Subaru were moving again. Once more, I hunched over the wheel, my gaze darting from the line of razor wire the farmer had strung across the boundary line to my rear-view mirror.

Suddenly, Liam filled my rear view. He was approaching low, wings flapping, body a long jet torpedo.

Wait. Don't do anything until you see the yellow of his beady eyes. . . .

Closer. Closer.

Now! I wrenched the steering to the left and slammed on the brakes.

A thud. Followed by a long rending scrape of hooked claws on paint.

I checked my mirror and gulped. The rear window's glass was crazed. In the center of the depression, a big, wet, remarkably ugly smear of blood. Where was he? Did I get him? I checked the side mirrors, then the back again. I listened for the flap-flap of his wings. Then, swallowing hard, I put the car into neutral and cracked open the door.

Please be dead.

I was hoping for roadkill.

But Liam had done what shifters do when one body was compromised and the other was in fine form. He'd transformed. My stomach dropped at the sight of the man crouched behind the back bumper, one knuckle braced on the ground. Feathers and goo clung to Liam's naked flesh, and stuff oozed from the gash on his hip. Looked red, smelled like blood, but I wasn't taking anything for granted. For all I knew the guy ran on motor oil.

Liam stood, favoring one leg. "You sacrificed them?" he said, jerking his head toward the car's empty passenger seats. "Or did you send them off with the decoys?"

"Let's make a deal," I said, backing away from him and the car.

"No deals," he said, limping after me. "Just play."

That's what I thought. I took to my heels, haring for the questionable safety of the pine, the cedar, and the clump of white birch.

"Run," he called after me. "I like it better that way."

I looked over my shoulder. Hands loose at his sides, he watched, letting me gain some distance. He was staring at me from under those wicked brows, and I knew, in another breath, he'd smile and come after me, bad leg and all.

What the heck. I skidded to a stop.

He cocked his head, the corner of his mouth lifting. "Chicken?"

"Nope. Coyote."

If he'd turned around, he'd have seen Cordelia creeping out of the garage. But he didn't—just as I'd gambled, he'd be too obsessed with the promise of hurting me to notice peripheral action.

Cordelia's rifle cracked, and his chest exploded. It was as simple and wonderful as that. "You got him!" I shouted as he slowly sank to his knees. *Don't you get back up, Liam. Don't change into a bird again.*

He fell sideways, mouth open, plucking at his chest.

I slipped the gun out of my waistband. His eyes were

struggling to change from a human's to a bird's. "You should have asked me what type of coyote I was." The end of the revolver fit nicely in the spot between those wicked dark brows. "Say good-bye to the Wile E. Coyote, Liam."

I pulled the trigger.

Chapter Twenty-One

The hotel was located near Union Station, a vast train depot that handles everything from the national rail lines to local trains. At any given time of the day, Front Street is jammed with cabs and commuters.

Cordelia pulled up as close as she could get, maneuvering in behind a minivan with a peeling bumper sticker. The corners of her mouth pulled down as she stared at the hotel's entrance. "Let me come with you."

I shook my head, absolutely firm. "We've gone through this."

"This is a hasty decision."

"No. I've thought it through to the end." Driving to Toronto had taken more than a frustrating hour. I'd used the time to look into the future and consider the ripple effect of those possible outcomes on the people I loved.

The "mines" in my life were slipping through my fingers fast as the sand slithering through the hourglass back at Brenda's house. Near the entrance to the highway, we'd come across Rachel's abandoned truck, parked on the verge, keys still in the ignition.

Heart curiously numb, I'd done a quick tour around the vehicle. There were no skid marks to indicate forced evacuation. No bullet holes either. I'd peered into the car, half frightened that I'd find their bodies in the backseat. But the interior was empty and the bag I'd tossed into Brenda's lap at the last minute was gone too.

I'd tested one door, then another. They were locked.

So, they'd made it to the highway. Biggs had slung the backpack weighted with twelve bottles of sun potion over his shoulder and Brenda had put out her thumb. Together, they'd hitchhiked into anonymity.

For the next few miles, I'd thought about ties and lies.

I hoped they got another year together. A lot of memories can be stored up in twelve months. Even longer if you're smart enough to spend summers in the Arctic where the sun shines for twenty-four hours a day. There had to be a reason it's called sun potion.

Be smart, Biggs.

Suddenly, a wave of commuters poured out of the train station. A few of the more foolhardy disdained the lights, instead threading their way through the cars driven by impatient drivers. The train that spat them out must have been one of the last covering rush hour.

It was 9:50 A.M.

Another thing I'd done during the long drive into town was to use spit and the car's upholstery to remove all visible traces of blood and gore from my arms and hands. Now, I flipped the sun visor down to check my hair. *What a wreck.* I finger-combed as best I could, then wet the tail of my T-shirt to deal with the grime my tears had missed.

The ferret chittered, and my niece— who'd done a terrific impersonation of a statue ever since our tête-à-tête— turned her head. A pair of green eyes studied my reflection. Pale as my own, but shaped like my twin's. I offered her a tepid smile. Anu pulled the ferret higher in her arms and returned to staring out the window. So, the reserve that had begun to melt was icing over once more. *Fool, "Trowbridge" and "Lexi" were the only two words she understood in that epic fail to bond.*

I snapped the visor closed.

It's probably better that way.

I reached for the iPad by my feet, wishing I could steal one of the backpacks bobbing past me. Even wrestling one of those all weather jackets from a commuter had its attractions. I was cold again. So was Merry.

One more glance at the dashboard. It read 9:52 A.M.

"Can you reach that scarf?" I asked Cordelia.

"What do you want with it?'

"I need to protect the tablet from my hands. Too much Fae woo-woo contact can fry the circuits."

"This is absurd." Cordie grunted, her body twisted as she stretched for the baby-blue knitted scarf lying on the seat beside Anu. "The council will have armed guards. You can't simply stroll in, unarmed and uninvited. Let me come as your witness."

"No." I started wrapping the device with the scarf. The pattern was complicated and perhaps too ambitious for the novice knitter. The bobbles were too loose, almost flattened.

"You need me."

"What I need," I said in hard voice, "is for you to fulfill a promise I can't." My fingers stilled, holding the swaddled iPad stable on my knee. *There. I've said it.* Time to do the thing I had turned in my mind ever since I'd watched Anu stretch to put Merry in the birch tree.

Her head turned. "What promise?"

I felt my mouth curve into a bleak smile. "One I made to my brother about his daughter." Commuters were pooling at the red light. Everyone carrying a burden. A briefcase, an overlarge purse, a backpack, or a shopping bag. They stood, shifting their weight on their feet, watching the red, anticipating the release of the green.

Like the pack before the moon.

Do it fast.

"I've had a lot of time to think during this endless night of drives. About brothers and promises. Alphas and councils. Bitches and bastards." I dug deep between the seats to excavate the plastic bag Brenda had shoved between them. "How I never want to see the 400 Highway again." I snorted, shaking out the crumpled bag. "I might get that wish. We've got evidence, but they might overturn it."

"Once they listen to you and see what you have to say, they'll know what questions to ask Whitlock. And if he tries to lie—"

"They'll smell it. I thought about that. But then it hit me—even if I manage to convince those old geezers that Trowbridge and I are completely innocent of any trade with the Fae, we're going to end up at war with the council. It's inevitable. My mate needs to rule without any interference. And he won't get that. Not after this. The council will be breathing down his neck, questioning his every move."

"There's no precedence for their involvement." She developed a sudden and intense interest in the three construction workers doing not much of anything with a piece of plywood.

Ah, Cordelia. I've looked ahead. Like you have.

"They'll make one," I said, inserting the woolen-cozied tablet into the bag. "It's all about money. And power. Who has what, and who wants what. Am I wrong?"

"No." A soft reply. Filled with regret.

"Well, the Alpha of Creemore has a lot of things to covet. Remember the first time I sent the pack off for their moon run?" I smiled, feeling wistful. "I almost felt like I was one of you for a little while. Just for a few minutes. Right after I used my flare to send the pack down the trail. Some of the younger wolves stretched their necks as if my flare felt really, really good. But after you all left, I went back to the trailer. On the table was Harry's map." I glanced to her for confirmation. "You know the one that shows all the packs and boundary lines?"

She jerked a nod.

"I'd never seen it laid out like that, Cordie. So much land to look after and so many small packs to watch over. How could I protect them? They were so far away. So spread out." My gaze left hers and drifted to the throng of humans on the street. "That's when I realized that all of those people were now my responsibility and all those boundary lines were mine to guard. I stayed awake all night thinking about it. Then I picked up a book and kept my head in one until Knox knocked on our door."

"Why?" she said, her voice low. "I never understood. You just . . . disappeared."

"I was scared. I'm still scared. But I won't run from my fears anymore." I wanted to stroke my ear, but my hands were busy. Tightening on the plastic handles. Making fists on my thighs. So very busy. "No matter which way you look at it, my heritage is going to be a problem for us. The council will note that Ontario is riddled with Fae portals and point out that he chose a halfling for a mate. And that will be their precedent."

"You're not a halfling."

"Semantics, Cordie. I am half blood. They'll use my Fae as a device to keep us under constant surveillance. All of us. Trowbridge and me. Anu. You too, Cordie. They'll be coming at us all the time and even when we're at Creemore, among our pack . . . there'll be no sanctuary. No safe place." I chewed my lip. "If Trowbridge and I ever get to return to his pack, I'm going to have to face Rachel. She's going to say that I made a promise to her and broke it. She'll be telling the truth."

And I hate the pack, Cordie. I truly hate them.

Cordie went back to digging under her wig, trying to

get that spot that bothered her so, then swore. She whipped the carefully cut red bob off her head and slapped it on her knee. Then she gave in to the demand to scratch.

No wonder she was at that spot like a poodle with a case of mites. She'd developed a nasty rash, haloing the stubble she buzzed every day with her electric razor.

"What is that?"

"I have no idea," she murmured, rubbing the back of her balding pate. "I think it's stress. My hair is coming out in patches."

"Well, stop going at it. You'll wear what's left of your real hair off."

"And you should stop making promises!" She gave it one more furious go, then sighed. She gripped the steering wheel and stared ahead bleakly. "What did Rachel want?"

"For me to go to Merenwyn and stay there." I shrugged. "She should have made me pinkie swear. I have no intention of staying in the Fae realm and I imagine she might be feeling a tad pissy when I return. With Trowbridge standing by me, she won't be able to do anything directly, but she's vindictive and she'll find a way to get her own back. She'll come at it sideways."

Her nod was more of a head jerk. "She'll take it out on Anu."

"I won't be able to give Anu the type of home my twin wanted for her." My hand traveled to my breast where Merry lay. She wrapped a gentle tendril around my thumb. "I don't want her name to be added to someone's list. I don't want her watched and ostracized. No—to do it right, Anu needs to be taken to a place where she can't be hurt by people who don't understand her."

Cordelia's knuckles were white. "I can do that," she said, her voice very low.

I turned back to watch the drones in the suits. "I want

her to go to school. I don't care how much grief she gives you about that—you make her graduate from high school anyhow." In the silence that followed that, I studied the young guy wearing a Queen's University windbreaker checking his cell phone. "College would be nice."

"That's a long time in the future," she said.

"Well, you'll be busy teaching her stuff in the meantime. Start with our language. Give her words to shout at you when you're being pushy or demanding. I want her to be capable of giving you as much trouble as I did."

"You never gave me trouble," she muttered.

"You're a bad liar." My throat ached. It *ached*. I took in a breath and another, breathing through my mouth until the urge to bawl eased.

Cordelia's scent was strong as it reached for me.

I slid my hand down inside my pants until I felt the golden links of my mom's bride belt, warm against my hip. "You're going to need some money," I told her, hooking the chain with a finger. Sucking in my gut was required to pull the soft leather pouch clear of my jeans waistband. "You're getting a little long in the tooth for the drag circuit."

"I have some cash hidden in my sock drawer back in Toronto."

"You don't have a sock drawer." I worked the jeweled clasp open, then sat forward to pull the chain belt free. Gold glinted in the early morning sun, catching the eye of a passerby. I gave him the finger. The human lifted his brows and huffed off. I sat back, head resting on the window. "I wish I had a scent," I said, tracing the gilt embroidery on the leather. "Anu won't remember me at all."

"You are unforgettable, Hedi, darling."

I winced. "Don't torture her with that song, okay? Not everybody likes grocery store music."

"It is a classic."

"So you say." I glanced at her. A fat tear hung from her lower lash, too proud to fall. I held out the bride belt. "Here. Take it. There are enough diamonds in it for you to buy a home and see both of you to old age."

"I won't take your tears," Cordelia said. "I can sew costumes. I can glue rhinestones onto tiaras. You won't have anything of your own if I take those."

I winked. "Never fear. There's more where that came from." And damned if my eyes didn't start to fill. "Cordie . . . I have the thing I wanted most in life—I am loved. I've been surrounded by it for half a year. It just took me a while to recognize that love comes in different flavors. It's not just One True Thing. It was a geezer that called me 'Little Miss.' It's a six-foot mother hen who never knows when to back off. It's a brother . . . a really broken twin . . . who loves me enough to swallow a bottle of sun potion." I watched a man in a fine coat stride into the hotel. "I want Anu to find that out for herself. I want to meet the council, knowing that whatever happens, you and Anu are going to be safe for the rest of your lives. Living at one address, not a whole bunch of them. In a house. A real one, made of brick, with a solid door that no wolf can huff and puff down."

"You'll be back," she said.

"I want it to have a wide bow window in the front room exactly like the one in the Trowbridge living room and a white picket fence like the one in that magazine you keep hidden under your satin knickers."

A flush crawled across her raw boned cheeks. "I *knew* you went through my drawers."

"It will have a garden exactly like the one in that picture."

"With sweet peas," she said thickly.

"And roses for my mum." I tapped the glove compartment with my knee and gave her a significant look. She'd

seen me take out the square of canvas and watched me
brood over Lexi's painted image for several exits. She
hadn't commented, but her scent had woven around my
seat—maternal warm and mother protective—until I'd
rolled it into a cylinder and put it in the glove compartment. Now, she flicked a glance toward that safe-deposit
box and gave me an infinitesimal nod. "Later, when the
time is right, you're going to tell Anu about her father.
You can start by telling her that he was brave."

"He was that."

"And that her eyes are shaped like his." Before age
tightened them. "Tell her that he didn't mean to become
what he was. That once he was so full of mischief and
light. That he liked to prowl the woods and pretend to
save damsels in distress—"

"You'll be back!" she repeated fiercely.

"Sure I will," I said, suppressing a shiver. Before I lost
my courage, I put the belt in the console's cup holder.
"Wagons ho, Cordie. Drive as fast you can, and get the
hell out of Ontario."

Her wig lay forgotten on her knee. "We'll go to B.C."

I smiled. "Where rogue Weres and society's discards
live in perfect harmony."

"Supposedly," she said, her gaze rigid on the side
mirror.

A cab driver honked.

I pivoted in my seat to look over my shoulder. I stared
long and hard, trying to take a mental picture that one
day I might share with my twin. Thin face, good bones
though. A promise of future beauty. "Good-bye, Anu. You
give her hell."

Her grip tightened onto the ferret. It squeaked and
squirmed.

One final glance at the driver. Her jaw was a rigid line
with a whole bunch of sagging skin below it. "You'll al-

ways be beautiful to me, Cordelia," I whispered. Then I
opened the door and slid out into the traffic.

By the time I crossed the boulevard and looked over
my shoulder, the green car had been swallowed by cars
heading west.

It is good. It is right.

Goddess, please watch over both of them.

Chapter Twenty-Two

The Royal Empress Hotel has old-world charm. Back in its heyday, it had lured in movie stars and princes with its opulence and attention to fine detail. It still had that, in spades. The lobby's ceiling could have been lifted from Windsor Palace. I'd circumvented the guys with the epaulets manning the front door by taking an entrance on the side of the building. A bellman looked askance at my bare feet as I walked past him.

My cologne was eau de flames, my clothing was street-person chic, and he was worried about my dusty feet? I lifted my brows in a perfect mimicry of Mad-one. "I'm with the band."

He looked away.

I got on the elevator. Stared at all the buttons. There were so many floors to search in very little time, and on those, perhaps more rooms than I can care to think of. But I had my nose, didn't I? And a wolf inside me, who was on high alert. I took my finger and started jabbing, from mezzanine all the way to fourteen. The round lights glowed at me.

I leaned back against the wall, thinking about Lexi and Trowbridge.

A man in a suit entered the elevator. He went to push

the buttons, stiffened, and then turned to glare at me before he exited in a huff.

Tinned background music played as the cab traveled up a floor. The doors opened. I leaned out and let my wolf do its job. She smelled cleaning products, and food, and human, human, human—but no wolves.

We didn't get lucky until the eighth floor.

Yes. There.

Not just a wolf, but at quick guess, at least five. I stepped out, my head back. Inhaled again. The scent streamed from the corridor to my left.

And then, once those doors slid closed, I followed the Alpha-ripe trail all the way down the hallway. Trowbridge's strand of scent was thick and heavy. Alive then, though the usual combination of woods, and wild, and sex, and him was muddied by the sweet tone of the sun potion.

A guard stood outside the room at the end of the short hall. Sparely built, wearing, incongruously, a three-piece suit. I could almost read his mind when he spotted me. "Small young female, round and unassuming, carrying a plastic bag and the scent of" . . . and that's when his brain skipped.

I smiled at him, knowing that I carried the signature of Cordelia, who smelled of perfume, wolf, and man. Confusion and suspicion creased the guard's face. He reached inside his suit—I've seen enough Bond movies to know that when a bodyguard reaches for his armpit, he's not bringing out a Subway sandwich—and began to walk toward me.

I am tired of guns and of men who want to shoot me.

My eyes, which had been burning since I left Cordelia and Anu, ignited into a full flare. Green light—as bright and magical as my serpent's, spiced with the fury of a woman who has been pushed beyond the pale—exploded from me.

It's the only way I can describe it.

Power, in the form of light. It came from my heart; it came from my soul. And it rolled down that hallway, a long ocean roller swell. My Fae-gift hit him with a slap, just like that wave you're not expecting, the one with an undertow and suck to it, the one that pulls your feet out from under you.

He stalled, right there, hand still tucked under his armpit.

Who's the tough guy now? I walked right up to him. "Give me your weapon."

His peepers were brown, and mostly, thanks to his conflicted feelings, had dilated pupils. My green light bathed his face—he grimaced as if struggling to swallow a very bitter draught.

I focused on him. On nothing but him.

He gave a shudder, and then he passed me his weapon.

"What is it with all the guns?" I shook my head. "You know we're Canadians, right?" I jerked my head toward the door. "You first, buddy."

I pushed Mr. Natty Dresser through the door. Two dark outlines turned to meet my flare.

One gasped.

The other's Alpha-blue light flashed, as unexpected and dazzling bright as a Ninja assassin's bomb. Someone gasped—not me—because I was bracing myself for the full impact. Joy, oh joy. A huge undulating breaker of delft blue surged down the narrow hallway to meet my green challenge. There was no soft hello of two bright hues, no merging into turquoise. Our respective flares met, a tidal wave hitting a rickety pier.

Thank Goddess, I braced. As it was, the slap of his

dominance rocked me to my underpinnings—my right knee felt distinctly wobbly. Fortunately, my left knee said, "You're not Robson Trowbridge. We only go weak for him."

But no sooner had I finished cheering my self-fortitude than the next wave hit. The bag holding the tablet slid from my fingers. How can such a weightless thing—a flare is light after all—feel so tangible? So heavy?

"Bend!" it demanded.

Shit! I was melting faster than the Wicked Witch. I put a lock on both knees. *Balls, Hedi. Grow some balls.* I had royal Fae blood in me, didn't I? I had a wolf who'd caught the wink of an Alpha's eye, hadn't it?

"Vraiment, vous me défiez?" asked my sparring partner before adding a little more oomph to the throw down.

Geeze. What was he? Obi-wan Kenobi?

A bead of sweat rolled down my back, then sluiced between my ass checks. "Don't give in," I told myself, wanting to do precisely that. "You are stronger than you think you are. Last night you stood toe-to-toe with evil. You killed two men. You yanked a bolt out of your own shoulder blade. You traveled to another realm. You outlived a car accident. You outthought a shapeshifter. You are strong."

I want to fold, I want to fold.

You see? It's too easy to listen to the voice that tells you that you're too weak, or too small, or that your resistance amounts to nothing in the larger scheme of things.

Hold on. My knees started shaking. Literally knocking together.

Oh Goddess, for how long?

That's when my Fae, who'd sat and listened to my good-byes, and who'd watched death and destruction, and observed humility and loss, and all things humanizing, stepped up. "Do not bow to him," she said. And without further ado, she merged her presence with ours, and so, together, the three of us—she, me, and my inner-bitch—held.

As Strongholds do.

"You are a very stubborn woman." I heard the French guy sigh from the other side of the wall of delft blue. "It is not my desire to hurt you."

People have been saying that for days. I lifted my hand, finger poised, because frankly, using my magic was starting to become second nature. I'd been tripping, choking, smacking, cracking, and killing with my Fae talent for over seven hours.

"To him," I whispered.

There was a delay. A very *important* delay in response time because my Fae was busy shoring up my dissipating flare.

The Alpha sprang. Or flew (after Liam, nothing was too improbable or impossible). Whatever. A split second after my command, he and I were up close and uncomfortable. His legs bracketing mine while his large hands circled my throat. Curled over me he was, like a dog hunched over a meaty bone. Wolf breath on my forehead. Hot. Flavored with brandy.

Why do Weres always go for the neck and humans always go for the head?

He squeezed. I squeaked.

Merry leaped.

She went, as per her custom, for his cheek. A flash of whipping vines, then pincers pinched his flesh. *"Merde!"* His sharp hiss feathered my hair. I had a brief moment of hope, but his rear of surprise didn't greatly interfere with his desire to choke the ever-living life out of me. He could rear and throttle simultaneously—the man had very long arms.

Oh crap. Spots were forming. *I'm fading.*

"What's going on?" I dimly heard someone say.

"Nothing," lied the Frenchman. Through his near-blinding flare, I got a hazy impression of high cheekbones. The scent of blood—*not* mine—bloomed between us.

"Who's there?" A Spaniard.

"I believe it is Hedi Peacock," answered the guy squeezing my neck. He leaned so close that Merry's looped chain tickled my chin. "I suggest a temporary truce, mademoiselle," he whispered. "Perhaps you'll ask your amulet—it is sensible to words, yes?"

I grunted, my vocal cords too abused to squeeze out words.

"Then I would be gratified if you would ask it to release me?" he inquired softly. The squeezing-python sensation eased a tempting fraction—the implication clear. Air was on the other side of compliance.

Someone spoke up in the background. "Shall we call for reinforcements, St. Silas?" A Russian, sounding amused.

"I have everything in hand," he replied.

"Let him go, Merry," I whispered.

My amulet reluctantly released her pinch-hold, then wetly dropped from his cheek, still pulsing a purple-red light of her own. Immediately, the choking pressure around my throat was removed.

Air. Sweet Goddess, air.

"Now, as to your flare," St. Silas continued in his silky whisper.

I'm still flaring?

"I am an Alpha and I cannot allow you to defy me much longer. It is not done, you understand? And so, your defiance will end here, and that which you seek—for I am sure you have come here for a good reason—will never be discovered by those on the Great Council."

"I have things to show you," I rasped. "Things you need to hear."

"Then put out your flare," he said in a hard voice.

It seemed like a loss to comply, and I needed a win, or at least a draw. There was only one option left: I stiffly turned my head and directed my flickering flare to the wall. From my perspective, it wasn't a surrender, it was a cessation of direct fire.

The wall colored green while my tear ducts streamed.

He laughed softly under his breath. "You are a very rude woman. We will both extinguish flares at the same time, agreed?"

Speech was beyond me. With a curt nod, I closed my eyes.

Goddess. I slumped against the wall. Could eyes smoke? Blindly, I knelt to pat the ground, searching for the iPad. I heard the crack of knees—so, the French Were had some cartilage issues—and a cloud of Alpha stink surrounded me. "Is this what you want?" he asked. The weight of Knox's tablet settled on my thigh.

I don't like smelling other Alphas. I don't like having their essence coat my skin. That intimacy belongs to Trowbridge, and no other wolf.

I rested my head against the wall and breathed through my nose. My head ached, my sinuses throbbed. I pressed my fingers over my eyelids.

I had a roomful of Alphas to face.

"Allow me to help you to stand, Mademoiselle Peacock," he offered.

Like hell.

Walls are multipurpose things. They hold up structures, they're useful to have sex against, and dammit, this one would do to help me spider-walk myself to a standing position. When I was more or less upright, I counted four Mississippis, then turned to face St. Silas.

The Frenchman was a surprise. Like most mated Weres, he didn't show his age. Plus, he was francophone cool—

the type of French Canadian male who can wear a battered leather jacket at any age, and look supremely urbane and elegant. Blue eyes, some facial hair—but a nice scruff, mostly dark though patched with sections of white. About a week past due his layered haircut, but he evidently had a very good barber.

Astute, though. With eyes that revealed no inner thoughts.

His weren't streaming tears.

"After you, Ms. Peacock," he said, with a courtly wave.

I blotted my face with my sleeve as I passed him. When I walked into the suite proper, I was assailed by quick impressions, coming at me fast as a handful of confetti thrown in my face. This was no committee meeting. The opulent room was too empty. The scent signatures too distinct for a mass of wolves. And there was a curious flatness of smell.

Trowbridge listed in a silk-covered chair, set in the middle of the room.

"Hey," he slurred. The flare he'd attempted to summon at the sight of me was brief and short-lived—the tiny flicker of a lightning bug against the backdrop of very dark night.

"Hey," I replied.

Somewhere between here and the Peach Pit, he'd been given a change of clothing: a gray hoodie and a pair of jeans that would fit a man far heavier. He wore no T-shirt under that sweatshirt, and there was a rust-colored stain smeared across his chest. More blood bloomed on his knuckles. Another caked and broken line of it ran from the corner of his full lip to the edge of his chin.

Mine.

Déjà vu. I'd been here before. Threat circling my battered Trowbridge. But this time, *I* wasn't duct-taped to a kitchen chair.

And I was not helpless.

"She shouldn't be here," said Reeve Whitlock.

My gaze jerked to the wolf, who stood to the right of my man, gripping the blade he'd brandished at the Peach Pit. And all the other bits and pieces of information? The perplexing absence of witnesses and jury. The guard with his gun. The French Alpha. All those other threats blew away. Specks of gray confetti gusting in the wind.

Hurt him.

My magic sprang from me. It hurtled across the room, aimed for the center of his chest.

Take his black heart. Squeeze it in your grip until it beats no more.

Intuiting that something wicked came his way, Whitlock sucked in his gut and did a half spin, effectively reducing the strike zone to a much narrower profile. Instead of skewering him, my magic grazed his ribs.

Hit him again.

Before I could snap my wrist, he slashed at us with his blade—the wide sweeping arc of a blind man. A lucky swipe. It severed the long thin coil of glittering green light neatly in two. And with that, my green serpent, so abused, so overused, broke apart into a cloud of shimmering green iridescence.

I inhaled sharply in shock. My own heart—so cold, so focused—slamming inside me. My magic was too tired to re-form, too spent to reshape, but my nostrils had picked up a saliva-inducing layer of copper over woods, wolf, and enemy.

My inner-bitch—she of the tucked tail—now knew the possessive satisfaction of resting teeth on the nape of her meal.

She slipped her leash. "I am hungry for a hunt."

Chapter Twenty-Three

I'd scented blood so many times. Oozing from skinned knees, hidden under cloth bandages, leaking from plastic-covered meat trays. I'd understood it not by the quiver of my nose hair but by my reaction to it. Howling horror—*Daddy's stomach is torn open!* Blunt pain—*Mummy is gone.* Weeping despair—*don't cut my Trowbridge again!*

But now . . . oh Goddess, now.

It was a multilayered missive to the animal within me. We could smell what Whitlock had eaten, we could sense the faint metal tone of his hidden fear, we could taste the brine of his loathing. We knew him on the most basic level.

I sank into a feral crouch. I could feel the stretch of my lips, the air on our exposed front teeth.

The hunt. We leaped.

Whitlock turned to face our attack, his face split with a lupine leer.

I'd forgotten about the knife.

My mate hadn't. Trowbridge lurched upward—the guy with eight beers and a couple of hot dogs tucked under his belt who dimly perceives the arch of a home run overhead. With more luck than skill, he managed to snare my waist as I soared past him.

Momentum carried us. We hurtled over his chair, and I

hit the floor with a bloodcurdling howl. Trowbridge top-pled heavily on me, his body covering mine.

Trapping us. Holding us back. My inner-bitch's frustra-tion exploded. Growling and moaning, we arched under our mate. Teeth snapping, claws raking at his broad shoul-ders.

"Eaasssy."

I think that's what he muttered. Hard to make it out. I was überbitch and his face was buried in our hair . . . *Our* hair? I froze under him, registering the fact that I was hovering on the brink of a change. A real change. My spine—it was suddenly too short. While my rib cage—oh heavens—it was getting tighter.

My skin. It's crawling. Goddess, is it moving? Will I become my wolf here? Now? In front of them?

Our enemies were threatening shadows in the periph-ery of my vision. No. I couldn't be vulnerable in front of them—naked as a newly birthed pup.

I whimpered. *Help me, Trowbridge. Help me push her back.*

His scent wove around me, reeking of sun potion, and of dried blood, and of dull, unfocused anger. But there—love and anguish too. And now, fear. Not for him, but the same sort of nagging worry for me that I'd sensed on his skin before we'd made love.

"Eaassssy," he breathed again.

Trowbridge. The start of all my "mines."

The heavy pounding inside my chest eased, searched for unity with the rhythm of his. Pulses melded and set-tled.

Till two hearts beat as one.

A tear snaked down my temple. With a dark wordless mutter, he pressed a kiss to the tiny hollow between ear and jaw. He turned his head so his cheek rested on mine. His breath warmed the sensitive whorls of my inner ear.

"What took you so long?" he mumbled.

I lifted my lids. Stared into glazed blue eyes. His pupils were too dark, too wide.

My magic curled over his unprotected head. Curious and covetous, it licked at the sweat coating his forehead. Tiny sips. Testing and tasting.

"Whazzat?" he asked, his brows pulling together.

I stroked his jaw. "Just me."

"Don't want you here."

Sharp hurt. I stiffened under him again.

"Can't watch them hurt you," he said thickly.

"Hush." I pressed my fingers to his mouth, sealing it. "Can't you see I've come to rescue you?"

He shook his head, widening his eyes with obvious effort. A strained and shaky grin. "Coming for you. Trying to come for you. But I'm so—"

"Hammered," I filled in. My gaze hungrily roamed over him. *The most handsome man in this realm.* "You okay?"

"Been better," he muttered. "They've got plastic."

"What?"

He nodded to the floor. My gaze followed his, and my gut suddenly clenched. Indeed, the Great Council had plastic. A large sheet of it, heavy gauge, about the size of a large area rug, spread over the hotel's wall-to-wall.

Some trial. Some open court of inquiry.

"Separate them, Mathieu," I heard St. Silas say. Then some dumbass—male, wearing a nice watch—tried to do just that. He leaned into our space and tried to pry my mate off me. Freakin' idiot. Talk about pulling a hungry dog off his favorite bone. Trowbridge, though hovering on edge of the twilight zone, was *still* an Alpha.

Holding his mate. Worrying about "the plastic."

Trowbridge rolled off me and snatched up the glass objet d'art on the nearby coffee table. Before I'd risen to my knees, Trowbridge was standing behind Mathieu.

Breathing hard. The piece of glass flummery broken in two, its jagged edge pressed meaningfully against the dumbass's jugular.

Ralph let out a beacon of white light. An Asrai "Come on."

There was a sharp intake of breath—which I swear came from the corner where no one sat—then a veritable mélange of voices and threats erupted.

Whitlock, having righted himself, shouted, "You want proof that she's Fae? She tried to use her magic on me. Look at my ribs! Look at those amulets!"

Trowbridge threw out a promise of his own. "I'll cut him!"

And other voices—their volume rising but somehow distant. No one was *there*. The room I'd expected to be full of Alphas only held three. Who was talking? Where were the voices coming from?

Merry shone, fire bright, as I scrambled to my feet.

Voices. Angry voices. Who was watching us? Were they protected by a ward of invisibility?

Oh hell no. Been there. Done that.

We have to get out of here. Now. Trowbridge had a fierce flare. Why hadn't he used it? My problem-solving skills stretched as I tried to figure out exit strategies that included disarming a guy with a gun while supporting my mate as we lurched for freedom.

I could raise another flare, couldn't I? Hang the burning eyes. Screw the stabbing socket pain. *I can do this. No. I* will *do this.* If we both fired up our flares at the same time—

"I will handle this," said St. Silas.

The babble behind us bubbled for a moment longer, then silence fell. A heavy one, ripe with expectation that was far more frightening than the disembodied voices that had unnerved me a minute ago.

The soft wisps of hair on my nape bristled.

St. Silas spread his hands. "Bridge, this is beneath you. Release Mathieu. He is a good soldier and I would be grieved to lose him in such a manner."

Plastic crackled as Mathieu—presumably the wolf with the neck about to be slit like an envelope—shifted his weight uneasily.

"Want your word," said Trowbridge, breathing heavily.

"What do you want?"

"No pain. Promise me she feels . . . no pain."

Oh Goddess. There's that word again. I tugged his arm, ever so lightly because his balance was obviously crap. "Seriously? That's what you're bargaining for? That I won't feel pain? People have been promising not to hurt me for days. I *always* end up in pain. Couldn't you have bargained for a long life, filled with kids and prosperity?"

"Shhh," he said. Not a soft shush. More of a "Son of a bitch, for all that is holy, cease talking!"

"Trowbridge," I replied. "I don't like the way this is going. Let's say we get out of here. What say we start backing toward the door?"

Trowbridge weaved on his feet, thinking it over.

"Where will you go?" St. Silas inquired of my mate. "Leave this room and you are no longer the accused, you are the hunted. You will be run to ground, I can promise you that. And then? Sadly, I cannot promise that she will feel no pain. Bridge . . . you are an Alpha. Your days as rogue are over. You are held accountable to us now."

"I know what I am," he growled.

St. Silas sighed, then shrugged and said to the other guard, "Louis, shoot Ms. Peacock in the leg."

Quicker than a ladybug facing a can of bug spray, I scuttled behind Mathieu.

"You promise me!" Trowbridge shouted, his neck red. "Give me your word!" I could smell my lover's sweat. Feel the faintest tremble in his limbs as he fought to keep himself standing on two feet. He let out a thread of air through his teeth when I snagged his waistband and hauled upward.

"Very well," said St. Silas. "She will not feel pain."

Trowbridge sighed. "Good." Without further warning, he sent Mathieu spinning toward St. Silas. My lover reeled on his feet, equilibrium lost. All that kept him from sinking to the floor was my grip on his jeans.

Weres. They're so heavy.

And my hands? They'd been abused. But letting him fall to his knees in front of them—whoever they were? No. *This shall not pass.* Even if my arms began to tremble under the strain of managing six feet of muscle and man.

Merry hot against me.

Hold.

My cable of magic saw the problem through my Fae's eyes and solved it for me. She streamed back to us, and did a lap around his lean waist—a safety belt of fluorescent green—then knotted herself around my wrist.

"That you again?" Trowbridge muttered.

"Yup."

Merry belayed up her chain, made a short leap to Trowbridge's shoulder, and sat there. Belly facing forward, her light a color I rarely saw—purple-red in the center, bleeding outward into fiery orange. With an expressive shudder, she untwined two vines. They did a circle over Trowbridge.

"Jesus," he slurred. "I really hate this sun potion shit."

Impasses are exactly that. Little time-outs while people talk with their eyes. I could tell that Trowbridge was using his—St. Silas's gaze rested heavily on him, engaged in a wordless communication with my mate.

Meanwhile, I had things to say to Whitlock.

I'm going to kill you.

Soon.

Chin lowered, Whitlock sent me his own death glare. I glowered back. The burn in my eyes intensified, and I saw the answering flicker of Alpha light in his.

"Merde," said St. Silas. "Reeve, extinguish your flare." There was hidden steel in those soft tones, and perhaps a history there too because Whitlock's jaw hardened with resentment.

But, after the faintest pause, the leader of the NAW complied. The small flame that lit his blue iris died, and I was left staring at a man who looked human and was not, who smelled of Were and threat, and who I knew, without any doubt in my heart, meant to see this day finished with me and my mate rolled into a neat package of plastic.

I'll kill you first.

"Louis," said St. Silas, "reset the chair for the Alpha of Creemore. And find another for his consort."

"Reeve Whitlock is lying," I said for the benefit of all who listened. "Neither Trowbridge nor I have had anything to do with the trade of sun potion."

"Make her go," said the unseen Russian, his tone bored.

My grip tightened on Trowbridge. "Who *is* that?"

St. Silas squeezed the bridge of his nose, then walked over to the desk. He pivoted the laptop resting on it.

"You video-conference?" I gasped. Son of a bitch. I hadn't seen that coming. There were four open windows. Inside each, respectively, from left to right: a vain blond stud, an effete tulip of fashion, a thickset brute with a bowl of nuts, and a guy with a face like a hatchet.

"But of course, Miss Peacock," replied St. Silas, with heavy sarcasm. "The Great Council forever stays abreast of technology."

"That is not her name." The Russian chose a pistachio from the bowl balanced on his thighs. "She is the get of

Benjamin Stronghold." His lip jutted as he concentrated
on splitting open a shell with his thick nail. "I remember
him. Good man. Strong. Could have been a second to the
Alpha of Creemore one day." He inspected the green meat,
gave a small grunt, then popped it into his mouth. Small
eyes studied me as he chewed. "Then he met the Fae
woman. And he became not so strong, not so good." The
Russian studied me for another brooding second, then
said heavily, "And she is the result." He tossed the husks
onto the discard pile. "Make her leave."

"I have a video!" Except, where was the iPad? I must
have dropped it preleap. "Also, a spreadsheet . . ." My
gaze darted, sweeping the floor, until I spotted the carrier
bag. The edge of the tablet peeked out of the neck of it,
still swaddled in wool.

"This is exactly why we don't let mates attend trials.
Too many countercharges. Too much emotion," said the
studly wolf reclining on a king-sized bed (bare chest
gleaming, brocade pillows propped behind his head). His
speech had a Nordic intonation, very faint. "Slows things
down. In the end it always comes down to the Alpha."

Oh, spare me.

"Who isn't fit to stand trial," I pointed out. "Much less
defend himself or me. Look, I can clear this up in a second." Trowbridge started to list to the left. I gave his
jeans another surreptitious upward tug. "Just pass me the
tablet."

"This is the Great Council," said Whitlock. "They deal
with Alphas here, not their consorts."

"Shut up, Whitlock," muttered Trowbridge.

A flicker—a spit of delft blue—gleamed in St. Silas's
eyes. "A valid point, Reeve." He studied me for a moment, then turned to my mate. "Bridge, this is not a family
court, you comprehend? This is a session of the Supreme
Alphas, and serious charges have been laid against you,

which you must answer to. Normally, she would be sent from the room. To wait, like any other, to discover the fate of her consort. But as your mate has pointed out, you are drugged and not entirely coherent." He moved to the tea cart where he righted a cup onto a saucer. "My esteemed colleagues are very busy men." Thoughtfully, he lifted the teapot. "Are you able to answer our questions?"

Trowbridge's jaw worked then he said slowly, "Whitlock drugged me."

"Again," yawned the guy in the bed. "This could stretch out forever. Can't we cut through this? What do you say, Gregori?"

The Russian placed the bowl on the table beside his seat. He scrubbed his head. "I have a business to run. If she will not leave the room peacefully, let her stand for her mate."

"That's entirely against protocol!" piped up the effete guy.

St. Silas poured a cup. "No, Charles. It is unusual but not completely against 'protocol.' " The tone he used for the last word spoke volumes about his feelings on that subject. "Bridge, consider what I put in front of you most carefully. If she speaks for you, then you may not. Not a single word, you comprehend? By giving your assent, you waive your right to speech inside these rooms." He added four sugars to his cup. "One would need to trust his mate very deeply to let her stand for you."

Trowbridge leaned back his head to stare through half-slit eyes at the Quebec wolf.

Don't look at him. Look at me.

What was he thinking? Was he even capable of logical thought? Or was he drifting along, encased in the happy bubble sensation that comes with multiple hits of sun potion?

Trust me.

St. Silas took a sip, then asked indifferently, "So, Robson Trowbridge, Alpha of the Ontario wolves, leader of the Creemore pack, what is your wish? Shall it be your mate who answers the charges or you?"

Choose me, Trowbridge. Let me speak for you. I'm a half-blooded Fae. My lies are not broadcast in my scent. Trust me, Trowbridge.

"You up to it, mate?" he asked, his gaze still resting on St. Silas.

I wanted to close my eyes in relief. Asking me if I was up to lying was like asking a washed-out former kid star if he was up to taking a line of coke. Or course I was. Spinning tall tales was one skill I'd taken the time to study and practice. "Yes."

He leaned back in his chair and let his head rest against the seat's pillowed back. "Works for me."

Whitlock started, and sought to cover his sudden agitation by pouring another inch of whiskey into his tumbler.

"Very well," said St. Silas in a brisk tone. "The formal inquiry is now open. Be it known that Robson Trowbridge has accepted the substitution of his mate. Her words will be his words. Her truths and lies, his. She will stand for him."

And this time I'll do it right.

St. Silas smiled. "Miss Peacock, many charges have been laid. In the interest of economy of time, let us move directly to the essential issue, which is—

"Her allegiance," growled the Russian. "Is she Fae or is she wolf?"

"That is not of immediate concern." St. Silas put down his cup. Crossed his arms. "The question is, has she or her mate engaged in trade with the Fae?"

"No," I said flatly. *There, subject done.*

"Never?"

"Never," I replied.

"Of any kind, whatsoever?"

"Nope." This was going to be easier than I'd thought.

"Test her scent," said the Spaniard tightly. "See if she lies."

I couldn't help it. The corner of my lip lifted ever so lightly.

Whiskey slopped when Whitlock slammed his glass on the table. "She's half Fae," he said in disgust. "She doesn't carry a scent and St. Silas knew it when he asked her to stand for Trowbridge."

"Not true," murmured St. Silas.

Whitlock's knee bobbed, telegraphing his building irritation. "That bit about Trowbridge being too soused to answer—what a crock of shit. St. Silas has effectively taken his ability to scent lies off the table."

The Frenchman inclined his head. "How could I possibly know she doesn't have a scent? I've never met her before."

Fumes of frustration rose from Whitlock. "But you've met other Faes. You know they're scentless."

"Never a half-blooded one." St. Silas's tone turned hard. "I based my knowledge on what I knew of halflings. And they carry the scent of their wolf from father to child." He glanced at the plastic carrier bag. "I, for one, wish to see this video now."

Trowbridge swayed as Mathieu unwrapped the tablet and passed it to his boss.

St. Silas turned it over in his hands, then pressed the button on the side.

He stared at the screen.

Then he pressed the on button another time. "It doesn't work," he said, lifting his gaze from the pad.

Karma fucking hates me.

* * *

St. Silas's pronouncement provoked a babble of voices, speaking over each other. They spoke so fast, and broke over each other so ruthlessly that I couldn't track who was talking. I could only listen, my gaze riveted to St. Silas's, my hopes draining as they argued. Team Trowbridge was losing.

"Maybe the battery's dead," I said to St. Silas.

"You dropped it, *ma chère.*"

The Spaniard observed, "This is exactly why we don't have mates testify on behalf of their men."

No, no. I gave it a shake. "There's a spreadsheet on it. A really—"

"Shall we vote?" said the Russian.

"It's their client list!" I shouted. Well, I'd meant it to come out as a shout, but I was anxious, and pissed. And I'm female. It came off as an earsplitting shriek, that clearly hurt at least one listener's ears because someone whined in protest.

Were hearing.

While I had their attention, I went straight into the good stuff. "Their clients were culled from the NAW's kill list. All the information is there, including payment history and credit card details. Neither Trowbridge nor I have access to the NAW's kill list," I said, mentally thinking, *Ta-dah!* "Only Knox and Whitlock would."

Whitlock picked up his glass. "You've got your facts wrong there. I've never accessed the kill list either."

Crap.

"Check the user logs," he said with a hard smile. "I've never logged in to the database. Not once." He wrinkled his nose to emphasize his overall distaste. "Not much of a fan of halflings. Let them die, that's what I say."

St. Silas considered Whitlock, then the tablet. "Perhaps our flares drained it. All the electricity . . ."

"That could be it," I said, working to infuse some confidence in my tone.

"Louis, have you a charger?" asked St. Silas. "It would be good to see the video."

"She's just jerking your chain. Wasting time." Whitlock crossed his leg and balanced his glass on his calf. "Gentlemen, everything she's said so far has just reinforced what I told you before." He jerked his chin in my direction. "Knox saw an opportunity when he met this one. The last of the Fae. Young and impressionable. Hungry for attention. But she couldn't open the portal with her amulet so he teamed her up with Trowbridge. She needed Bridge's amulet to reopen the portals."

Ralph took exception to that. He glowed, white hot.

Whitlock shook his head. "We've all heard what she did to get it. Killing the old Alpha of Creemore. Sacrificing her aunt. Mating with Trowbridge. That's all common knowledge. And she's never denied that she pushed him into the gate." He lifted the glass and swirled the ice. "My mate's healing in Merenwyn," he mimicked. "Yeah, right. Trowbridge needed a cover while he spent time with the Fae."

I let go of my mate's jeans. I stepped in front of him, Merry shining on my chest. "Trowbridge forbade me to send him to Merenwyn. I waited until he was unconscious and sent him there against his wishes. He never traded with the Fae. He never wanted to go to their realm."

"Blah, blah, blah," said Whitlock. "If that was true, he'd have been back in a couple of hours. Instead, he spent six months, living the good life, making trade agreements with his new buddies—"

"He was held captive by the Fae," I shouted. "He loathes them!"

Silence, of the particularly piercing kind, followed that announcement.

The Spaniard's pitch was soft. "Then why did he mate with you?"

Chapter Twenty-Four

Because I tricked him—that was the real answer. Because I didn't give him a chance to figure out who he was saying the words to—that was another truth. Because I'd have done anything to have kept him living.

Anything.

I'd stolen him from death's claws. Because I'd wanted his life woven into mine. His love wrapped around me. That's what I'd hungered for. Though that night, I hadn't allowed myself to dwell on what he'd wanted.

Since then, I couldn't seem to stop thinking about how all the things he'd wanted—a pack, recognition, his own lands—they'd all been dangled in front of him, then jerked away. *You want this? You can't have it.*

Death. Fate. Karma. One or all of those entities hadn't forgotten my theft. They kept coming at us. From the back, from the front, from the side. *Has it been worth it, Trowbridge? I know you love me. I've felt it in your touch. But have I been worth it?* I kept my gaze fixed on Whitlock as whatever warmth I'd had drained out of me. Thus, I sensed, rather than saw, Trowbridge turn his head to stare at me.

Don't look into his eyes. You may not want to read the answer waiting there.

His scent spiced. But I still wouldn't look at him.

So my mate spoke to me and to them, the only way he could.

Through touch.

Robson Trowbridge stepped closer, sliding an arm around my waist, drawing me back so that my hip rested against the juncture of his thighs. My body was stiff, telegraphing the insecurities that never left me. With a soft tut, he nudged the back of my knee with his. I fell against him, my head finding that place I'd started thinking of as another "mine"—that hard and welcome spot above the rise of his pectorals but below his collarbone.

Up came his other arm, to circle my shoulders, and to sweep aside the neck of my shirt. It laid bare to their gaze the base of my neck where there should been a permanent mark of the mate bond.

There was no silver half-moon scar.

Just my Fae skin. Smooth and pale.

Outwardly? I think I turned to stone. While inside? Mortal-me flinched, and railed, and cried too. For in that instant, My One True Thing had laid me more naked to the wolves than if he'd stripped the shirt off my back and slipped the jeans off my hips.

My Were stiffened inside me.

How could you? Before them?

The muscled arm around my waist tightened in reproof. Then Trowbridge slowly bent his head—warm breath on skin turned suddenly cold—and lowered his mouth to the sacred place, the hollow where mates leave marks and scars are formed. A swipe of his tongue sent a shiver along my spine.

Over the place he'd once toothed, he bit down. Not hard enough to break my flesh, but with enough pressure to make me take in a quick breath. A moment—he surely held his teeth in that gentle nip for no longer than one perfect moment.

Sometimes moments are all you need.

Heart of my heart. Mate for all my years. I offer you my life.

He turned the pantomime of mate-bite into the softest kiss. A gentle one, a visual demonstration to even the thickest, blindest, most doubting wolf that I was loved. I was precious. I was wanted.

I was his.

Tears blurred my eyes when Trowbridge lifted his chin. His jaw grazed mine—skin warming with the soft scrape of his stubble—then it found its customary place at my brow. He draped his heavy arm over the front of me, covering up the skin that belonged to both him and me.

Together then. We'll face it together.

My mate's final summation on the mate-bond topic was directed to Whitlock and executed with typical Trowbridge efficiency. Just one quick upward jerk of his jaw—a "see that?" and "screw you" all rolled into one.

No one can deliver a challenge as insolently as my Trowbridge.

I damn near cried when his callused palm flattened to rest protectively (and yes, perhaps possessively too) over the place he'd laid his mark.

I am loved.

And I am tired. Of some wolves and some men. Of doubts and fears. Of yo-yo destinies and taunting futures.

"Let me cut to the chase," I said. "I can give you the Safe Passage and the Gatekeeper." Amazing how a big honking dollop of self-confidence can clear your mind. Suddenly, I wasn't the game novice, stunned into silence by the complexity of the chess board. I was the Chess Master.

"The Gatekeeper will answer," I said. "We have never met and I will be a stranger to her." My lover's arm was a solid band of steel as I pointed to liar-liar-pants-on-fire.

"But she's met Whitlock. She's eaten pie with him. Let St. Silas read her face when she sees him. Let your truth sensor ask the Gatekeeper who she traded with. Trowbridge or Whitlock?"

Whitlock's flare was the car behind you on the highway. The one driven by the guy who used his high beams without prejudice.

It blinded me. So, I didn't have a chance to see him charge, blade drawn. If I had? I might have flinched or stiffened up. Any of those reactions would have made it harder for Trowbridge to toss me aside in time to face Whitlock's knife.

Lucky me. I didn't have time to react.

Whitlock went into a crouch, then he slashed at Trowbridge. A foolish move. A long swipe when he should have jabbed, rabbit-punch fast.

But he used the knife like a man accustomed to guns.

He'd never lived in a world where weapons were the rock by your hand and the sand by your feet. I'd imagine the only time he'd ever really fought was in his wolf form. Perhaps that's why he wasted so much time circling Trowbridge.

My guy didn't circle.

He didn't even turn his body. He just looked over his shoulder.

Whitlock lunged. My mate feinted to the right, then flowed right back toward Whitlock. So smoothly, so fluidly was his reaction. And then, with a thud, and smack, Whitlock was down, his neck pinned under Trowbridge's knee.

Kill him. Slowly.

St. Silas rapped out a string of French. Mathieu and Louis rushed in. Mathieu to press his gun under Trowbridge's jaw, Louis to position his above Whitlock's ear.

"You cannot kill him." St. Silas.

"Watch me," replied Trowbridge, indifferent to the gag rule.

"No, my friend."

"He's guilty! You can see he's guilty!" shouted Trowbridge.

"Yes, I can see and smell his guilt," murmured the Quebec Alpha. "But we have—"

Trowbridge snarled. "Don't you tell me you have some fucking protocol."

"Bridge. Your mate has stood for you. She must stand for you now." St. Silas exhaled, a man brought to a place he didn't want to be. "Miss Peacock, it is you who must mete out the final punishment. Your mate must stand back and allow you to finish this."

Yes.

"Tink?"

"I need to do this," I said, gazing at Whitlock.

"Stand down, Bridge," murmured St. Silas.

He did, reluctance and hurt for me written on his expression.

Louis snagged a chair, and positioned it onto the plastic. Whitlock was forced into it. Mathieu helped hold the leader of the NAW in place, while zip tics were used to secure his hands to the armrests. Whitlock began to protest but his cry was smothered by a hand over his mouth, and then that temporary gag was replaced by a length of duct tape.

Plastic crackled as St. Silas took up a position behind the chair. He placed an arm around Whitlock's throat, and positioned his hand so that it was over his head.

A choke hold.

Silence in the room, as I went to the table. I stared at Whitlock's knife. Picked it up. Felt its weight. Knew that once I finished using it, my soul and my hand would always remember the feel of the wooden handle, the heft of the knife.

"Nice balance," I said.

"St. Silas," said Trowbridge in a low voice. "Let me do it for her."

Afraid that it will change me forever? I am changed. Oh, Trowbridge, I already am.

"No, my friend," replied the Quebec wolf. "She must see it to the end."

"Don't fret, Trowbridge," I said, wishing that I was numb. "I can do this. I'm getting good at killing."

Though it was easier when the victim fought back. When he wasn't tied. When he was a direct threat to me and mine. This revenge? It was as cold as the knife's blade.

But it didn't sicken me.

Five steps to Whitlock. That's all it took.

I bent so that we were eyeball to eyeball. Then I said, "This is for Harry." I plunged the knife into his belly. Felt it slide in smoothly. Blood gushed. Not a neat kill.

Anguish in Whitlock's eyes.

I said, so softly, "And this is for Brenda."

And then I turned the knife in his belly, at the exact moment that St. Silas snapped his neck.

Now, I'm a multiple murderer. May Karma be kind.

Back on the highway again. Driving northward on the 400—a roadway that would from this point on be forever subtitled in my thoughts as Hedi's Highway to Hell. St. Silas was at the wheel of his rental. I sat beside him. We were alone in the sedan. That was a bit of an insult—I was after all the Fae with magic at her hands. Shouldn't St. Silas have entertained the slightest qualm that I might turn on him? Summon up the Fae in me and choke him with my magic?

Evidently not, because he knew, as I did, that my mate was in back of that van behind us. And that vehicle was loaded with two guards, one who was clearly motivated to prove that his indiscretion in the hall had been a blip. Louis had been unnecessarily rough with Trowbridge, slamming him into a couple of walls along the short path from the garage elevator to the van.

There seemed to be a direct correlation between how much I pissed someone off and how many bruises Trowbridge accumulated.

St. Silas drove well, his attention split between the road and his thoughts. We'd traveled for an hour, with not a word spoken between us. I was Marie Antoinette again. Sitting in my cart, traveling to the guillotine.

Whitlock's death hadn't led to a chorus of "Hail Robson Trowbridge and his Consort, the Fabulous Hedi Peacock." What had erupted after that . . . *oh Goddess* . . . those men would go down with their cruise ship, their lifeboat still attached to the davits, arguing over who manned the oars and who took the tiller.

Immediately following my dispatch of Whitlock, the Spaniard had aligned himself with the Russian, both voicing their original opinion that in the bigger scheme of threats, it mattered little who really traded sun potion. Of greater concern was the fact that the Alpha of Creemore's consort was a Fae.

Who could open portals.

Yeah, there's some irony there.

Too late to tell them I'd never succeeded in summoning one. Too late to back up. Hadn't I just stood there so proudly, so confidently, and told them that I could? I'd radiated confidence, hadn't I? Even the guards had read it on my face. I knew I would succeed in summoning a portal. I had the coin in my pocket, hadn't I? And MOTT's arm draped around me, right?

I could fucking jump tall buildings with one leap.

As soon as the Russian had launched his conspiracy

theory, Trowbridge had shifted me so I was less in front of his body and more to the side of it. "We're done," he'd told them, his tone definitely threatening. "Whitlock's dead. Let us go."

Gregori had cracked a nut. "No," he'd said.

"Agreed," the Spaniard had added. "Interrogate her. We need to know how to summon the portal."

And that's when Trowbridge went ballistic. He'd already put it together, right? While I was still rubbing my palms against my jeans, convinced I'd never get the smell of Whitlock off me, he'd been thinking ahead. And thus, he'd seen what I hadn't, and he'd anticipated what I hadn't gotten around to worrying about. The Great Council wasn't going to leave a portal unguarded and open to Fae travel. The Gatekeeper had to die, and her gates permanently closed.

They'd asked me to kill the Gatekeeper.

Lopping off someone's head (the Spaniard's suggestion) is the kind of proposition over which your brain should pause and linger. Sadly, I hadn't been as appalled at the suggestion as one might expect. Since (*a*) I didn't know her, and (*b*) I was already a mass murderer. Too late to grow a conscience now.

Besides, I never said when I'd lop her head. And personally? I was thinking that execution could wait. Until after Lexi's problems were solved. And Trowbridge and I had led the Raha'ells through the Safe Passage.

I'd said, "Okay."

Then, Trowbridge had said, "You bastards." Because he'd realized what would happen after I killed the Gatekeeper and permanently shut down the portal. Good-bye to Trowbridge and his Fae. Which is why he went berserk, and the reason, despite his balance issues, he'd attempted to tear St. Silas and his guards into two pieces. Or three.

But it always comes down to guns, doesn't it?

St. Silas had grabbed Louis's weapon and held it on me, shouting that Trowbridge's "Contempt of Council" would be answered by a bullet to my left arm. Followed by another bullet to my right arm. And so it would go. Legs following arms, torso points that didn't protect vital organs being next.

The threat had worked. Trowbridge had stopped his drunken rampage of furniture and face breaking. He'd subsided with a growl, though he'd still seethed, a smoking Vesuvius ready to erupt molten lava.

All this had taken less than a minute. Sixty seconds, give or take, where I'd stood there . . . confused.

I'd rescued us, hadn't I?

Solemnly, my mate wordlessly shook his head at me. Kind of the way the guy living at the bottom of the hill might have after the top of his pretty mountain blew off.

Oh.

Evidently, my flare-down with St. Silas had struck the Great Council as being less spunky than punky. And my physical attack on Whitlock (an Alpha of stature) and my subsequent verbal defiance to them (Bigger Alphas of Bigger Statures) had not been chalked down to a woman standing by her man. It was defiance. Pure and simple.

Okay. I got it: I was a threat to the Great Council. Worse, they assumed I had Fae friends.

Oh crap, I'd thought. *We're toast.*

Doesn't the good guy ever freakin' win?

We passed the sign for Bradford. I'd watched it grow from a small green square to something roughly the size of a small billboard, my gut clenching and unclenching. The next exit would be the Peach Pit's.

Soon, I thought. *One way or the other, it will all be over in less than a half hour.*

It was almost a relief. I could finally sleep.

Suddenly, St. Silas spoke. "Why did you assume leadership of the pack while your mate was in Merenwyn?"

Of all the questions he could have posed, that one threw me. I turned to study his face. He kept his eyes on the road and his scent neutral. "Why do you want to know?"

"After you sent Bridge through the gates, you stayed to live among his wolves," he observed, his tone reflective. "You could have gone back to your old life, among the humans. Why did you choose to wait there—in Creemore?"

My hands knotted. "Free us."

"I cannot free you," he replied. "We must deal with this gatekeeper. A portal between their realm and ours cannot be left open and unattended."

"So, I summon her, then I kill her. But the real question is, what happens after that?"

"You will seal the portal."

"And following that," I bit out, "what exactly will the Great Council do about me and Trowbridge?" There—that's the real question, isn't it? I turned my head away, knowing he wouldn't answer it.

The fields flashed by. The reaping long over; crops shorn to stubbled stalks.

It wouldn't matter if I swore on my mum's soul that there was only one portal that could be opened by yours truly. And that I'd never, ever, ever open another portal. They wouldn't believe me. They'd probably weight our bodies and toss them into the Peach Pit's fetid pond. My ghost forever taunted by the fact that I was *that* close to pie.

St. Silas returned to his earlier line of questioning. "You displayed no desire to lead a pack or aptitude for it before you sent Bridge to Merenwyn. I cannot understand why you chose to stay. The pack has not been your family."

"No," I said. "They've never been that."

"It must have been difficult," he said with a sideways glance, "to live among us and not be one of us."

Fishing, was he? I shrugged. "I'd thought if I stayed I could hold Trowbridge's position—make sure that he had something to claim when he returned." I went for my ear, finding the tip. Two strokes to soothe, a third to calm. "I didn't want him to have to start from zero again. He'd already had everything taken from him."

His family. His status. His future.

Maybe more than instinct and hormones had been at play when Trowbridge sparked my first flare. We'd been the same, hadn't we? Trowbridge and me? Adrift after the night Mannus and Lou had destroyed our families. Seeing him? He'd been the Bridge to my nostalgia, carrying me back to the days when I was part of something that amounted to "Us Against the World."

I would have sold my soul to re-create a facsimile of that life.

New love shouldn't be embroidered onto old memories. Those bittersweet recollections belong where they live—deep inside you.

I'd felt shame, and remorse. Love and longing too.

I'd wanted to make amends.

"There's so many things I couldn't give my mate," I said, thinking about it, "but I could give him that—a place to belong if he wanted to."

"But you hoped he would not want to stay with the pack," St. Silas said with surprising acuity.

"Yes." I turned my head to look at him. "I'd hoped he'd just want to be with me."

The Quebec Alpha tilted his head. "It could not be so. It is against our nature. Wolves need to live among the pack. Those who do not—they pine."

My gaze slid away from him, thinking about the day Trowbridge had walked into my Starbucks. I hadn't seen him in ten years. When he sat down at the table, my life changed. Right there, between one beaker of soy milk and a double shot of espresso.

I'd been wishing my brother would come back.

I'd been waiting for My One True Thing.

What had he been pining for? The pack? Is that why he'd returned to Mannus's territory? Examining it now, I realized that Rachel's request for some brotherly intervention didn't hold up. I'd seen Rachel with her brother. Neither of them loved each other the way I loved Lexi. Trowbridge must have seen through it. And yet, he'd risked all when he'd crossed into Ontario.

He'd returned. Not to the bosom of his family, but to the heart of the pack. Because the need to belong was greater than the need to preserve his own life.

I'd known it, hadn't I? Though unshaped and muddled, the thought had flickered on the edges of my consciousness. I'd waited by a fairy pond, instinct telling me that eventually he'd return to the place he belonged.

A wolf needs a pack.

And yet. By heavens . . . he loved me. His teeth on my skin—*his kiss*—it had said more to me than a thousand words.

Us against the world.

"Why are you interested in all this?" I asked testily.

"Because you never answered Gregori's question. Are you wolf or are you Fae?"

"You people keep asking me to define myself." Merry shifted slightly. I gazed at her, wondering what she saw when she studied me. "I don't even know what I am yet. I keep finding myself being pushed from one identity to another, and with every jump I'm a little different. I refuse to choose. I'm both. I am Benjamin's and Roslyn's daughter."

"Which makes you dangerous."

"Am I any more dangerous than you? All I want to do is to protect those that are mine."

"And yet, your definition of what is 'mine' keeps enlarging, gaining territory."

He had that right.

"Very much like a wolf," he murmured.

And the phrase echoed in my head, as the last exit sign flashed by us.

Like a wolf.

Chapter Twenty-Five

Money talks. And so does violence, or the threat of it. The owner of the Peach Pit spent ten minutes with St. Silas, then closed the business for the day. Employees were sent home. One of the wolves called in as backup muscle stood sentry down at the end of the long drive, ready to tell any pie lover that they'd have to travel farther on the 400 to satisfy their sweet tooth.

The vigilance against the curious struck me as unnecessary. We could have summoned the portal in front of a busload of tourists and they'd have just stood there, eating pie, thinking the lights and the smoke was yet another spiffy amusement offered by the Peach Pit.

Case in point: I'd held the faint hope when St. Silas pulled into the restaurant's parking lot that we'd find it cordoned off with yellow caution tape and damn near full to bursting with black-and-white cruisers. Why? Because Ryan's abandoned car was still there, parked where Liam and he had left it.

Now, if I'd driven up to work, and noticed a vehicle that had clearly spent a portion of the night sitting in the lot (the windows were dewed), I'd have thought to myself, "Gee, Hedi, I wonder whose car that is?" And then, I would have done what anyone with a scintilla of curiosity would have—I'd have moseyed over to the vehicle and peeked inside. That's when I'd probably have noticed the long trail of mud and blood leading from the pond to the top of the small hill.

Hello, crime scene. Didn't anyone watch *CSI*?

Humans. They're the mortal equivalent of a dray horse wearing blinders. For crap's sake, signs of a mortal struggle were right *there*. All they'd had to do was walk a few feet toward the animal pens to see it.

"Where is this portal, Miss Peacock?" inquired St. Silas, opening my door. "Over the pond?"

"No." I pointed to the fenced-in train ride. "It's down over there."

St. Silas's right eyebrow rose. "Interesting."

I looked over his shoulder to the gray van. Mathieu had pulled into a spot closer to the restaurant. He sat behind the wheel, watching us from his side-view mirror. The vehicle's ignition was off, but the engine ticked as it cooled.

The Alpha turned to follow my gaze. "You look for your mate? He will stay where he is until I get a sense for the land." Then he swept his hand. "Lead the way, *ma chère*."

I swallowed. *Call the gates. Kill a Fae. Today's to-do list sucks.* Wearily, I slid out of the car, and led St. Silas down the little hill, and past the go-cart track and the sign that said THIS WAY TO THE BEST PIE IN ONTARIO! Once we broached the cement walkway, I turned left.

Under sunlight, the kiddie ride was even more incongruous. A chain-link fence, the type used to surround municipal swimming pools, circled the cement pad. Six enormous wolves, set on plinths, provided the wow factor for the tiny-tot train riders. The actual train was missing. I supposed it was locked up in the adjacent shed.

"*This* is the entrance to the Safe Passage," he said slowly. He glanced at me, then at the enclosure again. Suspicion spiced his scent.

"If I'm lying, I'm dying," I said blandly.

He cocked his head. "Would that be black humor?"

"Oh yes." Jesting was preferable to shivering. I swore I felt the iron leaching from the rust, its numbing cold wicking up from the ground, chilling the soles of my feet. Being around so much iron—the only thing I hadn't done over the last eight hours was eat the stuff—had increased my sensitivity to it. I'd have to move fast. The longer I stayed inside the fence, the weaker I'd feel.

"Shall we call the portal?" St. Silas swung the fence gate open and gestured inside.

I hate we-jobs. The person who does the talking never does the walking.

Worry bit at me as I stepped inside. I'd never tried to call a portal in daylight, and Lou had always waited for dusk before she began her song. What if darkness and a moon were two open-sesame requirements?

St. Silas followed me inside, and shut the fence gate behind us.

Geez Louise.

It was spookier inside the place than out. The flatness of the concrete. The serpentine rails. The six statues. Seen close up in daylight, they packed a predatory punch. Partly due to their size, and partly due to the realism the artist had infused into the cast stone. The tendons, the bunched muscles, the teeth . . . *Talk about putting your head into the jaws of the wolf.* The smallest of them would loom over me.

I studied them hard, trying to figure out which of the six appeared the most hungry for a mouthful of coin. *One coin. Six one-armed bandits.* The majority were cast from the same mold, poised with their snouts open, their muzzles lifted upward for a howl.

The easiest thing would be to try each animal, but that would look lame. I took a moment to sort through Brenda's statements, then smiled. She said that you gave the coin to the *wolves,* not the wolf. How fortunate, then, for me. The statues were placed in pairs, like mates.

The first set was dismissed because they were too close to the steel tracks. A Fae would take one look at the rust and back away. The second couple was disqualified because of their positioning (shoulder to shoulder versus snout to snout) and aspect (poised too close to the restaurant.) They felt wrong.

Those two are guards, watching out for humans.

The final duet sat square in the middle of a large loop of track. They'd been posed in a playful montage. Significantly larger than his mate, the male stood, paws braced for challengers, as brave as Nanu of the north. His jaw was open—*hungrily* open.

The other half of the bonded pair was unique among the statues, as she'd posed in the act of giving her mate a shoulder check instead of mid-howl. Her mouth was slightly ajar, her dainty head coquettishly cocked sideways, as if she planned to nip his snout.

I chewed my lip. Was the oddly heart-shaped space between them large enough for a doorway to another realm? Possibly. Though the portal traveler would have to be a diminutive biped or a four-pawed canine.

The Fae had to have modest height. Hadn't Whitlock said she resembled a troll? According to Mum, they were short and ugly, and quicker-tempered than a dwarf who'd spent too long underground in the caves of Cairynglaze.

Goddess, don't be a real live troll.

My mouth dried. It took two hard swallows to acquire enough saliva to say, "I'll need Trowbridge."

"Why?" asked St. Silas.

"I need his blood. Mine isn't pure enough." Maybe it

was, maybe it wasn't. But I did need Trowbridge. Here. Beside me. Rescue got less complicated if I could pry him out of the van.

St. Silas considered it for a moment, then turned to call to Mathieu. "Bring the Alpha of Creemore." Then he turned back, his gaze sweeping the enclosure. "Your mate and I will go this far," he said, "and no farther."

Mathieu swung the van's back doors wide to reveal the Alpha of Creemore sitting on a tire, his arms braced on his knees, his thumb slowly working his palm. Trowbridge gave the guard a long look from under his brows.

He didn't move. He just looked.

Perhaps my lover's scent was particularly pungent. Mathieu took a quick step backward and raised his gun.

Trowbridge growled. "You think this puppy's going to keep me from my mate's side?"

"I am confident he cannot," replied St. Silas. "But I can and will." He pulled out a pair of handcuffs. Metal. The type you see hanging from a cop's belt. "Join us, if you will."

Trowbridge leaped out, all agile grace and coiled menace. He took a few steps down the slope, then paused, his gaze flicking from Mathieu to the mud slick I'd left. In daylight, the deep twin trail my knees had gouged looked worse—wider somehow. "That's my mate's blood," he said, lifting his head. Impotence and fury— never a good combination for my man. "Who dragged her up this hill?"

As no one volunteered the information, I said, "Liam."

"Where is he?" His tone was pitched so low I had to strain to hear it.

"Probably having tea with Lucifer. Because I killed him this morning."

The vein by his right eye pulsed. "Did you make him hurt?"

It saddened me to remember just how much I'd wanted to make Liam hurt. *Watching Newland's punishment had sickened me. Killing Liam had thrilled me. Knifing Whitlock had felt . . . so very right. There's a certain de-evolution going on here.*

I lifted my shoulders, Merry glowering orange on my chest. "Feathers flew."

Trowbridge's smile showed all his teeth.

St. Silas snapped one cuff to the chain-link fence and offered the other to my mate. "Will you do me the courtesy of attaching this to your wrist?"

A blue comet spun around my mate's dark pupil. "I'm not putting those on."

"Then I will instruct Mathieu to shoot both kneecaps. It amounts to the same. Your mobility will be compromised."

"Stop with this shit, okay?" The angry flush reddening Trowbridge's hollow cheeks went all the way to his throat. "You've got guns, we don't. We all know that this is a dead end. I'm not going out tied to a fence."

St. Silas sighed. "Though Gregori is of the opinion that your mate will dart through the portal at first opportunity, I believe he is wrong. She would never leave you here, alone to face our anger."

No. I wouldn't.

The Quebec Were shook the cuff impatiently. "Thus, the need of these restraints. Bridge, I am not, by nature, a man who enjoys the guns. Let us be civilized. It is obvious your mate will attempt to take you with her. Thus, I must anchor you to this realm. It is only practical."

Yes. St. Silas, you utter bastard. That's exactly what I'd planned to do—snatch my guy and make a break for it through the gates. My Fac powers had been on the cusp of full revival. All the time during the ride, growing, glittering bit by glittering bit, inside my belly. Preparing to

spring, a long thin coil of magic with which I'd hoped to
lasso my mate.

And now I couldn't.

It's over. My shoulders slumped. *I've played every ace
I had in my deck.*

Trowbridge gave me a searching look. "We don't have
to do this. You don't have to call the gates and you don't
have to kill the Gatekeeper. We've tried, sweetheart. We
really did. Let the Great Council take care of the mess
Knox left. Let them deal with everything that follows."

Tempting.

"We can end it here." His eyes blazed. "Right now."

"I know," I whispered.

Oh how I did. My pounding heart understood precisely
how much easier it would be to press myself against the
chain-link fence. To twist my arms around his torso. To
huddle under his chin while he wrapped those strong
arms around me. It would be so much less frightening to
let him hold me. I'd never see the death blow.

Dammit, dammit, dammit.

"I should never have lifted the *Tale of Two Cities*," I
muttered, shaking my head. Lines of confusion deepened
on his forehead. "Dickens, Trowbridge," I said helplessly.
"I should never have checked out Dickens."

Because that sentence fragment about self-sacrifice was
playing in my head. "It is a far, far better thing that I do,
than I have ever done . . ." I wished I'd never dwelled on
that line—even for a nanosecond—or what it took to be a
hero.

Far better thing . . . for whom?

Not for me.

What lousy timing. I was inches away from getting out
of life without having to test my sense of responsibility
any further.

I resent this.

It was so damn wrong. I don't like humans. I don't give a rat's ass whether or not their empire of humanity fell under a deluge of bad magic. And whatever seed of liking I'd cherished for the wolf packs of this world had withered over the last week. Hurt me once and I was naïve. Hurt me twice and I was a fool.

Try to kill me three times, and I was so fucking done.

Love is as dangerous as a virus. Someone spreads their love onto you, and you spread those x's and o's onto someone else. And before you know it, you love a lot of people.

Or just enough people to make you a better person.

I loved my family-that-was-not. Cordelia and Anu in their green Subaru. Even Biggs—*damn you for betraying us*—with his too long bangs and his silly shoes. And those dear people—half of my cherished mines—lived in this world.

My soul-lights in this realm.

Could I chance that Lexi and the Old Mage would succeed in killing the Black Mage before he opened the Book of Spells' final pages? Why not? Hate's almost as powerful a motivator as love. My brother and his mage wouldn't stop until they had their revenge.

So I shouldn't have to worry about a gatekeeper with a key to this world. Or a portal door being left forgotten and ajar for a mage with a black soul. I shouldn't need to squash that fear that he would destroy everything in his world and then . . .

Oh Goddess . . . I can't chance it.

Don't cry. Don't make it worse.

I bit down on the inside of my cheek and gave my mate a helpless smile.

"Tink, you don't have to," he whispered.

"Gotta," I whispered back. "Bad things might drip into this world."

He didn't say anything after that. Actions—they really do speak louder than words. Silently, he snapped the cuff over his wrist, his fierce gaze never leaving mine.

My anchor to this world.

My One True Thing.

He was looking at me like I was Boadicea, and Ripley, and Atomic Betty all rolled in one. Who knew seeing his pride in me would have made me want to howl like one of those damn stone statues?

I pulled the coin out of my pocket. It had warmed from my body. Then I turned to St. Silas. "I still need a drop of his blood."

The Quebec Alpha snapped his fingers. "The knife." There was movement in my peripheral vision, but Trowbridge and I . . . our eyes were talking.

I love you. Blue eyes, dark eyelashes, full of sorrow and love.

It will be over soon. Green eyes, pale as sea light, full of fatigue and love.

St. Silas said, "Bridge, your hand?" Trowbridge turned toward the Frenchman. He offered his damaged hand and didn't flinch when the other drew a thin line across his palm. Liquid welled, filling in those curving lines of heart and head, fate and life.

"I only needed a drop of his blood," I said.

"No, *ma chère,*" St. Silas replied quietly. "Your heart needs a quart of it, but this is the best I can give you."

"Shut the fuck up, St. Silas." Trowbridge's hand was steady, cupped and ready. "Do it, sweetheart."

I dipped the coin into the velvet-red pool. Without wincing or wanting to throw up. Or needing Merry to pinch me else I'd faint. *Look at me. I've matured into a badass.*

"What next?" inquired St. Silas.

"I'll need a weapon to kill the Gatekeeper."

The Frenchman turned the blade around, offering the

bone handle. Mathieu hadn't done a good job of cleaning it. The detailed engraving was tinted with something suspiciously reddish in hue.

"Well, I guess I'll get to it," I said.

Trowbridge looked like he wanted to do a thousand injuries to a thousand men. *Let's pretend,* I silently begged. *That I'm not scared, and you're not enraged.* His scent spiked but he nodded, so I pivoted to face my court of stone wolves.

One foot in front of the other. Don't think. Just do.

My skin goosefleshed. Despite the sun's rays beating down on the cement pad, it was a lot colder inside the enclosure. I took a circuitous route toward the heart of the course, hoping to minimize my body's reaction to the iron. But by the time we reached the double rail closest to the odd couple, shivers racked me, and my feet dragged.

How did the Gatekeeper tolerate it? It had to be much worse for her. And more to the point—how did she get herself over the tracks? The ties weren't wood, they were steel, and the track was a double ribbon of the same rusting metal.

It would be no worse than playing hopscotch. One jump, and a hop on one foot, then another jump. And then I'd be over them. Safe on the other side. Pretending that the scar on my wrist wasn't burning, and that the indents of the kid's teeth weren't faintly glowing.

While I considered the sad fact that wolf pups prefer games that don't include a rock and a piece of chalk, Merry shortened her chain until she rested in the hollow of my throat. She bristled with caution and worry as I bent my knees.

Screw hopscotch.

"Hang on, Merry. I'm going for the long jump."

One leap later, we were staring up at the stone plinths. *Goddess, even stone wolves are bigger than me.* I went up on my tippy-toes, stretching for the bigger wolf's mouth. Success. The coin fit neatly between the male's teeth.

With a hand balanced on the plinth, I counted to five. Then to six.

The bugger had *looked* hungry.

By twelve, I'd taken back my coin and moved to the lady wolf. Her snout was narrower, her lips almost sealed. It took delicacy and craft to get the coin posed on the tips of her canines. Hand braced on plinth, I started counting again. My calves screamed. The birds chirped. Cars whooshed by on the highway.

Crap.

"Is there a problem?" asked the Frenchman.

What do you think, genius?

I heard the fence rattle.

Portals. Why did saving this world have to depend on my personal plague?

Merry unfurled a tendril of gold to hook a hank of my hair. Tiny feet bit into the tender skin stretched over my breastbone. Her chain grew, lengthening from choke-Hedi to chest length. Now free to move, she did so. She minced across my collarbone, up my shoulder, to the faint mound of my almost nonexistent bicep.

She did this, without letting go of my hair. Which meant, as she turned, so did my head. And thus, I saw what I'd somehow managed to miss. "I see it," I whispered.

And I did. Sunlight highlighted the faint notch carved into the female's lower jaw. It wasn't large or deep enough to swallow the coin, but . . . my gaze flew to her mate. He had an identical cut, below his lip. *A mate's kiss.* My fingers shook as I repositioned the coin, so that an edge was balanced on either hairline crevice.

Positioned horizontally, Knox's piece of brass was the perfect bridge between two lovers.

No sooner had I sunk back to my heels than the coin began to glow. Dull brass warmed into a golden-reddish copper. And light, of the most exquisite brightness, streamed through the coin's keyhole.

I backed away.

The air between the two statues began to stir. The scent came next—a flood of floral. Then the lights, little pin-pricks hardly visible in the sun's glare. Sparking and spar-kling, they faintly burnished the wolves's stone ruffs.

The myst came last.

Goddess. There it was. Stripped down of grandeur. Set low, the window to Merenwyn was a simple heart-shaped opening, the view through its glass blurred by a vaporish film. Bending, I blew at it, and the smoke cleared, moving from the center to the sides of it, where it formed a living frame.

I stood back to get a perspective and found none. There was nothing but blue sky, gorgeous and frightening. No sun. No tree line. No rooftops. No mountains. Just a bril-liant sky that had seen no chemicals, no discharge from cars, no smog or pollutants of any kind.

"Does that look like Merenwyn to you?" I whispered to Merry. "Because it looks a helluva lot like the sky be-yond the drop-off in Threall to me."

Wouldn't that be a kick in the ass? Instead of some diminutive Fae who has a passion for rowan wood, we'd get Mad-one. Threall's Mystwalker buying groceries at Metro . . . checking out the hair products at Walmart . . . buying sweaters at Eatons . . .

"Mademoiselle," called St. Silas, "summon the Gate-keeper!"

I flicked him a glance of irritation. What did he want me to do? Stick my head inside and yodel, "Helloooooo?"

Pebbles. I could pitch pebbles through it. She'd hear them, wouldn't she?

I inched closer, cocking my ear. Had I heard something?

I strained to listen.

Yes, there. A hollow repetitive click. Boots on a floor? No. Not boots, but a woman's pair of heels. Tap, tap, tap.

She's coming.

Don't be a troll. I took a cautious half-step to the left, my grip tightening on the bone handle. The first sight of her could best be described as perplexing. A small round mound at the bottom edge of the heart-shaped window. It took me a full second to recognize it for what it was: the bun of a curly-haired woman. Fuzzy, wiry. Mouse brown.

Clearly, she was walking uphill, because with each of her hurried steps, we got to see more of her. The bun view gave way to a forehead with a too short fringe of corkscrew curls. Then eyebrows—quite average. Deep-set brown eyes under puffy lids, their gaze cast downward.

Those were her best feature.

Put baldly, the funny Fae lady was ugly.

There was no two ways about it. She had a mouth too wide in a face too narrow. A jaw too pointed. Skin that probably had come through the birth canal already battered and deeply pored.

But she was not a troll. Mom said they smelled like meat that had gone bad. And this Fae carried with her only the scent of Merenwyn.

She must be climbing stairs, I thought, noting her bobbing progress. She took the last one with a little hop that brought her itty-bitty foot to rest on the lip of the window. There, she paused to lift a pale hand—*Goddess, she's no bigger than a ten-year-old*—to shade her eyes against the sun.

There she was. The Safe Passage's Gatekeeper. The Fae who'd painted my brother against such a terrible backdrop. Who'd traded sun potion for an easel and a bunch of rowan twigs.

Why couldn't you have stayed on your side?

Her eyes widened. "Who are you?" she surprised me by asking in English.

"I'm Hedi." *The girl who'd been tasked with your death. Even though you've neither angered me, nor threatened nor hurt one of mine. But I have a knife. Which I will use because it's you or it's me. Just as it's this world or your world.* My grip on said blade turned utterly painful. Bone bit into my palm.

"You are his sister," she said, her voice both rough and low.

"Whose sister?" I asked innocently. *Kill her. Then seal the gates so bad things won't drip into our world.*

"The Black Mage's Shadow," she whispered, appalled.

Guess the green eyes gave it away. "You know him."

"He will bring death. Pestilence. War."

"No he won't."

"I've seen it," she whispered. "Our world will end. Life will—"

"End?" I shook my head. "There's a lot of that going around."

Humor was obviously not one of her strong points. Though, here's a funny thing about Faes. Most of them possess magic.

And when you have magic, you can have . . . oh shit. With a gasp of dismay, she summoned her talent and a sphere of light and flames burst to life to float above her fingertips.

They must cover fireballs in the 100-level classes. How to Bail with Balefire.

She flicked her wrist.

Incoming. I've seen fireballs whizzing toward me before. I know what to do. Basically, what you want is to duck, real fast. Sadly difficult to do when you're bent slightly over at the waist.

Our bodies? Sometimes they don't wait for your brain to catch up. I had a knife and a meteor heading for my face.

Estimated time of impact, almost immediate.

Reflexes I didn't know I possessed kicked in. My blade jerked up, ready to deflect the course of the sizzling hot thing hurtling toward my unprotected skin. Hell, a length of steel is better than a bare hand, right?

Damn right, it was.

With a hiss, the tip of Knox's knife went right into the center of the balefire.

This was when it would have been good for the ball of flame to divide in two, like a split walnut or a broken clamshell, before it broke apart to fall harmlessly to the cement pad. Instead the fireball remained relatively intact, save for that dribble of wet fire that scorched my tender knuckles and remained poised on Whitlock's blade.

A rather spectacular fiery shish kebob.

"Son of a bitch," I breathed.

The Fae's eyes widened until her lashes tickled the pouch of skin above them. "Blah, blah, blah, blah!" she shrieked in Merenwynian as she twisted the coin she wore around her neck.

Then, quicker than you could say "Alice in Wonderland," she spun on her boots and pelted back down those hidden stairs.

I'm not stupid. I had fire on my knife blade and a wrist as strong as hers. I flicked the balefire through the heart-shaped window. Heard it drop with a sizzle onto the stairs. Was momentarily blinded by a flurry of red sparks, blue flame, and dark smoke.

My brain caught up. Told me to duck.

I did, sinking into a frog crouch.

So, I was in a good position to watch the gray coil of smoke billow out of the window's opening. And the film over the gate to darken, then slowly clear itself.

Tender knuckles braced on the cement, I found myself ogling blue skies.

And nothing else.

The Gatekeeper had harried back down her rabbit hole.

Well, I didn't immediately leap through the gates after her. What I did—considering the sum strangeness of my evening and morning—was take a time-out.

I stared at the window blankly. That's what you do when you're looking at something that makes no sense— like a sky that is both up and down. You freeze, dumbfounded, giving your head time to wrap itself around the huge-ass differences between this portal—this *safe passage* – and what you knew of the Creemore portal that had swallowed first your Trowbridge, then your brother.

Apples and oranges. That's what I was comparing.

Or better yet, economy travel against a first-class ticket.

Behind me, I heard a click. Yesterday, I wouldn't have reconciled that noise to the snick-slide of a safety latch. Today, it was achingly familiar. I flicked a glance over my shoulder. Mathieu. Diamond in his ear winking in the sunlight. Wrist resting on the fence's railing. Snub-nosed weapon pointed my way.

Was that the same gun? It looked smaller.

"Oh fuck off," I muttered, turning back to the passage.

What should I do? Cry "Sy'hella!" and hope this gate would respond like the one over the fairy pond at Creemore? Because the damn Fae had left it open—any Merenwynian evil could slither through it. Where the hell was she? Waiting somewhere in those passages? Ready to pop out at will, lobbing fireballs again? Or maybe she'd already crossed to Merenwyn? Screw those pesky mortals! She was astride her pony, spurring her trusty steed to the castle.

Sound the alarms. The wolves just returned fire.

Crap.

St. Silas's boots echoed on the cement.

Just get it over with. Shoot me. Or better yet, let me go back to Trowbridge. Allow me to huddle in close. Let his chin cover my eyes. Then . . . shoot us. Yes. That's the better choice. Romeo and Juliet. Except Romeo had been a douchebag and Juliet . . . I'm sorry, Julie-girl, but you gave up way too easily.

How can I fix this? How can I make this better? Right?

"Leave her alone, St. Silas," shouted Trowbridge.

Unmindful, St. Silas crouched beside me. He scratched the stubble on his chin. "The Great Council will not let it end so."

"Of course they won't," I said, with bitter sarcasm.

The burning smell was gone. Rinsed in a wind I couldn't feel. Scent, sweet as freesias, drifted through the heart-shaped portal.

"Gregori and Salvador will demand that you travel to Merenwyn, *ma chère.* They will hold your mate here—a hostage, you understand?"

"Stop talking to her, St. Silas." The fence shivered and groaned.

"Yes," I replied dully. "I understand hostages."

The sky was so blue. Lexi was on the other side of that window. Waiting for rescue and an attitude adjustment. The Black Mage too.

And the gate . . . *oh Goddess* . . . it was still wide open.

"They will sweeten their demand with the promise of hope." He balanced his arms on his knees, hung his head in a manner almost doleful. "They will tell you that once you've returned with her head and both coins, that they—we—will let you go."

"But you won't."

"I would try, *ma chère*. But my appointment to the council is recent. My opinion does not, as yet, carry great weight." The wind ruffled his hair. Caught his scent and sweetened it with flowers. He lowered his voice, to the faintest whisper. "Do you recognize opportunity, *ma chère*? Sometimes it passes us so quickly . . ."

"I don't know the language," I said, my mouth dry. "I can't speak a word of it."

They have crossbows in Merenwyn.

He scowled at the window. "Perhaps the Gatekeeper has not traveled far. Perhaps she has fallen inside this . . ." He paused for a word.

"Rabbit hole," I whispered. *The Black Mage knows what I look like.*

A slow nod. "It is possible that she's wounded. Inside the passage. An easy kill."

"Or she's waiting for me on the other side. With a few dozen royal guards."

What about the Raha'ells? What if they found me first? Would they take a long look at my translucent green eyes and think that they looked awfully familiar? Would they hold the Shadow's sister as hostage or would I become the fox? Running ahead of the hounds.

"You can't send her!" shouted my mate. "She'll be defenseless."

We both pivoted. St. Silas on his heel, me on my knee. Trowbridge gave the handcuff securing him to the railing a furious yank. The chain-link fencing shivered.

"I will arm her with the knife," the Frenchman replied.

"You may as well put these fucking handcuffs on her and push her through hog-tied," he said, comets swirling. "They'll pick her off before she's covered half a league.

They have traps and hunters! It's a game to them, don't
you get it?"

"I will allow it to be her choice." The Quebec
wolf slanted his gaze away from my mate's growing flare.
"Stand down, Trowbridge. Or I shall instruct Mathieu to
commence target practice?"

I gave my lover a thin smile that tasted both sad and
sweet, then turned back to the gates. Staring at all that
sky—seeing that there was no land, no horizon, not a tree
in the distance—it was like being in Threall and looking
at the end of the world. Exactly like that. If I took that
first step through the window, what would I find? An endless plunge, or a short drop?

"Jesus," Trowbridge said despairingly. "Don't go, Tink."
I don't want to. I really don't.

"I have to close the gates," I said. "Have to."

"Just say the words. Stay with me."
Stay. His favorite word is "stay."

I thought of my brother's portrait. I thought of Anu
and Cordelia.

Then . . . I thought about me.

I am stronger than I think I am. Harder too. Death's
been trying to catch me for days, and I just keep . . . slipping between its fingers. And if I do go—if I take that
leap—I will buy some time. Things happen when time is
bought.

Pigs fly.

"Don't let her go!" yelled my mate.

Courage. It starts with one step.

"I'm going to do it," I said, getting off my knees.

"Sweetheart, don't. Not without me."

I bent over, put one hand on the frame. The myst rolled
over my knuckles. It was cool, and perfumed with a smell
I remember so well. My mother's land. "I'm no baby anymore," I said, staring at the blue sky.

"You'll always be mine."

Mine, mine.

I forced my lips into a weak smile. "This is where you're supposed to tell me to stay alive, Trowbridge."

A muscle jerked in his jaw. "Stay alive," he whispered.

I nodded, turned my back, and took that step.

Chapter Twenty-Six

I should have anticipated falling down the stairs. I knew they were there. But they'd been cut to fit a size zero foot, not a size six. Very narrow, very steep. And I was already disoriented. Everybody had told me portals were all about wind and walls that looked like smoke but felt wet. That there would be voices, long, echoing cries. And people behind the liquid walls. Lost souls. That's what I'd been told—portals were air, and smoke, and sound, and everything that scares you.

There was no wind, no smoke. No voices either.

I was alone. Utterly alone. On a rock landing pad of sorts, at the bottom of a slope of stairs that had been chiseled out of solid dark rock. If I rolled, just a bit, I'd drop.

Maybe three feet, maybe leagues.

Into a pool of blue.

Sky? Or water?

I can't do it. I don't want to fall. I don't want to be alone. Not again. Not now when I know what it feels like to belong to family that wasn't a family.

I swear—I didn't say it. I thought it but I didn't say it.

Merry spoke. With a pinch of tissue, and a bite of electricity, and a deep golden glow from inside her breast—she reminded me.

I was not alone.

And so, I took a deep breath, and I covered her with my palm, pressing her hard against the cushion of my own breast, and then . . . I rolled.

To find myself dropping into the air, not a chilly pool. Into the arms of a strong wind, not infinity. We were carried, blown like the leaf I'd always thought I was, by a breeze so powerful that my clothing flapped about me. My stomach roiled. I got impressions of others—hands pressed against the wall, mouths opened in cries—images set into undulating walls. A blur of faces too white, anguish too real.

Light ahead.

Blue, blue, blue.

The opening came up on me faster than I wanted it to—and for once, time did not slow down. We were sent— Merry bleating orange pulses—spewing into the void.

Goddess, take my soul.

A sense of falling. My mouth opened for another long shriek.

And then, with a thud that stole my breath, we landed. Hard, because one way or the other, all my landings are hard. No spongy moss beneath me this time. The ground smelled of earth and something else . . . sweet as my mum's breath. I lay where I was, facedown in very ordinary dirt, for far longer than I should have, temporarily robbed of courage. Merenwyn's earth tasted very much like ours.

Merry's ivy twined tight around my cold fingers. Gave them a reassuring and painful squeeze.

I rolled to a sitting position.

I'd landed on a small promontory approximately six feet in width. Wincing at the flaring hip pain, I turned and looked behind me. A solid wall of rock, and above that, a small cave. It would be difficult to spot unless you knew it was there. The entrance was shadowed. And the set of stairs carved into the cliff face had been sized to fit a very small foot.

Get up.

Nothing had broken, though my knee felt hot and I knew it would swell soon. I crab-shuffled to the edge. Below me was Merenwyn. Acres of untouched forest. Stretching out to the horizon, rolling with the swell of the land.

The Raha'ells waited there. And perhaps over there, down by that ribbon of a river, I'd find a royal guard or two. Or three.

Look at those trees. As massive as the ones in Threall.

How to leave this place? My gaze followed the line of the notched stairs and noted a trail, no wider than a couple of feet. It led down the mountain, and then disappeared into the dark woods. So . . . courage. It can begin with a simple action. One step that takes you to a place you'd never thought you'd go. But heroes? They're people who choose to keep moving forward. Even if they're frightened. They move toward a goal. They soldier on toward their destiny.

I will close the gate behind me. I will find shelter. I will meet Lexi and kill the Black Mage. I will see the Book of Spells destroyed.

From the tunnel came a faint strand of sound. The shiver of metal fencing, hollow and distant.

I stared at the vista, verdant and far-reaching.

Count to twenty-five then do it. Get up. Take the next step.

Suddenly, a gust of wind howled through the gash in the rock face. My hair lifted and whipped around my face.

My hand tightened on the knife hilt.

The noise grew terrible. The rattle of metal, the shriek of steel striking stone.

One final cataclysmic whoosh of sound and wolf-scented air.

Then a thud, coupled by the chatter of chain link.

And a curse, exquisitely mortal.

I closed my eyes briefly. Fect and fencing had landed in Merenwyn.

His scent reached for me first. Alpha and man, woods and salt, sex and that indefinable element that was sung to the wolf inside me. It wrapped around me and said, "This be my mate."

A thoughtful pause.

Down in the valley, the tops of the trees swayed.

"You always going to leave when I ask you to stay?" he asked.

I smiled through the tears. "What took you so long?"

Acknowledgments

My first round of thanks goes to those who volunteer to slog their way through the first draft read: Julie Butcher, Kerry Schafer, Rebecca Melson, and Victoria Koski. I'm endlessly grateful for both your comments and pat-pats.

My second round of applause is directed to those who help polish and present that draft: my editor, Holly Ingraham; my hidden resource, Mickie; and all those at St. Martin's Press whose work touches mine. Hugs to you all.

My final round goes to the readers. Though I write the books, my readers make the series. Thank you for hanging with me for the entire ride!